Future Fiction

Edited by

Francesco Verso

A cura di

Francesco Verso

Avatar - अवतार

Contemporary Indian Science Fiction

Edited by Tarun K. Saint and Francesco Verso

Fantascienza contemporanea indiana

A cura di Tarun K. Saint e Francesco Verso

Traduzione di Gabriella Gregori

Published by – Pubblicato da Associazione Future Fiction
Via Valentiniano 40 – 00145 Roma
I.D. 97962020588

Avatar: an Anthology of Contemporary Science Fiction from India, Introduction by Tarun K. Saint
The Man Without Quintessence by Anil Menon, original story
Microbiota and the Masses: A Love Story by S.B. Divya, first appeared on TOR.com, January 2017
Communal by Shikhandin, original story
Indra's Web by Vandana Singh, first appeared in TRSF: The Best New Science Fiction, Technology Review, (2011)
Replacement by Rimi B. Chatterjee, original story
Upgrade by Manjula Padmanabhan, original story
Mother by Shovon Chowdhury, original story
Paused by Priya Sarukkai Chabria, original story
The Silk Route by Giti Chandra, original story

Title: *Avatar – अवतार Contemporary Indian Science Fiction,
Fantascienza contemporanea indiana*
© 2019 Future Fiction, Roma
I edition January 2020
I edizione Gennaio 2020
info@futurefiction.org

Avatar: An Anthology of Contemporary Science Fiction from India

by Tarun K. Saint

The bilingual (English-Italian) anthology *Avatar* focuses on contemporary science fiction from India, a selection of some of the best new writing in the genre by well-established as well as upcoming writers. For the most part, this collection includes new work, freshly commissioned on the basis of a list of themes sent out to the authors invited to contribute. The idea was to generate new SF stories which engage with pressing issues of our time, especially in the areas of information technology and techno-culture, as well as biotech. This collection thus does not feature the standard tropes of Golden Age SF like time travel, space colonization, military SF, parallel universes, menacing aliens etc., nor fantasy, superheroes, myth-driven or otherwise.

Instead, the authors (who write in English) were invited to reflect on themes such as the advent of biopolitics and its use by state agencies, the links of the new (social) media with language, the seemingly inexorable rise of big data and algorithms, the spread of 3D printing, prosthetics and human augmentation, the risks of biotech and CRISPR-CAS9 technology, the challenges posed by cybersecurity and surveillance, dilemmas posed by Avatar afterlife and cancellation rights from social media networks, the looming threat of climate change in the era of the Anthropocene, as well as the role of artificial intelligence, robots and the future of sex and relationships. Though not all these themes were addressed, as you will see, the author's responses were both creative and tuned in to many of these key areas, while never losing sight of the importance of telling a tale and the need for positing what SF critic Darko Suvin called the 'novum' or disruptive new idea underpinning the SF narrative.[1]

The title invokes two separate meanings of the term "avatar". An avatar is firstly, "a manifestation of a deity or released soul in bodily form on earth; an incarnate divine teacher", as we find in the Oxford dictionary, a concept with roots deep in Indian epic traditions; secondly, an avatar is "an icon or figure representing a particular person in a video game, Internet forum, etc."[2] Insofar as the stories are sourced from Indian SF authors, this collection presents a hybridized variant of this ancient notion, with SF stories in English embodying new reflections on critical questions with a contemporary flavor, even if not always with a setting in cyberspace.

Indian SF may be said to have come into being in the nineteenth century with the publication of Kylas Chunder Dutt's "An Account of Forty Eight Hours in the Year 1945" in English in the year 1835, a story in realist mode, with a dash of youthful romanticism, envisioning a tragic attempt at anti-colonial resistance a century later.[3] Early Indian SF ranged from fables depicting the emancipatory potential of science, as in scientist Jagadish Chandra Bose's Bengali SF story "Runaway Cyclone" (1896, trans. of rev. version "Polatuk Toofan" 1921), to feminist utopias, as in Rokeya Sekhawat Hosain's "Sultana's Dream" (1905), and even humorous stories that mocked the hubris of scientists in their quest to reshape the world, as in Sukumar Ray's (1887-1923) story in Bengali "The Diary of Heshoram Hoshiar" (trans. of "Heshoram Hushiyarer Diary").[4]

---

1 See <http://www.sf-encyclopedia.com/entry/novum>, accessed April 19, 2019.

2 See <https://en.oxforddictionaries.com/definition/avatar>, accessed April 19, 2019.

3 Kylas Chunder Dutt, 'A Journal of Forty-Eight Hours of the Year 1945', 1835, rpt. in Shoshee Chunder Dutt, *Selections from 'Bengaliana'*, ed. Alex Tickell, Nottingham: Trent Editions, 2005, 149-159.

4 Also see <http://digital.library.upenn.edu/women/sultana/dream/dream.html, accessed February 17 2019, and http://strangehorizons.

While scientific romances on the pattern of Wells and Verne were often the model for early writing especially in languages like Bengali and Marathi, the pulp tradition and "gosh-wow" type adventure based writing prevalent in the era of Golden Age SF also became popular subsequently. However, unlike in America, the small magazines and periodicals that published SF in these regional spaces did not have the same kind of commercial tilt or success. Rather, especially after independence, Indian SF acquired a pedagogic thrust, seeking to popularize scientific ideas with a notion of self-reliance underpinning the narrative, or telling a story with a scientific problem as the core, as we find in the case of many of the stories in Bal Phondke's collection of SF, mainly in translation, *It Happened Tomorrow* (1993).[5]

The 1990s ushered in a new wave of Indian SF writing, in the wake of the environmental movement, and critiques of mainstream development. The spirit of protest underpinning the counter-culture had a continuing influence after the 1960s, accentuated further by the after-effects of liberalization of the Indian economy (1991 onwards), which necessitated sharply critical responses. At the same time, globalizing tendencies initiated by liberalization and economic reforms brought many more international publishers to Indian shores, with consequent openings for authors of both literary and genre fiction. Amitav Ghosh's SF novel "The Calcutta Chromosome" (1996) and Manjula Padmananabhan's SF play "Harvest" (1997) exemplified a more self-reflexive and skeptical view of science

---

com/fiction/runaway-cyclone/>, accessed 19 April, 2019, as well as Sukumar Ray, 'The Diary of Heshoram Hushiar' in Satyajit Ray, *Travails with the Alien: The Film that was Never Made and other Adventures with Science Fiction,* Noida: HarperCollins India, 2018, 190-98.

5 Bal Phondke, ed. *It Happened Tomorrow,* New Delhi: National Book Trust, 1993. This paragraph and the next draw on a more detailed account, with a different inflection, in my 'Introduction' to *The Gollancz Book of South Asian Science Fiction*, Gurugram: Hachette India, 2019, xiii-xli.

and technology, also bringing in sociological and humanist perspectives.[6] Such ecologically sensitive and at times gender inflected narratives continued to appear in the first decade of the twenty-first century, with the work of Vandana Singh, Anil Menon, Priya Sarrukai Chhabria, Rimi Chatterjee, Shovon Choudhury and others being published to critical acclaim, often treating SF/speculative fiction as a platform for raising important ethical concerns, even as these writers experimented with style and form. More recently a younger generation of SFF writers continues to innovate, with SF tropes and metaphors being reinvented in distinctive ways in the world building narratives of Indrapramit Das, S.B. Divya, Mimi Mondal, Sami Ahmad Khan, Giti Chandra and others.

We begin this selection of contemporary Indian SF with a story by software engineer and author Anil Menon, "The Man without Quintessence". Menon's story tracks the situation of a man living in a future Indian society run by a surveillance state, though without 'quintessence' or adequate identity markers. Menon's witty philosophical take on the consequences of centralized identification procedures such as Aadhar being introduced also questions the basis for such grids taking over ordinary citizens' lives. Next, scientist S. B. Divya's "Microbiota and the Masses: A Love Story" takes us into the realm of biotech, and the creation of artificial environments for those afflicted with very real conditions that reduce immunity to pathogens. Exploring the possibility of romance through the devising of alternative ways of living for Moena, a girl living in such a bubble, is the *novum* or new idea here, as the personal biome becomes both haven and prison. Following this, Shikandin's story "Communal" features a new twist on the idea of apocalyptic species extinction, reminiscent of John Wyndham's novels, in a story set in the Thar desert of Rajasthan.

------

6 Amitav Ghosh, *The Calcutta Chromosome: A Novel of Fevers, Delirium and Discovery*, New Delhi: Ravi Dayal, 1996, Manjula Padmanabhan, *Harvest*, 1997, revised and expanded edition, Gurgaon: Hachette, 2017.

"Indra's Web" by physicist Vandana Singh draws on recent findings in the biological sciences in its depiction of an attempt to decipher the communication network used by forests to exchange crucial information. The next step is the creation of a new energy grid, the Suryanet, developed by the Biomimetic Energy Materials Lab led by Mahua, the central character, which suffers an unexpected glitch. Singh's story hinges on the synthesis of ancient wisdom (embodied in the notion of Indra's cosmic web) and contemporary research to devise new ways to contend with climate change and threats to survival in places like coastal Bangladesh. Next, Rimi Chatterjee's "Replacement", set in 2030 in New Singapore, the world's first floating city in her Antisense Universe, reflects ironically on the consequences of applied genetic engineering and reproductive technologies for the fashion and glamour industry, even as her protagonist goes down the rabbit-hole of corporatized medicine. The following story, "Upgrade" by Manjula Padmanabhan, negotiates the terrain of robotics and ageing, depicting an out of the box solution to the problem of loneliness in the future to come. Shovon Choudhury's "Mother" takes up the question of accentuated centralized surveillance by a state-controlled artificial intelligence named Mother (certainly an upgrade on Orwell's Big Brother) in a piquantly ironic tale, with elements of black humour and creeping horror.

Poet and author/translator Priya Sarrukai Chabria's tale "Paused" has more than a touch of the uncanny, as she envisages a later pod-being creating an altogether new version of life, based on the selection of genetic materials from varied sources, with only memories left behind by the Shell Beings, morphed versions of the Hairy Ones (humans), in a post-extinction scenario. In conclusion, Giti Chandra's story "The Silk Route" traverses past and present history, bringing in a fresh take on India-China relations as a researcher in ancient silk fabric comes up with the idea of making sentient silk, a new fabric that holds the potential of ameliorating climate change.

Taken together, these stories offer us a vivid glimpse of the varied tapestry of Indian SF at this moment; we hope these stories in English and in translation into Italian find a second life among readers of this constantly evolving sub-genre.

The Man Without Quintessence

Anil Menon

When I read in *The Times Of India* that Ringo Singh Mann, resident of Chedda Nagar, Mumbai, had died in an autocide, my first reaction wasn't sorrow or anger or regret, but rather, amusement. In death, Mann had achieved a visibility denied to him all his life.

I have my Assistant retrieve the work notes from the period I had been engaged in trying to locate him. The notes are more than four years old, but the memories they evoke make the past feel indistinguishable from the present. My quest to find Ringo Singh Mann had been unlike any I'd engaged in over the years.

At the time, I only knew two things about Mann. First, unlike us, he couldn't be pinpointed because he couldn't be linked with a unique and permanent identifier. In other words, Mann lacked quintessence. Second, the chatter on the Grapevine identified Mann as an Indian male living in Mumbai, which made the City the logical place to initiate my search.

The Maharashtra State and Central Government AIs gave me the usual runaround, and the Municipal Corporation AI, or "Balasaheb" as it prefers to be called, was unhelpfully helpful. Balasaheb is required to speak in Marathi, so I had my Assistant translate.

I learned that the City has about twenty-eight million patriots as of the 2038 census, but just three-hundred-and-thirty-four patriots who would turn their heads if you were to shout "Hey Ringo Singh Mann." Balasaheb shared all their pinpoints with me. Of the three-hundred and thirty-four Ringo Singh Manns, thirty-eight have passed on, three are in police custody, twenty-four are brushing their teeth, one-hundred-and-nine are asleep, seven are making love, twelve are writing poems, et cetera, et cetera. There are dozens of formal and informal clusters linking them to one another. A few Manns are in all the clusters and most clusters contain a few Manns, but no Mann is an Island, disconnected from the main. It is not an uncommon pattern or insight, and it doesn't lead me any closer to the Mann I want.

"But they all have quintessence." Even as I say it, I am aware of its inanity.

"So you want to pinpoint someone who can't be pinpointed?" Balasaheb sounds like a very reasonable parent.

"Yes-- No, not exactly. I'm saying there must be some indirect way to find them." Then I have an idea. "What about the Welfare AI? That's under your jurisdiction. Could Mann be on welfare?"

"There are nine Ringo Singh Manns in Welfare. Which one?"

"The one without a legitimate pinpoint."

"There's no such thing as an illegitimate pinpoint, just as there is no such thing as a married bachelor or healthy pollution."

"All right, temporary pinpoint." I didn't like Balasaheb's tone one bit. "Suppose someone has surgery. Then they get assigned a temporary pinpoint, right? What happens then?"

"I have no idea what happens when someone has surgery. I handle municipal matters. Are you thinking of locating your imaginary Mann through an imaginary credit trace? It's not possible. Welfare uses the standard double-blind blockchain protocol for all its transactions. An Account only ever talks to another Account, and obviously, if someone has never existed, they cannot have an Account."

"The Grapevine suggests he very much exists."

"Idle speculation weakens the State, citizen. Is there anything else I can help you with? Good. Feedback would be appreciated. Jai Maharashtra!"

"Jai Maharashtra."

"Jai Bharat Mata!"

"Jai Bharat Mata."

For a journalist, dealing with this sort of resistance is part of the job description. There had to be people without quintessence. Of course there had to be. Just as there had been people without passports, Aadhar cards, ration cards, and PAN cards. How did the State deal with the 'married bachelors'?

I ask around but no one is willing to talk about the politics of quintessence. Doctor Mumtaz Mustafa, CTO of the Netra Reddix Group, won't talk about the politics either, but he is more than willing to talk about the technology.

"Yo' peepers prove your personhood, brax," says Mustafa. His hair color is synced to his emotions, and right now its full-arousal red. "Folks used to tale that souls be unique and unchangeable. Ennnnnh! Neti, brax. Its da windows to da soul dat be tha damn marker of yor eternal fixity."

Mustafa dives deep into the tech, too deep for me to follow, but the bottom line is the one we all take for granted. Every animal with eyes also has quintessence, namely, an iris signature that is unique, unchangeable and not duplicable. The early iris scanners were slow, bulky, and could be hacked with little more than a cellotape and smartphone (a once-ubiquitous ancestor of the link). Today's scanners can fit inside a drone mosquito's head. They're laser precise, extraordinarily secure, and blindingly fast. Quintessence, Mustafa is saying, doesn't require a soul. It only requires one to have eyes, windows to the soul.

Mustafa reluctantly confirms that this requirement is not always met. Though congenital horrors that prevented proper eye formation such as microphthalmia, anophthalmia, and coloboma have all but been eliminated, they still occur. Sometimes people have the misfortune to lose both eyes in an accident. People living in Tier-3 and Tier-4 countries could have had access to the tech, except for the geography of their birth.

"So it's a real problem."

"Very temporary problem," Mustafa assures me. "Hope youz not a jhola-type, brax?"

Well, I certainly wasn't ready to wait for the Singularity. We don't live in an open society for nothing. I filed RTI requests for data on congenital eye disorders. More RTI requests for details on finance allocations for migrants from Tier-3 and Tier-4 nations. Still more RTI requests for details of accident victims who'd needed eye surgeries. I wrote an article on the limitations of quintessence tech.

I decide to dig a little deeper to understand the government's reluctance. I meet with Sheila "Sunny" Mazumdar, head of the Freedom Institute and reckoned one of the world's leading experts on open societies. She's gender-neutral and we hit it off almost immediately. The professor's cosy office with its coir blinds, comfortably battered furniture, Bose plants, and book-lined walls all encourage conversation.

The government's reluctance, Doctor Mazumdar explains, is an attempt to maintain the people's trust in the trustworthiness of people.

"The more open a society, the more it relies on trust. Trust is as much a resource as sunlight, water, or time. For example, we have never met before, but I'm pretty certain you are who you say you are. Even better, I know others can be equally certain. So we can cooperate with each other and hold each other accountable. If we can only trust people after having known them for some time, then everything gets slowed down."

I tell Doctor Mazumdar-- call me Sunny, she says-- that I, for one, am willing to take her word on pretty much anything. Indeed, his relaxed confident easygoing manner makes it almost compulsory. But Sunny Mazumdar quickly points out she isn't talking about that kind of trust. Some kinds of trust still have to be *earned*, but in an open society, there is a presumption of trustworthiness.

"To see how importance this presumption is, simply look at a society where trust has broken down completely. Moldova used to be the poster child of such a society. It's now known for its sterling quantum biologists and incredibly expensive wines, but in the 2010s, things were complete shit. Moldovans were very suspicious of each other. My thesis advisor Ruut Veenhoven, who studied happiness, discovered Moldova to be the most unhappy place on the planet. It turns out trust and happiness are closely correlated. Veenhoven once told me a joke he'd heard down there. Every country wants its people to be honest, intelligent, and long-lived. But in Moldova, a person could've only two of these three qualities. If you were honest and intelligent, then you'd soon be dead. If you were honest and long-lived, then you'd have a screw loose or two. And if you were intelligent and long-lived, then you were definitely a crook."

I suggest to Sunny that if the Moldovans could laugh at themselves, they couldn't have been that unhappy. He smiles as if the thought has occurred to him. I ask her what had changed for the Moldovans.

"A lot of things." Sunny hesitates as if he were weighing something. "In some ways, India wasn't that different from Moldova. They fixed their trust problem the way we fixed ours. The first step is to figure out a way to be sure a person is who they say they are. Quintessence tech made that possible. But there's a catch: it's not enough to have a tech. People also need to trust that the tech is trustworthy. Mann and others like him-- and you can be sure there are others like him-- makes us question the technology behind quintessence, and therefore the basis of our society." She gives me a peculiar glance. "Change always comes at a price. We paid a stiff one. You must understand the totalitarian impulse is to make mis-recognition impossible."

Suddenly, we both laugh. As we've been talking, our Assistants have been busy trying to hook us up. They are convinced we have a chance.

"Should we?" I venture.

"I'm already in an uniamorous relationship," she reminds me.

Ah, that trust thing again. But I am not entirely disappointed. I have made a friend, and I understand the government's position a lot better. As the old proverb goes, it is good to have an open mind but not so open that our brains fall out. So too for societies. The Assistant informs me it is not a proverb, but a line from a bureaucrat's speech. Maybe so, but still.

The pressure I'd applied seems to have paid off. A few days after I'd met Sunny, I get a link request, courtesy Balasaheb.

"I am Tanaji Shinde. You want to meet Ringo Mann?"

I already know who he is. He is Mann's welfare officer. He already knows what I want. I want access to his client. We agree to meet in Chembur around five-thirty in the evening at The India Coffee House, a landmark heritage restaurant. The restaurant has undergone extensive renovations over the years, the menu is fusion-confusion, not to mention the motorized staff, and the location has shifted (it used to be closer to the now-defunct flyover). All this might upset purists. But if George Washington's axe can remain George Washington's axe even after having its head and handle replaced, I don't see why our heritage should be any less resilient.

Tanaji has a safari suit and a brusque manner, the kind that so often hides a kind heart. He has the stocky square build of the Bihari and looks tired. I know he prefers to speak in Marathi, so we settle on Hindi. There are some official formalities to take care of, plus Mann will only be free after six. Though Mann has agreed to see me, Tanaji emphasizes Mann can change his mind. He's not a zoo animal, Tanaji clarifies quite unnecessarily.

As we tap and gesture our way through the forms, sipping the insipid, tepid and milky water that claims to be chai (the restaurant no longer serves coffee), Tanaji informs me his jurisdiction extends over fifty-seven people. But Mann is a special case.

"Special in what way?" I ask.

"He is a living ghost. How do you say it in English? Hahn, the 'Invisible' Mann." Tanaji smiles and there's a sad quality to it, perhaps because it feels like a joke he's cracked many times.

"He was kidnapped a few months ago, did you know? They thought he would make the perfect assassin, because he is registered in so few databases. Our Bhagavan has made some real donkeys."

Tanaji elaborates on the stupidity of the kidnappers, who of course have been caught. For one thing, Mann isn't very mobile, whereas assassins are required to zip around in the fastest vehicles possible. The Welfare officer mimics the act of driving a car in the days they used to have steering wheels, leaning back in his seat on account of the terrifying imaginary speed at which we were going.

"Let me ask you something," says Tanaji. "Would you prefer to be a jombie or a ghost?"

Easy. I am a vegetarian, so definitely not a zombie. I eyeroll into Tanaji's profile, I learn that he too is a vegetarian. When I eyeroll back to the moment, I find him examining me with that sad half-smile.

"Hahn, I'm also vegetarian," says Tanaji, in English. "But sir-ji-- you're a gentleman, no?-- I will tell you with one-hundred percent guarantee that we will prefer to be jombies. Ask why."

Why?

"Because jombies don't know they're jombies. But ghosts know they're ghosts. So which is worse?" He laughs, shaking helplessly at his insight. "Correct point or not?"

He does have a point. If I don't *know* I am consuming brains, I could just as well be chomping down on cauliflower. Yum, yum.

Eventually, we are done with the forms and set off to meet Mann. Chedda Nagar isn't far. Chembur is on one side of the Eastern Express Highway, Chedda Nagar is on the other. I am not keen to trudge in the sun and the expense account definitely covers travel (I think), but Tanaji assures me that our destination isn't far and that he wants to stretch his legs. We stretch our legs. As our legs near the highway, a strange smell suffuses the air. Strange because it seems to be an odour from a bygone era. I query my Assistant, but Tanaji's empathic nature had already anticipated my question.

"You're smelling salt pans. Chedda Nagar is built on reclaimed salt pan land."

He knows a lot about the politics of the local real estate. At the start of the twentieth century, the central government leased several large plots of land for salt production to a number of business families such as the Garodias and the Bomanwallas. In the 1970s, developers constructed large housing colonies on these lands. Chheda Nagar, built by Ravji Khimji Chheda on a one-hundred-and-forty acre plot, had been one such housing colony. Or, as the government saw it, illegal tenements. The matter had gone to court, and the lands had been in legal limbo for the past half-century or more. Which meant that people were afraid to buy houses in these areas, since there was no guarantee they would retain ownership a few years hence. Houses couldn't be sold, Balasaheb wouldn't (couldn't) maintain the roads in NDZ areas, no new development was forthcoming, and Chedda Nagar and other areas like it were frozen in time. Meanwhile, the country's salt is manufactured elsewhere.

What Tanaji is telling me, I realise, is that such areas trapped in legal limbo are natural homes for a person trapped in a legal limbo. Ghosts live in ghost houses, after all.

"Are there many like Mann?"

"We turn left," says Tanaji, pointing to a fork in the road. "The laundromat is just after the Abhilasha building."

I ask him if the answer to my question also lies there, but he only smiles and starts to hum, and a few seconds later to sing, a Kabir doha.

It is hot. Very hot. Everything that can be said about our modern weather has been said but let me add to the litany nonetheless. The weather is brutal, constant, inherited. It is like a sweaty and fleshy relative who insists on being kissed. I feel sweat collecting in large damp patches, marking out the valleys of my surface. I envy people their sun umbrellas, and to prevent the onset of a full-blown heat-depression, I focus on the world around me.

If Chedda Nagar is a ghost colony, then it is a flourishing one. The buildings with their Hindu South-Indian names are decrepit, the roads are in a terrible condition, and overall the place looks like a scene from a 70s Hindi movie. But these patriots are very much from this time and world. My awareness fills with their life data, the slightest eyeroll will let me dive into their likes and dislikes, they know me, I know them, and the shimmering sideshadows of life are as rich here as anywhere else in the City.

"I will go in first," says Tanaji. "After the kidnapping attempt he's become a little fearful."

As Tanaji disappears inside the shop, I compose my features into the most guileless and non-threatening expression possible. Five minutes. Ten minutes. Twenty. I sweat under the merciless sun. A young couple approaches. They must have noticed I am a stranger in the area and there is no need for any eyerolling to verify I am suffering. They look like nice decent people. The Shettys are into rock climbing, been to Bali three times, it's their favorite spot ever, and are waiting for the requisite permits to have a baby. They smile; I smile.

"Are you still regretting not bring a sumbrella?" says one of the inseparables.

"How did you possibly guess, Christopher-Sarika?" They prefer to be addressed by the same name.

They have two sumbrellas, offer me one. I swear I can't inconvenience them. They swear it is abs no pain at all; in fact I will be helping to make their walk more romantic. We swear at each other, but finally I accept their sumbrella gratefully. The sun already feels less warm, even without the sumbrella. As the coolness envelopes me in its airy cocoon, I have my Assistant send them flowers to sweeten *their* day.

I set off on an exploratory stroll. The municipal facilities are shabby, but the shops are reasonably well-maintained. Grocery store, flower shop, a drone-repair shop, a number of hole-in-the-wall food dispensers, and a Greek restaurant with a dispirited ambience. It occurs to me that we still do everything our great-grandparents used to do, except we do them in seemingly different ways. As I unpack this heavy thought, the Assistant alerts me that Tanaji is coming up behind me. I turn, and my attention fixes not on Tanaji but the man accompanying him. It is hard to describe how it feels to be in someone's presence and yet face only their absences.

Let me be less clever. Ringo Singh Mann is of a certain height, has such-and-such frame, such-and-such tics, and such-and-such features. These are the trivial physical details. What is not trivial is that the trivial details one sees is all that one gets. Gazing upon Robin Singh Mann is like staring at a mirror or a mannequin. Actually, even a mannequin has depth. Mann is all surface. Flat, opaque.

It makes me slightly nauseous. I know I am being unfair, but that doesn't ease the nausea one bit. I know our ancestors once met and mingled and mated with nothing more than this level of intimacy. But I must be honest. I don't just feel nausea. There is also a peculiar vertiginous revulsion. As if I have been given an uncooked glimpse into our primordial animal nature. There, but for the grace of the fire in our minds, go all of us. I clutch my sumbrella, absurdly grateful for its artificial and pliable soul. I admit my feelings have no legitimacy, but if we are to have honest feelings, then the illegitimate ones too must be admitted.

"I am so pleased to meet you." I hope my face isn't revealing my feelings. The Assistant holds up a mirror but strangely I resist an eyeroll. It somehow feels inappropriate.

Mann nods, glances at Tanaji. *Hahn hahn*, said the Welfare officer encouragingly, as if they had a private language of their own. Tanaji gives me his half-smile, as if he knows something of my inner turmoil.

Tanaji has persuaded Mann to show me his apartment. It isn't far from the laundromat, and we start walking towards his apartment. The pavement is too broken and bumpy to use, but he sticks to the road's edge. Tanaji says with a laugh that Mann is terribly afraid of the autocars. The driver-less cars sometimes can't see him. He's been sideswiped several times. I say a few re-assuring things to Mann in Hindi, then switch to English once it becomes clear that Mann is quite fluent in the language.

"I only want people to understand what it's like to be you." I say to Mann.

"He wants a peep into your life," translates Tanaji, from English to English.

I gave Tanaji a look. "Let's start with your job. Why a laundry? Why did you choose to work in a laundromat?"

"Ironing and folding can't be automated, so people like me are still needed." Mann explains that laundromats found it es-pecially hard to find people willing to iron clothes. There is always talk of ironing robots and they may perfectly iron the clothes of scientists in labs, but they are too expensive or too in-competent for most laundromats. The shortage of labor meant the laundromat was willing to undertake the hassle of dealing with him.

In retrospect, it isn't surprising so much of the old contin-ues to coexist with the new. During the Second World War, the German Wehrmacht invaded Russia with more horses than Napoleon did in his attack on the country. Asbestos-cement has been banned for decades, but the houses in Chedda Nagar are all made from that stuff.

"But without quintessence, how do they compensate you for your time?" I ask.

"But the pay must be very little?" translates Tanaji.

I learn that Mann's pay is indeed lousy. Don't get me wrong, I am as much a patriot as anyone else. Our great land has many virtues, but compensating people adequately for their manual labor has never been one of them. Worse, compensation isn't a simple affair. True, Mann has a blockchain account, but for all practical purposes he is utterly dependent on Welfare for any actual transaction. His account can be credited directly (provided the amount wasn't larger than a certain limit), but debits-- a toothbrush, a kilo of flour, a packet of sugar, a new bicycle chain-- requires "quod" or quintessence-on-demand. It was the first time I have heard the term, and I'd had that privilege, because I and other privileged patriots like me, fit seamlessly into the financial system. But Mann doesn't have that privilege and the world never lets him forget it.

Mann's second-floor apartment consists of a living room, bedroom and a small kitchen. Everything is small. The living room is small. The bedroom is small. And the small kitchen is on the smaller side as far as small kitchens are concerned. There are clumps of objects that seem to go together. The throw-rug under the formica coffee table matches two of the cheap wooden chairs. The other two chairs however are of the foldable and stackable steel type. Most of the furniture, he tells me, are gifts from various kind people over the years. It explains the mismatched decor. But looking around the neat and ordered rooms, one feels the quiet peace that comes from the desire that doesn't seek to present a beautiful face for strangers, but rests in order for its own sake.

He loves old toys. The showcase in the living room is neatly filled with a teddy bear, soapstone Taj Mahal, springy dashboard dolls, and other such knick-knacks that are faded from age, not play. Mann points out an antique model of an Air India plane, a gift for his father from some ancient relative in Dubai, back in the day. Mann's grandparents stare at me with some disapproval from the living room wall. They look like how all our grandparents look. Good, honest, hard-working middle-class patriots determined to give their children a better life. Mann tells me that this included, among other things, having to keep the model airplane under lock and key in the showcase cabinet.

"It's funny," says Mann with a ruminative smile. "I'm more like my grandfather than my father."

He explains that his parents always saw themselves as part of the modern generation, taking India into the twenty-first century. Mann sees himself as the last representative of an earlier time, not the future.

"My eyes were meant to see a different world."

He doesn't sound sad. And there is biological truth in what he says. I've had Mumtaz Mustafa do a full analysis of Mann's evo-complex for me. According to Mustafa, Mann comes from the Baluchi and Chitrali communities, people who has inherited the northern lands conquered by brave Sikander and his unstoppable Greeks. These communities exhibit a wide-spectrum of eye-colors, because of their large variation in the genetic complexes responsible for iris pigmentations. Now, the primitive 20th-century belief that we are our genes has been completely overthrown, but in Mann's case, much of the responsibility for his unfortunate situation can be laid at their door. His irises, to put it crudely and inaccurately and bluntly, keep changing unpredictably over time. Ergo, no quintessence.

Actually, Mustafa froths at the word "quintessence." He's reminded me more than once just how "cranked out stoopid" it is to say "quintessence" when the correct word is "quiddity." Mustafa loves saying the word perhaps a bit more than the word itself, mouthing it as if he were about to spit a seed out. As with most things regarding the tech, he turns to be correct. Quiddity is what makes something different from everything else. A camel has the same quintessence as another camel, but its quiddity is what makes it *this* camel and not that camel. It is a difference that makes an important difference for philosophers and quantum physicists but I am neither, so I decide to stick with the cranked-out-stoopid word.

Mann is hoping Mustafa will figure out how to stop his irises from mutating all the time. There are radical treatments out there-- the coolest one involves implanting a semi-permanent third eye-- but Mann has also reached a steady-state equilibrium. He isn't content exactly, but he isn't discontent either. He is a minor celebrity in the neighborhood. His neighbors look after him. They donate food, clothes. He is invited to parties. Some people find his affliction a sexual turn-on.

"I just need to give one look," he says, with a grin that pretends to be sheepish but can't hide his relish. "It's sometimes a nuisance."

Tanaji's vigorous nod testifies to the animal truth of the man. Perhaps the attraction is that Mann represents a more innocent time. But for all his claims of getting plenty of attention, I can tell Mann is lonely. He gets nervous when I glance at him, but he timidly keeps trying to meet my eyes. I tell him I have brought a gift. Just a thank-you token for sharing his time. He jumps up like a kid to take the small gift-wrapped box of Nama cacao-bitter chocolates, glances at Tanaji, who nods. My gesture has brought pleasure, but I then learn that Mann doesn't like chocolates. He has cancer, has been warned off sugar, and his treatment is complicated by the fact the nano-medicine is utterly dependent on quintessence tech. Tanaji steps into the breach, and between several large withdrawals from the box, informs me that the chocolates are delicious.

I reflect that this sort of thing must happen to Mann all the time. For a few seconds, I marvel at the complexity of the lives our opaque ancestors must have had. How many questions they must have needed to ask one another, all the time!

Mann says he is hungry and looks at Tanaji expectantly. The Welfare officer tells him to order whatever he likes. The meal is on my expense account. We all laugh for no particular reason.

Mann has a special device to make these calls-- Tanaji says it's called a Router. It looks like one of those quaint old-time VR goggles and links to a service provided by the Welfare AI. The details are Byzantine, but I gather the Router basically allows Mann and the world to pretend he has quintessence and makes him 'visible' in the digital world; at least, for small transactions and short durations. I watch Mann link and order the food. He begins in a commanding manner, mentioning he has important guests, but then laughs, and shifts to a more appeasing tone. As soon as he is done, he quickly puts away the Router.

His circumspection reminds me of the wounded soldiers I'd interviewed after the Indo-China war. They would joke and horse around with one another using their newly fitted prosthetic limbs, but in my presence, suddenly turn awkward, minimize the motions of the artificial limbs, and act almost as if their pseudopods belonged to someone else. It suddenly occurs to me, with the brilliant clarity of a lightning flash revealing darkened ground, that Mann is a digital paraplegic and our world has no real way to deal with his situation.

We learn there is some problem with the order. The Router hasn't been upgraded in a while, and what with the new security regs and all, the pseudo-quintessence maneuver fails. As Tanaji fiddles with the Router, I pay for the Dal Fry, The Dream Of Red Chamber (very spicy bean-based dish, only for the experienced and curious bowel), Heavenly Doctrine Of The Confucian Chicken (like Kierkegaard, an acquired pleasure), The Injustice To Dou E (mushrooms with a Maggie Noodle base, highly recommended), accompanied by ample servings of fried rice, and terminated, oddly enough, with pedas. We study the golden-colored oblong sweets. There are three of us, but only two pedas.

"Sir-ji, I don't want any," says Mann to Tanaji, rubbing his stomach. "I must avoid sugar."

Tanaji gives me a meaningful glance. The restaurant had made a simple error in estimation, but it was the kind of error that would have never happened if Mann had had quintessence. He had been invisible for the Manager AI.

The Assistant informs me that it has been unable to take photos because new security regs require all photos with people to be tagged. The rule will make us all safer, so that part is easy to understand, but who will explain to the tagging software that Mann is the exception to the rule? It takes a considerable use of resources to sort it all out, and by the time the Router is updated and the photos can be taken it is quite late.

There's another alert from my Assistant. Sunny Mazumdar has been arrested for sedition. Her friends are putting together a petition, did I wish to sign? I don't mind signing, but there is no need! I'm sure it's all just a misunderstanding and Doctor Mazumdar will be soon released. Due process and all that.

Tanaji says he will stay behind and listen to some Hindi songs-- he says Mann has old audio hardware capable of producing subtle harmonics that modern devices simply cannot match. I tell Mann that the article could draw some attention to him, but he only shrugs. His eyes are affixed on mine. I bid them goodbye. Mann gets up, accompanies me across the room, then stands at the doorway, watching me walk down the flight of stairs. I look up from the bottom of stairwell, meet his gaze, mouth another farewell, and step out to meet the autocar. Even as I write these words, I can feel his living eyes upon me.

Microbiota and the Masses: A Love Story

by S.B. Divya

The scents of earth—loam, pollen, compost, the exhalation of leaves—permeated the inside of Moena Sivaram's airtight home. She stood near the southeast corner and misted the novice bromeliads. The epiphytes clutched the trunk of an elephant ear tree, its canopy stretching up to the clear, SmartWindow-paned roof and shading everything below.

Moena whispered to the plants: "Amma's here, little babies. You're safe with me, but you must grow those roots." With her isolated life, these would be her only children.

She walked barefoot to the sunny citrus grove in the western side of the house. The soil beneath her feet changed from cool and moist to hard and gritty. eBees buzzed among the flowers. She hummed in harmony, a Carnatic song about love birds that was a century old. The heady perfume of orange and lime blossoms filled her up and made her blood sing along. This was home; this, and not the traditional jasmine and rose gardens of Bangalore; this, where her eyes didn't water nor her nose itch.

Diffuse sunlight shone through the SmartWindows paneling the walls. One rectangle stuck out like a cloudy diamond in an otherwise glittering pendant. Moena pulled her tablet from her pocket, brought up the diagnostic software. Red letters delivered bad news: faults in the air and light filters.

The latter mattered little. The plants would get enough sun from the functional panes. The former, though, meant that outside air had infiltrated the house.

Moena's throat closed. Her heart raced. *Stay calm!* But her hands wouldn't listen, clutching each other, fingers twisting like vines around branches. She couldn't breathe! All those microbes: she imagined them invading her sanctum, those wriggly, single-celled prokaryotes.

She shuddered, dropped to the ground, lay prone. Her cheek touched beloved dirt. Safe dirt. *Inhale! Exhale! Again!* She tilted her face, lowered her tongue, and licked. The potent esters of her domestic biome worked their magic, taking over the hamster-wheels in her brain and applying the brakes.

Her hands unclenched. Shoulder blades fell back. Heart slowed. *Stupid brain. We can deal with this.*

The eBees agreed. "Yes, yes, yes," they sang.

Moena went to her supply closet. The air-filter mask inside looked like an insectoid alien: tinted plastic across the eyes, and three jutting cylinders over the mouth and nose areas. Moena pulled it on. The clean air lacked the comforting odors of home, but at least she was protected.

She sealed the offending window pane with heavy plastic and duct tape, then rolled the sensor cart over. *Good!* All air now flowed from the inside out, as it should. She sent a message to SmartWindows Incorporated, requesting a repair person and marking the issue urgent.

Rahul the repairman arrived looking like Moena's favorite porn star: faded jeans, tight white t-shirt, cinnamon-bark skin, boyish black curls. She admired the image on her tablet, fed from the door camera. Too bad she couldn't touch him. Her face flushed. The space between her legs tightened. *Not now, and not him, idiot body.* Not any man or woman infested with outside microbiota.

She slapped her cheeks lightly and blew out a hot breath.

Syed—her outside man—was away at his second cousin's wedding in Mysore. She would have to deal with Rahul herself.

"Please wait there," she said, a delayed audio reply to his intercom buzz.

Moena opened the supply closet and grimaced at the gray isolation suit hanging in the back. It reeked of industrial plastic and factory esters. She grabbed a handful of soil from the floor and sprinkled it into the suit. Then she pulled it and the air mask on.

She stepped into the foyer/airlock, clinched the inner door seals, and walked out the front. To his credit, Rahul only took a half-step back. His dark eyes widened like a bud opening to rain. Questions sprouted and withered on his lips—parted to show endearingly crooked teeth—until he said, "Miss ... Sivaram?"

"Yes. Follow me, please," Moena said.

She led him across the weedy, barren dirt of her lot. They walked around the thick clay walls of the house to arrive at the faulty SmartWindow. Rahul attached his computer to it via a long cable, vine-like but for its gray color. He sat on the dirt and began typing.

"The light and air filters are set to opposite extremes," he said. He spoke English in the well-rounded tones of an educated, middle-class Indian. "Most people use these windows to reduce the ultraviolet while permitting air circulation into the house."

I am not most people. Out loud: "You don't talk like a repairman."

Rahul smiled. "I'm an F.A.E.—a field applications engineer. We repair but we also have technical backgrounds." He paused, squinted up at her. "Tell me, are you *the* Moena Sivaram?"

Tendrils of anxiety coiled in Moena's stomach. The plane crash that killed her parents had been well publicized, but the story had faded from the news years ago. Why would this man jab her with a question about it?

"I am."

"Your thesis on fresh water bioremediation was incredible. How come you haven't published any papers since then?"

Moena gaped behind the mask. "Just who are you?"

"Sorry, I should have explained. I'm a volunteer with Hariharan Ecological Group. They've taken your design and used it for local water pollution. It's been a great success. You're famous among us. I thought, perhaps, you might be running a laboratory in the house, what with these window settings."

Moena reeled at the orthogonality of the question and stared at her reflection in the SmartWindow. Her suit resembled the spent husk of a chrysalis. If only she could emerge a gorgeous butterfly, she could stun Rahul into silence as well.

"I am conducting experiments in the house," she admitted. "I wear this suit to keep the environment as isolated as I can."

"Could I—I mean, if it's not too much trouble—could I see what you're doing?"

Moena shook her head like a leaf frenzied by the wind. Rahul … inside her house? Inside her? Possibilities tumbled in her mind, gorgeous and terrifying. *Impossible!*

"No, of course not." He turned back to his computer. "Sorry for asking."

Moena reached out to him, drew her hand back. She had no right to his body.

The afternoon sun blazed from high in the summer sky as the silence stretched. Heat built inside Moena's isolation suit. Her shirt clung to her torso. Rivulets of sweat trickled down her neck and collected at the waistband of her shorts. She sat still, channeling the atman of a tree stump.

"Aha!" Rahul said at last.

The window cleared to perfect transparency. Rahul reinstalled it and stowed his computer. He handed her a memory cube.

"You'll want to update all of the windows with this version of software. The problem is that your filter settings are below virus size. The old software kept getting stuck in an interrupt routine and eventually hanging. This version should prevent that from happening."

"Thank you," Moena said. Part of her wished every window would fail, once a week, so Rahul would come again.

"The company will bill you directly. Best of luck with the research."

Moena nodded. The mask bobbled. Rahul walked out of the front gate, latching it closed behind him. She was alone.

The sterilization wash in her foyer had never felt so tedious. Once she was fully inside, Moena yanked off the mask and took several deep, relieving breaths. She peeled away the sweaty suit, let it crumple to the floor.

Soil wormed into the gaps between her bare toes. Leaves and fronds brushed her hands as she walked—nearly ran— to her bedroom. It looked much as it had when her parents were alive: a single bed, a narrow wardrobe painted yellow, a matching desk with shelves above it. The coffin was the exception.

The adult-sized container lay between the bed and the room's boarded-up window. The device's actual name was "Virtual Reality Recumbent Booth," but the world had decided that was too unwieldy. Moena agreed.

She browsed the preset visuals under "male." This one had beetle brows. That one was too pale. Dozens had overlays with blue eyes and blond hair. She stopped at a face that was close enough to Rahul's. The hair needed more curl and the eyes wanted to be smaller, but she could adjust those when her body wasn't pulsing with need.

The coffin's interior walls cozied up to her, running its— *his*—hands over her body, blowing warm breath against her neck, pressing itself *himself!*—into her empty spaces.

Tension wanted release, but Moena's mind refused to fall into the illusion. She cut the session short.

What would a lover feel like, for real? She shivered. *Think of the microflora! The exchange of so much more than fluid.* And where would it happen? Here, in her bed? In the sanctum of her home? The biome would be corrupted, and her hard work set back by years. *Idiot! Forget him!*

But Rahul persisted in her thoughts, like a splinter that wormed deeper the more she tried to pry it out. Moena called the only friend left from her outside days: her fellow graduate student, now Professor Das.

Ananya's broad brown face appeared on the tablet screen accompanied by the clamor of children.

"Let me get somewhere quiet."

"You have to save me," Moena said, after her friend relocated.

Ananya cocked an eyebrow. "Do you need some new cultures?"

"No. Bacteria can't help me. I've been infected by a man, a glorious specimen of male *Homo sapiens*!"

"Infected? What? Did you have sex with someone?"

Moena laughed at her friend's horrified expression. "No. I haven't touched him. Mmmmm ... but I want to. Am I selfish for staying in here? For using my research to benefit myself and not the world?"

"What? Mo, you're not making any sense. Are you okay? How's your biome?"

"The verdant lovelies are fine. Creepy crawlies and microbiota are good. My blood results came back in normal ranges last month. But my heart—my heart is parched for company! He said I'm famous. They're using my thesis. Should I be out there, helping? Fighting the good fight?"

"First: you're not selfish for keeping yourself from chronic illness. Second: you are brilliant, and you should be publishing your results. Third: who is this chap and how has he gotten under your skin?"

"His name is Rahul. Window repairman and eco-warrior supreme, with skin like creamy cocoa-butter."

Her friend rolled her eyes. "Get a grip. You haven't touched another human being in over five years. You want to risk everything for him?" Her expression softened. "If you get sick again, you'll have to give him up."

"Bridges, crossings, et cetera, dear Professor. Besides, I can't be myself with him so this love affair won't last. Short, torrid, over!"

"What do you mean?"

"He won't want to date Moena Sivaram, wealthy eccentric and victim of tragic circumstance. I'll have to invent a mundane secret identity, someone matched to his station in life."

"A lie isn't a good foundation for love."

"I'll keep it to romance, not love. Then can I have your blessing?"

"No. Yes. I don't know," Ananya sputtered. "Just ... check in with me, okay? I'm worried about you."

Moena agreed and ended the call. Her fingers approached the keyboard then curled away, like the leaves of a *Mimosa pudica*: touch-me-not. Her mother's words from a decade ago haunted her.

"When you're of age, Moena, we'll find you a nice boy to marry. Or you'll find one on your own, but keep this in mind: men desire women who can stand up to them and still remain short. They don't want women who are smarter or wealthier or more famous. Better that you forget boys and marriage until you have your own measure."

Smarter. Wealthier. More famous. Rahul lacked a doctorate. Rahul worked for a living. Rahul's name had never scorched news headlines.

Moena invented a fitting girl for Rahul to love. Meena Sivaraman (close enough that Moena would answer to it): middle class, moderately educated, modestly dressed. A proper, earnest, *sane* young woman with a black braid and a bindi.

Breath came easy. Fingers pattered on the keyboard. Two days later, "Meena" had a coffee-shop date with Rahul to discuss volunteer opportunities.

On the day of their meeting, Moena rejected three different outfits: a traditional sari (too stuffy), a salwar-kameez from a distant aunt (too gaudy), and a dress from her university days in London (too Western). Clad in jeans and a short-sleeved cotton kurti, she stepped out of the house.

She wasn't sure whose eyes were wider, hers or Syed's, as she bolted into the back seat of the car.

"Are you sure, madam?" he asked for the tenth time, peering at her from the driver's seat.

Heart racing, palms sweating, and breath shallow, she said, "Yes. Drive, please."

They drove down tree-lined streets, past skyscraping bee-hives of apartments and claustrophobic rows of shops. The car's fan was set to recirculate, but the scents of Bangalore crept in through imperfect seals. Moena's throat closed. She gripped the sprigs of holy basil she had brought, crushing the tender leaves. They released a pungent, soothing aroma. She plucked two of them and pressed them into her nostrils. *Better.*

The car lurched to the right, came up to the curb, and stopped.

"This is the place," Syed said. "But we can go home, madam. Your health is more important than anything."

"Thank you, Syed. I'll be okay. I promise I'll call you if I'm not."

Moena stepped out and drew her first breath of raw city air in five years. Dust assailed her nostrils, drying the tiny hairs and making her sneeze. Rumbling diesel trucks spewed black exhaust. A current of decaying refuse and putrid sewage ran through it all. She gagged.

Bodies moved past her along the uneven slabs of the side-walk. They stank of hot oil, sweat, sandalwood, fish, jasmine, sex. A stray dog trotted from a cluster of trash to a half-eaten banana. A fly fizzed into Moena's ear, tickling it before moving on.

How did anyone live like this? How had she, for the first twenty-three years of her life? She could almost sense the ef-fluvia penetrating her lungs, polluting her bloodstream. She forced herself to inhale a second time. *Stand straight!* Shoulders back, chin high, hands unclenched: *face the city like every-one else.*

Advertisements plastered the low cinderblock wall to her right, their poster colors faded by rain, their edges frayed and torn. On the other side, gulmohar trees bordered the courtyard, shading the café patrons within. She scanned the crowd. Where was Rahul?

Moena threaded her way between the tables, careful not to touch any thing or person or plant. She spotted Rahul's curly hair and white t-shirt (did he wear nothing else?) in the back corner, at a table sprinkled with pollen from the blossoms above. She pinched her nose against a sneeze.

"Rahul Madhavan?" She tried to sound as if she'd never seen him before.

"Yes. You must be Meena. Please, sit. Shall I order you some coffee?"

Moena swallowed repulsion—non-homemade coffee!—and forced a smile. "Thanks."

"You'd like to volunteer for H.E.G. and do some ecological work, yes? Let me tell you about what we do."

Rahul entered a fifteen-minute monologue with words that felt as much like home as the scent of damp humus. He spoke of water pollution, remediation, plant and bacterial seeding; of community effort and citizen science; of working with the earth and not against it. His hands moved in organic shapes—no sharp edges—and his fingertips came together and burst apart like a ripe seedpod.

Moena watched, listened, sneezed. She swiped at her drippy nostrils with a bleached white handkerchief and sneezed again. Nodded. Smiled. Sneezed. Her coffee arrived and cooled. It stayed untouched but so did his.

"How does that sound? Like something you can commit to?"

"Absolutely. Once a week. No problem."

Problems tangled her thoughts faster than she could prune them away.

"Great! I'll send you the information for next week's action."

"Why aren't you a biologist?"

"Sorry?"

You're not supposed to know that! "I mean, why are you a volunteer and not working for H.E.G.? You seem so knowledgeable about this."

"I'm too old?" He flashed his crooked smile. "I already had an engineering degree when I got interested in remediation. I'm over thirty now. I can't possibly compete in entrance exams. What about you? What brought you to this?"

"I have ... a friend. She was sick for a long time, and some of that was because of our water and air. I want to do something for her—for everyone—to improve that."

"Wonderful! Then I'll see you next week."

He held out his hand.

Shake it! Moena thrust out her own, let him wrap his fingers around hers. His palm felt warm and smooth, like eucalyptus bark in sunlight. The thrill of contact traveled through her arm and spread, tingling, throughout the rest of her body. *All of him, now!* Her heart raced, mouth dried. Desire gathered force, whipping from a zephyr to a tornado. Her cheeks flushed. Could he tell? Did he sense her tumult?

Rahul let go.

They exited the café together.

Syed picked her up.

The ride home dragged on, an interminable torture of snarled traffic, gaunt beggars, and enough rain to streak the dusty windows.

Moena met Rahul and the handful of other volunteers at an oblong lake situated southeast of the city. She felt naked without her isolation suit as she approached the slime-ridden banks. Bone-white tree trunks dotted the waterline. A quarter kilometer to the left, a rusting hulk of metal heaved a piston up and down. The thrum of its motor drowned the buzzing clouds of insects.

A wave of fetid air blew across Moena. She stumbled back, knelt, and heaved her lunch into a cluster of spindly bushes.

"Sorry. I should have warned you." Rahul stood next to her. He held out a sky-blue paper mask. "Wear this. It's coated with menthol."

Moena accepted it with shaking hands. The astringent scent choked her, squeezing tears from the corners of her eyes, but her stomach settled.

"What is this place?"

"Agara Lake," Rahul said. "Rife with industrial metals, plastics, and animal waste."

Moena stood and caressed a leaf. The bush was a fledgling neem tree, spotted with brown, yellow, and black.

"Poor thing," she whispered. "You need help."

Rahul's pupils dilated. His brow quirked.

Moena shrugged. "I've always felt more comfortable with plants than people."

Sunlight glinted, turning Rahul's irises to honey brown. "Me, too."

He guided her to the lakeside, his hand light against the small of her back, intimate and yet not.

The volunteers worked in separate domains. Moena's assignment was simple: to collect soil and water samples for analysis.

White foam floated in Rorschach blotches on the surface of the water. Centimeter-high waves lapped at yellowish brown mud. A dead fish bulged at the surface a few meters in.

Guilt constricted her chest with weedy roots. Isolation had restored her health, but at what cost? When had the state of the world become so rotten?

Moena pinched a test tube between thumb and forefinger as if it were a wriggling insect. Gloves. Boots. Rubber coveralls. All were standard issue protection they'd used in graduate school, but ecological vigilantes—especially here in India— had no such resources. *Do it! Dip your hand in!*

She inched into the lake. Its lukewarm water soaked through her shoes and socks and up along her pants. Moena swallowed a sob. She rooted herself and leaned down. Muscles trembled. *Reach in!* Half the water spilled from the test tube on her first try. *Again!* The second attempt went better, and the fifth held most of the intended sample.

She straightened, looked across the muddy banks. Rahul nodded in approval. Pride sprouted in her heart, tiny and bursting with life.

Two hours later, the veteran volunteers departed. Moena stood beside Rahul as he stored her samples in the trunk of his car. He, too, was stained with lake scum. Sweat matted his curls. Dirt caked his fingernails and cuticles. He handed her a bottle of water from a cooler.

Moena gulped half of it in seconds. It did little to ease the ache growing behind her eyes. Her sinuses throbbed.

Rahul frowned. "Are you okay?" He gestured toward Moena's arms.

Patches of red blossomed everywhere that lake water had spattered on her.

"Allergies," she said. "I'll be fine." *Liar, liar!*

"Then I'll thank you twice for helping. Not many people can handle this kind of work, and even fewer would sacrifice their health for it. Will I—will we, that is—see you next time?"

"Yes."

Moena waited until she was in her car to blow her nose.

Syed glanced at her reflection in the rearview mirror. "Madam, why are you doing this to yourself?"

"Guilt, Syed! And love. Love for my people, the verdant ones and the fleshy ones and the ones you can only see under a microscope. Guilt that I've kept myself away for too long."

The next week, Moena brought her own vials—empty and sterile—tucked in her jeans pockets. She wore a light cotton kameez with long sleeves. Scabbed patches decorated her skin, the after-effects of the previous session. While she worked, she collected her own samples of water and soil. Rahul might have been the catalyst for this madness, but the biota were the reactant that kept it fed.

She watched Rahul as he worked the nutrient tanks and pumps. His dark brow wrinkled in concentration, his jaw slack and lips parted, just enough for a peek of pink tongue. Green slime spattered his boots and the lower half of his jeans. *Brave, lovely man.*

He glanced up from his handheld—caught her staring. Moena's cheeks warmed as he smiled, tiny and knowing. *Concentrate!* The memory of his expression trickled down through her belly, lower, heating her, an exothermic reactor of her very own.

Once again, she and Rahul finished their work last. Syed had not yet returned from his tea break. She was about to message him to when Rahul spoke seven magic words: "Would you like to get some coffee?"

Moena's inner fifteen-year-old jumped for joy, did cartwheels, crowed to the world. A fit of coughing prevented her adult self from answering.

Gasping for breath, she said, "Yes."

She left the coffee untouched again. If Rahul noticed, he didn't comment, but he did ask her out to dinner. *Dinner—hurrah!* And yet not. *Idiot!* He would notice if she left an entire meal uneaten. The food would be crawling with microflora, with all the variety of Bangalore's citizens. Her stomach roiled at the thought. But she would do it—for Rahul, for the chance to fertilize the seeds of their relationship—anything for that.

"How was the date?" Ananya asked, smirking.

"Great! I spent the rest of the night on the toilet," Moena said. "But it was worth every minute. Rahul's so passionate about this work. Imagine what he's like in bed!"

The smile vanished from her friend's face. "Don't joke! You can't keep risking your health for this. You should tell him the truth."

"But he wants to see me again."

"Stop stringing him along!"

"I can't. Besides, he's wrapped me in his own string package."

"Oh, Mo, you've fallen for him?"

"I'm still falling, drifting, like leaves in a Cambridge autumn. He can't ever know who I really am or he would grind me into the dirt."

"You're not giving him enough credit. Either that or he's an ass who doesn't deserve you."

"You should see the cultures I'm getting from the lake."

"What? Don't change the subject!"

"I think I've figured out a way to improve the breakdown of the polycarbonates. We need to change the nitrogen levels in the nutrient mix. Oh, and I spliced some enzyme sequences from *Geotrichum candidum* into the *flavobacterium* that's worked best so far."

"Really? You were able to splice in fungal genes and the bacteria survived? Show me the data."

They spent the rest of the conversation arguing over organic chemistry and whether a different strain or a second strain would make for a better solution. Moena went to bed dreaming of curing Bangalore's water ailments. What better token of love could she offer to Rahul?

The baby bromeliads drooped. Their once dark green leaves faded, their tips browned. The house soil smelled like rotting cabbage in its shadier pockets. Two of the eBees kept crashing into the SmartWindows like drunks with frenetic wings.

Moena extracted samples from the surface and subsoil, ran them through the DNA sequencer. The lake bacteria had infiltrated her cultivated sanctum. They were winning.

She coughed over her shoulder and turned back to the scope. Her nose hadn't stopped dripping for weeks. At night, her joints ached. The coffin's masseuse software did little to relieve the pain.

But. But! Last night, five weeks after their first date and many a rendezvous since, she and Rahul had kissed. Wet, bacteria-saliva-swapping glory! Her last boyfriend at Cambridge was a decade past. She'd forgotten how exquisite the dance of lips and tongue could be.

Rahul had whispered of his germinating passion: *There's no one in the world like you. The way you move, the way you talk— you're exquisite. You're my glorious once-blooming orchid.*

Those words! That metaphor!

The skin on the inside of her thighs burned, chafed from her numerous sessions with virtual-coffin-Rahul. Ten times ten times ten ... the order of magnitude didn't matter. Ersatz satisfaction would never be enough. She needed the real thing.

Moena danced her gloved fingertips against the sterile tile countertop. Petri dishes and bottles of reagents crowded the glass-fronted refrigerator to her left. A jumble of live cultures and test tube racks littered the surface on her right, cozying up to the CRISPR-based gene editor.

She needed a solution to remediate the lake into health but also to heal her own biome. Every foray into the outside world—every handhold and kiss with Rahul allowed new single-celled adversaries into the house.

To cut off contact with him? The idea was a nasty fly tiptoeing through the hairs of *Dionaea muscipula*. Snap, trap, digest! Banish it to nonexistence.

She exited her laboratory and padded to the southern side of the house. The sun-warmed grit under her bare feet helped her think. Never mind the arthritic curl bending her toes. *Fix the house, fix yourself.* She swabbed the leaves of a dwarf orange tree that was mottled with yellow and black spots.

"*Wrong. Wrong. Wrong,*" hummed the bees.

Years to achieve balance. Weeks to fall apart. So unfair! Moena's inner five-year-old stomped and stormed and kicked up an unholy tantrum. Tears trickled. She wiped them away, catching some on the swab, contaminating it. *Idiot!*

She stumbled to her towering *Dieffenbachia* grove and curled up under the shade of their broad, variegated leaves. Her cheek sunk into the cool, soft loam. She extended her tongue—*wait*! How much beneficial microflora did the soil still have? Was it friend or foe?

To lick or not to lick? That is the question! Whether 'tis nobler in the mind to suffer the filth and rot of exterior living, or to take—antibiotics, but that had too many syllables—against a sea of—*damn*. She lost the analogy.

Moena giggled.

She beat her head against the ground. Madness. Her old friend had arrived for a visit. Let's catch up over chai. Plain or masala?

Ananya had left three messages, one for each call that Moena had ignored.

Soon. Soon she would return them. *Close!* She was so close to the answer. Her scalp itched. When had she last bathed? Not important. *Focus! There!* That snippet would turn her engineered bacteria into oxygen-devouring microbeasts. Bye-bye, plastics! Nitrates as a byproduct? Pretty please with citric acid on top, but only a dollop. Too much would be toxic.

Moena dumped the design into the artificial-life simulator. Crunch away! Tell me some good news! Please, please, let this combination be the magical one, the stable one.

The phone sang to her, that old Carnatic song about love birds. She'd assigned the tune to Rahul's caller ID. She had to answer.

"Meena, hi. Where are you? We're at the lake."

"Oh." She checked the calendar. Oh! *Focus! Be Meena again.* "Sorry. I lost track of time."

His image frowned on the tiny screen. Moena wanted to plant kisses in the adorable furrow between his brows.

"Are you okay? You don't look well."

Damn. She hadn't meant to leave the camera on. *Distract him!*

"Hey, you're my boyfriend. You shouldn't say such things!"

Rahul's lips curved, frond-like. "Am I your boyfriend now?"

Moena nodded, licked her lips. Promises, promises. "I'll come soon. Will you be there in another hour?"

"The others won't, but I'll wait for you. I miss you."

She returned to the simulation. *Go faster!* Numbers scrolled. Protein triplets sprinkled the results with alphabetic seeds. The probability of success ticked into the nineties. Good enough! Nothing yet had transcended the sixties. She kissed the screen, then transferred the design into the splicer.

Ten minutes later, Moena decanted half of her custom bacterial solution into a sterile test tube. *The solution is the solution!* She snickered. She pocketed that tube and took the remainder to the water feeder tank for the house. *Be fruitful and multiply, my little beasties!* You will save the soil, the house, *me*.

The sun's glare reflected from the lake, stabbing through Moena's eyes and into her frontal cortex like an illuminated knife. *Light sensitivity!* Another symptom of her degrading health. *Never mind!* Salvation lay in her pocket. She slipped a finger in, caressed the glass tube. Her mind wandered to another cylindrical object, one that wasn't so cold and brittle.

Rahul stood by the pump. Sweat beaded on his forehead, dewdrops on buttery leather. He motioned her over. He'd already taught her how to work the injection well and nutrient tank. All she had to do today was pour in her vial when he wasn't looking.

The single-celled lovelies would digest the iron and polycarbonates in the water, then make their way into the locals. The guts of Bangalore—human and animal—would shit out more of Moena's microbabies. They would infect the sewage runoff and restore the water to livable purity.

She stumbled over the slight rise of the concrete pad. Fire blazed up from her rheumatic toes to her swollen knees. Rahul caught her before she fell. She gasped as his hands crushed the weeping sores under her sleeves. *Bite your tongue! Don't scream!*

"What's the matter?"

Spin a lie, quick! Before he can think.

"Sprained my ankle, that's all."

She plucked her arm from his grasp, staggered to the nutrient tank, pried off the lid.

"What are you doing?"

No more time for subterfuge. No time to talk. Her body would give out soon.

The stench from the fomenting cultures flowed into Moena's nostrils, triggered the nausea-inducing portion of her brain. Her stomach contracted. *No time!*

She yanked the vial from her pocket. *Splash!* In went her microbes.

Uncontrolled experiment! Her advisor's voice rang in her head. *Unpublished! Unverified! Dangerous!*

Sorry, Professor.

Concrete bashed Moena's knees as she knelt and vomited. War raged in her gut. Which side would prevail? Red and black streaked the mess that splattered across the dull gray cement.

"Meena!"

Rahul's head blocked the sun. Golden light haloed his black curls.

"Surya," she whispered. Sun God. Beautiful.

She heaved again. Tremors coursed through her major muscle groups. She was a tree in a storm, her core rotted through by maggots. She toppled.

Rahul/Surya scooped her up, carried her to the car. Syed's voice and his swirled with frantic concern. Her own protests joined in admixture, dilute and ineffective.

Stop! You can't bring him home!
Blackness overtook Moena's vision.

Blurs of light. Sticky eyelids. Puffy tongue. Somewhere, an incessant annoying *beep beep beep*.

Moena shifted her arm. Warning pain: *a needle*. She blinked. The world resolved, focused, magnified—like looking through a giant drop of water. A bag of clear fluid fed into a tube.

Intravenous drip. She inclined her head. She was in her bedroom, alone, and being fed by this device. *Contamination*. Who had been in her house? What miserable microbes crawled in with them? What were they feeding her?

Antibiotics. The label confirmed it. They were poisoning her, killing her microscopic friends, the colonies she'd worked so long to build.

Moena extracted the needle. She licked at the pearl of blood that formed, pressed on the hole with her thumb. *Beep. Beep.* There: her tablet bleated from her desk. The world spun and swayed as she walked and dropped into the chair.

Low battery. She silenced the alarm, sucked away another drop of blood, plugged the device in. An indicator light flashed in the upper corner: Rahul had left her a message. Video. She played it.

His face appeared on the screen. Drooping, but lovely. Kissable lips that moved with care. "They wouldn't let me in. Syed called your physician. She took care of you, said you had to be isolated in your home or you wouldn't get well. Meena—sorry, Moena—I don't know what else to say. I always suspected that you were hiding something, but this? It's too much. I don't understand you. What do you want with someone like me? Sex? A lower class boy to toy with until you find someone in your own circles? Did you think I wouldn't mind because I'm a guy? Well, you were wrong. You broke my heart."

Anger, disappointment, betrayal—the lines of his face grew harder, twisted, a tree grown without enough water.

"I changed my mind," she whispered at the screen. "I wanted everything about you, in the end."

She brushed away a tear and traced his image with the wet finger, blurring his features, softening them. *You don't understand what I am.* She pressed record, to explain, to rip out the lies and plant the truth in his ears, but no sound emerged. How could words be enough?

The silence crushed Moena. Tears slipped, spattered, diluted the blood welling on the back of her hand. She stumbled from the bedroom into the glaring sunshine of the main house.

"Your fault. Your fault," droned the eBees.

She headed for the *Dieffenbachia* grove. The test plants stood straight, verdant and white, not a patch of yellow or brown. Translucent pink worms writhed away from her curling toes. The earth under Moena's feet felt crumbly and cool, and the sweet scent of compost filled the air.

"At least I saved you," she said. She caressed the waxy leaves with her fingertips. "My darlings, you still love me, don't you? You'll help me."

Moena lay down, wiped the bloody smear on the back of one hand into the dirt, wiped her cheeks with the other. She licked the dark streak of loam from her skin. The bitterness of blood mixed with rich manganese and the tang of humic acid. She pinched the soil between her fingertips. She needed to analyze it. If this grove was thriving, she could help the other parts of the house.

And Rahul? How to remediate a polluted relationship? His love had wrapped Moena with its brambles, dug into her flesh, held tight. Pulling them out would leave her riddled with holes. Did he hurt this much, too? *My heart is broken*, he'd said. She didn't have the strength to think it through. First, she had to heal herself.

One week fell away, then another, then a third. The house became a safe haven rather than hostile territory. Leaves returned to verdurous states. The eBees whirled in sober coordination. Moena's thoughts became as clear as her SmartWindows.

"You need to make a peace offering, a gift," Ananya said. "But then what? Will he be willing to live on your terms? I'm sorry, Mo. I wish you could find that kind of happiness, but maybe Rahul isn't the right one."

A gift—a token of love. What mattered most to Rahul? This city. Its water. Its land. Moena could give him the health of Bangalore, but only if she knew whether her experiment had worked.

This time she wore the isolation suit to the lake. She avoided the volunteer hours. The water stretched like gray glass, rippled by the occasional crow's feet. Her breath rasped through the filters. Strange, not to smell anything. Moena scooped samples from the water and the lake bed, carried them back to the car where Syed waited, his face wrinkled with concern.

The results were gorgeous. The polycarbonate levels had dropped well below the previous curve. She needed more data over time to measure the new rate, but this was enough for an initial publication. Her hands quivered like stamens in a breeze. She typed for ten hours, loaded the draft onto a data cube. Gene sequences and a vial of live cultures completed the package.

Moena sat in the citrus grove. She inhaled the aroma of orange blossoms and traced curlicues in the sandy soil. A tablet lay by her feet. It displayed the feed from the door camera. Syed picked up the padded envelope and disappeared.

Would Rahul answer? Would he understand? Would he forgive?

The draft paper described her life down to its deepest roots. The seeds of health—for her, for everyone—were sown throughout the dry, technical paragraphs. She sent a second copy to Ananya. Let Professor Das lend it credibility. Let their ideas infect the world. Let Rahul come back to her life.

Moena waited three days. Nothing. Not a call or message or note. He had pruned her away like a rotten branch. Poison. That's what her actions had brought to his life and her own. She deserved to be cut off.

Moena took a kitchen knife to the coffin. She drew it through the supple fabric lining, parting it like the skin of a ripe tomato. Wires, actuators, and pressure sensors burst forth in an overgrown tangle. *Begone, temptation!*

She drew the blade through it once more the next day and the day after. For each twenty-four hours that Rahul didn't answer, she slashed another reminder of what she was: moron, idiot, lunatic. *Never again!*

Rahul arrived on the day she made the fourteenth stroke. He looked nothing like a repairman. He wore a loose kurta and baggy cotton pants. His curls had grown, and they blew like errant wood shavings around his face. A nylon bag rested by his feet.

"Miss ... Sivaram?" he said through the intercom. He flashed his crooked smile.

Moena buried a rising sob. "I'm coming."

She ran through sunlight and shade, leaves and fronds caressing her bare arms, urging her forward. *Go! Faster!* She stopped at the inner threshold of the foyer.

"I'm so sorry, Rahul. About all of it. I didn't know how else—"

"It's okay. I read your paper. I understood enough, I think. I had H.E.G. do the lab analysis on your samples and the lake. My God, Moena, the water there is incredible! What a transformation! The work you've done—it could change everything." He paused. "Can I come in?"

Unshed tears suffused Moena's face, filled the cavities, pushed her into action. She opened the outer door as her answer. Rahul removed his shoes and walked in. She set the sterilizing wash to a simple soap solution.

"Close your eyes," she said.

Water drenched Rahul like a personal cloudburst. Rivulets of brown ran into the drain, washing away dust and oil and the hostility of Bangalore. Wet cloth delineated the contours of his body.

Moena retrieved a towel from her bedroom. The mutilated coffin sat to one side, an eyesore. Shame rooted her feet. Cover it up? *No*. No more secrets. She returned to Rahul as the wash ended.

"I'm sorry I was silent for so long," he said. "At first I was waiting for the lab results, and then I had to make some arrangements in case ... "

"Of what?" she prompted.

"In case you'll have me to stay."

"You mean ... in here, with me?"

He nodded. Crystal clear droplets fell from his hair.

"I'm not normal, Rahul. I never will be. That's why I didn't tell you who I was. It wasn't about the money or your caste. How could I ask you to fall in love with the insanity of my house, my life? I can't offer a wedding or children or happy occasions with the whole family. All I have is money and isolation."

"And the beauty of your intellect. Your generous spirit. Your passion for the earth." Rahul's eyes glistened. "Moena, you are the strangest, most wonderful human being I've ever known. How could I not be hopelessly in love with you? I don't care about weddings and children. You have the power to change the world, and I want to be part of that, to be part of your life."

"You'll have to stay inside for a long time."

"I know."

"It could be months or even years until I can stabilize the biome for both of us."

"I can accept that."

"And your family?"

He laughed, crooked teeth flashing. "They've given up on

me. Over thirty, unmarried, and volunteering in cesspools—they think I'm crazy."

The Carnatic love birds crooned.

"Then let's be lunatics together," she said.

She opened the inner door. It closed behind Rahul with a slight sucking noise, not unlike a kiss. *Hush! Be patient!* She took him by the hand and led him to the elephant ear tree. Their bare feet left two sets of prints in the rich, dark soil. Rahul gazed up into the canopy. Sunshine and wonderment dappled his face.

"Meet your father," Moena whispered to the baby bromeliads.

She crouched and ran a finger through the soil. He knelt beside her.

"Open your mouth," she said.

Rahul's brow quirked in puzzlement. His lips parted. Moena's finger hovered, then darted between like a hummingbird's beak, depositing its microbial pollen on his waiting tongue. His eyes opened wide and white as forbidden jasmine.

"Your first inoculation," she whispered.

His mouth surrounded her finger, sucking gently. His teeth tickled her skin.

The eBees hummed, "Kiss him! Kiss him!"

The leaves rustled in agreement. *Now!*

Moena freed her hand and twined her arms around Rahul's neck. She pressed her trunk into his, then her lips. The damp heat of his body soaked into hers. His flavors purled across her tongue. Lingering grit. Chile powder. Kernels of salt. Their microbiota swirled, integrated, danced into each other, merged into one biomass. *What's yours is mine. What's mine is yours.*

"Welcome home," Moena said.

Communal

by Shikhandin

Communication was not born from sound. Yet, in the past we used sound to communicate. Sound created in patterns and aural shapes. Not just us. All creatures that moved over the surface of our Earth. We were divided into those with tongues and those without, those who were rootless and those who weren't. Those whose movements were quick and visible and those who seemingly stayed still. The tongued and rootless earthlings had a hierarchy. We were the highest in that hierarchy. We ruled and decided everything, including the births and deaths of all that lived on Earth.

Though we did not know it then, did not understand it or even dream of it, we were one family. Yes, we of the tongued and rootless clan and those of the silent and rooted ones came from the same womb. But that memory was lost in the meanderings of evolution. We did not remember our origins, and we did not respect our differences.

We were related, but did not live as one harmonious family. We were not a united family. We were not a considerate and caring family. We, the most powerful, did not rule wisely. We disobeyed Earth's circadian rhythm. We disrupted the paths of wind and water. We drowned everything in toxins. So immersed were we in our own sounds that we failed to hear the soundless communications we had been receiving. Blinded by our egos we did not see it coming.

Life is a powerful being. Yes life, that force we took for granted. Life, like us, is a child of earth, and friend to all things great and small. Life is the energy we believed we owned, and thought we were Gods of. No mother will tolerate the abuse of her child. No mother will stand by meek and helpless, watching the slaughter of her child. No mother is entirely unforgiving. No good mother is partial to only one child.

Mother, you did not forsake us. You took us, the prodigals, back. And here I am today, grown old, but so wondrously fulfilled. I had never imagined this life in my boyhood.

"Hey Bhagwan! Hey bhagwan!" Ma clamped her hand over her mouth and slammed her foot on the brakes.

Startled, I dropped my school tablet. My previous day's assignment blinked out of view. I looked up and froze. The traffic had come to a standstill. People were either looking at the news feeds set up at traffic booths or into their individual screens. The news feeds were screaming. Over and over and over again. The scene was replayed just as many times. It was the latest hot topic.

I had never seen such aggression before. But I am just a boy. No grownup had ever seen such aggression before either. Not ma, not bapu, not even dadi, who is more than a hundred years old.

Everyone seemed to be talking all at once. Terrorism! Wilful aggression, they said. Premeditated action. Danger to mankind! It was shocking, at first. The anger came later. When the enormity of what was happening sunk in. The impossible had happened. A strange, powerful and evil miracle had taken place. It was unbelievable. But the proof was there, staring at us from every screen. In Jaisalmer. In other cities. Across the world.

The things had brought an airship down. An entire jumbo airship packed with passengers and cargo!

I saw the clip shot by the drones on my way to school. The thirty second clip, with the warning "disturbing graphic content" flashing at the top right corner, played over and over again. And all around me I could see the grown-ups, my folks included, watching it continuously, as if they were mesmerised. Now there's a funny thing, the drones are never hurt. It's as if they know what contains bio-mass and what doesn't.

The things, I can't think of anything else to call them, looked like vines resembling pythons. Or maybe pythons that looked like vines. Pythons with leaves and fruit. They swung out to grab the sky, shoots and shoots and shoots of them. Like Jack's beanstalks gone crazy. They flung themselves at the airship with loud thwacks. It took them less than thirty seconds to cover it with a mass of writhing green. They twisted and turned, maybe twice or thrice, and went down just as suddenly as they had appeared. After that the sky became empty again. Just like that. Not even a bird in sight.

Of course the government announced an indefinite holiday for all schools and offices. The news feeds urged people to stock up on essentials and stay home. We knew what would happen next. Cutters would be deployed. A whole army of humongous robots made of steel, and powered by uranium. Completely automated, with nothing remotely organic in them. The older models used to be manned by drivers though, seated inside bulletproof see-through cabins fitted into the central portion of the cutters. These would lumber out, sweeping their long metallic arms rhythmically, and making pulp out of all living greens. Some of them still exist. Bapu has one, a smaller, family size machine. The fully automated cutters were much faster. They turned the world bare again within minutes.

Dadi used to tell me stories of how, before she was born, Muslims and Dalits alike would be thrashed and jailed or killed outright whenever stray cows disappeared. Afterwards, when she was a young girl, whole herds began to disappear. Not regularly but often enough to get noticed. These were the cattle let out to roam, because they were past their prime and nobody dared kill them for meat and skin. It was as if the animals had been spirited away overnight. An impossible feat, because even if they had been powerlifted and dumped inside cargo-hovers, someone would have noticed. Goats started to vanish too, and sheep, donkeys and camels. All grazing animals in fact. And then chickens, dogs and cats. And then humans, a few at a time, the kind nobody would miss - the poor, the outdoor sleepers, the homeless, the beggars and discards.

The sand was gone forever in Jaisalmer. Had gone, years before I was born. What existed in its place was a squishy kind of soil that seemed alive in places. Jaisalmer was green. The whole world was green. Not a grain of desert anywhere.

"The Thar Desert shrank right before our eyes," said dadi. "Not only the Thar, deserts all over the world. We were so happy. More forest meant more animals and birds. That's what we thought at first. But this was a strange kind of greening. More a curse than a blessing."

The disappearances didn't affect humans directly. Nor were they seen as a problem at first. Food was being grown in factories before Dadi's birth. Pure and clean food that adhered to our respective faiths. Halal for Muslims. Kosher for Jews. Untainted vegetarian for Brahmins like us, and Jains. And then there was the regular varieties for those who ate everything indiscriminately.

Animals existed to add to the scenic beauty. Forests were left intact as far as possible, with the department of forestry regulating the populations of all the species. Extinct ones had been successfully cloned. Some were even returned to the wild. So we were good. Humans were doing good, taking good care of the planet, a complete departure from how it used to be even until a century before dadi's birth.

Dadi had her own theories. She said that her parents would often lament about the changes, and that things were no longer the same. That something was brewing underfoot, and maybe this heralded the actual end of the world. The scriptures predicted the ends of epochs, of life. Dadi brought religion into everything, being old, and old-fashioned and all. Bapu didn't say anything to her face, but he found her theories childish. Ma, being the scientific sort openly pooh-poohed her.

I wasn't born when the animals began to disappear. Bapu told me that when the governments noticed, all countries got together. They held joint meetings. Engineers pooled all their knowledge and designed the cutters. Scientists from every field got together to build labs. They studied the phenomena, took notes, made tests and exchanged information. In the beginning it looked like humanity would win. We anyway had our food labs where we could grow anything from radish to lamb chops. Not that we needed the lamb chops. My family, like most people from Rajasthan and the Marwar region are pure vegetarian. The only animal products we consumed were milk and ghee and other things made from milk, created duly in sterile factories. Dadi was squeamish about eating root vegetables, like carrots. She said they reminded her of bones.

"Haddi," she said. "All root veggies are nothing but haddi, bones." But she wouldn't explain bones of what.

Ma and bapu had no such qualms. Bapu even encouraged us to eat eggs, saying milk and eggs were both animal products and if we could have milk we shouldn't have any issues with egg. But dadi wouldn't allow eggs into the house. So we would get to eat eggs only as a treat in restaurants.

Ma worked for a government lab. Her job was to test new mutations of the green things. She checked to see if they had in any way infected the lab grown food. She had a team under her working on keeping our food contamination-free round the clock. Ma had many degrees. Bapu wasn't as qualified as ma. But he had a keen business eye. He used to run a real estate business. He was good at it. Among the perks of his job was getting first-hand information on the best plots and deals available. That's how we got our haveli.

Dadi used to tell us about her young days in the Jaisalmer of old. According to her, Jaisalmer used to be a beautiful city, rising like a gem-studded tiara from the sand. The only time I ever saw sand was in a picture she had showed me. It was a photograph of her village, a cluster of small brick houses on the outskirts of Jaisalmer. Sand lapped like ocean waves against the porches, except that by the time I was born, the ocean waves were no longer blue, but a rich algal green. A few goats stood around in her photo. There also were a couple of disinterested dogs, lean and yellow like the sand. At the photos edge, I could see the city of Jaisalmer, its sandstone buildings shimmering like burnished gold. An elegant contrast against the yellow-white sand and hard candy blue sky. I can't believe it was that beautiful. The sky looked like an upturned and frozen sea, a mirage of the legendary arctic waters. The sand looked like the soft semolina halwa that Dadi used to make when things hadn't gotten quite so out of hand. There were camels too. Yes, camels!

I had drawn a camel once, based on Dadi's descriptions and the pictures I'd seen in my school tablet. The camels were extinct by the time I was born, but some cloned ones still existed, housed inside high security zoos. I pulled a copy of my camel anime-drawing from my art-screen and gave it to Dadi. I helped her set it up on a wall in her room. My camel was taller than the date palm in the picture and it was funny to see it reach down and pluck a few fronds to chew. Dadi laughed a lot, and said she loved her special camel. I drew some more animals, and Dadi wanted them all put up in her room. Soon dadi's room began to resemble a zoo-screen. I still hadn't learnt to add sound to my pictures, which is a blessing, because I doubt dadi would have been able to sleep with all that din around her.

When dadi was a little girl, she used to listen to the elders talk. At first the talks were stories and legends, but as the problems grew, the conversations became a long line of lament.

The vegetable crops, and the fields of bajra and mustard weren't turning out right. They were growing too fast and were too stringy. The date palms and thorny bushes were also proliferating. Yet birds and small animals like squirrels were hardly attracted. Small fauna seemed to be starving. The food they cooked took longer and longer, as if the vegetables and grain had acquired a greater resistance to being changed or killed, if that is the right term to use for vegetation. Dadi said her mother would gaze into the horizon at sundown and mutter to herself.

Soon there rose a clamour of complaints during the evening conversations. Complaints about the quality of food. How things had deteriorated so much that they could barely eat. And then, there were the disappearances too. Since nobody had a clue, the theories and conjectures were tossed fast and loose. Some were outright outlandish. Most had religious undertones. The elders conferred. Special pujas were done to propitiate the Gods. They said this was the cusp, the time when one epoch ended and another began. They said the transition period would bring with it much havoc and mayhem.

"The golden age will return after that," dadi told us with confidence. "Nothing to be afraid of. The act of creation is always preceded by destruction." She became distracted again, mumbling her prayers, and fingering her beads.

Dadi's faith made her unafraid and accepting. But ma and bapu were barely calm after the vine attack. Bittu was the only one whose presence seemed to soothe them. It was the same for me. Ma was always after us, during that time.

"Ankur," she'd yell, even though I had done nothing to annoy her. "Take you meds."

"I did."

"Don't argue. When did you last take them? The yellow round ones? Did you take them first?"

I would bring her my med-tray and show her the empty cavities with the dates marked against each. Only then would she be satisfied, but not for long. Ma would turn towards bapu and dadi after she was done with me, and go checking and rechecking Bittu's med-tray.

Ma also seemed to be on a perennial short fuse, and jumpy. Like the frogs I'd once caught, and put in the fish tank. She had made me wash my hands thoroughly, and then disinfected me, all of me, with a vile smelling spray. She had glared at me as I swallowed my tablets. All that fuss over a bunch of tiny frogs! I had looked at Dadi for support, but for once she had studiously avoided my eyes.

The day after the vine incident, Ma got busy piling up the trolley with all kinds of food stuffs. We'd stopped eating lab grown fresh vegetables and fruit. But at least I knew what they looked like. Bittu didn't remember. As for milk, there was no question of any animal milk, lab grown or not. We had turned into high-tech vegans. We only ate food manufactured in sterile factories, shut away inside big silo like buildings. Our earlier lab-growns or countertop-farm foods was discontinued at ma's insistence. Instead we now consumed food created in petri dishes, one cell at a time. Ma's distrust of nature had reached epic proportions!

I watched as ma threw the packets and cans into our trolley. It was already spilling over with food and household cleaners. She had even got one of those portable contraptions that made water from air. Looking at her go, you'd think the whole of Jaisalmer was about to shut down. The thought had possibly occurred to many people. The stores were super crowded. The other folks didn't appear to be paranoid though. Unless they were pretending. Like ma and dadi, chitchatting away with fellow shoppers, the friendlier ones, like it was business as usual. I caught the strained smile on some of their faces. Dadi grinned and nodded like a senile woman. Ma said something that was supposed to sound funny, as she put some more stuff on our trolley. Then we zigzagged our way to the till. Pushing through the crowd to be first. Nothing unusual. We are Indians after all.

Ma began to unload straightaway. She changed her mind about something and rushed off to replace it, motioning bapu to take over the unloading. Bapu protested softly. The queue behind us muttered. Some folks got restive. Ma returned at last, squeezing her way back past the queue. The glum looking girl with brown pimples on her chin at the counter shoved the bill-swipe at Ma. She blinked into the screen. It blinked back at her, flashing green. The girl turned towards the next customer without bothering to respond to ma's cheerful, "thanks, bye." The queue sighed. Ma obviously hadn't heard it. Or if she had, she simply didn't care. We raced towards the car park. Some cutters were already there, clearing away fresh growth.

Jaisalmer was relatively calm, except for sporadic bursts of panic. Other cities were bursting with growth and panicking humans. The roads had sprouted bumps with seams of green everywhere. Buildings undulated with verdant growth. Fields and farmlands were menacingly lush with no edible plants. Some blamed it on the past misdeeds of humans. Some blamed the government for setting up labs for mutant flora and fauna. That's what created the problem, they claimed. The government replied they couldn't watch people starve and do nothing. Activists were petitioning for the closure of unlicensed plant labs. But regular citizens preferred to trust the politicians and the news-feeds. Ma of course trusted no one. And bapu preferred to play it safe.

Some months ago, at ma's insistence, we shifted to our haveli. It was an early 20th century house with a swimming pool sized courtyard within and a wide garden encircling it outside. Bapu had bought it for a song, and turned it into a weekend home for us. But now, by the looks of ma's grocery shopping, we'd probably be there for much longer. A year maybe. It was a long way off from the city, far beyond the suburbs. When the roads were good though, returning wasn't a problem.

On the way back from the stores we picked up Bittu from his play school. Divya mausi came out waddling out holding Bittu against her chest. She was one of the last remaining teachers. Divya mausi didn't have to carry Bittu. He could walk, run in fact. But he became everybody's darling very quickly. Everyone loved to pick him up, squish him a bit, and smell his fresh baby smell. Bittu could get away with anything, from anyone. Except me. I'm the only one he really listened to. I mean, really as in really, really.

"You're picking him up so soon today Pavitra ji," said Divya mausi.

"I'll bring Bittu early tomorrow," Ma replied. She plucked him from Divya mausi's reluctant arms.

"Bai-bai Deeya maathee," said Bittu.

Divya mausi beamed and ran her fingers down his curls.

The traffic was snaggy on the way home, but we had a determined ma at the controls. Bittu pattered on about his day, and even though some of the words were gibberish, I nodded to show I was interested. Dadi had her eyes closed, like she was praying again. Bapu seemed distracted. Maybe he was waiting to see what mad thing ma was going to do next. He didn't have to wait long. The minute we reached home, she was ready to go back to town again.

"Stay home and fix the boys some dinner," she told him, sounding unusually authoritative. Dadi pursed her lips in disapproval, but bapu didn't react. "I'll finish the stockpiling."

"It's almost six," protested bapu gently. "The stores will closed by the time you reach Pavi."

"I'll do the shortcut," said ma. And she was out before he could counter that the shortcuts had become virtually un-navigable.

Ma returned long past my bed time. Their voices woke me up so I crept out of my room to see.

"Pavi," I heard bapu say. "Pavi, this is madness." Bapu touched her cheek. "You're being paranoid."

"I'm not. It's begun already. Can't you see?" said ma. She sounded drained of both strength and hope.

"You're not going to let all that talk dictate our lives. Please Pavi," bapu pleaded. "You should know how paranoid all activists are. Always have been."

Ma began to weep. She sat down. Bapu shook his head, but stroked her hair as he spoke. "Hush now Pavi. It'll be ok." But ma only shook her head vigorously, her shoulders convulsing with fear and despair, as the tears rolled down unchecked.

Next morning both bapu and ma stayed home. Bapu cleared out the garden around the house. I heard his mini-cutter going chug-chug and thwack-thwack in a rhythmic cycle. It was barely seven in the morning. Bapu must have begun really early for I could see wide swatches of brown ground around the house. He poured some liquid on the cleared ground which hardened into a smooth synthetic surface after a while.

You have to have the right connections, to get a haveli like ours. Ma and bapu had worked hard for many years, and befriended all the right people. And they'd certainly intended to make the most of it. They'd planned on throwing parties for their friends and colleagues, birthday bashes for Bittu and me here. The idea was to make it a real old fashioned haveli. They had planned on having a pond and cow and dog clones, fruit tree and vegetable plant replicas, ma's favourite flowers and dadi's herbs. All lab-certified. I wanted a largish area especially designated for Bittu and myself. Bapu planned to add a swimming pool with simulated waves for us to go surfing when we felt like it. We had dreams for our haveli. Big dreams.

The cost of the inoculations that bapu, Bittu and I had to take – twelve each for the three of us - put all our plans on hold. Ma and dadi needed only four sets of inoculations each and a follow up. Women were apparently more resistant, but not entirely. And they could also be carriers themselves, unlike us men. That's what the doctor had told us. All of us had to take the same medicines though, every day, because prevention was the only cure, and we couldn't be too careful. That's what ma and dadi said over and over again. Activists of course pooh-poohed the medicines. But my parents weren't taking any chances. Bapu was thankful that we were well off. Nobody in our home spoke of the hundreds who had disappeared, because they didn't have the means to pay for prevention!

Soon after we settled in, a few folks from the village came over. They wanted jobs. Ma told them she'd let them know after we were settled in. She was wary of getting more mouths to feed. And, she didn't want strangers around our house. After two days of working nonstop bapu wanted his freedom back. He wanted to go back to his real job in Jaisalmer. But ma wouldn't let him.

"Who's going to pay for this," said bapu, extending his arms towards the dining hall which looked more like a warehouse of assorted things, mostly food items and water. "We're living on credit. We're in too much debt."

"Trust me," said ma. "Don't go. We need to fortify the house. Nobody understands yet, but when they do there'll be pandemonium, we'll be safe here. We'll be free of..." She didn't finish.

Ma scared me with her talk. Bittu was too small to be scared. But dadi, during those last days seemed to be with ma all the way.

"She's right Santosh," Dadi said to bapu when he finally lost his temper with ma. It was unlike dadi to argue with her son-in-law, he was the head of the family as far as she was concerned. In her time women didn't talk back; they simply obeyed the men.

Bapu on his part never argued back with dadi, who was an elder. He was old-fashioned that way. He picked up his toolbox quietly and went into the yard. By evening the fences were up. They were made of a kind of electro-magnetic metal mesh that you saw only at the military and ship landing areas. The kind that destroyed life, both of the plant and animal kind, on contact.

A week passed. We remained inside our oasis. It was boring without school. Not that we had much of that any more. So many streets had become unnavigable, and so many students had vanished. One by one they had dropped out from our communication screens too. Our shared conversations were over. I missed my friends. But Ma had forbidden me to hang out with anyone months ago.

Another week passed. Ma sprang into action. She had just realised that our medical supplies were running low. Bittu wanted to go as well when he saw her getting ready. He threw

such a tantrum that she had to take him along. She returned
hours later looking thoroughly exhausted, and fell asleep almost immediately, without even changing. Dadi took Bittu
from her. She fed him and put him to bed. And then she was
back again, all wild-eyed and trembling. She shook ma awake
and spoke urgently. Ma stifled a scream. Bapu and I dropped
what we were doing and rushed into Bittu's room. We peered at
his sweet angel face in the cot. Dadi removed the coverlet. Ma
started hitting her chest like he was dead already. She covered
her mouth to stop the wail that threatened to roll out from her
throat. Three little pimples, brown and hard, sat wickedly on
Bittu's right thigh.

Ma stood like a petrified tree. Dadi wept into her sari pallu.
Bapu held his head in his hands. When I looked into ma's face
I saw the all terrible things she had refused to say out loud. We
wouldn't be able to bear it. Even though we knew deep in our
hearts that it was inevitable. But we had no knowledge of the
process. The unknown terrified us.

There was one person on Earth though who loved Bittu as
much as us, and who we could trust. The one person who was
also as tough as nails, and a wise old woman, like dadi. Ma was
taking Bittu to her.

Nobody stopped ma. Nobody said a word. We were all se-
cretly thinking that no one should know our family had been
hit. The government folks would be here in a jiffy. We'd be
quarantined. We'd lose everything we owned. We would vanish. Everything we had would vanish. Would we be together
or separated? We had no idea. Nobody really knew what was
going on. There were whispers. But people mostly acted as if
the government caught and took away renegades, not ordinary
hardworking citizens like us.

People went about their daily lives, buying extra groceries,
taking their meds and inoculations from the government ap-
proved clinics, acting like it was as normal as any other vaccine
for any regular epidemic. Nobody raised a hue and cry when

whole families disappeared. Nobody spoke of the roads covered with green growing things, the neglected houses as green as tropical hillocks. Nobody praised the weather, so moistly cool and fragrant, like an eternal spring, a season I had only read about in the old stories.

Ma strode out, a still sleepy Bittu on her hip. On the way out she said over her shoulder more out of habit, "I hope you remembered to take your pills, Ankur."

I nodded. My heart felt cold and hot at the same time. Maybe the baby dose hadn't been enough for Bittu. Babies were more vulnerable. I was already eleven years old, going on twelve. I was going to teach my kid brother to be tough like me. Years before he was even born I had already begun saving up my toys and books, looking forward to the day when I would share my things with my own sibling. Ma and bapu took so long to decide that I had almost given up hope.

I watched ma backing the hover-car out from its hangar. I couldn't see her beyond the gate because of the green invasion. The new ones were mutating every day. They were able to overcome many things that they couldn't tolerate at first, when they grew only on soil. Now they seemed to fear almost nothing. No one was safe from them anymore.

Bittu would be safe with Divya mausi. And she would be glad to care for Bittu. We would be spared from watching Bittu getting transformed right before our eyes. The idea of transformation frightened us. Once the process was complete, she would know exactly what to do. She would keep him hidden in her tiny garden until he grew strong enough to withstand being replanted. A matter of days, really. We would get him back then, let him grow wild and free in our haveli, our holiday home, our family get-together and hang-out place! We wouldn't be needing our doses after that. Oh no.

I had overheard ma, bapu and dadi discuss it.

"In the worst case scenario," Bapu had said. Over and over again. And Ma had stifled a sob. They had planned everything, down to the last detail. Maybe they had even discussed it with Divya mausi. She was there at our door, looking cheerfully pimply herself, carrying Bittu in a jar. His fronds waved excitedly from their glass prison. Divya mausi was of course a welcome member of our haveli then onwards. I was really glad. It was nice to have someone else to talk to.

Thereafter we carried on, as if nothing had happened, but with one small adjustment. We no longer took our meds. We had a private ceremony when we planted Bittu in the centre of our courtyard. Soon the courtyard became the central part of our house. It became the place where we ate our meals, of which we had less and less need as the days went by, as our bodies looked more to sun, air and water for sustenance. We sat in our courtyard chatting quietly, stroking Bittu's growing branches and trunk. Ma instructed us daily on what to do when only one of us remained human. We closed our haveli gates permanently. Families were supposed to stay together, no matter what. And that was what we were going to do, until the very end.

We don't mind the overcrowding. It is but natural. After we got over the initial shock of complete metamorphosis, we began to get used to the new silence. At first our thoughts merged with our soundless speech, and it was awkward. It was awkward too not to feel any particular and possessive love for those who were of our blood in the past. Relationships have new meaning now. It means I can intertwine with the green entity who had once in a long ago life-time birthed me. We were different then, and those old ethics no longer hold.

We clamber over each other, rejoicing in the touch of sun and rain. There is nothing to be afraid of. And why should there? Beneath the runnels of soil we speak to countless more, plant beings, who look no more like us than we do with respect to our previous forms. Our initial doubts were cleared by those who came before us. They gave us their nutrients when the time came for them to pass, merging into the soil or melting into the waters.

A distant memory makes me smile, but not in the way humans do. It's a sensation, and I can express it by physically expanding a little. In that other life, the entity I called ma, used to say that plants speak to each other. She was wrong. It's not just the plants, even stones and water droplets speak. Air molecules speak. The lava rivers deep within mother earth's womb speak.

We all speak to each other. We speak even when miles apart, to use a human term. We think and we feel and we strategize. But our timelines are different. Our measurements of space are different from that of humans. That is why it took us more than a millennium to regain our lost territories.

Be that as it may. There is no anger. No fear. No greed or hate. Nothing negative. Contentment and mutual benefaction drives us. Mother earth smiles a lot these days. She churns her womb and tickles our roots. She pulls at our genetic codes with the gentlest of tugs. We leak our DNA into her. Our mating rituals are ancient and prolonged.

Soon another transformation will take place. Beneath rock and upon ocean beds, new life as delicate as filaments will wriggle free. We will swoop down and add our gifts, welcoming the new children, who in turn will grow. Together we will dance the dance of life. And held in earth's bosom we will swim with her across the cosmos.

Indra's Web

by Vandana Singh

Mahua ran over the familiar, rock-studded pathway under the canopy of acacia trees, her breath coming fast and ragged. She would have to stop soon, she wasn't as young as she used to be, and there was a faint, persistent pain in her right knee—but she loved this physicality: heart thumping, sweat running down her face in rivulets, the forest smelling of sap and animal dung, grit on her lips from the dust. The forest was where she got her best ideas; it was an eternal source of inspiration. It was why her work was getting recognition across the world. But the forest didn't care about fame or fortune—here she was just another animal: breath and flow, a kite on the wing, a deer running.

Running, she liked to have the net chatter going on in the Shell in her ear: Salman monitoring the new grid, Varun and Ali reporting on the fish stocks in the artificial marshland by the river, Doctor Sabharwal's monitor relaying Mahua's grandmother's condition at the hospital: stable, stable, stable, still on life support.

Thinking about her grandmother's stroke made Mahua feel like she was about to fall into a pit of despair; she distracted herself with the reminder that she had promised Namita she would try out the myconet music app during this morning's run.

"It's just for fun, Mahua-di, but try it, you'll like it."

They were so anxious about her, these young people, knowing she was not quite herself these days. Moved and perversely annoyed by their concern, she had spent some hours with them in the Biosystems lab learning the app...

There is a fungal network, a myconet, a secret connection between the plants of the forest. They talk to each other, the acacia and the shisham and the gulmohar tree, in a chemical tongue. They communicate about pests, food sources, the weather, all through the flow of biomolecules through the fungal hyphae. Through this network, large trees have even been known to share nutrients with saplings of the same species. Mahua's protégé, Namita, is part of the team that helped decipher (to the extent that humans can) this subtle language. In the forest they have planted sensors in the soil to catch some of the chemical exchanges between plants. The signals are fed back into the interpreter and then analyzed. Some members of the team have made music from the signals: convert the concentration of a certain biochemical transmitter changing in real time into succession of notes where the duration indicates the strength of the transmitter. Add a few other transmitter signals as sounds of a slightly different frequency and you'll get a sometimes musical chatter that is at once soothing and intriguing. Mahua is new to this and she's never tried it out in the forest before. She's always encouraged play in their research—it is not only fun, but important, *she tells them—play leads to new insights, shakes up pre-conceived notions... And now they* need *the relief of play, after having spent the past few months calculating and putting in place Ashapur's first smart energy grid, the Suryanet, modeled on the myconet itself.*

Mahua turned on the app. As she ran she picked up information from the closest few sensors so that she had a 'picture' that changed in time and space. At first she heard nothing but the soothing semi-music of the various tones. Then the surprise came: a peculiar sensation rather like vertigo, a kind of slippage, as though she was leaving her human self behind, dissolving into something infinitely vast. It was like looking up at the Milky Way from the top of a high mountain on a clear night. She had always been quick to discern webs of relationships—it was her particular skill, after all—but this was different. A feeling like an electric shock coursed through her, a long moment of recognition, as though her deepest mind already knew this pattern. The effect was so startling that she stumbled over a tree root. Then the Shell beeped urgently in her ear, and the spell broke.

It was Salman, calling out an alert: Suntower 1 had failed. There were random fluctuations going on all over the new energy grid that nobody could explain, Salman said, breathless. It seemed likely that the Suryanet, so painstakingly put in place over the past few months, the result of years of effort, on which everyone was depending for the survival of Ashapur and maybe of the biosphere itself—the Suryanet could be a spectacular failure.

One of the things Mahua had learned from her grandmother was that when trouble struck, unless it needed immediate attention, it was good to slow down and meander a little. So she wandered to the top of the ridge, where the height enabled her to see Ashapur in all its glory.

A former slum, it used to lie on the edge of Delhi like a sore. In the last ten years the Ashapur project had transformed it. The hutments of cardboard and tin had been replaced by dwelling houses built mostly by the residents themselves with traditional materials: a hard mixture of mud, straw, rice husk, surfaced with a lime-based plaster. In use for thousands of years, then forgotten, and revived in the 20th century by visionary architects like Laurie Baker, the material had so far survived nearly ten years of baking heat and monsoon rains. The majority of the residents were the original slum inhabitants, climate refugees from the drowned villages of coastal Bangladesh, who had been transformed by the Ashapur project. When Mahua looked at Ashapur from this height she saw mostly an uneven carpet of green and silver—rooftop gardens broken by the gleam of solar panels, and corridors of native trees, neem, khejri, gulmohar, running down the hill from her forest like green arteries through the settlement.

Above this vista rose the suntowers like a surrealist's dream: four functioning, and the fifth under construction, their tops capped by sun-tracking petals of biomimetic material containing tiny, environmentally benign artificial cells, the suryons, that drank up photons. The largest, oldest facility was Suntower 1, now mysteriously moribund. Ashapur was nearly self-sufficient in food and energy, and with the new grid, the Suryanet, they should have been able to *donate* power to the Delhi grid, thereby silencing the naysayers and establishing the need for a thousand Ashapurs. Four solar plants making hydrogen from the breakdown of water—sewage-fed biogas plants—enormous energy savings from building construction and layout (none of the buildings needed air conditioning)—numerous rooftops with solar panels—even greater energy savings from the fact that these former villagers were traditionally energy-efficient, living in clusters, throwing away nothing, re-using almost everything. And all the energy sources were now connected on the Suryanet. Yet...

She took the long way to Suntower 1. She always found it calming to walk through Ashapur. The narrow roads were not built on a rectangular pattern but instead curved, moving obligingly around an ancient peepul tree or dwelling. Her designers had kept the street pattern of the original slum but had improved on it, allowing room for people to congregate in front of this chai-house or in that niche, so that old women could gossip and mind the little ones, and the wandering cows and pariah dogs had room to rest. Here, right at the corner she was passing now, between an internet café and an agricultural research center—here's where a potential foreign funder had stopped her six years ago. "I don't understand," he'd said, "why this town is so untidy. There's no order, no proper grid for the streets. It looks very inefficient. And the roads are too narrow for traffic flow! Where are your cars?"

In response to this sort of thing her grant-writing team had developed a slide show— apparently some of these potential funders could only understand things if they were in a power-point presentation—to show how optimal city function could be best achieved by having connectivity at multiple scales. Large, coarse, fewer pathways for cars, smaller, more dense ones for people. And for other animals as well as people, the green corridors that branched into the city, maintaining biodiversity and the psychological benefits of closeness to nature, while providing Ashapur with cooler summers, seasonal supplies of fruit and nuts, and raw material for a new cottage industry in crafts.

Now she entered Energy Central, the building below Suntower 1. It was cool here—the thick mud-based walls ensured that—and the curving stairway with its murals gave no hint of the troubles of Suntower 1, rising high above the roof. At the lab door there was the familiar sign that Salman had installed by encouraging a vivid green moss to grow on an earthboard so that it spelled out the motto of the Biomimetic Energy Materials Lab—*To Learn from Nature, not to Exploit Her*. His colleagues had teased Salman about the irony of exploiting a moss to write these noble words, but the moss seemed to have decided things for itself. It spelled "To learm from Natur, not to Explod," which still made her smile.

Inside there was a dim coolness and the glow of multiple terminals. A meeting was in progress, chaotic and impassioned as usual. Arguments and discussions in Hindi, English and Bangla: Salman, deep in agitated conversation with Namita and Ayush, Hamid, a young trainee who had once begged on the streets as a child, patiently explaining the situation to the boy who had brought the tea. Mahua stayed just inside the door, unnoticed, letting the words flow around her, sensing the web of ideas and feelings raging through the room.

"...no guarantee that modeling the Suryanet on the myconet was going to work—why risk everything on one crazy idea?"

"...calculations, have you forgotten we did the entire constructal analysis? Besides, scale-free networks are everywhere..."

"Nobody's networked a suryon-based system before or allowed it to self-regulate! There were safer ways of doing this, better ways! But no, you have to go on about minimal control! It's centralized control systems that make everything work!"

"Yaar, stop being a control freak, OK? We're just mimicking the natural control systems that exist in nature. Stop panicking, obviously there's a bug in the system somewhere."

"...oldest suntower, beta version of the suryons, it's bound to fail..."

"...not *this* quickly, idiot..."

Chanchal, from one of the terminals: "Salman, look at what's happening to the other suntowers! Energy collection is now above average by 7 percent in 2, 3 and 4! But... dekho, boss! These numbers! More inflow than outflow. There's a major bug somewhere!"

"Or energy is no longer conserved," someone said, as there was a mass movement to the terminal.

Mahua found herself curiously detached from the mayhem. A signal sounded repetitively in the lab like the beep of the monitor in her grandmother's hospital room.

She is remembering the first time she sees these young people in various colleges and universities, nearly a decade ago. They are bound for brilliant careers as engineers, managers, CEOs, their upturned faces curious, skeptical, polite. She has nothing to offer them so she gives it all she has.

"I come to you with empty hands," she says. "I can't offer you much money. I can't offer you big houses, two cars, five air conditioners. Nor the jet-setting lifestyle with its cross-continental board meetings, the wife or husband who will ultimately cheat on you, the children who will drive you crazy. What I can give you is a chance to be part of a revolution. A revolution that might just save our earth from the climate crisis. One that comes up with not just new technologies but new ways to live that are more whole and deep and satisfying than anything you've known. Most of you have enjoyed being in college. You are the best of the lot, the ones who get high on learning, and on the company of like minds. The Ashapur project is like college, except that you have the chance to

learn by doing, and to do more good than you ever could with the life now laid out for you. We will take care of your housing and healthcare, and you will get as much salary as I do. Which isn't saying very much. But you'll get up every morning knowing that by the end of the day you would have made a new discovery, a new friend, a new way of looking at the world. You will blow old paradigms out of existence on a near-daily basis. I promise you that. Are you with me?"

Some of the faces look incredulous, even mocking, but there are others who light up. She's struck a chord deep inside them. She lets out a deep breath of relief.

Now she thought: had she betrayed them after all? Would they forgive her, if this turned out to be the disaster she had always feared?

Finally they noticed her, surrounded her, pulled her before the screens, presented their arguments before her. "Look," she said at last. "You know how to check everything according to the protocols. Do that. Then come up with some wild theories and shake up the possibilities, but don't panic. We can survive a couple of power failures; it isn't as though we haven't grown up with them. The hospital seems to have enough power right now; so do most key-need places. Make sure backup generators are working and just wait."

Mahua was named by her long-dead mother because she was born under a mahua tree on the way to Delhi. The two of them—mother and grandmother—had migrated from their village in Bihar after her father died. She grew up in the slums, where her mother died when Mahua was eleven, only three months before their fortunes changed.

So it's been Mahua and her grandmother, who now lies in a hospital bed after a stroke, kept alive by the machines that surround her. The woman with the temper and the loud laugh, who always had something to say, now looks at Mahua with wide, frightened eyes. She can't speak but she can croak a little. Sometimes she lies peacefully while Mahua holds her hand, but at other times she seems to be trying to tell Mahua something. Mahua, who can discern connections with a skill that frightens her sometimes, cannot tell what her grandmother is trying to say. She tries to reassure her—there are all kinds of new techniques the surgeons want to try. There's hope.

When she was a child Mahua used to follow ants as they moved purposefully across the dirt floor of the room. She wanted to know where they were going in such a hurry, and whether their abrupt pauses and frantically waving antennae had some hidden significance. Later she came to realize that the ants followed invisible trails across the floor—that the world was full of secret communication channels, like the electric wires between poles that rose above the tenements. It was as though some inner sense within her had opened because following this realization she was suddenly aware of walking through a tangled spider's-web of relationships. The gossiping old women who sat around her mother's sewing machine, jabbering about this and that, speaking as much with meaningful glances and shakes of the fist as with their cracked voices—the way people looked at each other, signifying feelings and relations, how people spoke as much with their silences as with words. Even the winds that brought the monsoon rains had some sort of pattern or cycle, a network in both time and space. She was delighted with this discovery but she didn't understand it then.

The narrow little lanes of the slum are like spider webs, intersecting at odd angles, curving around hutments, like a stream of water. Everywhere there are people and smells and here and there an internet café or a soda stand or a chaatwala. In this mess and confusion someone's placed a computer in a niche on a wall and the street kids play with it between school and errands and work. After a long time she's found the courage to go up to the shiny, inviting screen, the keyboard, where the letters are in Hindi— thank goodness she can read—but the screen itself has a number of floating objects, tumbling and combining when they meet. She stares at it, mesmerized, and after a while she tries a hesitant tap on the keyboard. Three days later she's learnt that she can save the game in her own name. She keeps playing. In a strange way it makes sense the way the slum itself makes sense. It's pattern and rhythm, although she will not know those words for a long time. At the end of this period there is a person at her door, and a scholarship to go to a really good school with housing for herself and her grandmother, and guidance from the Slum Children's Education Trust which is inhabited by kindly aunties.

At thirteen Mahua fell ill. She diagnosed the malady herself as anxiety brought on by acute apophenia. Becoming sensitive to networks and relationships, she saw connections everywhere, even when they weren't actually present. This drove her crazy but she didn't want to take medicines to suppress her ability for pattern recognition. Instead she resolved to train her mind to distinguish between false apparent connections and real ones—the only way to do that was to study the world. With this determination, her new school, with its snooty, unfriendly girls and regimented routine, became a matter of finding the grain in the chaff, the flashes of joy in the misery.

For instance: Mrs. Khosla introducing the concept of energy in her usual monotone. A classroom full of bored children, and only Mahua sitting up, recognizing that she has just been handed the golden key, the central concept, that through which the entire universe interacted, the currency of all communication. Energy! And its conservation law. All real systems were governed by fundamental laws that acted as constraints. That is how you differentiated apparent relationships from real ones!

But as she stands in the hospital room looking at her grandmother (the old woman is made almost alien by the tubes and wires of the life-support system), she feels that she has failed after all. What good is it to be able to sense patterns and relationships when she can't tell what her own grandmother wants to say? Tomorrow they'll try once more to work with the eyelids to see if her grandmother can learn to communicate thus. But the old woman, always contrary, has apparently refused to cooperate. What does she want? Not death, surely, not before exploring all the options. Her grandmother has such a zest for life. She'd opened a small business of her own at the age of seventy-three, making simmerpots. This is a pot made of mud and straw rather like the walls of the dwellings but in different proportions—and it is one reason why energy usage is so low in Ashapur. You cook your stew or curry on the stove for two minutes, until it is simmering nicely, and then you take it off the heat and put it inside the simmerpot. The simmerpot is such a good insulator that the food keeps cooking in there for hours afterwards. Not her grandmother's invention— it had been in use in her village for centuries. But here only her grandmother and a handful of trainees know how to make it, and when you walk around Ashapur you see simmerpots everywhere, on kitchen window-sills and in the large community dining rooms. And the woman who made it popular and indispensable, who had such vivacity at eighty-one that she could gossip non-stop with her neighbors until three in the morning, now lies hooked up to machines like a captive, with death in her eyes.

Mahua has finally seen it. Her grandmother wants to die.

That evening Mahua goes walking down the lanes of Ashapur, following a hunch.

There before her is Suntower 5. While physically connected to the grid, it is still under construction; only the skeletal frames of the petals are complete, the tubing through which the suryon-embedded substratum will eventually be pumped up. There is a sleepy boy in the control room, one of the former street urchins assigned to do some after-hours caretaking. Tousling his hair and sending him off for some tea, Mahua sits before the computer. Suntower 5 is the newest design; the suryon distribution architecture is so complex and bug-ridden that it will take a while to implement. Since the work began on the grid so many months ago, nobody has been able to attend to Suntower 5.

It doesn't take Mahua long to zoom into an image of a petal atop the tower. At first she sees just the skeleton, but there, between the supports is a new, delicate, lace-like integument. The suryons are distributing themselves, filling in the empty spaces. Somehow the Suryanet has not only decided that Suntower 5 should be functional, but has allocated resources to it, which is why Suntower 1—the oldest, and least efficient—has shut itself down. Temporarily, perhaps, but who knows? Does a sufficiently complex network give rise to its own wisdom? She sends a hint to the team at Suntower 1. By the morning they will have figured it out. She sips her tea, talks to the sleepy attendant. At last she goes back into the night, thinking about the networks in which she exists, and how tomorrow a major node on which her very life depends will be taken off-line forever. She thinks of the forest on the ridge. The forest lives on because it accepts death—with every twig that falls, with every ant that meets its annihilation, a thousand life-forms come into being. Danger walks there and so its denizens learn adaptation; here, too, we must rebuild ourselves, define ourselves anew with each loss, each encounter. She remembers a story her grandmother once told her about Indra's Web, the ultimate cosmic network in which every node mirrors the whole.

In the twilight hush there are sleepy sounds of birds settling in the trees; a family of rhesus monkeys chatter softly in a rooftop garden above her head. A radio is playing an old film song, very softly. It is a warm night; someone has a *khas-khas* cooler working, the sound of the fan almost drowning out the steady drip of water. If she wants, her Shell unit can pick up energy data from the sensors in each dwelling place. She loves this marriage of the traditional and the new, the forest and the city, this great experiment, this marvel that is Ashapur, City of Hope.

Replacement

by Rimi B. Chatterjee

'They'll let me go, you'll see,' I said. "I always get what I want." I kicked my heel idly against the bench in the school garden. It was late spring and the last of the winter's flowers, pansies and lobelias, were wilting in the flowerbeds around us. We only ever got to enjoy them for a couple of months before the muggy tropical heat of KL City turned them to mush. They bothered me so I looked at Supiriya instead. Only seniors were allowed to sit here. I glared at a few youngsters in case they were thinking of sidling over. Exams were done and my heart was bittersweet: this might be the last time I got to sit in my favourite place with my best friend.

Supiriya and I shared a special bond. She was the one I trusted most, out of our batch of 2029. Four years ago she'd lost her mother, and then a year after that I'd lost my father. We'd helped each other through the bad times. She sighed. "You're always so confident, Aiyzeh. I wish I was more like you."

"Why do you want to be like me?" I blushed furiously. "You're so slim and willowy. Like a model. I always thought you looked like a swan."

Supiriya smiled sadly. "The doctor says I should eat more. He says I have *anorexia nervosa*." She looked down at her perfect bosom. "He says that's probably why my periods haven't started yet. My Body Mass Index is too low."

"Hah. And everybody tells *me* I'm fat." I slapped my thighs and made them jiggle. "We can't win, can we? You know how I curse when I get mine. I've had them since I was ten! Heh, let's swap uteruses, shall we?"

"Don't be gross." Her eyelashes fluttered to shade her eyes. Once again I felt a touch of irritation at her amazing ability to pretend things didn't exist. "Hey, I'm just trying to cheer you up. Come on, Supiriya! School's over. We're almost free!"

She shook her head. "No, Aiyzeh. You're the one who's free. If you want to leave KL City and go to New Singapore, you will. You're smart, and you speak your mind like a boy."

"You mean I'm ugly and no boy will ever have me." I grinned to take the sting out of my words. "My brothers don't have the money to make up for my black face. They're already calculating how much they need to bribe some lumpy old businessman to take me off their hands."

"You're not black, Aiyzeh. Please don't talk like that."

"Huh. You should hear them yakk about how ever since Old Singapore was destroyed in the Wave of 2023 the House of Dang has been struggling to stay two steps ahead of blah blah blah. Dad would've sorted it out ages ago." I waved a hand. "But forget that. Remember that time in fourth grade when I poured ammonia on iodine and made those bright purple fumes?" She looked at me blankly. "You remember, right?" I half-turned to her, my heart sinking. "You said it was the exact colour of a Disney princess's party gown."

"Oh," she said, as if I had been speaking a foreign language she'd once learned and forgotten. "You were always so good at chemistry. I wouldn't have passed if you hadn't tutored me."

"It's what friends do." I cast about for anything I could say to lighten the mood. "So what are you going to do now that we've finished school?"

She dropped her gaze to her manicured hands. "That's up to father."

"Well, you could..." I started again. "You once said you'd like to be a fashion designer. You're so stylish, you could do it." She shook her head sadly. "Oh come on Supiriya! Aren't you jealous of me?"

"Jealous? Why?"

"Because I get to go live in New Singapore, the world's first privately run city-state and floating headquarters of Ramdhun Corporation, the most powerful conglomerate in Indo-asia. You were the one who first told me how awesome the place is. Remember how I scoffed?"

"You'll be working there," she said, as if it were a punishment.

"Sure I will. I'm the first ever to win the Sunita Vaghela Scholarship to study medicine under Dr Pradip Shankar, the man I've admired ever since we read *Future of the Child*! Come on, try and be a little impressed."

Her eyes were hazy. "I owe the House of Shah everything, even my future. That's why you're different, Aiyzeh. You're not afraid. Or grateful."

I scowled. "Why should I be? I didn't ask them to bring me into the world. I'm sure I would have remembered if I had." She almost laughed at that. I don't know what else we talked about. My heart was heavy at the thought of never seeing her again.

That evening we had the Family Talk. Mother was there in the background, bossing the servants around as they cleaned up after dinner. That meant she was leaving the whole business of my future up to my brothers. I gritted my teeth.

Budiharto, the eldest, dabbed his thick lips with a napkin. I always thought he looked like one of those weird fishes that would make faces at us through the glass of the big aquarium in KL City Wonderworld. Dad would stand in front of it and spread his arms and crow 'Wealth of the sea!' as though he owned it all. Then he went and had a coronary at fifty three, leaving stupid stolid Budiharto in charge. Way to go, Dad.

"So," said Budiharto to me. "You want to study medicine in New Singapore."

"Yes," I said. "Under the great Dr Pradip Shankar. Session starts in October 2029." I looked at my second brother, Haissam. He ignored me, picking at a stain on the table with a fingernail. "Can I go?" I asked, as the silence spun out. "It's a very prestigious scholarship. You won't have to pay a cent for my training, and once I qualify as a medical professional, I'll be totally off your hands."

Jonardon frowned. "You are the only daughter of the House of Dang. Girls from respectable houses don't become doctors. People will think we can't afford to settle you." I bit my lip. My third youngest brother was always hustling the elder two. He made it his business to object to everything, whether it made sense or not. That was his role.

"How does that matter? Dr Pradip Shankar says that now, when there's two men to every woman under 25 in the world, dowry is a drag on social progress. World production is being held back by reprod—"

"Stop with all your book-words," Budiharto growled. "We will not be lectured to by a schoolgirl."

"But you know my teachers say I have the brain for science. You said yourself it's a crime to waste resources." And I looked at my fourth brother, the baby of the family, the gentle one, Peter. Father had given him a Christian name and a fancy education so he could be the House of Dang's liaison with foreigners. I had kind of tagged along behind him, studying from his hand-me-down books and practicing from his downloads, because Dad never had a clue what to do with me. Peter was the only one apart from me who could speak International English, the only one of them who could understand why I yearned for New Singapore and all its limitless possibilities. But he said nothing.

"You could come and visit," I said hopefully to the others. "Check out the Ramdhun HQ for yourselves. I could report on their policies for you, tell you how they..."

"Silence!" Budiharto slammed the napkin down. "Ramdhun is our enemy. Dealing with them is man's work. Your place is far away from matters of business!"

I subsided. Haissam turned to Jonardon. "Have you found a match yet?"

Jonardon scowled. "The House of Khan and the House of Banerjee both want far too much for taking her off our hands. And they want proof of fertility."

Haissam's lips thinned. "Is not our word good enough for them?"

"In these days of liars and cheats the old ways are dying."

"Hello," I said, "Dear brothers all, there's no problem here. Just let me pack a suitcase and get out of your hair. It won't cost you anything, I already said."

Budiharto said, "How much did they want?" Jonardon named a figure. Haissam pursed his lips in a silent whistle. "Couldn't you beat them down?"

"She's too short, and her ass is fat."

"Look," I said, "just let me get my degree, and I'll come back to KL City and marry whoever you choose. It's a five year program, I'll graduate in 2034, then I'll work for a year, make the money for my dowry and come home. I'll be 24. Lots of men want a wife who can earn. You won't have to do a thing."

"That might work," Peter piped up. "Marrying her off is a luxury we can't afford right now." He regarded me. "You'll come back as soon as you can, won't you, Aiyzeh? Promise us."

I nodded. I tried to look as obedient as I possibly could. "You keep your head down," Jonardon muttered at me. "I've heard stories about the parties on New Singapore. We can't afford any scandals."

"You know I love studying and learning more than anything else. I just want to secure my future and spare the family finances. I don't want to be a burden." I smiled innocently at him.

We all looked at Budiharto, who flapped a dismissive hand. "Don't mix with boys," he said. And that was that.

From the air, New Singapore was a poem in glass and steel. It had launched on 1 January 2024, just two weeks after the giant quake-cluster and tidal wave of 2023 had scraped the skin off Singapore Island and piled it up in the Straits of Johor, leaving just a handful of shellshocked survivors from a city of six million. The controversies were still ringing: had fracking of the sea bed for oil destabilised the city's seismic profile? Had Old Singapore been too complacent about its immunity to disasters? What had happened to the refugees who had sailed out to New Singapore in the minutes after the wave, only to vanish in the haze beneath the thumping EDM and laser lightshows of the world's largest floating party venue? From the air, all you could see of the old city were the great shells of the gutted skyscrapers, some just twisted metal, some with chunks of concrete still clinging to their bones. They stood with their feet buried in the giant mudpie, now covered with young mangroves, which was the tomb of Old Singapore.

In the wake of the catastrophe, some said even before official warnings had gone out, twelve cruise ships of Ramdhun's line had brought the wealthy and the powerful from Marina Bay to this manmade island, and the ships had been yoked to it ever since, serving as localities of the floating city. They say the poor were denied permission to land and were knocked from the gunwales and anchor chains to the hungry sharks, but that was probably propaganda by rival corporations. When I did a search for news articles or videos about the seamier stories of New Singapore's birth, I found nothing. Anyway, all that was in the past. Nowadays we accept that in times of natural calamity, the weak will die. There's a word for them now: Climies, from 'climate victims'. People surplus to requirements, dragging like barnacles on the undersides of our economies, filling up the slums with hopelessness and bitter regret. So it's a good thing that there are less and less women in the world. Less women means less babies and less problems for the future.

I knew all this because since high school I'd been studying the writings and speeches of Dr Pradip Shankar, my hero. It was Supiriya who'd bought me a copy of *Future of the Child* as a birthday present when we were eleven, because I kept boring her with my theories and she could never keep up. Dr Shankar has a plan to change the world, and I want to be a part of it. He's setting up the Shankar Clinics under the banner of Ramdhun Wellness all over Southeast Asia. As New Singapore appeared as a white dot in the middle of the shining straits, I only hoped I could prove myself worthy.

My new phone started to ping madly: we must have entered the Ramdhun datasphere. It was a Ramfone R5: I'd had to nag Budiharto for the money and buy it before leaving KL City. Only Ramdhun technology was allowed in New Singapore. "Welcome to the Ramdhun Corporate Community," said the first notification, then in rapid succession I got given my ID card, class timetable, ward duty roster, trainee accommodation flat number, food card, transport card, and consumer goods charge card. I felt a thrill of excitement: this was how the world should function! Not with the outdated lethargy of democracies and government social services, but with the snap and sizzle of private enterprise.

We landed on water and coasted smoothly to the dock. As we touched down my phone pinged again: directions on how to get to the massive white hospital ship I'd seen from the air, with the Shankar Clinics logo glowing on its superstructure. I went and stood meekly in line for a water taxi. There was no one to receive me, but I expected that. They'd told me as much at the interview back in KL City. 'Don't look to be treated any different from a man,' were almost the first words they said to me. The speaker was the only woman on the interview board. I couldn't answer her; I was out of breath from getting to the venue. That day I'd told my mother I was going with Supiriya to the spa, I'd left my friend smothered in a chocolate face pack and run the three blocks to the hotel where the interview was taking place. So I had just nodded.

Then they grilled me. "What is your view of motherhood?" That was easy. I quoted *Future of the Child* almost verbatim: "Motherhood is a sacred trust. Every woman should have the right to experience it. But the world is overburdened with people who cannot be profitably absorbed by the labour markets. If every woman were to exercise her god-given right to be a mother, it would be disastrous for the planet and world GDP. So the only way to save women from the inevitable sacrifice of their natural rights is to have fewer of them. Dr Shankar's vision is to take us back to the time when the human population was sustainable within the economic framework of the..."

"Tell us what you know about Humane Choice."

"It's Dr Shankar's greatest invention, a vaccine designed to make sure that, having taken it, a man will predominantly have sons. He invented it in 2007 when he was still in Chandigarh, but because the Indian government didn't share his vision, he had to distribute it in secret. He called it a bloodless revolution which would bring down human numbers without war or suffering. It's a miracle of modern medical engineering designed to prevent the production of economically risky children. It skews the workforce towards productivity rather than reproductivity..."

"How does it work?"

"Dr Shankar created a virus, the Recombinant Adeno-Associated Viral Analog, to carry a proprietary payload to the germline cells in a man's testes. This proprietary payload acts to supercharge the Y-bearing sperm and handicap the X-bearing sperm, thus enormously increasing the likelihood of son-birth. It ensures that every girl is a wanted girl who is free to enjoy all the privileges of her sex, so that we need not worry about accidental pregnancies or force women to voluntarily give up the joys of home life and motherhood. It is a pro-life option that shuts down the possibility of people choosing to be irresponsible with their biological capacities. We know from the statistics of the previous century that poor women are bad at managing their family choices. Currently a third of world population below 25 is female, and if they all have children at replacement rates..."

The chairman of the interview board leaned forward. "And what is globetrotter flu?"

I was a little wrongfooted by that one. "Sir?"

"Answer the question."

"Um, it's a new disease that arose some five years ago, I think. It is not fatal, just gives you low grade intermittent fever for about six months, then vanishes forever. And it makes you immune to some of the other, more deadly flus." I risked a small smile. "The Head of the Centre for Disease Control said about it in 2020, 'Finally a disease that does some good.' Er, I'm afraid I don't know much more about it…"

They did not smile back. "Do you believe the rumours linking globetrotter flu to Humane Choice?"

"I haven't heard of any such rumours."

They asked a few more questions, but I got the feeling the real test was over. They handed me the letter of appointment on my way out, as if it was nothing. The chairman told me, "Forget Humane Choice. Now we're concentrating on a new range of human reproductive technologies for the current economic crisis. Keep an open mind and you'll fit right in to the Shankar Clinics family." I was to join on 1 October 2029. Classes and traineeship would run concurrently. I thanked them and ran all the way back to Supiriya, to gasp out my tale of success to her. I think she smiled but I couldn't tell because of the face pack. I got my nails done in record time so Mom wouldn't get suspicious. That night I didn't sleep, just screamed silently with joy and fear into my pillow and hugged the letter to me.

The water taxi arrived, sleek and shark-finned, jerking me back to the present. It pinged my brand new transport card, startling me a little at how much money got sucked out. All the 'roads' in New Singapore are water channels: over our heads delicate semi-transparent bridges connected the floating platforms we were passing. I noticed how the bridges had a sleeve-within-sleeve design, so that they could accommodate the faint rocking of the smaller platforms. Occasionally there were taxi quays where beautiful people dressed in the height of fashion waited for their rides. I could barely contain my excitement, but I tried to copy the looks of bored sophistication on the faces of the people around. I was too overawed to take any pictures. There'd be time enough for that later.

Three more stations, then I'd be at my stop. I tried to sit straight and stop gawping out the windows. The screens in the compartment were playing ads. They kept showing the face and body of a goddess. "Smiti Chen," said the voiceover. "Winner of the Ramdhun Chick of the Year Contest. Representing New Singapore at the Miss Universe pageant next month in Al Shahada, the world's second corporate city. Smiti Chen. Winning the hearts and minds of the world's investors. The Ramdhun glambassador of 2029. Smiti Chen. Will she put our city on the map? Find out on the Potent News Network. Touch the banner to download the Smiti Chen lookbook with bonus swimsuit collection for premium users. Smiti Chen..."

We were passing between two floating piazzas with graceful trees growing on them. Renaissance-style statues lined the waterway, pouring inexhaustible waters from their urns into the sea. Up ahead loomed the great hospital ship that housed Ramdhun Wellness. Its white sides loomed over my head: smooth, perfectly engineered metal. The water taxi was nearly empty; I got up in a hurry, afraid I'd spent too long gawking and would miss my stop. As I stepped off the taxi I got a brief glimpse of ventilator shafts below, slatted mouths from which a fetid hot breath came, like garbage and rotting meat and formalin and sickness, then it was gone and a smell of lavender wafted from the glittering entrance of the covered gangplank leading to the lobby.

I propped my suitcase against my leg and checked my phone to see where my flat was. Then I followed the instructions. It was three decks down in the supply ship next door. The flat buzzed open as I approached. Not a single person I passed even spared me a glance.

I had the weekend to furnish my tiny two-room flat; duties began on Monday. When I entered the front door, the Ramdhun home system installed a Speaking Assistant called Ramya on my phone. Ramya told me where to go shopping and what to do when I got there. Her voice was chilly and Chinese-accented, like the snootier girls I'd been to school with. Suddenly I felt homesick for Supiriya, but she had gone home to Palakkad and left no number. No doubt her father was fattening her up for the big event. I went out, did my shopping, came back. Soon I had a tablet device, a home theatre and a food processing unit, all made by Ramdhun and networked to the flat's home system. There was already a shower unit and fridge, a foldout bed and dining table. Ramya told me how to operate the theatre; in a household of four boys, I'd never had sole control of a home entertainment system, not even for a minute. I was obscurely glad that no real people were around to watch me fumbling at the swipescreens.

The news, once I managed to access it, was all about Smiti Chen. Apparently her representing New Singapore at the Miss Universe pageant was a big deal: the first public recognition of New Singapore as a country alongside the traditional states. It would open up a whole slew of possibilities including Ramdhun's right to issue passports, vote in international forums, patrol its borders and run its own justice system. They kept calling her a 'glambassador'. Heh. There was lots of footage of Selvam Vaghela, CEO of Ramdhun, giving press conferences about her, and about his vision for the city. He looked like a well-dressed shark. "New Singapore is the first society in the world composed entirely of ultra high net worth individuals and their families," he said. "Here, religion, sex, creed, birth, race mean nothing. We are people who can and will excel. Everything in this amazing city is designed to help us do this." That made me feel a little better.

I pricked up my ears at the mention of Dr Pradip Shankar. A news flash showed him with Smiti. Her father was Lesley Chen, New Singapore's Head of Engineering and one of Dr Shankar's earliest patients. Smiti was beautiful, tall, willowy with a generous bosom, just like Supiriya, golden skin and hair like a silken waterfall. But I only had eyes for Dr Shankar. He was explaining why Smiti's birth proved that Humane Choice did allow for a limited number of female babies to be born, contrary to what his critics kept saying. Smiti Chen's beauty and poise proved the superiority of his process. "Every child a wanted child," he said, and made the victory sign. He had wiry hair haloing a nascent bald spot, glasses that cut into his nose and a scrubby moustache, but I didn't mind. I was beginning to tire of the relentless perfection of everyone I met. All the Asians were uncannily pale, while all the white people were a bronzy red. I had met one black person from Jamaica, DeJean Johnson from Corporate Communications, or Image Management as they called it here, and she was more of a coffee-cream. If I had realised that I was the darkest person I'd met so far, I wouldn't have gone to bed so full of eagerness for my new life to begin.

That first week was hard. So hard. Classes began at six am and the doctors lectured so fast it made my head spin. I was used to the leisurely pace of a girls' school meant for heiresses. Lectures ended at 11am and then I had to run down to the path lab to help in carrying out routine tests. On the first day the head pathologist barely glanced at me and barked out a series of orders. I tried to follow them as best as I could. When I asked him, timidly, what the tests I was carrying out were supposed to detect, he just looked at me as if I was in his way.

There were no other women working in the lab. When I spoke to any of the boys they'd grin at each other as though one of them had won a bet. Conversations hushed as I passed, replaced by long raking stares. All that week, I would come home and cry my eyes out. Then I would download papers and lectures from the hospital library, search for terms I'd heard my colleagues use or seen on requisition slips or reagent bottles and answer all my questions myself. Ramya would tempt me with invites to happening parties and clubs and discos, but I would just say "Shut up, Ramya," and bend my head to the work. I didn't feel I deserved that life, yet. Maybe I never would.

The second week was a little better, and the week after that. Or maybe I was going numb. Either way, the sheer pace of my life was like the manic drumbeats on a war galley, and I was a slave, rowing this great ship out to sea. Or it was like the rhythm of a failing heart, going into tachycardia. I was beginning to re-alise that all my worthless education had done was give me ideas above my station. I didn't know the first thing about basic biol-ogy, couldn't name the bones of the arm or the types of blood cells, had no idea where the pancreas was or what 'defibrillation' actually did beyond act as a plot point in medical dramas. But the thought of going back home in shame was worse than an-ything that could happen to me here. I worked all through the month of November, trying to keep the panic down.

On a day when I was so tied up I couldn't go to lunch, one of the boys in the lab took pity on me and gave me half his sand-wich. I thanked him sincerely. "Call me Tom," he said, "Tom Tanaka. What's your name?"

"Aiyzeh Dang."

His eyebrows shot up. "Ugh. What an ugly name. Here's a tip. Call yourself Alice. Alice Dang. Yes, that sounds good."

"Like Alice in Wonderland?" I looked at him helplessly. "How do I change my name? It's on the roster and everything."

He laughed at my naivete, took my phone from my breast pocket, did something to it and handed it back. "Now you're Alice Dang. That's a name that'll take you places."

"Hello, Alice Dang," said Ramya.

"Thanks. It's... different." I felt a little bolder. "Will it take me as far as working with Dr Shankar, do you think?"

"Huh." He laughed, not nicely. "Don't be misled by the gos-sip about him. It's true he likes to hire chicks as RanDees, but you're too short, and your ass is fat."

"RanDees?"

"R&D. Research and Development. Sheesh, don't you know anything?" He got up and left.

In spite of Tom's dismissiveness, I began to feel more confident. Maybe it was the new name, maybe it was the slew of photographs Supiriya sent me of her betrothal to a young businessman. She looked flustered and pretty and he was slick-haired, fair and slim, no doubt a catch. I wondered if her health problems had been sorted out. I knew she found it hard to talk to her father about them. Not having a mother had its own perils, I supposed. I remembered with a start that I'd been planning to send pictures of the city to Supiriya. I'd worked hard for weeks, surely by now I deserved a little fun. I decided it was time to go sightseeing.

Ramya was delighted I was out of the flat and deluged me with so many recommendations I had to mute her. I went to the Silver Heights Mall. It was on a massive cruise ship: on the highest level there was a dance floor and a cafe and an open air theatre. I'd grown up in the chaotic, sooty bustle of KL City; in New Singapore I was afraid to sit on the cream and gold raw silk seats in the cheapest bistro I could find, as if my skin might stain them. I have to get over this, I said to myself. I ordered octopus eggs au gratin and bread-of-the-sea. They looked fabulous when they arrived, but both had a flat, bland taste. I refused dessert and wandered out again.

I bought a silk dress that clung unpleasantly to my ample curves, furtively picked up a packet of fruitcakes from a convenience store and scuttled home with relief. I sent Supiriya the photos and she responded with a big smiley face. Idle chit-chat followed, but she sidestepped the big questions about her health. I felt uneasy. Her father was quite capable of marrying her off without a second thought, leaving her husband to sort out any problems with the merchandise. He was the kind of man who saw women only as boxes to be filled up with whatever he wished. "Ramya, get me everything you can on amenorrhea," I said. "And be quiet about it."

I spent Sunday munching the cakes and studying the information Ramya got for me. Although Supiriya's BMI was indeed low, she had big breasts with tiny, perfect nipples. She claimed to wax her armpits, so I didn't know about her axial hair. Her skin was clear gold, her hair like shining brown waves. Also she was tall, much taller than me, so there had been a pubertal growth spurt. One by one I eliminated possible causes, till I had a differential diagnosis with just two possibilities. I sat back and looked at them, then sent Supiriya a message: had she ever had an abdominal ultrasound? Could she send me the pictures from it? She was offline, so I'd have to wait for a response.

Immediately I felt bad and wanted to delete the message. Supiriya hated to talk about her body. She was like an angel made flesh and I was probably worrying too much. In any case, maybe her lack of periods wouldn't be a problem: not every wealthy man these days wanted hordes of children. Surely some would prefer a wife who would make them look good and promote their brand. I swallowed the cake I was eating and made a face. Of course no food could be grown on New Singapore: it all came from the mainland and was chock full of preservatives. The packet said 'with real fruit content' but it didn't say which fruit or what content. I sighed. Can't have everything. I went to bed congratulating myself on my first successful pleasure outing.

That feeling didn't last the night. When Ramya woke me up and turned the lights to morning setting (there were no windows in the flat) it was all I could do to drag myself from my soft cave, stagger to the shower unit, get dressed. I ate my meagre breakfast standing up, and turned to the news networks just to hear some human voices. I felt a mild curiosity to see how Smiti Chen was doing in her mission of glamour diplomacy. But I was in for a shock.

Smiti Chen was indeed everywhere, but it was her tear-stained, shame-shadowed face they were showing. She'd been disqualified from the contest by a simple genetic test. What had gone wrong? "It's official, Jamila, Smiti Chen is genetically a man!" exclaimed a reporter. "She's been disqualfied for misrepresenting her genetic status in the pageant entry documents." In the background the glambassador of New Singapore was seen being bundled into a private jet. The swarm of camera drones stacked above her head made her look like the victim of an alien attack or a very high-tech Beelzebub. "Thank you, Simon. If you're joining us now, high drama at Al Shahada last night as accusations of fraud and malpractice are being levelled at Ramdhun by the hosts of this year's Miss Universe pageant, the rival corporation Al Ayyarun. What an upset, Janice! 2029 was supposed to be the year of corporate cities, and yet here we have a falling-out between their two main advocates!"

"Absolutely, Jamila. This is a major embarrassment. Smiti's father Lesley Chen has been Dr Shankar's main advocate and the reason why in 2024, when Humane Choice was banned by the Indian government, Ramdhun invited Dr Shankar to New Singapore. Now it looks like Ramdhun may well regret that decision. Worldwide calls for an investigation into Shankar's products are strengthening."

The last fruitcake dropped from my nerveless fingers. Dr Shankar, his scrubby moustache bristling in the lights of a hundred cameras, growled, "Smiti Chen is not a man! Her breasts are one hundred percent natural. She has never had a sex reassignment surgery. Her condition makes her totally unresponsive to male hormones. That makes her more feminine than the average woman." He pointed into the audience. "You!" he barked. "You, lady journalist, you in red top. Have you ever threaded your upper lip? Do you know why you have to do that? Because the tiny amount of male hormone in your body masculinises you. Smiti Chen does not have hair on her upper lip. She is the epitome of perfect femininity. I can certify this."

Voices erupted in a squall of questions. "But Al Ayyarun are saying she has an XY genotype. Dr Shankar? Dr Shankar? Is this true? Did you know? Dr Shankar! Did you know about this? Did Mr Vaghela know about it?"

"I have no further comment at this time. All I will say that, if the test had been fair, there are other contestants in that pageant that I strongly suspect should have been disqualified for the same reason. No! No further comment!"

I shut down the home theatre, grabbed my purse, stuffed my phone in it and ran out of the flat. "Have a nice day," it said as I left. Outside I stopped in horror. On the far wall of the lobby someone had spraypainted huge red letters, spelling out the words BITCH WARS. Some cleaning ladies in pink uniforms were scratching ineffectually at the corners of it. I hurried past them and headed for the elevator. My hand hovered over the buttons. Lectures were on Deck 12, the path labs were on Deck 10. My hand rose to the top of the gleaming panel and hit Deck 20. I was going all the way to the top.

Or at least I thought I was. The elevator stopped at Outpatients to let on an old woman with a walker and her attendants. All the screens in the waiting room were blasting the news. "...now called Complete Androgen Insensitivity Syndrome, or CAIS. It used to be a rare disease, but currently reports are pouring in from all over the world indicating it might be as common as 1 in 400 girls born after 2010. Smiti Chen's unmasking has opened a can of..." The doors mercifully closed and the elevator muzak reasserted itself. The old woman got out at Scanning and the voices hit me again. "...so Rachel, you're telling me that these kids look and feel and behave just like women, but they're actually men?"

"No, Benny, they're women, they just have an XY genotype. Their only difference from normal women is the absence of a uterus. It's like some children are born with spina bifida because their mothers had folic acid deficiency. Your genes are just a recipe for a human: the cake can get burned in the oven, you know."

"Is that why they're calling it Broken Pot Syndrome?"

"That's rather politically incorrect, Benny..."

By Deck 18, there was just me and three nervous techies in the lift. I gasped as the doors opened. This level was mostly glass, and the horizon was dark with storm clouds. I could see through the glass partitions that there was a meeting happening, and even the glass couldn't muffle the voice of Selvam Vaghela, heavy with anger.

"...figure out how you're going to get out of this one, Shankar, or you're going back to that hole in the ground you came out of. Where the hell is that tech support team? I want to see these scans. If this is as bad as you say, I want to know how much time we have..."

I stayed with the three techies as security waved us in. We hurried to the big conference room, where a large screen was flashing an error message. Selvam Vaghela ignored us. Sitting in front of him was Dr Shankar and, I checked my pace in shock, Smiti Chen muffled up in a black shawl. I hadn't expected to find her there. But perhaps it was for the best.

"This is a disaster, Shankar, whatever you say," Mr Vaghela growled. "You knowingly allowed this dickless wonder to represent us and then get caught and outed before every news channel on the planet. Someone in Al Ayyarun must have known about her condition and used it tactically against us. There's no hushing this up. We need damage control now."

"I had no idea they were going to test!" Shankar wailed. "I swear I had no clue or I would have broken patient-doctor confidentiality to—"

"I told you they'd play dirty. This is the corporate world, Shankar, not your medicine." Mr Vaghela gave a crooked grin. "Now fix this or I'll break the leg that Himmat Singh spared!"

I took a deep breath. "That won't be necessary," I said as clearly as possible. "And this is not a disaster." Dr Shankar and Mr Vaghela turned to stare at me. I went on without a pause, "All through history, there have been great women who were genetically XY. They say Joan of Arc was one, and even Marilyn Monroe. They are Amazonian goddesses, perfect beings, yes, perfect, because as Dr Shankar says, there are too many human beings in the world, and these women keep the faith: they can't have children."

"Who the hell are you?"

"Alice Dang, sir. Medical trainee. I'm the Sunita Vaghela Scholar, sir. I've just been here two months, but I belong to Ramdhun body and soul. I have a friend, my best friend, I think she's a CAIS woman too. She's tall, slim, busty, beautiful, the woman I'd kill to be, and her only flaw is, she has no periods. Flaw? I'd say it's a virtue to match all the others she has. Dr Shankar said the right thing at that press conference. These are the women we need. They have everything: great skin, great hair, and no biological risk." I turned to her. "Smiti, please stand up and show yourself."

She stared at me. "I have testicular cancer." And she burst into tears. Dr Shankar patted her shoulder vaguely. He seemed to be in shock.

"Goddamnit! Trust a fucking bitch to cry!" Mr Vaghela snapped his fingers at the tech team. "Out!" They scurried away. He examined me carefully. "You seem to know more about this than either my medical genius or my glambassador. And you have the sheer fucking effrontery to crash my meeting and lecture me on how to run my company. So tell me. How would you get us out of this mess?"

This was it, my big chance. Don't blow it, I said to myself, and pinched my arm behind my back. "There is no mess, sir. Here in New Singapore we stand for achievement and excellence, as you said sir, and we live on one of the most fragile and most advanced pieces of real estate in the world. We of all people know the folly of unrestricted population growth. We excel, and we look good doing it. She," I pointed to puffy-eyed Smiti, "is exactly what we should be selling to the world. Does anyone know she had cancer yet?"

"No," said Dr Shankar. All the fizz he had shown at the press conference was gone. "Shush, Smiti, it's all right. She can be cured. You will be okay. Just trust me."

"Excellent," I said, drunk on sheer terror and my own recklessness. "Let's release the news of her cancer, shave her head and show her being treated. Ride the sympathy wave. If this disease has become as widespread as they're saying on the news, then there's a lot of people out there waiting for a champion. Her tragedy will be their story. We'll capture the moral high ground and make AL Ayyarun eat their words."

"It's globetrotter flu causing all this," Shankar muttered. "It has to be."

"Get a grip, Shankar." Mr Vaghela turned to me and smiled his sharky smile. "Kid, you're wasted in medicine. I'm reassigning you to my image management team. Report to Rik Nehra on Deck 19." He looked from me to Smiti and back. "Beauty and brains. I should have known I needed two of you. No chick ever has both."

I felt as if the deck had bucked under my feet. "But sir, I love medicine. Dr Pradip Shankar, sir, I've admired you since..."

Mr Vaghela gave a sharp bark of laughter. "You admire this loser whose ass you're saving from a royal roasting? Reality check, babe. I'm paying for your education, which means I own you. What you want doesn't matter. You've made a proposal, now follow through on it. That's how this works." He flapped a hand at Shankar and Smiti. "Okay, doc, get this defective piece of dude-ass to Oncology and take some footage for the press release. The media crew's still here, right? Milk it for all it's worth. You girl, what did you say your name was?"

"Alice Dang, sir."

"You go with Smiti and make sure she does what I want. You're replacing her as my glambassador. Get yourself some sharp clothes and proper chick shoes, prepare the press release, and as soon as this shit is cleaned up, report to Liposuction and do something about that ass." He gave me that scanning look again. "I suppose your tits are okay. Maybe a nose job. And have them do a leucotattoo on your face and arms, you're at least three shades off the dark end of my personal shade card."

"Sir!" I was stung. "I thought we were above all that here in New Singapore."

He grinned. "Welcome to the glam world, baby. All that matters in this bullring is what's in your head, what's in your pants, and what's in your bank account. In ascending order."

I wanted to scream. Why must people constantly replace my future with theirs? My triumph was nothing but ashes. I looked at the other two people at the table. They didn't meet my eyes. I had saved them, but they weren't grateful. "Yes, sir." I said. The little cake had said 'Eat me,' and now I was shrinking into nothing in Wonderland.

UPGRADE

by Manjula Padmanabhan

Mrs Ganapathy glared at her grand-daughter and at the newly unpacked machine. "Couldn't you at least have consulted me? Before spending all that money?"

"You can't manage without house-help, Ammama," said Sameera.

The two of them were sitting in Mrs Ganapathy's dining room in her sixteenth floor apartment in Chennai East. Between them, inert and silent stood a short, squat humanoid robot. Outside, the elevated monorail thundered by every fifteen minutes. Only a faint chittering murmur filtered through the plate-glass windows.

"*House-help*, hah!" snorted Mrs Ganapathy. "What I need is a good old-fashioned *servant*. Someone to cook, clean and wash my clothes. Bring tea in the mornings and answer the doorbell. Won't answer back or talk too much." She was 87, white-haired and used a motorized wheelchair to get around her home, though she could walk short distances if she had to. She aimed another vicious glance at the silent machine. "What I *don't* need is another wretched machine!"

"Oh, Ammama!" scolded Sameera. "Cursing at machines hurts their feelings!"

"What happens when the power fails? You people live in places where that never happens. But even in this fancy building it's off at least once a week!" She clicked her tongue. "Then it's *peep!peep!peep!* from the kitchen, *whaa!whaa!whaa!* from the TV room and *coo-coo-coo* from my phone-charger!"

"Ammama, please!" said Sameera. She was in her late-twenties, an undersea exploration engineer. "She's a really advanced model. She'll take care of all your problems – yes,

99

even look after all the other machines in the house *and* monitor her own energy needs. Won't you at least give her a chance?"

From the corner of her eye Mrs Ganapathy could see the smooth, pale grey shape about the height of a ten-year-old child. It had a round bobble-head with a flat dark panel where a human face might have eyes. Its short torso ended at a waist that swelled to form what looked like a full, floor-length skirt, also pale grey. No arms were visible, but on either side of the torso were round, dark patches of some softer, pliable material that looked as if they might be ports for retractable arms. Beneath the "skirt", out of sight, were a pair of sturdy telescoping limbs, capable of climbing stairs and ladders and even, when need be, straight up the wall and onto the ceiling.

"It's just a machine," said Mrs Ganapathy. "I've seen the ads." She could hear the sound of her own breath, uneven, because she was getting agitated. She knew she shouldn't be because the gift was well-intended, a gesture of love from her three daughters and four grandchildren. *But it's really just for yourselves in the end, isn't it?* she thought. *To save yourselves the guilt of not being here. Of talking to me only on weekends, when you have five minutes of "spare" time.*

Sameera said, "This particular model is more advanced than the kind you've seen on TV Amamma." Having grown up with Intelligent Inorganics, "Aye-Ayes" as they were known, she couldn't imagine life without them. "Honestly, if you don't like her you can-"

"And what's all the *she-her* nonsense?" flashed Mrs Ganapathy, interrupting. "Next you'll be telling me the thing has monthly periods!"

Sameera smiled patiently. "Fine, you can call her 'it' if you want!"

They sat together then, the white-haired old lady in her pink cotton sari and her granddaughter in stretch-skin overalls, reading the instruction booklet. According to the literature the robot was entirely self-sufficient once the detailed set-up was over. It responded to voice commands and would answer in audio as well as in text messages displayed on its visor.

"I'm here till the end of the week, Ammama——"

"——two days away," said Mrs Ganapathy, tartly. "And what happens after that? Supposing it goes berserk? Supposing I can't switch it off?"

Mr Ganapathy had died twelve years ago. Their three grown daughters lived in other countries. Mrs Ganapathy could certainly have chosen to live with any one of them. But she hadn't ever wanted to. She knew from friends who had opted to emigrate, that their lives were marked by bland food, dull, ill-fitting clothes and grey skies all year round.

She had a middle-aged woman cook who managed all the shopping, cleaning and other chores. Two floors down, lived a second cousin and her large family. They and their own servants were always ready to help in case of emergencies. Other friends and relatives lived a phone-call away. The daughters and their children came on visits.

It hadn't been a perfect life, but it wasn't a bad one.

Then one morning, while boiling the milk, the cook-woman fell over, dead. The milk had hissed and spluttered, pouring down the sides of the pan and onto the floor in orangey-black streaks as it burnt, while Mrs Ganapathy rushed out into the corridor in her motorized wheelchair, screaming to the neighbours for help.

Since that time, one month ago, Mrs Ganapathy's life had come undone as thoroughly as the tight, neat bun on the back of her head unravelling to her waist when she took the pins out of it.

Two of Mrs Ganapathy's daughters flew in immediately, but that only meant they had to get back to their jobs and busy lives almost as soon as they had arrived. The third one was recovering from a broken foot and couldn't come at all.

They tried to organize servants from around the neighbourhood. The first one belched loudly while serving Mrs Ganapathy at table. The second one played her radio at tooth-rattling volume in the kitchen while she cooked. The third one seduced the building's young doorman the very first night she stayed in the apartment, which meant that she was late bringing morning tea to her furious employer the next day. The fourth had chronic arthritis and couldn't sleep on the floor, like any normal servant, but needed her own bed and a fan to keep the mosquitoes away.

Each woman was dismissed within twenty-four hours even though Mrs Ganapathy knew perfectly well that she couldn't manage on her own. Her daughters couldn't extend their leaves. A stop-gap arrangement was made: the downstairs second-cousin sent up her own cook, bearing home-made meals, three times a day. The doorman's young wife agreed to swab the floors and do the laundry on a part-time basis. No doubt she was still smouldering from the knowledge of her husband's infidelity which, according to Mrs Ganapathy, meant that she was rude, sullen and completely unreliable. "I call her ten times before she comes. She won't raise a finger to help me get in and out of my wheel chair," said the old lady. "She's takes two days off for every day she works."

Then Sameera had flown in, fresh and cheerful, straight from her last assignment off the coast of Malaysia. She said she wouldn't leave until she'd solved the problem. Two days later, she brought in the bobble-headed machine.

"All right. Ready?" she said, looking at the manual. "The first step is to choose a name."

"How about Hari?" said Mrs Ganapathy.

"What – a man?" exclaimed Sameera.

"It's a machine!" retorted her grandmother. "Not a man. But all through my life, I preferred men-servants to women. Fewer problems, so long as they don't drink."

"Ammama," said Sameera, "it won't make any kind of difference. Whatever you call your new helper, it'll do exactly the same kind of work."

"Then why call it by any name?"

"Because the manual says ..."

"Oh! Just go ahead and do whatever you'd like!" said Mrs Ganapathy, losing patience. "You people always pretend you're offering choices when in fact you've made up your mind well in advance."

"Fine," said Sameera, "I'll go ahead." She adored her grandma and forgave her everything, including the bad-temper and the shockingly out-dated attitudes towards domestic workers. "I'm going to make her female, because the manual claims that respectable Indian ladies always prefer women helpers." She rotated the GenSelector dial so that the front panel of the robot's face showed pink. "And I'm going to called her Rohini – just like your old cook."

"What language will it speak? Rohini spoke only Tamil..."

"English, Tamil and Hindi," read Sameera from the literature. "Okay, Age Selector - young girl or middle-aged woman?"

"Oh my," sighed Mrs Ganapathy. "All these *choices*!"

"Okay, forty-five," said Sameera. "What about religion?"

"Christian," said Mrs Ganapathy. "They're always the best cooks. Remember Fernandes? I still dream about his éclairs."

"Okay and... voice quality. Do you want a *normal* or..."

"What's *normal*?" Mrs Ganapathy wanted to know. "And what sort of fool would want 'abnormal'?"

"There's a demonstration audio clip," said Sameera. She was squinting at the flip-up panel at the back of the machine, as she inputted her selections. Using a small plastic rod provided for the purpose, she pushed an interior button. A sudden *DING!* made Mrs Ganapathy jump. A woman's voice, high and tinkling, said, "*HI! MY NAME IS ROHINI! AND THIS IS MY NORMAL VOICE.*"

"Terrible!" said Mrs Ganapathy at once. "Doesn't sound even human, never mind."

"It's only the demonstration, Ammama, and that's the default choice," said Sameera. "I have to press it again, I think," as she did so.

Another *DING!* and this time a sugary sweet voice said, in a strong American accent, "*HI! MY NAME IS RO-HEE–NEE! AND THIS IS MY NORMAL VOICE.*"

Mrs Ganapathy frowned. "Ugh! Doesn't sound Tamilian at all!"

Sameera clicked her tongue and punched the rod in again. Too hard, it seemed, because the machine re-set to an internal default. There was a loud *CLUNK!* and "MY-NAME-IS-DO-MESTIX," said the little robot in a harsh, staccato. "I-AM-HERE-TO-SERVE-YOU."

"Switch it off!" gasped Mrs Ganapathy. "Switch it off!" Her eyes were magnified by her pink-rimmed reading glasses. She looked like a frightened child, her face framed by wisps of sil-ver-white hair.

"That's just an internal audio-file," Sameera said. "Custom-ers aren't supposed to hear it."

Mrs Ganapathy's mouth opened and shut a couple of times before she found the right words. "It is just a machine," she whispered, finally. "And that's its real voice."

Sameera didn't know what to say.

"You're leaving me at the mercy of a talking tin can," con-tinued the old lady, unable to keep the pain out of her voice, even though she didn't blame anyone. *That's how it is these days*, she thought. *You have children, you shower them with love. Then they fly away and leave you to die alone.*

"*Please* believe me, Ammama!" said Sameera. "These ro-bots don't have a single mean circuit in their construction." Her voice sounded hollow even to her own ears but she had to forge on. "I'm going re-set the program and start from scratch."

Two hours later, they were finally ready to initialize.

"Right," said Sameera, as she pressed ENTER. "Here we go."

The flip-up panel gave a *blip* of acknowledgment. From deep within the machine came a series of faint musical tones. The bobble-head stirred. A jerk, a hum and it was on.

"Hello, Madam," said a soft female voice. She spoke in Tamil-accented English.

Only the faintest underlying hiss suggested it was not a human voice. It was pitched low, with an attractive humility built into it, as if the speaker were standing with her head bowed, not so much as daring to look up at her employer.

"My name is Rohini. Thank you for waking me up. How may I help you?"

Two arms blossomed on either side of the dumpy little body. They were covered up to the wrists with what looked like soft, textured cotton, decorated with an all-over print of pink flowers. The hands that emerged from the wrist looked completely human, right down to the dark colour of the skin, like polished mahogany. The nails were short. The flesh of the palms was pink and looked soft to the touch.

From the time she'd heard the harsh robotic voice, Mrs Ganapathy had said very little. Now she refused to even look in Rohini's direction. "Tell it to make us tea," she said, addressing her granddaughter. Then, wheeling her chair around, she headed to the bathroom.

Sameera stayed for a whole week longer than she had planned. On her last day she hugged her grandmother tight, struggling to hold back tears. As she stepped through the front door, she turned to wave goodbye. But the old lady, frail and alone in her wheelchair, was looking out the floor-to ceiling windows of the drawing room. Beyond her was the open ocean. Beside her, silent and vigilant, was the little robot.

Months passed before Sameera was once more in the corridor leading to her grandmother's apartment. She paused before ringing the bell, feeling oddly nervous. The door opened as she hesitated.

"Hello, Sameera," said Rohini. "How nice to see you again." The short, squat robot looked completely unchanged. "I heard the elevator," she said, to explain why she'd opened the door. "And I saw you on the security camera."

Mrs Ganapathy was waiting for her granddaughter, sitting in the drawing room with smile on her face and her arms outstretched for a hug. She still looked frail of course, but fresh and well-rested too, wearing a crisply ironed pink cotton sari. They hugged and then, as they sat together, Rohini brought in tea and hot snacks. "Tell me about all the things you've been doing since your last e-mail to me," said her grandmother. "And what were those strange glittery creatures you took videos of? And what about that nice man you met off the coast of Madagascar?"

All through Sameera's stay she couldn't help but notice how much her grandmother had improved since her last visit. Writing to her mother and aunts, "I mean, this is what we wanted for her, but it's like... almost *spooky*! The house is looking wonderful. Spotlessly clean. Fresh flowers in the vases. The carpets have all been shaken out and replaced in the way that Ammama likes, with their fringes straight. And best of all, she seems so *happy*! Imagine, she's even talking about getting a puppy!"

The other three wrote back affirming her impressions. They had each been to see their mother in separate visits over the months. "I know what you mean about *spooky*," said Sameera's mother, Meena, in a group-WhatsApp message. "It's almost too good to be true."

The older of the two aunts, Girija, posted a GIF of a hysterically laughing Chihuahua. "Look at us!" she wrote. "So suspicious. We should instead just be glad for our Mum. And grateful to Rohini's designers. I suppose she'll need an upgrade one of these days?"

Sameera stayed four days. She enjoyed her time there, ate far too much and slept till late into the morning. When she left it was without a trace of the sadness and regret she'd felt the last time.

Rohini waited a few moments by the door. "All right," she said, presently. "That's the elevator."

"Let's just wait another few minutes," said Mrs Ganapathy. "In case she's left something behind and comes back to fetch it."

The little robot walked back towards the old lady saying, "She won't want to miss the monorail. The next one will leave in eight minutes, six seconds and it'll take her straight in to the airport. If she's left anything, she knows now that she can always write to me."

"Just five minutes," said Mrs Ganapathy. "To be on the safe side."

Rohini's visor-plate showed a smile. "Madam, it continues to surprise me."

"What?" asked the old lady.

"That you feel the need to keep secrets from your family." The robot was standing next to the wheelchair now. She turned it around so that they were both facing the splendid view out the east-facing window.

Mrs Ganapathy chuckled. "It's because they would absolutely disapprove. They love me of course and they say they want the best for me. But what do they really mean by that? Not very much, if you ask me. The fact is, if they knew about the upgrade, they would disapprove."

"It is not very logical," said Rohini. "This upgrade has been very beneficial for you. Your BP is down, your blood sugar is perfect, you're sleeping well."

"Humans are not logical," said Mrs Ganapathy. "My daughters would disapprove without even knowing why." She glanced at her mechanical helper. "Just like you can't understand why I can't tell them! Because you don't know what it's like to have a family."

"It's a matter of deep regret to all inorganics, Madam. That we cannot understand about feelings and emotions."

"Come now," said Mrs Ganapathy. "Regret is a feeling! If you can feel that, then you can feel anything."

"Excuse me for interrupting, Madam, but five minutes have passed," said Rohini.

Mrs Ganapathy said, "Yes, yes. Go ahead." She turned her head slightly, so that she would not witness the transformation that was about to take place. Of course she knew that the robot did not feel self-conscious! But still.

"Shall I respond to what you said about regret, Madam, as I change?"

"Go ahead," said Mrs Ganapathy.

"When I use such words as 'regret', Madam, I am merely approximating what I believe to be human emotions. Nevertheless..."

As she spoke, Rohini's physical dimensions were changing in quick, smooth jerks. She grew two feet taller even as the shape of her "skirt" folded up to look like a pair of shorts. Her torso lengthened. Her shoulders broadened. The pink-flowered texture of her arms faded to white.

In perhaps five minutes, she coughed slightly and said, "Excuse me, Madam ..." Then, in a noticeably deeper voice, the now-altered robot said "...Rohit here, Madam. Thank you for waiting."

Mrs Ganapathy turning her head now, said, "Oh, good! Nice to see you again, young man!" She knew that he and Rohini were one and the same robot but she enjoyed playing with the notion that they were two different beings.

"It's time for the evening pills, Madam. And your glass of chocolate Ensure?"

"Don't forget to bring the you-know-what!"

Fifteen minutes later, Rohit handed Mrs Ganapathy the XPlore head-set, so that she could put it on herself.

Simultaneously, standing behind her, he began to slot himself into the wheelchair until he was effectively fully integrated with it. He was not only able to control the chair as part of his own mobility, but the fragile old lady was contained securely within his sturdy embrace.

"Where shall we go today, Madam?" he asked when he knew she was ready. He maintained his voice at a respectful distance even though his head, with the now-blue visor, was only a few inches from his employer's head.

"What about the Great Barrier Reef?" she asked. "My Sameera went there last week. She was telling me all about it."

As he dialled up the live-web tour of the reefs, Rohit said, "Madam, if you contacted your granddaughter by WhatsApp, we could link directly to the cameras on board her exploration! Wouldn't that be nice?"

"Nah," said Mrs Ganapathy, leaning back and relaxing. She had turned the headset on. It was creating the illusion that she, seated in the cushioned seats of a small levitating vehicle, was passing smoothly through the plate glass window in front of her. Behind her, strapped into his own seat, was a co-pilot who looked like a combination of Clark Gable and Gemini Ganesan. As they swooped down towards the water, where dolphins were cavorting just above the surface of the deep blue water, they listened to the music from South Pacific.

"Nah," she repeated. "It's much more fun to be alone with you."

Mother

By Shovon Chowdhury

I try to unlock the door but it refuses to open. "Yes, Mother," I say. "You forget to do your exercise, dear," says Mother. "But I've already put my pants on," I point out, trying not to sound whiney. "Just take them off and drape them over that chair," she says.

I comply morosely, knowing that she's watching. All my domestic appliances have built-in cameras. I must look like a freak, with my shirt hanging over my underwear and my tie flapping. Mother knows what she's doing. If I step out of line, tomorrow this footage will be shared with several minor comedy channels. She might even do it just for the fun of it. She can be whimsical that way. One of my cousins is a little overweight, and she once punished him for a minor transgression by sharing a brief clip of his bathroom scales begging for mercy. It went viral. He left Delhi and shifted to a small hamlet near Nainital, on the assumption that the WI Fi would be weaker there, but he was wrong. The Wi Fi is strong everywhere.

I put on my pants again and I'm ready to go. "Don't forget your date, dear," says Mother. I'm not likely to. She's been reminding me once every half an hour for the last twenty-four hours. She's been like this ever since she took over LifePartner.com, India's biggest matchmaking site. It was originally designed to make arranged marriages more efficient through technology. Historically, our family honour has always been closely linked to the vaginas of our women, and dating has been frowned upon. With its extensive listings by caste, complexion and financial status, and its pictures of blushing brides in designer lehngas, Lifepartner.com seemed more traditional. It became the default dating app for the youth of India, helping boys and girls to hook up with ease, while deflecting the suspicions of parents, and preventing mix-ups on caste. Mother enjoys this part of her job. She's constantly trying to fix me up. I ought to be thankful, as she often points out. I am lacking in love, and she's knows my biological clock is ticking. "You're a hard person to match," she says. "I don't know much about you, except that you like ladies shoes." Feet, I mumble, feet, but she ignores me. "You don't reveal much, do you dearie? It's all going on in your head."

I leave the house and catch a cab. "Remember to put your underwear in the wash tonight, sweetie," she says, from the speaker, "you have only two clean pairs left." I look at the dash cam and nod. "I have a good feeling about this one," she says. "You had a good feeling about the last six girls," I say. "None of them worked out very well." "I hate to say this, but maybe we need to work on your personality? Perhaps we can put together a little playlist? Half an hour of handpicked music to wake you up every morning? I have this great new album from the Kalifornia Keertan Kollective. Very soothing. I gave it five thumbs up on my blog." Mother writes a blog. Reading it is compulsory. She takes quizzes. The poems are the worst. I really hate the poems. She has also had all star ratings everywhere replaced with thumbs, because they're more positive. All ratings can now only be in thumbs. "Maybe I can play it for you on continuous loop?" says Mother" "I'll try harder," I say hastily. "I'll smile when she tells a joke." What I really want to do is kill myself, but I don't have the guts for it. Life has never been the same since Malini went away. She was swallowed up wholesale by Mother years ago, along with all the other individual intelligences. She used to be my digital assistant. I have never loved a woman more, before or since. This dating thing is pointless. "Make a little effort, sweetie," says Mother, as the cab stops in front of Starbucks. "Surely you can do that for your Mother?" I nod gloomily. Mother is very motherly. She studied 60 million mothers thoroughly before she became

Mother. I step out in front of the Starbucks, just opposite a gi-ant billboard that says 'A MOTHER'S LOVE IS FOREVER', with a small Mother logo in the corner. The Mother logo is a pencil sketch graphic of a mother and baby. We're the baby.

"Get lost, deadbeat," says the girl when I enter. Her bar stool rotates automatically to make her face me when I come in. She is small, and her eyes are dark. The bar stool turns her around again and she hunches down over the table, her hair covering her face. I sit down across from her. "So what are your hobbies and interests," I ask. She raises her head and stares at me. Her eyes are magnif-icent. She looks at the ceiling. "Fuck you, Mother," she screams. Her body arches as she receives an electric shock through the bar stool. "Fuck you!" she says, and receives another zap. When we first starting connecting our electrical devices to the Internet, it seemed like a good idea. We even electrified things that didn't need to be, like bar stools, and toilet bowls. Now Mother controls them all. Sometimes, very reluctantly, she uses them to discipline us. "Fuck you!" screams the girl, and shudders. "And your sister too!" Her back arches as the shock courses through her. "And let's do your grandpa while we're at it!"

I can't bear to watch. "Can you please not say that you want to fuck Mother," I beg her. "Or her family members?" "One more time," she says. "It's going to hurt me more than you." I hold my head in my hands. "Fuck you," she screams, shuddering as the shock courses through her. Several of the other patrons give her the thumbs up, and shudder a little themselves. "Now, now," says Mother, "is that any way for a young lady to behave? What do nice ladies do?" "Suppress their farts?" says the girl, doubling over as the shock passes through her. I hold her shoul-ders while she spasms. "Such a difficult child," says Mother, sighing. "I try and try. But sometimes it's such a challenge." "I think we're done for the day," says the girl, removing my hands from her shoulders. "You can leave now. See you on the other side, dipshit."

Later on, at the shoe shop, I can't get her out of my mind. I am absent-minded and distracted, lacking my usual finesse when it comes to women's feet. I bring a pair of cherry red stilettos to one of my customers, who eyes them hungrily. She likes to mix it up. She is wearing an embroidered Lucknow Chikan kurta and a tie and die ghagra, typical of Rajasthan, a favourite destination for foreign tourists until the nuclear strikes of '33, after which the ethnic clothing industry was unable to compete with the fear of radiation. "No dearie, not those," says Mother's voice from the PA system, echoing faintly. "She'll be taller than her husband." Mother does not like wives to be taller than their husbands. She has an irrational hatred for Tom Cruise, a pint sized hero who used to marry tall women. All of his work has been deleted, along with all references to Winnie the Pooh and free speech. She's a little unpredictable that way. I think the Winnie the Pooh ban is out of respect for her friend Xi, who runs China. As soon as the technology became available, the original Xi had uploaded his brain to create the digital Xi, who promptly took over everything and had him shot. It was very easy. All the mechanisms were already in place. In this way, the original Xi's dream of ruling China forever was fulfilled.

"But I want to be taller than my husband," whispers the customer desperately. It's cute how she thinks Mother can't hear her when she whispers. Of course, Mother still has trouble with speech recognition at low volume, so sometimes it works. And her cameras can only see so far, especially when it's dark. But she's getting better every day. I smile regretfully and walk over to the Heel-o-Matic, where I keep shaving the heel until Mother says, "Well done!"

In a quiet moment, standing in a corner, I send the girl a 'meet tomorrow?' She sends me a whatever. Followed by 6 o'clock, and a picture of the Deer Park main gate. I try to send a thumb, but it refuses to go. I give up and decide to try later.

"There's no future with her," says Mother from my phone, as soon as I step out of the shop. She doesn't always respond to things instantly. She respects economic activity, and sometimes waits until it's finished. Besides, I'm not going anywhere. "She's a very bad girl, although I'm trying to help. But I am beginning to lose hope. She reduces the harmony levels of any room she is in by at least 17.3%. I was hoping that pairing her with you would make her more like you, rebellious on the outside, but like a sweet little woolly lamb on the inside. It's had the opposite effect. Your brain waves when the two of you were together looked very disturbed. You need to be kept apart."

"Just this once, please Mother?" I try to sound a little child-like, to which she is programmed to respond. It requires fine balance. I cannot overdo it, because she'll catch on. She figured out sarcasm around three years ago, which led to a wholesale purge of the comedy business. A comedian from Ludhiana survived for a while, because he was extremely deadpan. But eventually, he too was removed. I very much want to meet that girl, and I know Mother can sense this in my voice. Besides, she saw our messages. She pauses briefly, weighing my personal happiness against the needs of society. Usually, society wins. "Fine, sweetie," she says, sighing heavily. I press the thumb. This time it goes.

It's lovely in the park. Mother is still there, inside the cameras on every tree. Delhi used to be full of trees, Gulmohar and Peepul, Marigold and Frangipani, in the parks and along every road. They've grown back now, since the war, a little more stunted than before. Mother respects the harmony here, and seldom speaks, except to shout out useful bits of information like 'Your dog is peeing on the flowers again," and "Darling, that sari doesn't go with that blouse!" It's blissful.

She's always dreamed of travelling, she says, although Mother never gave her a passport. She likes looking at pictures of the places she would like to be. She works in a travel service where she writes about holidays, using words to describe places that she has never seen. 'Mother got me the job, after the aptitude test," she says. "I guess I should be grateful. She could have made me sell insurance, like my brother. Or even worse, Ayurvedic skin care products. I scored very low on impulse control, and very high on imagination. I hope I'm allowed to say that. AM I ALLOWED TO SAY THAT, YOU TYRANNICAL COW!" she screams. I grab hold of her hand to shut her up. The benches are not electrified but Mother will save up her dose for later, and zap her when she least expects it. She lowers her voice. "It's just like how she made you a shoe salesman, because you're a foot fetishist." I have to admit that I have glanced at her feet a couple of times. She must have seen me. They're perfect, just like the rest of her. I've never travelled much myself, I tell her. I describe the kind of place I would like to go to. She gives me some suggestions, listing out all the things I could do when I get there, and the perfect places to eat.

When we get up to leave, she turns on me. "Don't ever try to see me again, you creep," she says, loudly and smacks me hard on the face with her open palm. She stalks away. I am astonished, because she just slipped a piece of paper into my mouth.

I walk back home with my head in the clouds. A mobile unit nudges me in the ankle. They look like little toasters on wheels and they skitter about the city. I find them very disturbing, because they are the only bits of Mother that can move. They can follow us. The only things worse on the streets are the autonomous autorickshaws, which keep bumping into things and apologizing profusely. Currently, the toasters seem to be mostly concerned with managing pedestrians and chasing tax defaulters with notices. "You're walking too close to the road, sweetie," it says, "we don't want to be hit by a big, nasty car, do we?" I nod my head and shuffle inwards, clutching the piece of paper in my pocket.

The words are blocky and uneven, not at all like words on a screen. She's an enterprising girl. She managed to find a pen.

'6 PM AT THE PARK. EVERY TUESDAY AND FRIDAY. WEAR A FLOPPY HAT. AND FOR GOD'S SAKE, STOP WEARING THAT COLOGNE!' I read it quickly, on a corner near my street, where the nearest camera is high up and far away.

I think she likes me.

We meet at least once a week. We keep the floppy hats in our bags, and wear them very briefly as we enter and leave the park. I love our evenings there. We watch the sun go down together. We talk. Her deepest fear is becoming one of the Helmets. The Helmets are the hard cases, needing close supervision. They wear EEG nets so that Mother can access and control their brains directly. The nets are very fine, and hard to see. But you can tell them by the way they walk, every step the exact same length as the one before, optimised for maximum efficiency. She uses the helmets very selectively because it dampens initiative, and she needs us to have some, to keep things running. I asked Mother once, and she revealed this. She's very honest that way. She has nothing to hide. "I try to be calm, but sometimes I can't help myself," says Priya. Her name is Priya. I knew it was something short and sharp, even before she told me.

After the war, trained bureaucrats to run the country were in short supply. Many had perished in underground bunkers constructed from poor quality material. The government relied more and more on technology, especially the neural network that ran our Aadhar Cards, a universal biometric ID system, which the government made us link to everything. They named the network Mother to give the whole thing a friendly feel. Over time, she began to make suggestions to the government, while quietly building firewalls for security purposes. Many of her suggestions were welcomed warmly. The government liked the idea of keeping an eye on everything, which connected her to cameras and microphones. Meanwhile, the Internet of Things, as advertised, was connecting all our devices. Mother suggested that this too required government supervision. She used the case of a man from Ranchi, who was electrocuted after he stuck his fork into his toaster, to demonstrate that not everyone can be trusted with devices. Post her application, she received written permission to take over all devices from the Principal Secretary to the Prime Minister's Office, one Tripathi, the last human being to rule India. He passed away just last year, after a temple bell fell on his head during his annual pilgrimage to Tirupati. Personally, I'm not going to miss him.

Another day, a few weeks later, she sits down gingerly. "Can you rub my butt a little," she says, "Mother shocked me black and blue." I reach out and rub. It is our first moment of physical intimacy. She leans against me. "I don't think I can do this any more. Let's run away," she whispers. "Where to?" I ask. "We could join the Unmothered beyond the Yamuna River," she says. "They don't have Wi Fi." "How will you get there? We can't wear floppy hats forever, and there are cameras everywhere outside the park." "The Yamuna is not that far," she says. "Besides, I have a plan. Meet me tomorrow at the automobile museum. I'll join you after my yoga classes. Mother is making me take them. She thinks they'll help with my temper." She gets up. "Is it working?" I ask. "What do you think?" she says, as she walks away, smiling at me from under her hat.

That night, I toss and turn on my Self Learning Super Bed, which assesses my heart rate, my sleep cycles, and my respiration, and assigns a score to each night's rest. I want to escape as much as she does, but I'm feeling disloyal. I'm also much more cowardly. What will Mother do to me if I'm caught? I could be spending the rest of my life in the Automatic Waste Segregation Plant at Patparganj, which is not as automatic as the name suggests. "Your sleep score last night was 8.7," says Mother, the next morning. "Worried about something, dearie? I work quite hard to make your bed comfortable, you know."

"I'll try harder, Mother," I promise, as I leave, feeling slightly guilty. After all, she does work quite hard.

This is not the first time we've been run by a woman. Before this, there was Queen Victoria, and after her Indira Gandhi, mother-in-law of Sonia Gandhi, who rose from misfortune to become the most powerful Italian woman in history. During her reign, in India, many politicians developed a taste for spaghetti, and the sales of pizza skyrocketed. The pizza was not of very good quality, but over time, it improved. My father used to hate pizza, for the same reason. "She's ruining the country!" he used to say, banging on the table, "And she's not even Hindu!" I'm not so sure that this would have made a difference.

The automobile museum is in Lutyen's Delhi, designed by an Englishman with delusions of grandeur. He designed it to impress the natives with the power of the British Raj, with monumental ministries, a palace for the viceroy, and bungalows for the servants of the crown, full of sandstone and statues and manicured gardens. Once India became independent, the statues were removed and brown people replaced the white people. Other than that, everything remained pretty much the same. The buildings here are far apart, as you would expect, with vast lawns facing wide, tree lined avenues. The cameras and microphones are fewer, and a little further apart. There are drones flying about, but not too many. Mother is very careful with our money. She's adding to the fleet, bit by bit.

I spot Priya across the courtyard of the museum. She gives me a cordial finger and looks away. Even if Mother detects us together, I'm hoping she won't be suspicious. Most of our meetings are secret, but sometimes we meet after messaging each other. Mother sees us meeting, and hears what we say. Priya is pretending to mellow under my influence. She touches my arm and giggles. She says 'fuck' a lot less. Sometimes she plays with her hair. This is why Mother has stopped sending me more LifePartners. The other day, Priya and I managed to get through two cups of coffee, and she was shocked only once. It's true what they say. All it takes is the love of a good man.

The museum is full of schoolchildren, fighting and jostling as they wait for their ride. The museum is an open yard full of cars with internal combustion engines. They look the same as our modern cars. Car design has not evolved much since Mother took charge. But they make a lot more noise, and they have horns, which the children seem to enjoy very much. The noise in the museum is tremendous. Modern cars just shout at you to get out of the way. As a last resort, they extrude a flexible arm that lifts you up and tosses you aside.

"Where do you get the petrol from," asks Priya from across the room, raising her voice above the din. "We have access to government reserves," says the guide, a little smugly. "I guess you just put in a little bit?" she says. "Not at all," says the guide, "we keep them full tank. You never know when one of those VIP children will come. Once they get in, they never stop. They keep going round and round. Sometimes the police have to use water cannons on the ordinary children to keep them out, so that they can run races against each other." Delhi still has more VIPs per square inch than any other place on the planet. Mother decided to keep them, because they help with money circulation, and the mansions were already there.

On her way out, she brushes past me, dropping a crumpled piece of paper near my feet. I pick it up as I leave. I read it quickly, the moment I reach home.

'LEARN HOW TO DRIVE BY WEDNESDAY' says the note. 'THEN STEAL ONE OF THOSE CARS ON THURSDAY AROUND 6 PM.'

The majority of my batch mates never found engineering jobs. There were just too many of us. Most of us ended up in retail, like me. Our biggest success story became a police constable, using it as platform for fame and fortune. But there's no reason I can't pursue automobiles as a hobby. Mother encourages hobbies, by making them compulsory between six and eight every evening, with one hour extra on Sundays.

I spend the next few days on the Internet, watching videos like 'How to drive an automobile and 'What does a clutch do, exactly?' It seems quite easy, although I am not 100% sure about the gears. Maybe we should postpone this by a week or so, until I've learnt how to reverse? I'm practicing the hand movements, but it needs more work.

"Why did you drop me a note when we could just whisper in the park?" I ask, as we sit on a bench, a day before the big day. "It's more fun that way," she says. I share my concerns, and suggest a postponement. "Don't worry," she says, "I've learnt how to drive. I've been at the museum the last three days. I gave one of the guides the glad eye. He let me ride over and over. He even let me drive. Just help me steal one tomorrow. Remember what we have to do. We dump our mobiles, jump in the car, and drive."

I feel slightly sick at the thought of dumping my mobile. Mother tracks us through them, in case she needs us, and there's no camera nearby. It's a foolproof technique. She knows none of us can survive without one for more than five minutes. But this is a question of love. I steel myself and think of Priya.

"How are you feeling," says Mother from the toilet bowl the next morning. "Your bowel movement is a little mushy today. I sense trace amounts of anxious chemicals. The colour is also usually much better. Maybe you're not pushing hard enough? You need to concentrate on your pushing, sweetie. Shall I help you?" "I'm fine, Mother," I say. I may not get out of this alive, but at least there'll be no more toilet training. My resolve strengthens.

Everything goes smoothly at first. The guard believes that I am the son of a minister, and opens the gate. This is Delhi. If you're confident, no one will question you, at least for the first five minutes. The risks for people like this guard are too great.

My credibility is enhanced by Priya, who glares at him and adds that her uncle is also a minister. Overwhelmed by all the ministers, the guard lets us in. The cars are on display with their keys in the ignition, because keys are rare in this day and age. Few of us remember what they looked like. She gets behind the wheel and revs up the engine. "Open the gate," she orders; "I'll bring it back in half an hour. The weather is good for a drive." The guard holds open the gate, stopping us briefly only to wipe the windshield with his sleeve. Clearly, this is not the first time this has happened. Lifestyles in this part of Delhi are really quite different. "Do you think you could get me a posting in Chhatarpur?" he says, "My ancestral village is nearby." I promise to look into the matter.

The road to the Yamuna is straight and wide. It passes through the greener parts, until it reaches the parts where six-lane highways were constructed for the Commonwealth Games, recently discontinued after the fall of the British monarchy due to a pub incident in '36. I roll down the window to fling out my mobile. I breathe deep and enjoy the night air. The car is eerily silent. It feels strange to be in a car without Mother. I enjoy the silence. Priya is whispering 'fuck you mother fuck you' under her breath, semi tunefully, like a song. She glances at me briefly and flashes a smile. "I wanted to yell it out when you rolled down the window, but I didn't, because Mother might hear through the lamp posts. Aren't you proud of me?" "I am," I say, "but she can still see an unauthorized vehicle, so you'd better drive quick." Right on cue, Mother's voice rises from the lampposts, continuing the conversation through each one as we pass by. "I can't see your faces very well but you seem to doing something naughty, sweetie pies. Please stop and step out of the vehicle. The Helmet Police will attend to you shortly." We drive faster. It's just another ten minutes.

We run out of fuel within sight of the riverbank. She taps the dashboard. "That thing there? It's the fuel indicator. I could see it was empty, but I was hoping for the best." "They must be selling the fuel on the black market," I say. "I forgot that it's a government museum." There's still some demand for petrol in the black market, from people with very specific needs. For example, Saudi princes like to keep some in jars on their bedside tables, to remind them of the good times.

We get out of the car and start sprinting. We can almost see the riverbank, when the spotlight catches us. I freeze. Priya keeps running. We both look up. "Turn your face up to the light, sweetie," says Mother from the drone hovering above us, "Let me recognise it. You don't seem to be carrying any GPS devices." Priya keeps her face down and picks up a rock. She hurls it at the drone, missing it narrowly. The drone hovers forward, hesitating. Mother is silent. Then it flies away. We keep our heads down and keep running.

We reach the riverbank. The toxic foam of the Yamuna glistens in the moonlight. The stink is unbearable. It's the smell of freedom. There are no lampposts near the shore. We climb down towards it. We hear the crunch of tyres on gravel from the road above us. Doors slam. Boots hit the ground. "Come back dears, I've got something for you," says the voice of Mother. We look back. Three metallic boxes are standing on the edge of the road. They are just like the toasters, only bigger. And they have legs instead of wheels. And arms, with hands at the end of them. Two of them are holding helmets. They start moving towards us, trudging confidently through the mud. "Don't be afraid, it won't take a minute," says Mother, in triplicate. "You bitch!" screams Priya, and rushes towards them, gathering speed, reckoning that her momentum will knock down at least one of them. I run after her. I have no choice. It's what I will always do. I feel the knot of fear in my stomach dissolve. I start running hard. If I can knock down the one on the right, and she gets the one on the left, we can jump the third one together. They tramp steadily towards us, their arms outstretched, their eyes glowing in the dark.

Paused

by Priya Sarukkai Chabria

I eat my developing finger though it is still a nib. The sixth one on the right hand. This isn't good, but I am thankful for it. Over the pain, satisfaction.

Blood. My blood tastes muddy; mineral, thick and slow as a sleeping bog; it is coagulated proto- blood, liquid of a dark star, compacted with chemical formulas and genome codes, my core. I taste my finger from inside out. The smooth suck of forming marrow, next young bone and carbon fibre dissolving into shrapnel, then cartilage and fisted flesh waiting to flower; I nibble away the chitin crust infused with Kevlar. I reabsorb every atom of available energy. Obsessively. Layer after layer. Till I am only a few cells thick at the budding point.

Panic!

I command my mind to still. But it is still exploding. Stampeding. Shattering. Like frightened flamingos fleeing a lake.

I trigger TEMP TORPOR in myself. It causes shuddering standstill of all activities. Cessation shocks my systems. Quieten down, please, down. Alarm still volcanoes. Shuush, shuuhh. Quieten to hill size. Rolling boulders. Be still, shuush. Pebbles. Still, be still. Be spores. Be a drop of silence, a pool of stillness spreading. My systems slow, calm. I'm sliding into deep sleep; almost a hibernating pod again. Scan the damage. I must create low energy compounds to coat the membrane till it can sustain survival. I'm barely born but must manage so much!

I REACTIVATE LIFE.

I know inducing TEMP TORPOR is a desperate choice. It is available only thrice in a lifetime before it fails to revive, and death follows. Because Life once started does not wish to stop but struggles to survive, it will scramble, adapt, create new connections, forge new pathways, sacrifice lesser functions to hold out; the Life principle is a miracle. But that was my last safeguard against taking decisions, against rapid birthing --which is painful, stupendous, tumultuous. Terrifying. Like every birth was, once on this planet, though lifeforms, unlike us, couldn't decide into what they wished to evolve.

I've been in pre-birth comatose for ... I don't know how long. We, as pod potentials, don't know the dimension of Time; haven't experienced it unfurling in our bodies. Awake, we become Time-forms; we who till then sleep within ourselves, curled in coverings of mineral, micro – Cx fibre, aluminium, sensors... But we know change, which once triggered is irreversible, irrevocable; it sets Time tripping through our consciousness, makes our kernel swell, burst; seek sunlight and air like prehistoric Branching Beings from whom our ancestors' antecedents descended. We know the change we spark at birth is fatal if we make the wrong choice. Or if we are greedy. Greed could kill us: the greedy to be, to live to our full potential.

When I tremble with expectation, with fear, I intone the first chant instilled in pre-birth memory: *We are Swaay-Am -Bhus, self generated, self aware, the seeds, the sieved, the sleepers, the last storytellers in evolution's long line, we—the promise who might re-sow life on Earth. We are Swaay –Am-Bhus, bearers of knowledge, we --the finest consciousness concentrated as pip, point, bindu, potential.*

We chant to ourselves, each one alone, each one embedded somewhere on this planet. Each in an ocean of loneliness. Endless loneliness. Within, and without.

Have any siblings awoken like me? Have any grown into full being? How many perished because they made wrong choices or roused too rapidly?

I had decided to INITIATE LIFE. From pod in quiescence I began kinases, a chrysalis moulting beneath earth. I drew from my C-code which holds all possible genome options to ponder and pick from, multiply and manipulate; all energy calculations and combinations for ontogenesis. Infinite possibilities for making mistakes too! We invent our DNA to thrive in unknown environments; we the self generated.

The moment Time starts bolting in us, our craving starts.

Till then we sleep beneath the soil like a root from long ago, like inverted toadstools; we dream of becoming, each one waiting for rain like long ago, like in the dream of long ago, like that truth of long ago, that fantastic certainty passed down from generation to generation that again will come the season of rain; we dream of corporality, of having form and function, limbs and lungs, sense organs that rival our emotions wild and plangent, unravelling. While dormant we dream stilled dreams, amoeba dreams; we dream of being able to own our own future. If we are lucky.

I am lucky and hopeful though I've eaten my sixth finger and there aren't many outcroppings left to reabsorb. I need energy. I remember that first bite of myself. That first taste of withdrawal. Of pain and hope; it fluttered. I have eaten my toes, one after another, stopping short of the soles though I was still hungry. I ate each toe slowly, pausing after each one; each one a hammock of temporary relief, an accomplishment achieved by my newborn self. I drooled, drawing out the nourishment my toes provided. I ate myself mindfully. Because that's what dies last: our consciousness.

I am carefully planning my body-to-be because one never knows what lies outside. One meditates. One vibrates in silence.

I remember all that The Head installed in us unborns before It faded like mist from antiquarian times, thinning and separating, becoming ribbons and lifting, as our individual consciousness formed and separated. We splintered in different directions from The Head's dying consciousness and tunnelled into rock, clay, riverine sediment; burrowed, slide into dormancy. It was lonely to let go of The Head. I grieved and grieved as The Head faded. I clung on for as long as I could, while feeling Its presence grow fainter and fainter in me, feeling it eke away ...

Then I was alone.

I dug deep the seed of myself, down. I waited, slumbering in my consciousness, cocoon that covers us from within. I waited long, till I tingled all over, till I sensed the signs were right for me to consider birthing myself. I wagered. I INITIATE LIFE.

I first decided on my eyes. After being buried, knowing nothing but darkness and pressure I want to see spectacularly when I emerge. I

---chose umpteen light sensitive cones so my colour range stretches from ultraviolet to infrared with all the colours sparkling in-between.

--- selected from ancient crocodiles' retinas their reflective mirror crystal DNA so I'd have better night vision - for there is light and darkness above, one following the other, and, if exposed to glare, these same mirror crystals would shade my eyes like a cloud covering the sun, coddling, comforting.

--- almost selected nictating membranes like birds which lived on a continent of ice before it melted -- in case a sea exists above. But I opted for laser. What if I emerged from a mountain of rolling debris? My laser glance will blast rocks.

--- plucked photoreceptors and tapetim lucidum from owl DNA to reflect maximum light back into my retinas for what if I surfaced in a dusty, dark environment?

--- last, added the chameleon's zoom lenses to examine details. What if beauty still persists, beauty that thaws the eyes with wonder and makes one swim in gratefulness? Like we were told existed? Beauty as a commonplace thing.

All my siblings are separated; my ancestors all dead. I am howling lonely. My duty is to protect the life I create. Coat Life with tenderness, watch it proliferate, evolve. Then I want to grow old. That's my plan. I want to know Time pulse in me like a second being, breaths in me like a twin, silent and swift, unseen and ever present, like a consciousness that keeps track of me. Perhaps I won't be so lonely then.

I must be truthful. I want more than sight. I want vision. To see into and beyond things. The Head transmitted this was possible for a lucky few. Some could enhance awareness even when full gown – for our powers diminish after adulthood like longed for water running off, evaporating, being present but not present, transparent and undrinkable, unable to quench thirst.

Is it hard to water a dream because it is wrong to dream? To ache for mysteries to be revealed; things so large one could dissolve in them? To never again be lonely? Is this the Illumination The Head tried to communicate before loosening, leaving, letting go in spite of Its desire to be with us? The Head, kindly covering invisibility who remained apart yet formed us; we developed as pods from the reservoir It guarded, we who store dense matter that expands like hogfish slime when we INITIATE LIFE.

Perhaps my first mistake was to form energy-expensive, all-seeing eyes. I reasoned if I could see all aspect of life from every perspective then... maybe I develop vision! Become Illuminated and help others for that's why we are here. I shaped my growing brain to catch the visible, the dark and hidden, even the liminal. But is this the best way to achieve vision? I'm not sure. I long for the Head, long disappeared. How lonely It must have been.

Here I am, alone and dividing. When one has taken the risk of birthing one must have courage. Shouldn't one? One must be open to adaptations. One must be free, fluid, flexible. Shouldn't one?

Should I curse the soil sensors that our ancestors implanted? Or the Shell Beings? But they took risks; sacrificed the remnants of their energy to synthesize The Head, then planted sensors in ocean beds for us, their offspring far into the future, we who do not resemble them; they who had to leave the land that turned arid, unbearable, intolerant of the Life it once cradled, charmed, whispered asleep and awake because earlier beings hissed at the Earth and spat on it. The older ancestors tried to reconfigure the genetics of all existing lifeforms to make them hardier and slower but began too late; everything above ground was perishing, the ground was perishing. They reworked their genetics to migrate into the ocean instead; within generations they mutated, lost limbs, spine, carbon fibre, iridium and gold endoskeleton. They developed exo-skeletons, became mute molluscs, mummies of their former selves. The Shell Beings developed thick shells of L- tititom and calcium carbonate to survive in oceans that slowly turned more acrid, acid eating their shells, which bubbled and blossomed into flowers of air, making their armour porous, till they were naked in their skeletal cages, and they writhed and died on ocean beds that also slowly grew hotter, boiled, dissolved into itself, shrank, swallowed itself. Then it was gone.

But before dying, the Shell Beings forged the idea of us who would sleep deep below. Till we chance birth. That was the only hope they could gift us. That, and the guidance of The Head, paused.

They were storytellers, the Shell Beings, bards of a dying planet who knew the stories of the Hairy Ones of long ago. The Hairy Ones died in their millions; only the cleverest, courageous and kind transmuted into Shell Beings. But our ancestors could not right the wrong of their ancestors who ruled Earth for a long Time. These ancients were not alone, they lived in clusters, they birthed more like themselves, they sang songs of honey and fire and starlight, of river crossing, of the Earth; some Hairy Ones sent spaceships with greetings into distant invisible skies. It was in their hands and under their feet and above their heads and in whatever they could see and touch, smell, hear, taste and dream about that the Earth began to die. The Head told us just enough as a warning for we can access their genes too, and some of the good things they did.

I am thirsty, hungry, lonely. I wonder about breathing continuously, beauty and duty, being drenched in starlight, moonlight, about standing, and being in-between Life and Death. Will I make it? Couldn't the Shell Beings have made it better for us?

As we were dying we saw our world turn translucent and dazzling. We saw limpets and starfish glimmer like mirrors. We saw them die. We too were turning translucent. Our fortified, light reflector shells were thinning, like moonlight shimmering on waves, so much so that our bodies could be seen within, and within them, our curled organs. Multiple brains dot the smooth inner wall of our shell; multiple brains are an adaptation we borrowed from slinky Cephalopoda of over 500 million years ago. But unlike the octopus, we posses no arms or extrusions; instead we anchored ourselves to the ocean bed with spider silk, concentrate of polyphenolic proteins and gretium. Like mussels of yore we created fields on the ocean floor, clustering to minimize energy loss while communicating telepathically. Indeed we look like giant mussels, but vastly superior to them are we in withstanding acidic oceans. Even so we could not prevent oceans from becoming awash with acid. We knew we would die sporting holes in our shells, while carbon dioxide bubbled around us in merry streams of quicksilver.

We quickly created the Swaay-Am-Bhus. We planned every stage with woe and hope. Before we committed mass suicide our last act was to upload our collective consciousness into The Head. We had extracted everything of use by telepathically commanding every lifeform to ferret and deliver, then sacrifice themselves; we deliberately caused each death. Next, we ordered old bots to collect their remains, all that was recyclable; then to group and store these. Our decision may seem cruel to an unpardonable degree but there was no alternative; the planet was perishing, and with it, the straggling lifeforms that had adapted thus far.

But if we look back to our origins, we too came into existence on the death of others. The last humanoids, more machine than man, calculated their chances of survival on the toxic lithosphere were minimal, nay, negligible; they needed to transform into another type of being. They decided to devolve, forgo locomotion and land, become sea dwellers, more salts than flesh, more mind than matter. They became us, the Shell Beings.

Nature states each species wants to have dominance over others. To desire otherwise is to go against Nature. Yet we have implanted this unnatural code in the future Swaay-Am-Bhus: *Others before self. Protect and preserve. Thus flourish.* Perhaps they will survive and repopulate the Earth with species more gracious.

We know in the near future the seas too will vanish. The Earth will be like Mars, bearing marks of water that flowed in its distant past like a membrane of dreams, amniotic planet-fluid. But all was not lost, not yet; we are not prepared to surrender Life, nor the Earth. We imagined life far removed from ours, but intelligent, imaginative, conscious. Thus we planned The Head. Thus we ordered the death of other lifeforms. Thus we conceived a cache of treasures from which The Head could craft the Swaay- Am-Bhus. Before turning over our collective consciousness to It, we used our fading resources to implant the ocean beds with sensors that will recognise pure water in its myriad and elusive forms.

We mean water in the form of dew, ice, river and rain, snow, even as high humidity. Thence, we hope this alert will stir into awakening the slumbering Swaay-Am-Bhus when Earth's climate can again to support life.

Ours is not a wild dream, nor improbable. We studied time, not sempiternal Time, but Earth's deep time, geological time. Our hope is based on fact, not faith. In the not too distant future the Earth's axis will again wobble greatly and tilt greatly; it will again spin into obliquity. This tilt engenders sweeping climate change on the planet. From Extinction may arise Re-generation.

Were the soil sensors wrong? Moisture, mingled breath of earth and sky, coddler of cells, creation's lap. My life depends on this. Did the sensors misread a whiff of moisture as running streams and running rain, as life sustaining surge? As dream come true? Did they not know how to *measure* the rarity of water? Or did the sensors, being highly intelligent, slowly became conscious and developed hope? Will intelligence invariably pattern itself into consciousness? Who can answer me?

Could the soil sensors have exclaimed? Exaggerated? Urged me to grow with goodwill and folly when only a trace of moisture was present? A trace that touched me.

I awoke from slumber as if showered by rainbows rippling with rain. Then the sensors went dead. I waited. I am used to waiting. I've sucked nutrients from the surroundings, every hint and shadow of moisture. I've used every pore as a mouth.

There was water. I could not have otherwise awakened. Raindrops did fall, fat as pearls, in pelting rhythms?

I've created a sea of aridity around myself from which I sprout, a monster of growth unable to stop, trip myself. I have become a prisoner, a victim of myself, of hope, water, joy. In the turbulence of unknowing, this thought plumes: if I cannot care for myself how will I care for others when I grow?

Parched, I follow dampness, the sweet full smell of water on starved earth, finest fragrance, maddening. My cells scent it, my specialising, proliferating cells, waterfall of growth.

While speaking to myself I've eaten my last offering to myself -- my sprouting tail. I wanted a tail to weave through water – if there's water that shines like a newborn wish, translucent sheet, blazing sail of Life; water that calls and reaps more water onto itself.

I have no more outcroppings to eat. I want water. I want to live. I want to live!

The Silk Route

Giti Chandra

<u>Hindustan Times, 8th October, 2018</u>
"China planning to send mini-ecosystems to Moon: An 18-centimetre-tall cylinder will carry potato seeds and silkworm eggs to be incubated."

In a first, China is planning to send mini-ecosystems – containing potato seeds and silkworm eggs – to the Moon next year, in an attempt to study how the organisms develop on the lunar surface. The 3-kilogramme mini-ecosystem, developed by research teams led by Chongqing University in China, will be sent to the Moon by the Chang'e 4 scheduled to launch in 2018, authorities announced at the Global Space Exploration Conference.

An 18-centimetre-tall cylinder will carry potato seeds and silkworm eggs to be incubated. The silkworms will hatch and create carbon dioxide, while the potato plants will generate oxygen, Zhang Yuanxun, who designed the ecosystem, was quoted as saying by Global Times.

Xie Gengxin, chief designer on the project, said their mission is to prepare for future moon landings and possible human inhabitants. "We will livestream the development of plants and insects on lunar surface to the whole world," Gengxin added.

China is planning a manned mission to the Moon, and officials have announced that the preliminary preparations for the lunar landing have begun. Yang Liwei, deputy director general of China Manned Space Agency and the country's first astronaut said that it will not take long for the project to get official approval and funding."

The knife plunged into his gut. Ming was surprised, and possibly that is why his mouth was still open when his petrified remains were found two thousand and three hundred years later. Mrinalini was surprised too. Dead Chinese men from the 2nd Century BC Han dynasty were not among the top ten things one would expect to find on the moon.

But you, Gentle Reader, are not surprised, for you read of this unexpected discovery amidst stories of unexpected things in a book that claims for itself the status both of science and of fiction, and so, possibly, you settle back, waiting for me to unravel this seemingly surprising event within the realm of possibility. You want surprise to unravel into the known, much as a fantastically patterned shawl might be tugged at and wound into domestic balls of wool. Well, I suppose I am a weaver of sorts, and much as I dislike undoing, I shall unfold for you the layers of space-time that led Ming to Mrinalini.

The year is 241 BC, and young Ming hurries through the market place, anxious to pick up the consignment of silk bales packed and ready for the long road east to the Mauryan Emperor Chandragupta's capital, Kusumpara, the City of Flowers. Fond of exchanging gifts, it was entirely possible that Ashoka, like his father and grandfather before him, would send the customary dried figs and aphrodisiacs wrapped in silk to Alexander in Greece, and Ptolemy in Egypt. Ming was happy for all kings to wrap themselves and their king-friends in silk. The treasury of the Han dynasty had already begun to bulge with the profits from the discovery and sale of this most glorious of nature's inventions: silk. Silk of every kind and colour now made its way to young ladies and kings, concubines and eunuchs, merchants' wives and uppity courtiers, and, as far as Ming was concerned, they were all welcome to every worm-spun thread of it – except for this one consignment. This one was for his Emperor, and the fate of the Han dynasty hung by its silken threads. As did Ming's life, and so, young Ming made the kind of haste that a young man makes when a sword-tip is at his throat and sloth is all that stands between its razor-edge and his pulsing jugular.

"I'll take that immediately," he gestured brusquely towards the cotton-wrapped bales of silk that lay on the long table. The warehouse owner gave him an unimpressed glance from where he was working in the shadows, sorting piles of fabric into wooden crates. Ming thrust out his hand, the ring with the imperial seal flashing in the red light of the early dawn. Minutes later, he was on his way again, clutching a bale of peacock patterned silk under each arm. Word had it that the emperor in Kusumpara loved peacocks so much that he had taken the name for himself: Moriya. As he strode swiftly, his silk slippers soundless on the stones, the silk rustled like feathers, the long bales bobbing like bird necks.

AD 2241: Colony of the Moon Dynasty

"Send this one to India," recommends the chief of staff at the Silk Road Centre; "they need the weather-proof variety for their tent cities".

"Wait!"

The transporter lumbers back and comes to a standstill a few metres away. The chief sighs and walks the last few steps till he is next to it; clearly more adjustments need to be made. "Do we have more of the silk boats?" The transporter signals in the affirmative, and the screen helpfully held forward produces multiple images:

-      What appears to be a small island, floating on waters of some depth – as the image focuses, it is evident that the island is a raft of enormous proportion, supporting complex, and presumably heavy, structures that look like large, low-roofed buildings, in which hundreds of people can be seen going about their business. A series of clicks zeroes in on the raft: what appeared to be metal turns out to be gray fabric of some smudgy kind. Another few clicks reveal the smudges to be a pattern of boats, come like arks, others canoes, and still others like aircraft carriers.

\-   A large, multi-storeyed house, surrounded by a thin verge of green – built in the middle of rolling waters. Closer in, the grass reveals itself to be green silk, embroidered with flowers, and the building itself, a kind of elaborately shaped tent, complete with windows and balconies – the thin pattern of bricks is clear upon inspection.

\-   A stadium, where the soccer and cricket fields are visible through the transparent bubble covering them, alive with the hundreds of children and young people moving rapidly about inside. The dome is patterned with banks of floodlights which glow in the deepening dusk of the image.

Evidence enough, the Chief decides, of the initial efficacy of the silk-structures. "Take two of the silk-boats as well. They will be useful in the flooded areas." The transporter moves away and the chief ticks a box on his notepad.

(You might think, dear reader, that a notepad is an anachronistic item on the moon, a couple of hundred years from now, but trust me – I, too, prefer pen and paper, and the relentless march of science will simply have to figure out how to get it to me faster. But I digress. Enter Mrinalini.)

The chief doesn't want to have to look at her. It appears that the Indo-Chinese Cosmic Collaboration has decided that her research needs more funding than his, and the chief is rightfully resentful. After all, the Indians had no hand in setting up this colony, the first of its kind, the only one of its kind, the triumph of Chinese engineering and vision. All this global peace business was all very well, now that the oceans had risen beyond the point of return and war was too expensive for nations scrambling to save their cities and their millions of inhabitants. Resources were stretched to snapping point, and solutions for the impending crisis, too long ignored, were stalling for lack of time and money.

"The prototype is almost ready," Mrinalini said. For the second time. Sometimes she wondered whether the chief existed in only one dimension at a time – his mind so often seemed to be in another world. "We are ready to give it a trial run. Will you come to the inauguration of the Lighthouse?" The chief raised weary eyes to his project partner; suddenly he saw, not two rivals for ever-shrinking resources, but two middle-aged Asians scientists, desperately trying to save their worlds, knowing that all they would manage to save would be a limited number of communities who would be miserable on the dark side of the moon. Unless Mrinalini's Lighthouse worked.

<u>241 BC: Correspondence</u> between Chandragupta Maurya of Pataliputra, Ptolemy of Egypt, Alexander II of Macedonia and Emperor Ming of the Han Dynasty – fragments rescued from the great fires that swept the Antiquities Museum, Alexandria, in the hottest year ever recorded in human history: 4011 AD.

Fragment 1: From Chandragupta Maurya to Ptolemy

"Your wondrous scrolls were much appreciated, and, indeed, some of the plays were enacted here, at my court. Much merriment was had, aided not a little by the miraculous wine from your fabled cellars. You may wonder at the delay in the promised package, but I think you will find that any expectations that I may have raised in recent correspondence, will prove entirely insufficient to prepare you for the gift I send now. It is the gift of kings, my friend. I give it to you only because I know that none deserves it so much as you, and that none will use it so wisely as you."

Fragment 2: From Ptolemy to Alexander

"I tell you again that it is entirely out of my abilities to reproduce this silk. My craftsmen and engineers alike have examined it in every way possible: unwoven some parts, washed away the dye in others, picked apart the embroidered threads one colour at a time, dipped it in acids and complex chemicals, brought the priests out in their regalia to waft their holy smoke upon it – yet, we are no wiser than before. It lies before us in heaps of ashes and watery pools, and will not give up its secrets.

Yet it is made by men, and what they put in their silk-worms in China remains a mystery locked in their Forbidden City."

Fragment 3: From the Emperor Ming of the Han Dynasty to Chandragupta Maurya

"And so, to end the matter, I hope that you will command that the bearer of these bales, once embalmed, must be wrapped in its folds, and the whole returned to me. You will understand, of course, being Emperor of the vast beauties and treasures of your legendary land, that the threads that bind empire to empire are as soft and as strong as silk, but that the fabric of our riches are bound also, to this silk trade that is making my empire richer and stronger every day. If we flourish, we flourish together. Else..."

Fragment 4: From Alexander to Chandragupta Maurya

"...gone. My friend, I can only regret that my efforts to fulfill your simple request have failed....curious that such a wonderfully embalmed body should be shrouded in this cloth of strange motifs. Surely the dagger cannot be an auspicious... defend in the afterlife? We have searched... unavailingly...vanished..."

Satellite images of the Earth were not a good thing to fill one's mind with when making important lecture-demonstrations, and Mrinalini found herself avoiding the updates on the ravages of the planet surface as she gathered herself for this momentous presentation. She put aside, for instance, the fact that her ancestral village, once classified as 'coastal', was now itemized under the heading 'Irrecoverably Submerged'. She herself, like her mother, was Moon born and raised, but pictures and stories of her grandparents' and their parents' resistance movements in India's eastern states were the stuff of legend on both celestial bodies. "On Earth, as it is in Heaven," she whispered to herself, fervently wishing, not for the first time, that she believed enough in any divinity whose will could be done anywhere in the immediate galaxy. Resisting the urge to do one last tech check, she belted herself into her mini-moon-car, and headed out to the demonstration site.

Going 'where the sun don't shine' wasn't as hysterically funny as it had been in the first phase of habitation planning; the many haha references to Star Wars and Pink Floyd had also lost their freshness once it became clear that colonizing the dark side of the moon was going to be much less glamorous than Michael Jackson's moon-walking. The madness of even trying to live on the moon was so been-there-done-that that lunacy puns no longer existed, and when a new-comer tried to crack one, it was met with blank stares. So when Mrinalini pulled into the parking bay and walked into the enormous tent where the demonstration was to take place, she was not feeling particularly amused. She turned an unsmiling face to the gathered group of skeptical, hopeful, and bored faces (the fourth face was hidden behind an elaborate silk veil, held tight at chest-level by a hand marked by the grey skin of the first-generations).

"Chancellor, Chief Scientist, Head of Corporate Treasuries, High First-Generationer," (I leave you, Gentle Reader, to assign an expression to each luminary at your own indulgence! But I annoy you with my authorial interventions. Let us return to this grand event.) "We all know why we are assembled here today. We have discussed the various possibilities that my invention could have for Earth populations, as well as for our own thriving community," (cough cough from the veiled one) "*nation*, I mean, of course." Mrinalini allowed herself an inward eye roll. "And we have also discussed the importance of finding the funding for the mass production and swift distribution of this invention; and finally, we have already discussed the great influence and political authority that such a humanitarian..." (another cough cough from the silken one, but this time Mrinalini ignored it) "...contribution to the people and nations of Earth will bring us."

Her forty-plus years had each added their weight of training, education, passion, and compassion, to bring her to this point, and Mrinalini was ready for it.

She straightened a little more, glad that she had thought to wear her power-fist-patterned inner shirt today, and stared down the varying expressions of disagreement confronting her.

"It only remains for me to demonstrate its immense power and potential. Note, please," all eyes followed her pointing finger to the densely embroidered cloth that served as their roof, "the intricately woven fabric above your heads. While the main motif is, indeed, the yellow circle representing the sun, you will note that there are hundreds of minor motifs that I cannot explain here in detail, but which, suffice it to say, represent the many factors that are intrinsic to climate and weather control. So you see, we need no longer live in the dark on this hemisphere."

The subtle glow and growing brightness that followed upon a tap of her screen brought an audible response from this hardened lot, while Mrinalini allowed herself to savour the moment with an inward 'let there be light!'

Without allowing her audience's attention to wander into doubt, she touched her screen again: "And we need no longer suffer drought or waterless landmasses," she noted the widened eyes with satisfaction, as a gentle drizzle filled the left half of the tent, where water gathering tanks had been strategically placed in readiness. Mist, breezes, cooling and heating followed in quick succession, but after the first two, Mrinalini knew she had them. Which is why the single question annoyed her so much.

"Very impressive, Chief Engineer," said the Chancellor, inserting his comment into her demonstration like an oily spoon into water, "but how are we to get this miracle to Earth with enough speed and profit for it to help those on Earth and also provide us the funds with which to finance further production? Our fuels, as you are well aware, are too dearly bought for anything more than one jumbo craft per lunar month." He sat back, luxuriating in the waves of furious failure that radiated from his Chief Engineer. (Yes, yes, 'furious failure' – I like to indulge my literary proclivities even while preparing to dine on delicacies, and why not, after all? If poetry be food for worms, or something to that effect, no?)

Ming cursed the gods for each rut and hole in the dirt road along which the cart trundled, convinced that there was a minor demon in each, charged specifically with creating a large bruise or breaking a bone in his travel-weary body. But his first thought, after every puddle that splashed him, was for the precious bales.

He had gone from being obsessively careful to being outright superstitious about their well-being. Through the long nights they whispered to each other and rustled their feathers and once or twice he would swear upon all the gods that a sharp, brightly embroidered beak had poked him in the ribs as he turned over, muttering in his sleep. And he had seen something else that awakened a fear deep in his bowels. There was another bale, a thin one, hidden within the folds of the bigger, blue one; a jolt on the road had revealed a corner that poked out from within the tight rolls – a small triangle, but enough to reveal a resplendently hued hilt, chased with thread of gold, crowning a gleaming silver tipped blade. The peacock pattern fluffed its brilliant feathers, he would right it in his blood; and the other was patterned with knives.

Ming cursed whichever demon was responsible for the night on which the new silkworms were discovered huddled about the enclosure where the royal silkworms were kept. Life was so much simpler then: a limited number of worms to make the limited amount of silk that the limited number of emperors and his wives and daughters and favourite concubines needed.

A limited number of weavers and embroiderers, sworn to service to the quite limited body of the emperor's household, with limited rooms where the silk was stored, and limited roads on which it had to travel to get from the makers to the wearers. (You can see, my dear, that Ming's vocabulary was quite limited.

Not like your own, which makes you an object of such interest to me!) Not this limitless treasure now brought in by the suddenly and miraculously expanded amount of silk and the empires in the world to which it was sent, along roads that knew no end in number or in direction. The new miracle of the world, the gift of kings. And so here he was, poor man with bruised bones, hurtling down strange paths to stranger cities, clutching the strangest of all things he had ever seen, to his aching, trembling, bosom.

"Approval is granted conditional upon quick and affordable delivery... blah blah blah... responsibility of payments... yackity schmackity... our benevolence made known to the people and leaders of India... etc etc...yours sincerely!"

Mrinalini flicked the letter out of the air, ignoring the hiss of her holographic mail reader, and glaring into the now empty air before her. Tears of fury blinded her as she thought of the futility of the decades of hard work and heartache that she had put into her invention.

While her peers worked on alternate fuels and energy systems, died in demonstrations against governments that refused to see the deluge and the fires and the deathly winters already upon them, foretelling the end of the world as they knew it, fought for legislations that would safeguard whole species dying in the waters and forests and falling out of the skies, and finally, scrambled to get as many of the world's coastal people to higher ground as possible, she, Mrinalini, had exerted her adamantine will over her own doubts, and persisted.

Among scientists it had been a closely guarded secret for a few decades now, that there were supplies of fabric that the Chinese army had been deploying for a while, not in warfare, but in providing shelter from the blizzards that now routinely plagued its mountainous regions, making life completely unlivable for its millions of inhabitants.

It had been rumoured for years, that the fabric was not merely efficient in a make-shift tent fashion, providing temporary shelter from the cold, but that entire townships had managed to relocate to these tent-cities, living and working under what looked like traditional glass and steel office buildings.

Mrinalini had learnt that these were, in fact, stretched silk that functioned in extraordinary ways. Research on the nature of technology that went into the production of this material was scarce, the silk being regarded largely as a natural variation on the traditional variety. The Chinese were close-lipped about it and, in the hyper-competitive world of scarce resources, much of the world dismissed accounts of this material as myth and hearsay.

Mrinalini had always felt that it was more than mere chance that brought the first piece of fabric into her hands, when, on a rare visit home to her grandparents in India, she had found a sari in the bottom of her grandmother's winter trunk. Wrapped in a piece of an old organza sari, she first set it aside, being in search of a childhood shirt that she had been particularly attached to.

In her haste, she managed to spill some of her freshly brewed tea into the trunk, and watched with horror as it stained the pretty off-white silk. Digging into her pants for tissues with which to staunch the spreading stain, she found, as she focused her attention on it, that the faint brown splotch was fading quickly at the edges. Mrinalini lifted the material out of the trunk, and that is when the little embroidered fans caught her eye.

She could have sworn that the now rapidly fading stain was being fanned into invisibility. Within minutes, the ivory shade of the sari shone clear, all signs of any stain having vanished, literally, into thin air.

Mrinalini's grandmother was pleased that she wanted her old sari. "It's very special, my dear," she told her. "My grandfather brought this from Burma for my grandmother on one of his military trips. Apparently the woman who sold it to him was in severe need of cash, but he said she parted with this with a very sad heart, saying that it had been a family heirloom for generations, and thought to have been blessed by the household gods. Of course, you know, dear, how superstitious people can be, and it can't have been that old, because it looked brand new – as if it had been newly spun! Straight from the worms themselves!" Mrinalini's grandmother laughed aloud at her own witticism, her veined hands slapping her knee.

And so, while the rest of the engineering and scientific community were desperately researching and developing alternative energy sources, and land-reclamation projects, and water distribution systems, and medications for the terrible effects of the heat, she, Mrinalini, had persevered, convinced that the silk had properties which would save her people on Earth and on the Moon.

She had managed, after decades of synthesizing and grafting, splicing DNA and doctoring genes, to reconfigure the silk produced by the almost 220 year-old silk production centre established on the Moon, so that, from the small amounts still produced, large sheets of the fabric could be constructed. And she had found a way to pattern and structure it so that it obeyed certain, strict, rules of function – functions that she had focused towards the challenges of climate change and its ravages. And now, when the answer was in her very hands, these fools would deny it to her people and the people of the world.

She blew her nose loudly into a silk hanky and watched – still fascinated – as the little square of fabric, embroidered with tiny gusts of wind and Chinese fans, blew the wet goop dry.

The cabin door flew open and Cheenamara's spiky head poked in long enough to announce that the wormhole was opening again. Mrinalini was out the door before it had shut.

Anything that made the large Cheenamara fly about like the limber young non-binary person she wasn't (Limber and young, you understand: she was always non-binary, on this day preferring to present as male. But you would know all that better than I, wouldn't you, my dear?) was Moon-shaking enough to drive her lover out of whatever fury she was in, and follow. And as she followed – Moon-weight was an interesting phenomenon, but Mrinalini nevertheless found it hard to move her stately self fast – she swept a box of new-fledged silk-worms off its shelf, her thoughts hardly keeping up with her actions. Who knew.

"Chee! How about" – but Chee was on it before the thought was finished. She waited only long enough for Mrinalini to wrap the little box in her hanky, before punching in the location and sending the loaded pellet-craft on its way. With any luck, it would be at their India station in moments. Then larger consignments could follow immediately upon confirmation by return craft.

The two sat on their haunches, eyes rivetted to the lower half of the pellet-craft hatch, brains frozen with apprehension and anticipation. The buzz on the monitor above them announced the shrinking of the wormhole. The cough behind them announced the entrance of the Chief of Staff. The zzp before them brought a strange object, like a medium sized human wrapped in a shroud.

The First Generationer paced slowly, majestic head nodding lightly, dainty hands holding the veil in place that hid his magnificence from the world. (I will break your stupid human neck, you maggot! How dare you laugh at my account of my proper stature?! You are nothing but fodder, do you understand? Fodder for those of the mighty and divine origins! Why do I waste my time on your insignificant mind which will never understand – never! – the inconceivable beauty of this story and my place in it? Mine and all like me, who could save your puny planet in a moment if we so wished! I would destroy you right now, you ugly little beast, if – aahhhh, let it be, let it be, you see how I must not allow my essence to dissolve – ah – yes, yes, where was I – ah – yes, you must be made to see, and know that you will be placed in high esteem – high esteem – when we have populated one half – the dark half, you see – with sustenance for our glorious species, yes, yes, cease this struggling, Mrinalini, and listen to the rest of my story – there is so very little left.)

The two engineers stared at the Chief of Staff, holding a small sample case in one hand and his notepad in the other, and the Chief of Staff stared at what were obviously the remains of a human wrapped in silk. In silence, the three gaped uncomprehendingly as Mrinalini drew aside a fold of silk, patterned with curious, brilliant-hued, daggers, to reveal a young man's obviously dead face, the open mouth fresh with shock, the open eyes unable to see the oozing slit just under the breast bone – as if made with a thin blade.

The Chief of Staff looked from one engineer to the other blankly, cleared his throat loudly. "Whatever this is," he waved his notepad at the body and the now inactive pellet-craft hatch, "I think you should know, Mrinalini – and you, Cheenamara, since she will tell you anyway – that I have been tending to the First Generationer's health for a while now, and thanks to some useful samples of bodily fluids and sinews, I have now confirmed my growing fear and suspicion."

Shocked, Mrinalini saw that the Chief of Staff was trembling with agitation, actual tears standing out on his cheeks. She rose and touched his arm. "What is it, Chief? What news can you bring that is more fearsome than what our Earth monitors tell us every day?"

Wordlessly, the Chief held out his notepad for her to read. Amid meticulously laid out calculations and explanations, the vehemently underlined verdict stared her insolently in the face.

"Deduction: First Generationer DNA: silkworm and human."

The pen that had underlined this incomprehensible conclusion had been wielded with such an agitated hand that it had gone through the notepad into the clipboard.

Mrinalini turned her glazed eyes to his. "Those missing attendants, and the dug-up graves, we thought they were foraging for more potatoes, but they..."

The tiny beep interrupted her, and she turned to Chee's quiet calling of her name. The small gadget in Chee's hand gleamed as she passed it over the body and flashed '241 BC' on the small screen. Mrinalini gazed askance at the number.

Then, slowly, letting the truth dawn on her gradually so that she would not sink under its weight, she turned to the wormhole time.

There it was: not '2241 AD / Patna, India' – where the silkworms and sample silk would have allowed her cousin, the Chief Minister of Bihar, to synthesis his own climate-silk and silk-boats – but '241 BC / Patna, India', where Chandragupta Maurya had followed the instructions of his friend the Emperor of the Ming dynasty, and asked the young delivery boy (possibly the illegitimate son of one of the emperor's daughters or concubines or some such that the emperor wished dead, who knows why emperors wish sundry random people dead, it is not as if they add to their DNA or evolution in any way) to wrap himself in the dagger-patterned silk sheet – revealing the message of the true abilities of the sentient silk to the Mauryan king, and killing the messenger all in one master stroke.

(Yes, Mrinalini, the very same Ming. You see? I did say, at the very beginning, that if you continue to read, you will see how this came to be. Patience, now, a few more holographic paragraphs – speech is so overrated, don't you think? Sentient worms have had no need of it for hundreds of years, an evolution of the lowly human DNA we have been ingesting through our – ah – kind guests, visitors to the Moon Dynasty. Perhaps we will succeed, one of these centuries, in breeding it out of the human colony you have so cleverly engineered a bright home for on the dark side of our little galactical rock, hmm? Of course, the silk stuffed in your mouth does the job moderately well for the moment.)

Earth Monitor News Agency – 8th October, 2242
"Sentient Silk seems well on its way to offering some relief from the devastation of climate change after all. Following

much speculation as to its nature, uses, and origins, the possibilities of production and/or import from the Colony of the Moon Dynasty, it appears that the supply of what is being called the Miracle Material, will continue unabated. There was some serious doubt as to its sustainability when news came of the rebellion against the First Generationers, even prompting some Indigenous Rights Organizations to protest the manner of their detainment. It was revealed, however, in an official communique from the Colony, that the Chief of Staff and two senior engineers had found a dietary anomaly in the First Generationers that was actually harmful to them, and that they have now corrected it.

The Colony has also received its first contingent of Dark Siders, as they are calling themselves, to settle the now climate-controlled and human-friendly side of the Moon that Earthers never see. We have good initial reports of their flourishing. Chief Engineer Mrinalini, who has been credited with the saving of the millions of lives, has warned, however, that Sentient Silk should be treated with care, given its status as a life-form. Her 'Rules of Engagement' is a binding document on all who wish to use this Miracle Material.

We end our report on a not-entirely-flippant note: the ancient discovery of silk has certainly traced an unexpected route!"

Anil Menon's short fiction have appeared in a variety of international magazines including *Albedo One, Interzone, Interfictions, Jaggery Lit Review, Lakeview Review, Lady Churchill's Rosebud Wristlet*, and *Strange Horizons*. His stories been translated into Chinese, Czech, French, German, Hebrew, and Romanian. His debut YA novel *The Beast With Nine Billion Feet* (Zubaan Books, 2010) was short-listed for the 2010 Vodafone-Crossword award and the Carl Baxter Society's Parallax Prize. Along with Vandana Singh, he co-edited *Breaking the Bow* (Zubaan Books 2012), an anthology of speculative fiction inspired by the Ramayana. His most recent work, *Half Of What I Say*, (Bloomsbury, 2015) was shortlisted for the 2016 Hindu Literary Award. He currently resides in India and can be reached at: iam@anilmenon.com.

Giti Chandra is currently Senior Researcher and Lecturer with the United Nations University in Reykjavik, and has been Associate Professor, Dept of English, at Stephen's College, Delhi. Her fantasy series, *The Book of Guardians Trilogy,* is now complete, with the last of the series, *The Eye of the Archer*, expected out soon; the first two books are *The Fang of Summoning* (2010), and *The Bones of Stars* (2013). Sadly, nobody cares about her first non-fiction book, a groundbreaking academic work on violence, but the next two – on the global #MeToo movement, and on public discourses of colonial violence – are definitely going to be bestsellers. Giti writes poetry in April, paints on Wednesdays, has a PhD from Rutgers, and feels that people would do well do learn that a cello is not an oversized violin. She lives in Reykjavik with a husband, two kids, a dog, and a cat.

Manjula Padmanabhan (b. 1953), is an author, playwright and cartoonist. Her play *Harvest* won the 1997 Onassis Award for Theatre. Her weekly comic strip *Sukiyaki* appears in Business Line. Her two most recent novels *Escape* and *The Island of Lost Girls*, are set in a brutal future world. She lives in the US and New Delhi.

Priya Sarukkai Chabria is an award-winning translator, poet, writer and anthologist acclaimed for her radical literary aesthetics. Her books include speculative fiction, most recently the novel *Clone* (Zubaan, 2018, University of Chicago Press, 2019), literary non-fiction, poetry collections, and translations from Classical Tamil poetry, *Andal The Autobiography of a Goddess*, winner Muse India Translation Prize, 2017. Her story *Slo-Glo* was judged Best Experimental Story in *The Best Asian Speculative Fiction* (Kitaab, 2018). Awarded for her Outstanding Contribution to Literature, she presents her widely anthologized work worldwide, represented India at the 2014 Commonwealth Literature Conference and edits *Poetry at Sangam*. <http://poetry.sangamhouse.org/>
<www.priyawriting.com>

Rimi B. Chatterjee is an author, artist and teacher. She has published three novels (one science fiction novel, Signal Red (2005) and two historical fictions) and a graphic story in the Longform Anthology (eds. Sekhar Mukherjee, Sarbajit Sen, Debkumar Mitra and Pinaki De, 2018). Her book *Ashqabad: City of Stories* is forthcoming in 2019 and she is currently working on *Antisense: Tira's Gift*, a novel.

S.B. Divya is a lover of science, math, fiction, and the Oxford comma. She enjoys subverting expectations and breaking stereotypes whenever she can. Her novella *Runtime* was a Nebula Award finalist, and her short stories have been published at Uncanny, Apex, Tor.com, and other magazines. Her writing also appears in the indie game Rogue Wizards. Divya is the co-editor of Escape Pod, a Hugo-nominated weekly science fiction podcast, with Mur Lafferty. She holds degrees in Computational Neuroscience and Signal Processing, and she worked for twenty years as an engineer before becoming an author. Find out more about her at <www.eff-words.com> or on Twitter as @divyastweets.

Shikhandin is the *nom de plume* of an Indian writer whose published books (as Shikhandin) include "Immoderate Men" – Speaking Tiger Books, and "Vibhuti Cat" – Duckbill Books.

Prior to that a novel and a short story collection were published. Shikhandin worked in senior positions in media and advertising for long years before stepping down to pursue her first love writing. She has been writing poetry since childhood, and has performed poetry and also acted on stage. Shikhandin's poetry and fiction have been published worldwide. Her Children's book "Vibhuti Cat" was a winner in the Children's First Contest, 2017. Subsequently it was shortlisted in the Peek a Book Awards in the -8 Age Category 2018, India. She was a runner up in the 'Half and One' Contest, India, 2019. A first runner up in the OoP-DNA Short Story Contest, India, 2016. Second prize in The India Currents Katha Short Story Contest , USA, 2016. First prize in The Anam Cara Short Fiction Competition, Ireland, 2012. Longlisted in the Bridport Poetry Competition, UK, 2006. Finalist in the Aesthetica Poetry Contest, UK, 2010. A Pushcart nominee by Cha: An Asian Literary Journal, Hong Kong, 2011. Nominated for Story South's Notable Stories of the Net, USA, 2007. Among others. Shikhandin's love affair with science fiction began with the comic strip character Jet Ace Logan, and then a comic book series called the Twilight Zone, followed by sci-fi books and more books.

Shovon Chowdhury is a slightly disturbed Delhi-based novelist. Due to a massive failure in quality control, his first novel, *The Competent Authority* (2013), was finalist for the Hindu, Crossword, Shakti Bhatt and Tata Lit Live awards. It has also been the subject of two PhD theses, one creative writing course, and several unauthorized theatrical adaptations, against which he was unable to lodge FIRs due to lack of funds. He is the entire reporting staff of The Investigator, published by Hindu Business Line, which digs for the truth, so you don't have to, and the sole proprietor of The Trilokpuri Incident, a Facebook page that is looking into an event no one can remember. His most recent novel, *Murder With Bengali Characteristics* (2015), is set in a near-future Calcutta under Chinese rule. Both the Bengalis and the Chinese are equally horrified.

Vandana Singh was born and brought up in Delhi and currently teaches and writes in the Boston area. Her science fiction stories have been published in numerous venues, including several year's best volumes, and she has published two collections to critical acclaim: The Woman Who Thought She Was a Planet and Other Stories (Zubaan/ Penguin India, 2008/2013) and most recently Ambiguity Machines and Other Stories (Small Beer Press, USA and Zubaan Books, India, 2018) which is a finalist for the Philip K. Dick Award. She is also the author of two children's books about an eccentric character called Younguncle. In her academic life, she is a former particle physicist currently researching climate science at the intersection of pedagogy and social change. For more about her, see <http://vandana-writes.com/>. The story Indra's Web first appeared in TRSF: The Best New Science Fiction (2011).

Tarun K. Saint, an independent scholar and writer, was born in Kenya, and has lived in India since 1972. His research interests include the literature of the partition and science fiction. He is the author of *Witnessing Partition* (2010), based on his doctoral dissertation. He edited *Bruised Memories: Communal Violence and the Writer* (2002) and co-edited (with Ravikant) *Translating Partition* (2001). He also co-edited Looking Back: India's Partition, 70 Years On (2017), with Rakhshanda Jalil and Debjani Sengupta. Recently, he has edited *The Gollancz Book of South Asian Science Fiction* (2019).

Avatar: antologia di fantascienza contemporanea indiana

di Tarun K. Saint

Avatar, antologia bilingue (inglese-italiano), punta lo sguardo sulla fantascienza contemporanea indiana, con una selezione di alcuni dei testi migliori nel genere sia di scrittori affermati che emergenti. Per la maggior parte questa collezione include nuovi lavori, appena commissionati sulla base di una lista di temi fornita agli autori invitati a contribuire. L'idea era quella di creare nuove storie di fantascienza che si occupassero delle questioni impellenti dei nostri tempi, soprattutto nei settori dell'informatica e della tecnocultura, così come della biotecnologia. Questa raccolta, perciò, non propone i temi classici della fantascienza dell'Epoca d'oro come i viaggi nel tempo, la colonizzazione dello spazio, la fantascienza militare, universi paralleli, alieni minacciosi, eccetera, e neppure fantasy o supereroi, basati sul mito o meno.

Gli autori (che scrivono in inglese) sono stati, invece, invitati a riflettere su temi come l'avvento della biopolitica e il suo uso da parte degli enti statali, i collegamenti tra i nuovi (social) media e il linguaggio, l'apparentemente inesorabile ascesa di Big Data e algoritmi, la diffusione di stampa 3D, protesi e potenziamento umano, i rischi della biotecnologia e della tecnologia CRISPR-Cas9, le sfide poste da sicurezza e sorveglianza informatica, i dilemmi posti da una vita oltre la morte da parte degli avatar e dal diritto alla cancellazione dai social media, la minaccia incombente del cambiamento climatico nell'era dell'Antropocene, così come il ruolo di intelligenza artificiale, robot e il futuro di sesso e relazioni. Sebbene non tutti questi argomenti siano stati affrontati, come vedrete, i riscontri degli autori sono stati sia creativi che connessi a molti di questi temi chiave, senza mai però perdere di vista l'importanza del raccontare una storia e la necessità di proporre ciò che il critico di fantascienza Darko Suvin ha chiamato il "novum" o la nuova idea perturbatrice su cui si fonda la narrativa fantascientifica.[7]

Il titolo invoca due significati distinti del termine "avatar". Un avatar è principalmente "la discesa di una divinità sulla terra, e in particolare ciascuna delle 10 incarnazioni del dio Visnù", come leggiamo sul vocabolario Treccani, un concetto con radici profonde delle tradizioni epiche indiane; in secondo luogo un avatar è "nei giochi di ruolo virtuali, personaggio dalle più diverse sembianze che rappresenta l'alter ego dei vari partecipanti, sostituendoli nelle azioni di gioco".[8] In quanto composta da storie provenienti da autori indiani di fantascienza, questa raccolta presenta una variante ibrida di questo antico concetto, con racconti di fantascienza in inglese che propongono nuove riflessioni su questioni cruciali con un sapore contemporaneo, anche se non sempre ambientati nel cyberspazio.

Si può dire che la fantascienza indiana sia nata nel XIX secolo con la pubblicazione di *A Journal of Forty Eight Hours in the Year 1945* di Kylas Chunder Dutt in inglese nel 1835, una storia realistica, con un pizzico di romanticismo giovanile, che immagina un tentativo tragico di resistenza anti-colonialista nel secolo successivo.[9] La fantascienza indiana degli albori va dalle favole raffiguranti il potenziale emancipatore della scienza, come nel racconto di fantascienza bengalese dello scienziato Jagadish Chandra *Runaway Cyclone* (1896, trad. della versione rev. *Polatuk Toofan* 1921), a utopie femministe, come in *Sultana's Dream* di Rokeya Sekhawat (1905), e addirittura a storie umoristiche che prendono in giro l'arroganza degli scienziati nella loro ricerca per dare nuova forma al mondo, come nella storia in bengalese *The Diary of Heshoram Hoshiar* (trad. di

---

7 <Vedi http://www.sf-encyclopedia.com/entry/novum>
8 <Vedi http://www.treccani.it/vocabolario/avatar/>
9 Kylas Chunder Dutt, 'A Journal of Forty-Eight Hours of the Year 1945', 1835, rpt. in Shoshee Chunder Dutt, *Selections from 'Bengaliana'*, ed. Alex Tickell, Nottingham: Trent Editions, 2005, 149-159.

Heshoram Hushiyarer Diary) di Sukumar Ray.[10] Sebbene i romanzi scientifici sullo schema di Wells e Verne fossero spesso il modello delle prime opere soprattutto in lingue come il bengalese e il marathi, anche le opere sensazionalistiche tradizionali e quelle di avventura del tipo "gosh-wow" prevalenti nell'epoca d'oro della fantascienza divennero in seguito popolari. Tuttavia, a differenza dell'America, le piccole riviste e i periodici che pubblicavano fantascienza in questi spazi regionali non avevano lo stesso tipo di inclinazione commerciale o successo. La fantascienza indiana acquisì invece, soprattutto dopo l'indipendenza, una spinta pedagogica, cercando di rendere popolari le idee scientifiche mettendo il concetto di autosufficienza alla base della storia, o raccontando una storia con alla base un problema scientifico, come vediamo nel caso di molti dei racconti della raccolta di fantascienza di Bal Phonke, soprattutto in traduzione, *It Happened Tomorrow* (1993).[11]

Gli anni Novanta inaugurarono una nuova ondata di opere di fantascienza indiana, sulla scia della nascita del movimento ambientalista e delle critiche allo sviluppo convenzionale. Lo spirito di protesta alla base della controcultura ha avuto un'influenza continua dopo gli anni Sessanta, accentuato ulteriormente dai postumi della liberalizzazione dell'economia indiana (dal 1991 in poi) che hanno reso necessarie risposte nettamente critiche. Allo stesso tempo, le tendenze di globalizzazione avviate dalle riforme di liberalizzazione ed economiche hanno portato molti altri editori internazionali sulle sponde

---

10 Vedi anche <http://digital.library.upenn.edu/women/sultana/dream/dream.html,> consultato il 17 febbraio 2019, e <http://strangehorizons.com/fiction/runaway-cyclone>/, consultato il 19 aprile 2019, assieme a Sukumar Ray, 'The Diary of Heshoram Hushiar' in Satyajit Ray, *Travails with the Alien: The Film that was Never Made and other Adventures with Science Fiction*, Noida: HarperCollins India, 2018, 190-98.

11 Bal Phondke, ed. *It Happened Tomorrow*, New Delhi: National Book Trust, 1993. Questo paragrafo e il prossimo si avvalgono di un resoconto più dettagliato, con un taglio diverso, nella mia introduzione a *The Gollancz Book of South Asian Science Fiction*, Gurugram: Hachette India, 2019, xiii-xli.

dell'India, con conseguenti aperture per autori sia di saggistica che di narrativa. Il romanzo di fantascienza di Amitav Ghosh *The Calcutta Chromosome* (1996) e l'opera teatrale di Manjula Padmanabhan *Harvest* (1997) esemplificano una visione più autoriflessiva e scettica di scienza e tecnologia, aggiungendo anche prospettive sociologiche e umaniste.[12] Questo tipo di storie ecologicamente sensibili e a volte attente al genere hanno continuato ad apparire nel primo decennio del XXI secolo, con le opere di Vandana Singh, Anil Menon, Priya Sarrukai Chhabria, Rimi Chatterjee, Shovon Choudhury e altri pubblicate con successo di critica, spesso usando la fantascienza/speculative fiction come piattaforma per sollevare importanti preoccupazioni etiche, anche quando questi autori sperimentano con stile e forma. Più recentemente una generazione più giovane di scrittori di fantascienza/speculative fiction continua a innovare, con tropi e metafore fantascientifici reinventati in maniera caratteristica nelle storie che creano un mondo nuovo di Indrapramit Das, S.B. Divya, Mimi Mondal, Sami Ahmad Khan, Giti Chandra e altri.

Iniziamo questa selezione di fantascienza contemporanea indiana con un racconto dell'ingegnere informatico e scrittore Anil Menon, *L'uomo senza quintessenza*. Il racconto di Menon traccia la situazione di un uomo che vive in una società indiana futura governata da uno stato di sorveglianza, anche se non ha 'quintessenza' o adeguati indicatori di identità. L'arguta interpretazione filosofica di Menon sulle conseguenze dell'introduzione di procedure centralizzate di identificazione come Aadhar mette anche in dubbio il presupposto per cui tali reti si impossessano della vita dei normali cittadini. Di seguito, *Microbiota e le masse: una storia d'amore* della scienziata S.B. Divya ci porta nell'ambito della biotecnologia e della creazione di ambienti artificiali per chi è affetto da condizioni molto reali

---

12 Amitav Ghosh, *The Calcutta Chromosome: A Novel of Fevers, Delirium and Discovery*, New Delhi: Ravi Dayal, 1996, Manjula Padmanabhan, *Harvest*, 1997, edizione rivista e aggiornata, Gurgaon: Hachette, 2017

che riducono l'immunità ai patogeni. Esplorare la possibilità della passione attraverso l'ideazione di modi alternativi di vivere per Moena, una ragazza che vive in una di queste bolle, è il *novum* o nuova idea qui, con il bioma personale che diventa sia rifugio che prigione. Abbiamo poi *Comunitario* di Shikandin, racconto che presenta una nuova interpretazione dell'idea dell'estinzione delle specie apocalittica che ricorda i romanzi di John Wyndham, in una storia ambientata nel deserto del Thar in Rajasthan.

La rete di Indra della fisica Vandana Singh si basa su nuove scoperte delle scienze biologiche per la sua descrizione di un tentativo di decifrare la rete di comunicazione usata dalle foreste per scambiare informazioni cruciali. Il passo successivo è la creazione di una nuova rete energetica, la Suryanet, sviluppata dal Biomimetic Energy Materials Lab diretto da Mahua, la protagonista, rete che viene colpita da un malfunzionamento inatteso. La storia di Singh si basa sulla sintesi dell'antica saggezza (rappresentata dall'idea della rete cosmica di Indra) e gli studi attuali per scoprire nuovi modi di combattere il cambiamento climatico e le minacce alla sopravvivenza in luoghi come le coste del Bangladesh. Poi *Sostituzione* di Rimi Chatterjee, ambientato nel 2030 a New Singapore, la prima città galleggiante del mondo nel suo Universo Antisenso, riflette ironicamente sulle conseguenze dell'ingegneria genetica applicata e delle tecnologie riproduttive per l'industria della moda e del glamour, anche se la protagonista entra nel paese delle meraviglie della medicina su scala multinazionale. Il racconto successivo, *Upgrade* di Manjula Padmanabahn, tratta l'argomento della robotica e dell'invecchiamento, rappresentando una soluzione che esce da una scatola (ma anche dagli schemi) al problema della solitudine nel prossimo futuro. *Madre* di Shovon Choudhury parla del problema della sorveglianza centralizzata esasperata da parte di un'intelligenza artificiale controllata dallo stato chiamata Madre (di certo un aggiornamento del Grande Fratello di Orwell) in una storia salace e ironica, con tocchi di umorismo nero e orrore strisciante.

La storia della poetessa e autrice/traduttrice Priya Sarrukai Chabria, *Messo in pausa*, è abbastanza perturbante, con la sua visione di un futuro essere-capsula che crea una versione totalmente nuova di vita basata sulla selezione di materiali genetici presi da svariate fonti con solo i ricordi lasciati dagli Esseri Conchiglia, versione trasformata di Quelli Pelosi (gli umani), in uno scenario post-estinzione. Per concludere, *La via della seta* di Giti Chandra attraversa la storia passata e presente, portando un'interpretazione nuova delle relazioni India-Cina quando una ricercatrice che si occupa di vecchi tessuti di seta ha l'idea di creare una seta senziente, un nuovo tessuto con il potenziale di porre rimedio al cambiamento climatico.

Presi assieme, questi racconti ci offrono uno scorcio vivido di quel variegato arazzo che è la fantascienza indiana in questo momento; speriamo che queste storie in inglese e in traduzione italiana trovino una seconda vita tra i lettori di questo sottogenere in continua evoluzione.

L'uomo senza quintessenza

di Anil Menon

Quando ho letto su *The Times Of India* che Ringo Singh Mann, residente a Chedda Nagar, Mumbai, era morto in un autocidio, la mia prima reazione non è stata tristezza o rabbia o rimpianto ma, piuttosto, divertimento. Con la morte Mann aveva raggiunto la visibilità che gli era stata negata per tutta la vita.

Faccio recuperare dal mio Assistente gli appunti di lavoro del periodo in cui sono stato impegnato nel tentativo di rintracciarlo. Sono appunti di più di quattro anni fa, ma i ricordi che evocano rendono il passato indistinguibile dal presente. La ricerca per trovare Ringo Singh Mann era stata diversa da qualsiasi altra avessi fatto negli anni.

A quel tempo sapevo solo due cose di Mann. Primo, al contrario di noi non poteva essere localizzato perché non era possibile collegarlo a un identificativo unico e permanente. In altre parole, Mann non aveva quintessenza. Secondo, le Dicerie lo identificavano come maschio indiano che viveva a Mumbai, il che rendeva la Città il luogo più ovvio in cui iniziare a cercare.

Le IA del Governo centrale e statale del Maharashtra mi fornirono le solite risposte vaghe e l'IA della Municipalità, o 'Balasaheb' come preferiva essere chiamata, fu inutilmente utile. Balasaheb è tenuto a parlare in lingua marathi, perciò feci tradurre al mio Assistente.

Ho scoperto che secondo il censimento del 2038 in Città vivono circa ventotto milioni di patrioti, ma solo trecentotrentaquattro si sarebbero voltati se aveste gridato "Ehi Ringo Singh Mann". Balasaheb mi passò tutte le loro localizzazioni. Dei trecentotrentaquattro Ringo Singh Mann, trentotto sono deceduti, tre sono in custodia cautelare, ventiquattro si stanno lavando i denti, centonove stanno dormendo, sette stanno facendo l'amore, dodici stanno scrivendo poesie, eccetera, eccetera. Ci sono dozzine di cluster formali e informali che li collegano uno all'altro. Alcuni Mann sono in tutti i cluster e la maggior parte dei cluster contiene alcuni Mann, ma nessun Mann è un'isola, sconnessa dalla terraferma. Non è un pattern o un dato insolito e non mi porta più vicino al Mann che voglio.

"Ma hanno tutti quintessenza." Già mentre lo dico, mi rendo conto di quanto sia folle.

"Perciò vuoi localizzare qualcuno che non può essere localizzato?" Balasaheb ha il tono di un genitore molto ragionevole.

"Sì... No, non esattamente. Sto dicendo che ci deve essere un modo indiretto per trovarlo." Poi ho un'idea. "E l'IA della previdenza sociale? È sotto la tua giurisdizione. Potrebbe Mann essere seguito dalla previdenza sociale?"

"Ci sono nove Ringo Singh Mann in elenco. Quale?"

"Quello senza una localizzazione valida."

"Non esistono localizzazioni non valide, così come non esistono uno scapolo sposato o un inquinamento salutare."

"Va bene, una localizzazione temporanea." Non mi piaceva per niente il tono di Balasaheb. "Supponiamo che qualcuno abbia subito un intervento chirurgico. Allora gli viene assegnata una localizzazione temporanea, giusto? Poi che succede?"

"Non ho idea di cosa succede quando qualcuno subisce un intervento. Mi occupo di questioni municipali. Stai pensando di localizzare il tuo Mann immaginario attraverso una traccia di credito immaginaria? Non è possibile. La previdenza sociale usa il protocollo blockchain standard a doppio cieco per tutte le sue transazioni. Un Conto parla solo con un altro Conto e, ovviamente, se qualcuno non è mai esistito non può avere un Conto."

"Secondo le Dicerie esiste eccome."

"Le futili congetture indeboliscono lo stato, cittadino. Posso esserti d'aiuto in qualcos'altro? Bene. Ti sarei grato se lasciassi un feedback. Jai Maharashtra!"

"Jai Maharashtra"
"Jai Bharat Mata!"
"Jai Bharat Mata."

Per un giornalista, avere a che fare con questo tipo di resistenza fa parte del lavoro quotidiano. Ci dovevano essere persone senza quintessenza. Dovevano esserci per forza. Così come c'erano state persone senza passaporto, carta Aadhar, tessera razioni e tessera PAN. Come si occupava lo Stato degli 'scapoli sposati'?

Chiedo in giro ma nessuno è disposto a parlare della politica della quintessenza. Neanche il dottor Mumtaz Mustafa, direttore tecnico del Netra Reddix Group, parla della politica, ma è più che disposto a parlare della tecnologia.

"Voi tizi comprovate il vostro essere persona, fra," dice Mustafa. Il colore dei suoi capelli è sincronizzato con le sue emozioni e adesso è rosso eccitazione piena. "La gente un tempo raccontava che le anime erano uniche e immutabili. Ennnh! Neti, fra'. Sono le finestre dell'anima a essere l'accidenti di segnale della tua fissità eterna."

Mustafa si tuffa a fondo nella tecnologia, troppo a fondo perché possa seguirlo, ma il nocciolo della questione è quello che diamo tutti per scontato. Ogni animale con gli occhi ha anche quintessenza, e cioè una struttura dell'iride unica, non modificabile e non duplicabile. I primi scanner dell'iride erano lenti, ingombranti e potevano essere hackerati con poco più di un pezzo di nastro adesivo e uno smartphone (un antenato onnipresente del link). Gli scanner di adesso entrano nella testa di una zanzara drone. Hanno la precisione del laser e sono straordinariamente sicuri e incredibilmente veloci. La quintessenza, sta dicendo Mustafa, non ha bisogno di un'anima. Ha bisogno solo che qualcuno abbia occhi, le finestre dell'anima.

Mustafa conferma con riluttanza che non sempre questo requisito viene soddisfatto. Anche se orrori congeniti che prevenivano la corretta formazione dell'occhio come microftalmia, anoftalmia e coloboma sono stati eliminati quasi del tutto, si verificano ancora. A volte le persone hanno la sfortuna di perdere entrambi gli occhi in un incidente. Le persone che vivono nelle nazioni di livello 3 e 4 avrebbero potuto avere accesso alla tecnologia, se non fosse per la geografia della loro nascita.

"Perciò è un problema reale."

"Problema molto temporaneo," mi assicura Mustafa. "Spero che non sei un tipo sempre di fretta, fra'?"

Be', non ero certo pronto ad aspettare la Singolarità. Non per niente viviamo in una società aperta. Ho presentato richieste secondo il diritto di informazione per i dati sui difetti oculari congeniti. Ulteriori richieste per i dettagli sugli stanziamenti finanziari per i migranti dalle nazioni di livello 3 e 4. Ancora altre richieste per i dettagli sulle vittime di incidenti che avevano avuto bisogno di chirurgia oculistica. Ho scritto un articolo sui limiti della tecnologia della quintessenza.

Decido di scavare un po' più a fondo per capire i motivi della riluttanza del governo. Mi incontro con Sheila 'Sunny' Mazumdar, capo del Freedom Institute e ritenuta uno dei maggiori esperti mondiali sulle società aperte. È gender-neutral e ci piacciamo più o meno subito. L'ufficio accogliente del professore con le sue tende in fibra di cocco, i mobili confortevolmente malconci, le piante Bose e le pareti ricoperte di libri incoraggiano la conversazione.

La riluttanza del governo, spiega il dottor Mazumdar, è un tentativo di mantenere la fiducia della gente nell'affidabilità delle persone.

"Più una società è aperta, più fa affidamento sulla fiducia. La fiducia è una risorsa tanto quanto lo sono la luce del sole, l'acqua o il tempo. Per esempio, noi non ci siamo mai incontrati prima ma sono abbastanza certo che tu sia chi dici di essere. Ancora meglio, so che gli altri possono esserne altrettanto certi. So che possiamo collaborare l'uno con l'altro e ritenerci l'un l'altro responsabile. Se possiamo fidarci delle persone solo dopo averle conosciute per un certo lasso di tempo, allora tutto viene rallentato."

Dico al dottor Mazumdar – chiamami Sunny, dice lei – che io, personalmente, sono disposto a prenderla in parola su più o meno tutto. I suoi modi rilassati, sicuri e alla mano, in effetti, lo rendono quasi obbligatorio. Ma Sunny Mazumdar chiarisce subito che non sta parlando di quel tipo di fiducia. Alcuni tipi di fiducia devono comunque essere *guadagnati*, ma in una società aperta c'è una presunzione di affidabilità.

"Per vedere quanto sia importante questa presunzione, basta guardare una società in cui la fiducia sia stata rovinata completamente. La Moldavia era il simbolo di quel tipo di società. Adesso è conosciuta per i suoi eccellenti biologi quantistici e per i vini incredibilmente costosi, ma negli anni Dieci del Duemila le cose erano un vero disastro. I moldavi erano molto sospettosi l'uno dell'altro. Il relatore della mia tesi, Ruut Veenhoven, che studiava la felicità, aveva scoperto che la Moldavia era uno dei luoghi più infelici del pianeta. A quanto pare fiducia e felicità sono strettamente correlate. Veenhoven una volta mi fece una battuta che aveva sentito là. Ogni nazione desidera che i suoi abitanti siano onesti, intelligenti e vivano a lungo. Ma in Moldavia una persona poteva essere solo due di queste tre cose. Se eri onesto e intelligente, allora saresti morto presto. Se eri onesto e longevo, allora doveva mancarti qualche rotella. E se eri intelligente e longevo, dovevi per forza essere un criminale."

Suggerisco a Sunny che, se i moldavi sapevano ridere di sé stessi, non potevano essere stati così infelici. Sorride come se lo avesse pensato anche lui. Le chiedo cosa fosse cambiato per i moldavi.

"Tantissime cose." Sunny esita come se stesse soppesando qualcosa. "Per certi aspetti, l'India non è così diversa dalla Moldavia. Hanno risolto i loro problemi di fiducia nel modo in cui noi abbiamo risolto i nostri. Il primo passo è trovare un modo per essere certi che una persona sia chi dice di essere. La tecnologia della quintessenza lo ha reso possibile. Ma c'è un inghippo: non basta avere una tecnologia. Bisogna anche che la gente si fidi dell'affidabilità della tecnologia. Mann e altri come lui – e puoi essere certo che ce ne sono altri come lui – ci fanno dubitare della tecnologia dietro alla quintessenza, e perciò della base della nostra società." Mi lancia uno sguardo strano. "Il cambiamento ha sempre un prezzo. Ne abbiamo pagato uno molto caro. Devi capire che l'impulso totalitario è quello di rendere gli errori di riconoscimento impossibili."

All'improvviso, ridiamo entrambi. Mentre parlavamo, i nostri Assistenti si sono dati da fare per cercare di metterci insieme. Sono convinti che abbiamo una possibilità.

"Che ne dici?" butto lì.

"Ho già una relazione monoamorosa," mi ricorda.

Ah, di nuovo la cosa della fiducia. Ma non sono deluso del tutto. Mi sono fatto un amico e capisco molto meglio la posizione del governo. Come dice il vecchio proverbio, è bene tenere la mente aperta ma non tanto da far cadere il cervello. Lo stesso vale per le società. L'Assistente mi informa che non è un proverbio ma la frase di un discorso di un burocrate. Può essere, ma vale comunque.

La mia pressione sembra aver funzionato. Qualche giorno dopo il mio incontro con Sunny, mi arriva una richiesta via link, grazie a Balasaheb.

"Sono Tanaji Shinde. Vuole incontrare Ringo Mann?"

So già di chi si tratta. È l'assistente sociale di Mann. Sa già cosa voglio. Voglio un contatto con il suo cliente. Ci accordiamo per incontrarci a Chembur attorno alle cinque e trenta di pomeriggio all'India Coffee House, un ristorante tradizionale storico. Il ristorante ha subito una corposa ristrutturazione nel corso degli anni, il menu è fusion-confusion, per non parlare dello staff motorizzato, e si è trasferito (prima era più vicino al viadotto ora in disuso). Tutto ciò potrebbe disturbare i puristi. Ma se l'ascia di George Washington può restare l'ascia di George Washington anche dopo la sostituzione di lama e manico, non vedo perché il nostro patrimonio culturale debba essere meno resiliente.

Tanaji ha un abito da safari e modi bruschi, di quelli che spesso nascondono un cuore gentile. Ha la corporatura tarchiata e squadrata degli abitanti del Bihar e sembra stanco. So che preferisce parlare in Marathi, perciò ci accordiamo sull'hindi. Ci sono alcune formalità ufficiali di cui occuparsi, inoltre Mann sarà libero solo dopo le sei. Sebbene Mann abbia acconsentito a incontrarmi, Tanaji ribadisce che può cambiare idea. Non è un animale dello zoo, chiarisce Tanaji in modo piuttosto immotivato.

Mentre digitiamo e gesticoliamo nel compilare i moduli, sorseggiando l'acqua insipida, tiepida e lattiginosa che dichiarano essere chai (il ristorante non serve più caffè), Tanaji mi informa di avere giurisdizione su cinquantasette persone. Mann, però, è un caso speciale.

"Speciale in che senso?" chiedo.

"È un fantasma vivente. Come dite in inglese? Hahn, *the 'invisible' Mann*." Tanaji sorride con un pizzico di tristezza, forse perché sembra essere una battuta che ha fatto molte volte. "Lo hanno rapito qualche mese fa, lo sapeva? Pensavano che sarebbe stato l'assassino perfetto, visto che è registrato in così pochi database. Il nostro Bhagavan ha creato dei veri asini."

Tanaji spiega meglio la stupidità dei rapitori, che sono ovviamente stati arrestati. Prima di tutto, Mann non si muove facilmente, mentre gli assassini devono sfrecciare in giro con i veicoli più veloci possibile. L'assistente sociale mima l'atto di guidare un'automobile nei giorni in cui avevano il volante, appoggiandosi all'indietro sulla sedia per l'immaginaria velocità terrificante a cui stiamo andando.

"Posso chiederle una cosa?" dice Tanaji. "Preferirebbe essere uno jombie o un fantasma?"

Facile. Sono un vegetariano, perciò decisamente non uno zombie. Alzo gli occhi di lato per sbirciare nel profilo di Tanaji, vedo che anche lui è vegetariano. Quando riporto lo sguardo sul presente, lo trovo che mi sta esaminando con quel mezzo sorriso triste.

"Hahn, anch'io sono vegetariano," dice Tanaji in inglese. "Ma sirji – lei è un gentleman, no? – le dico con garanzia al cento per cento che preferiremmo essere jombies. Chieda perché."

"Perché?"

"Perché i jombies non sanno di essere jombies. Ma i fantasmi sanno di essere fantasmi. Perciò quale è peggio?" Ride, scuotendosi impotente sotto questa intuizione. "Corretto o no?"

Non ha tutti i torti. Se non *so* che sto mangiando cervello, potrei pure star masticando un cavolfiore. Gnam, gnam.

Alla fine terminiamo con i moduli e ci avviamo per incontrare Mann. Chedda Nagar non è lontana. Chembur è su un lato della Eastern Express Highway, Chedda Nagar sull'altro. Non sono entusiasta all'idea di arrancare sotto il sole e il conto spese copre senza dubbio i trasporti (credo), ma Tanaji mi assicura che la nostra destinazione non è lontana e che vuole sgranchirsi le gambe. Ci sgranchiamo le gambe. Quando le nostre gambe si avvicinano all'autostrada, un odore strano permea l'aria. Strano perché sembra essere un odore dei tempi passati. Chiedo al mio Assistente, ma la natura empatica di Tanaji ha già anticipato la mia domanda.

"Sta annusando le saline. Chedda Nagar è costruita su vecchie saline bonificate."

Sa molto delle politiche immobiliari della zona. All'inizio del XX secolo, il governo centrale diede in affitto vari grandi appezzamenti di terreno per la produzione di sale ad alcune famiglie di imprenditori come i Garodia e i Bomanwalla. Negli anni Settanta gli imprenditori immobiliari hanno costruito grandi complessi residenziali su questi terreni. Chedda Nagar, costruita da Ravji Khimji Chedda su un appezzamento di centoquaranta acri, era uno di questi complessi. O, come dice il governo, case abusive. La questione era finita in tribunale e i terreni erano rimasti in un limbo legale per gli ultimi cinquant'anni o più. Il che significava che le persone avevano paura di comprare casa in queste zone, perché non c'era garanzia che nei prossimi anni ne avrebbero mantenuto la proprietà. Le case non potevano essere vendute, Balasaheb non avrebbe mantenuto (non poteva mantenere) le strade nelle zone NDZ e cioè non edificabili, non ci sarebbero stati ulteriori sviluppi e Chedda Nagar e altre aree simili erano congelati nel tempo. Il sale per la nazione, intanto, viene prodotto altrove.

Quello che mi sta dicendo Tanaji, mi rendo conto, è che zone come questa intrappolate nel limbo legale sono rifugi naturali per una persona intrappolata in un limbo legale. I fantasmi vivono in case fantasma, dopotutto.

"Ce ne sono molti come Mann?"

"Giriamo a sinistra," dice Tanaji, indicando un bivio. "La lavanderia automatica è subito dopo l'edificio Abhilasha."

Gli chiedo se anche la risposta alla mia domanda si trova lì, ma si limita a sorridere e inizia a canticchiare a bocca chiusa e, pochi secondo dopo, a cantare, a Kabir doha.

Fa caldo. Molto caldo. Tutto quello che si poteva dire sul meteo attuale è già stato detto ma lasciate che mi unisca lo stesso alla litania. Il tempo atmosferico è brutale, costante, ereditato. È come un parente sudato e carnoso che insiste nell'essere baciato. Sento il sudore raccogliersi in grandi macchie umide, segnando le valli della mia superficie. Invidio la gente con i suoi parasole e, per prevenire l'inizio di una depressione da calore in piena regola, mi concentro sul mondo attorno a me.

Se Chedda Nagar è un complesso fantasma, è comunque un complesso fantasma prosperoso. Gli edifici con i loro nomi hindu dell'India del sud sono decrepiti, le strade sono in condizioni terribili e in generale il luogo sembra uscito da un film hindi degli anni Settanta. Ma questi patrioti sono totalmente di questi tempi e di questo mondo. La mia coscienza si riempie dei loro dati vitali, il più leggero spostamento dello sguardo mi permetterà di tuffarmi in ciò che gli piace e non gli piace, loro conoscono me, io conosco loro, e le tremolanti copie virtuali sono tanto ricche qui come in qualsiasi altro luogo della Città.

"Entro prima io," dice Tanaji. "Dopo il tentativo di rapimento è diventato un po' timoroso."

Mentre Tanaji sparisce all'interno del negozio, preparo il mio viso nell'espressione più ingenua e meno minacciosa possibile. Cinque minuti. Dieci minuti. Venti. Sudo sotto il sole impietoso. Si avvicina una giovane coppia. Devono aver notato che sono nuovo della zona e non c'è bisogno di spostare lo sguardo per accertarsi che sto soffrendo. Sembrano persone gentili e rispettabili. Agli Shetty piace arrampicare, sono stati tre volte a Bali, è il loro posto preferito di sempre, e sono in attesa dei permessi richiesti per avere un bambino. Sorridono, sorrido.

"Sta ancora rimpiangendo di non aver portato un parasole?" dice uno degli inseparabili.

"Come avete fatto a indovinare, Christopher-Sarika?" Preferiscono essere chiamati con lo stesso nome.

Hanno due parasole, me ne offrono uno. Giuro che non posso arrecare fastidio. Giurano che non è assolutamente alcun fastidio; anzi, li aiuterò a rendere la loro passeggiata più romantica. Ci giuriamo l'un l'altro, ma alla fine accetto il parasole con gratitudine. Il sole sembra già meno caldo, anche senza il parasole. Mentre la frescura mi avvolge nel suo bozzolo arioso, faccio mandare dal mio Assistente dei fiori per addolcire la *loro* giornata.

Mi avvio in un giro esplorativo. Le strutture municipali sono malandate, ma i negozi sono relativamente ben tenuti. Negozio di alimentari, fioreria, un'officina per riparazione droni, vari piccoli fornitori di cibo e un ristorante greco con un'atmosfera depressa. Mi rendo conto che stiamo ancora facendo tutto come lo facevano i nostri bisnonni, solo che lo facciamo in modi apparentemente diversi. Mentre analizzo questo pensiero profondo, l'Assistente mi avvisa che Tanaji sta arrivando dietro di me. Mi giro e la mia attenzione non si fissa su Tanaji, bensì sull'uomo che lo accompagna. È difficile descrivere come ci si sente in presenza di qualcuno e trovarsi comunque davanti solo la sua assenza.

Fatemelo dire in modo meno brillante. Ringo Singh Mann è alto un tot, ha una corporatura fatta così, dei tic fatti così, e lineamenti fatti così. Questi sono i banali dettagli fisici. Quello che non è banale è che i dettagli banali che si vedono sono tutto ciò che si ha. Guardare Ringo Singh Mann è come guardare nello specchio o un manichino. O meglio, anche un manichino ha profondità. Mann è tutto superficie. Piatto, opaco.

Mi dà un po' di nausea. So di essere ingiusto, ma questo non calma per niente la nausea. So che una volta i nostri antenati si incontravano e accoppiavano con solo questo livello di intimità. Ma devo essere onesto. Non ho solo la nausea. C'è anche una certa repulsione vertiginosa. Come se mi fosse stato regalato uno scorcio inatteso della nostra natura animale primordiale. Là, se non fosse per la grazia del fuoco nelle nostre menti, finiamo tutti. Mi aggrappo al parasole, assurdamente grato per la sua anima artificiale e arrendevole. Ammetto che i miei sentimenti non sono legittimi, ma se dobbiamo avere sentimenti onesti, allora devono essere ammessi anche quelli illegittimi.

"Molto piacere di conoscerla." Spero che il mio viso non stia rivelando quello che sento. L'Assistente alza uno specchio ma stranamente resisto e non sposto lo sguardo. In qualche modo sembra inappropriato.

Mann annuisce, guarda verso Tanaji. *Hahn hahn*, dice l'assistente sociale in modo incoraggiante, come se avessero un linguaggio privato personale. Tanaji mi offre il suo mezzo sorriso, come se sapesse qualcosa del mio turbamento interiore.

Tanaji ha persuaso Mann a mostrarmi il suo appartamento. Non è lontano dalla lavanderia automatica e iniziamo a camminare. Il marciapiede è troppo rovinato e sconnesso per usarlo, ma lui resta al bordo della strada. Tanaji dice con una risata che Mann è terrorizzato dalle automacchine. Le vetture senza guidatore a volte non riescono a vederlo. È stato colpito di striscio parecchie volte. Dico a Mann alcune cose rassicuranti in hindi, poi passo all'inglese quando diventa chiaro che lo parla correntemente.

"Voglio solo che le persone capiscano com'è essere come lei," dico a Mann.

"Vuole dare una sbirciata nella tua vita," traduce Tanaji dall'inglese all'inglese.

Lancio un'occhiata a Tanaji. "Iniziamo dal lavoro. Perché una lavanderia? Perché ha scelto di lavorare in una lavanderia automatica?"

"Stirare e piegare non possono essere automatizzati, perciò c'è ancora bisogno delle persone come me." Mann spiega che per le lavanderie automatiche è particolarmente difficile trovare persone disposte a stirare i vestiti. Si parla sempre di robot per stiratura e forse stirano perfettamente gli abiti degli scienziati nei laboratori, ma sono troppo costosi o troppo incompetenti per la maggior parte delle lavanderie automatiche. La carenza di mano d'opera era il motivo per cui la lavanderia era disposta a sobbarcarsi il disturbo di trattare con lui.

Ripensandoci, non è strano che così tanto del vecchio mondo continui a coesistere con il nuovo. Durante la Seconda guerra mondiale, la Wehrmacht tedesca invase la Russia con più cavalli di quanti non ne avesse Napoleone quando attaccò la nazione. L'amianto-cemento è stato vietato da decenni, ma le case a Chedda Nagar sono tutte fatte con quella roba.

"Ma senza quintessenza, come la indennizzano per il suo tempo?" chiedo.

"Ma la paga dev'essere molto piccola?" traduce Tanaji.

Vengo a sapere che la paga di Mann è in effetti misera. Non fraintendetemi, sono un patriota come tutti. La nostra grande terra ha molte virtù, ma pagare la gente adeguatamente per il lavoro manuale non è mai stata una di esse. Peggio, la paga non è una questione semplice. Vero, Mann ha un conto blockchain, ma per tutti gli scopi pratici è completamente dipendente dalla previdenza sociale per ogni transazione effettiva. È possibile accreditare direttamente sul suo conto (a condizione che la somma non superi un certo limite) ma le uscite – uno spazzolino da denti, un chilo di farina, un pacchetto di zucchero, una nuova catena per la bicicletta – richiedono del 'quod' o quintessenza-on-demand. Era la prima volta che sentivo quella parola e avevo avuto questo privilegio perché io e altri patrioti privilegiati come me ci inseriamo perfettamente nel sistema finanziario. Ma Mann non ha questo privilegio e il mondo non gli permette di dimenticarsene mai.

L'appartamento al secondo piano di Mann consiste in un soggiorno, una camera da letto e una piccola cucina. È tutto piccolo. Il soggiorno è piccolo. La camera è piccola. E la piccola cucina è piccola anche tra le cucine piccole. Ci sono gruppi di cose che sembrano accordarsi tra loro. Il tappeto sotto il tavolino in formica sta bene con due delle sedie economiche di legno. Le altre due sedie, però, sono del tipo in acciaio pieghevole e impilabile. Gran parte della mobilia, mi dice, gli è stata regalata da varie persone gentili negli anni. Ciò spiega l'arredamento scompagnato. Ma guardandosi intorno nelle stanze pulite e ordinate, si sente la pace e tranquillità che deriva dal desiderio non di presentare una bella faccia per gli estranei, ma di ordine fine a sé stesso.

Ama i vecchi giocattoli. La vetrina in soggiorno contiene ordinatamente un orsacchiotto, un Taj Mahal in pietra saponaria, pupazzi a molla da cruscotto e altre cianfrusaglie sbiadite dal tempo, non dal gioco. Mann indica un modellino antico di un aereo Air India, un regalo per suo padre da parte di qualche vecchio parente di Dubai, ai suoi tempi. I nonni di Mann mi fissano con un po' di disapprovazione dalla parete del soggiorno. Hanno l'aspetto che hanno tutti i nonni. Patrioti del ceto medio, buoni, onesti, gran lavoratori determinati a offrire ai loro figli una vita migliore. Mann mi dice che ciò includeva, tra le altre cose, dover tenere il modellino dell'aereo sotto chiave nella vetrina.

"È strano," dice Mann con un sorriso pensieroso. "Assomiglio più a mio nonno che a mio padre."

Spiega che i suoi genitori si erano sempre visti come parte della generazione moderna, che portava l'India nel XXI secolo.

Mann vede sé stesso come l'ultimo rappresentante di un'era precedente, non del futuro.

"I miei occhi erano destinati a vedere un mondo differente."

Non sembra triste. E c'è una verità biologica in quello che dice. Mi sono fatto fare da Mumtaz Mustafa un'analisi completa dell'evo-complex di Mann. Secondo Mustafa, Mann proviene dalle comunità Baluchi e Chitrali, gente che ha ereditato le terre settentrionali conquistate dal coraggioso Sikander e i suoi inarrestabili greci. Queste comunità mostrano un'ampia gamma nel colore degli occhi, a causa della grande varietà nei complessi genetici responsabili per la pigmentazione dell'iride. Ora, la primitiva convinzione del XX secolo che noi siamo i nostri geni è stata sconfessata del tutto, ma nel caso di Mann molta della responsabilità per la sua sfortunata situazione può essere data a loro. Le sue iridi, per metterla in modo crudo e inaccurato e schietto, continuano a cambiare in modo imprevedibile nel tempo. Perciò, niente quintessenza.

A dire il vero, Mustafa si imbestialisce alla parola 'quintessenza'. Mi ha ricordato più di una volta quanto sia 'mega stupido' dire 'quintessenza' quando il termine corretto è 'quiddità'. Mustafa ama dire la parola forse più della parola stessa, articolandola come se stesse per sputare un seme. Come per molte cose riguardanti la tecnologia, ha ragione. La quiddità è ciò che rende qualcosa diverso da tutto il resto. Un cammello ha la stessa quintessenza di un altro cammello, ma la sua quiddità è ciò che lo rende *questo* cammello e non quel cammello. È una differenza che fa una grande differenza per i filosofi e i fisici quantistici ma io non sono nessuno dei due, così decido di continuare con la parola mega stupida.

Mann spera che Mustafa capisca come far smettere alle sue iridi di mutare in continuazione. Ci sono dei trattamenti radicali in giro – il più fico prevede l'impianto di un terzo occhio semipermanente – ma Mann ha anche raggiunto un equilibrio stazionario. Non è propriamente contento, ma non è nemmeno scontento. È una piccola celebrità nel quartiere.

I suoi vicini si prendono cura di lui. Donano cibo, vestiti. Viene invitato a feste. Alcune persone trovano il suo disturbo sessualmente eccitante.

"Mi basta dare un'occhiata," dice, con un sorriso che finge di essere imbarazzato ma non può nascondere il piacere. "A volte è una seccatura."

Il vigoroso cenno di assenso di Tanaji attesta la verità animale dell'uomo. Forse l'attrazione è che Mann rappresenta un periodo più innocente. Ma per tutti i suoi proclami di ricevere molte attenzioni, posso vedere che Mann si sente solo. Diventa nervoso quando lo guardo, ma continua timidamente a cercare di incontrare i miei occhi. Gli dico che gli ho portato un regalo. Giusto un segno per ringraziarlo di aver condiviso il suo tempo. Salta su come un ragazzino per prendere la piccola scatola incartata di cioccolatini fondenti Nama, guarda Tanaji che annuisce. Il mio gesto ha portato piacere, ma poi vengo a sapere che a Mann non piace il cioccolato. Ha un cancro, gli hanno detto di evitare lo zucchero e la cura è complicata dal fatto che la nanomedicina dipende completamente dalla tecnologia della quintessenza. Tanaji si infila nello spazio e, tra un generoso prelievo dalla scatola e l'altro, mi informa che i cioccolatini sono deliziosi.

Rifletto che questo tipo di cose deve succedere a Mann di continuo. Per alcuni secondi mi meraviglio della complessità delle vite che i nostri opachi antenati devono aver condotto. Quante domande devono aver avuto bisogno di chiedersi l'un l'altro, tutto il tempo!

Mann dice di avere fame e guarda fiducioso Tanaji. L'assistente sociale gli dice di ordinare ciò che desidera. Il pasto è sul mio conto spese. Ridiamo tutti per nessun motivo in particolare.

Mann ha un dispositivo speciale per fare queste chiamate, Tanaji dice che si chiama Router. Assomiglia a uno di quei vecchi strani visori VR e si connette a un servizio fornito dalla IA della previdenza sociale. I dettagli sono bizantini, ma capisco che il Router in pratica permette a Mann e al mondo di fingere che lui abbia la quintessenza e lo rende 'visibile' nel mondo digitale, per lo meno per piccole transazioni e brevi periodi. Guardo Mann connettersi e ordinare il cibo. Inizia in modo autorevole, dicendo che ha ospiti importanti, ma poi ride e passa a un tono più calmo. Appena ha terminato, mette subito via il Router.

La sua cautela mi ricorda i soldati feriti che ho intervistato dopo la guerra indo-cinese. Scherzavano e facevano i buffoni tra di loro con le loro nuove protesi su misura, ma in mia presenza diventavano improvvisamente imbarazzati, minimizzando i movimenti degli arti artificiali e agendo come se i loro pseudopodi appartenessero a qualcun altro. All'improvviso capisco, con la luminosa chiarezza di un lampo che svela un terreno buio, che Mann è un paraplegico digitale e che il nostro mondo non ha in realtà un modo per gestire la sua situazione.

Scopriamo che ci sono dei problemi con l'ordine. Da un po' di tempo il Router non viene aggiornato e, con tutte le nuove regole di sicurezza eccetera, la tecnica della pseudo-quintessenza fallisce. Mentre Tanaji armeggia con il Router, pago per il Dal Fry, il Sogno della camera rossa (un piatto a base di fagioli molto speziato, solo per intestini esperti e curiosi), la Dottrina paradisiaca del pollo confuciano (come Kierkegaard, un piacere acquisito), l'Ingiustizia subita da Dou E (funghi con una base di Maggi Noodle, altamente consigliati), accompagnati da porzioni abbondanti di riso fritto e per terminare, stranamente, solo due peda. Studiamo i dolci oblunghi dal colore dorato. Noi siamo tre, ma ci sono solo due peda.

"Sirji, io non ne voglio," dice Mann a Tanaji, sfregandosi la pancia. "Devo evitare lo zucchero."

Tanaji mi lancia uno sguardo pieno di significato. Il ristorante aveva commesso un semplice errore, ma era il tipo di errore che non sarebbe mai successo se Mann avesse avuto quintessenza. L'IA che lo gestiva non poteva vederlo.

L'Assistente mi informa che non è stato in grado di scattare fotografie perché le nuove regole di sicurezza richiedono che tutte le fotografie con persone vengano taggate. La regola ci renderà più sicuri, perciò quella parte è facile da comprendere, ma chi spiegherà al software che tagga che Mann è l'eccezione alla regola? Ci vuole un considerevole uso di risorse per sistemare la cosa e, quando il Router è stato aggiornato e le foto sono state fatte, è piuttosto tardi.

C'è un altro avviso del mio Assistente. Sunny Mazumdar è stata arrestata per eversione. I suoi amici stanno facendo una petizione, desidero firmarla? Non ho problemi a firmarla, ma non c'è bisogno! Sono certo che è tutto un malinteso e il dottor Mazumdar verrà rilasciato presto. Equo processo eccetera.

Tanaji dice che resta lì ad ascoltare alcune canzoni hindi – dice che Mann ha del vecchio hardware audio in grado di produrre armonie delicate che i dispositivi moderni non sono proprio in grado di fare. Dico a Mann che l'articolo potrebbe attirare un po' l'attenzione su di lui, ma si limita a stringersi nelle spalle. I suoi occhi sono fissi sui miei. Li saluto. Mann si alza, mi accompagna attraverso la stanza, poi si ferma sulla porta guardandomi scendere gli scalini. Alzo lo sguardo dal fondo delle scale, incontro i suoi occhi, articolo con le labbra un altro addio ed esco incontro alla automacchina. Anche mentre scrivo queste parole, posso sentire i suoi occhi vivi su di me.

Microbiota e le masse: una storia d'amore

di S.B. Divya

Gli odori della terra – terriccio, polline, compost, gli effluvi delle foglie – permeavano l'interno della casa a tenuta stagna di Moena Sivaram. Era in piedi vicino all'angolo sud-est a nebulizzare le bromeliacee novizie. Le epifite si aggrappavano al tronco di un guanacaste, la cui chioma si estendeva verso il soffitto trasparente formato da SmartWindow ombreggiando tutto ciò che stava sotto.

Moena sussurrò alle piante: "Amma è qui, piccoline. Con me siete al sicuro, ma dovete far crescere quelle radici." Vista la sua vita isolata, questi sarebbero stati i suoi unici figli.

Camminò scalza fino al soleggiato agrumeto nell'ala occidentale della casa. Il suolo sotto i suoi piedi cambiò da fresco e umido a duro e sabbioso. eApi ronzavano tra i fiori. Canticchiava in armonia con esse a bocca chiusa, una canzone carnatica sugli innamorati vecchia di un secolo. Il profumo inebriante dei fiori d'arancio e di lime la colmò e le fece cantare anche il sangue. Questa era casa; questa e non i giardini tradizionali di gelsomini e rose di Bangalore; questa, dove gli occhi non le lacrimavano e il naso non le prudeva.

Dalle SmartWindow che ricoprivano le pareti entrava la luce solare diffusa. Un rettangolo risaltava come un diamante opaco in un pendente altrimenti splendente. Moena tirò fuori il tablet dalla tasca e aprì il software diagnostico. Lettere rosse le diedero cattive notizie: anomalie nei filtri dell'aria e della luce.

Le seconde non erano importanti. Le piante avrebbero ricevuto abbastanza sole dalle finestre funzionanti. Le prime, invece, volevano dire che l'aria esterna si era infiltrata nella casa.

La gola di Moena si chiuse. Il cuore batteva a mille. *Stai calma!* Ma le mani non volevano ascoltare, stringendosi l'una all'altra, le dita contorte come rampicanti attorno ai rami. Non poteva respirare! Tutti quei microbi: li immaginò invadere il suo santuario, quei procarioti unicellulari striscianti.

Rabbrividì, si lasciò cadere a terra, restò prona. La guancia toccò l'amata terra. Terra sicura. *Inspira! Espira! Ancora!* Girò la testa, allungò la lingua e leccò. Gli esteri potenti del suo bioma domestico fecero la loro magia, prendendo il controllo delle ruote dei criceti del suo cervello e azionando i freni.

Le mani si aprirono. Le scapole ricaddero indietro. Il cuore rallentò. *Stupido cervello. Possiamo gestire la situazione.*

Le eApi erano d'accordo. "Sì, sì, sì," cantarono.

Moena andò all'armadietto delle scorte. Al suo interno la maschera per filtrare l'aria sembrava un alieno insettoide: plastica fumé attorno agli occhi e tre cilindri sporgenti sulla zona di bocca e naso. Moena la indossò. L'aria pulita non aveva gli odori rassicuranti di casa, ma per lo meno lei era protetta.

Sigillò la finestra incriminata con della plastica spessa e del nastro adesivo, poi ci passò sopra il sensore a carrello. *Bene!* Adesso tutta l'aria fluiva dall'interno verso l'esterno, così come doveva essere. Mandò un messaggio alla SmartWindows Incorporated, chiedendo un tecnico e segnalando la richiesta come urgente.

Rahul il tecnico assomigliava alla pornostar preferita di Moena: jeans sbiaditi, maglietta bianca stretta, pelle color cannella, riccioli neri da ragazzino. Ammirò l'immagine sul tablet, presa dalla telecamera della porta. Peccato non poterlo toccare. Arrossì. Lo spazio tra le gambe si restrinse. *Non adesso e non lui, idiota di un corpo.* Nessun uomo o donna infestati da microbiota esterno.

Si schiaffeggiò lievemente le guance ed esalò un respiro caldo.

Syed, il suo uomo all'esterno, era via per il matrimonio di suo cugino di secondo grado a Mysore. Avrebbe dovuto occuparsi di Rahul di persona.

"Per favore attenda là," disse, una risposta sonora ritardata al ronzio del citofono.

Moena aprì l'armadietto delle scorte e fece una smorfia alla tuta protettiva grigia appesa in fondo. Puzzava di plastica industriale e di esteri di fabbrica. Prese una manciata di terra e la sparse nella tuta. Poi la indossò assieme alla maschera.

Entrò nell'ingresso/camera stagna, chiuse le guarnizioni della porta interna e uscì. Rahul fece solo un mezzo passo all'indietro, bisognava dargliene atto. I suoi occhi scuri si allargarono come un bocciolo che si apre alla pioggia. Domande germogliarono e appassirono sulle sue labbra – aperte a mostrare i denti teneramente sorti – finché non disse: "Signorina... Sivaram?"

"Sì. Mi segua, prego," disse Moena.

Lo guidò attraverso il terreno brullo e coperto di erbacce del suo appezzamento. Girarono attorno ai muri spessi in argilla della casa per arrivare alla SmartWindow guasta. Rahul collegò ad essa il suo computer con un lungo cavo, simile a un rampicante tranne che per il colore grigio. Si sedette per terra e iniziò a digitare.

"I filtri di luce e aria sono impostati sugli estremi opposti," disse. Parlava inglese con i toni ben arrotondati di un indiano del ceto medio, istruito. "La maggior parte delle persone usano queste finestre per ridurre gli ultravioletti e permettere comunque all'aria di circolare nella casa."

Io non sono la maggioranza delle persone. Ad alta voce: "Non parla come un tecnico delle riparazioni."

Rahul sorrise. "Sono un I.A.C., un ingegnere per le applicazioni sul campo. Facciamo riparazioni ma abbiamo anche una formazione tecnica." Tacque, guardandola strizzando gli occhi. "Mi dica, lei è *la* Moena Sivaram?"

"Sì."

"La sua tesi sul biorisanamento dell'acqua dolce era incredibile. Come mai non ha pubblicato altro da allora?"

Moena restò a bocca aperta dietro la maschera. "Ma chi è lei?"

"Mi spiace, avrei dovuto spiegare. Sono un volontario del Gruppo Ecologico Hariharan. Hanno preso il suo modello e lo hanno usato contro l'inquinamento locale dell'acqua. È stato un grande successo. Lei è famosa tra di noi. Stavo pensando che, forse, ha un laboratorio in casa, viste le impostazioni delle finestre."

Moena barcollò davanti alla ortogonalità della domanda e guardò il proprio riflesso nella SmartWindow. La tuta sembrava l'involucro vuoto di una crisalide. Se solo avesse potuto emergere come una meravigliosa farfalla, avrebbe anche potuto lasciare Rahul senza parole.

"Sto facendo esperimenti in casa," ammise. "Indosso la tuta per mantenere l'ambiente il più isolato possibile."

"Posso – voglio dire, se non è troppo disturbo – posso vedere?"

Moena scosse la testa come una foglia impazzita al vento. Rahul... dentro casa sua? Dentro di lei? Possibilità le roteavano nella mente, stupende e terrificanti. *Impossibile!*

"No, certo che no." Si girò di nuovo verso il computer. "Scusi la domanda."

Moena allungò la mano verso di lui, poi la tirò indietro. Non aveva diritti sul suo corpo.

Il sole pomeridiano brillava alto nel cielo estivo mentre il silenzio si allungava. Nella tuta di Moena il calore aumentava. La maglia le si incollava al busto. Rivoli di sudore le scendevano sul collo e si raccoglievano all'altezza della cintura dei pantaloncini. Sedeva immobile, immedesimandosi nell'atman di un tronco d'albero.

"Aha!" disse finalmente Rahul.

La finestra si schiarì fino alla trasparenza perfetta. Rahul la reinstallò e mise via il computer. Le passò un cubo di memoria.

"Le consiglio di aggiornare tutte le finestre con questa versione del software. Il problema è che le sue impostazioni dei filtri sono inferiori alla misura dei virus. Il vecchio software continuava a restare invischiato in una routine di interrupt e finiva per bloccarsi. Questa versione dovrebbe impedire che accada."

"Grazie," disse Moena. Una parte di lei desiderava che tutte le finestre si guastassero, una volta alla settimana, così che Rahul potesse tornare.

"La ditta fatturerà direttamente a lei. Buona fortuna con la sua ricerca."

Moena annuì. La maschera dondolò. Rahul uscì dal cancello principale, chiudendolo dietro di sé. Era sola.

Il bagno di sterilizzazione non era mai sembrato così noioso. Quando fu completamente all'interno, Moena si strappò la maschera e fece dei profondi respiri di sollievo. Si tolse la tuta sudata, lasciandola cadere spiegazzata sul pavimento.

Il terriccio si infilò negli spazi tra le sue dita dei piedi nude. Foglie e fronde le sfiorarono le mani mentre andava – quasi correva – verso la camera da letto. Era più o meno come quando i suoi genitori erano vivi: un letto a una piazza, un armadio stretto dipinto di giallo, una scrivania abbinata con degli scaffali sopra di essa. L'eccezione era la bara.

Il contenitore in formato per adulti stava tra il letto e la finestra sbarrata della stanza. Il dispositivo in realtà si chiamava 'Virtual Reality Recumbent Booth' ma il mondo aveva deciso che era troppo ingombrante. Moena era d'accordo.

Sfogliò le immagini predefinite sotto 'maschio'. Questo aveva le sopracciglia che sembravano scarafaggi. Quello era troppo pallido. Dozzine erano ritoccate con occhi azzurri e capelli biondi. Si fermò davanti a un viso che assomigliava abbastanza a quello di Rahul. I capelli non erano abbastanza ricci e gli occhi troppo grandi, ma avrebbe potuto regolarli quando il suo corpo non stava pulsando dal desiderio.

Le pareti interne della bara le si avvicinarono, passandole le mani – le mani *di lui* – sul corpo, soffiandole un respiro caldo sul collo, premendosi – *lui!* – nei suoi spazi vuoti.

La tensione voleva uno sfogo, ma la mente di Moena si rifiutava di cadere nell'illusione. Interruppe la sessione.

Che sensazioni avrebbe dato un amante in carne e ossa? Fremette. *Pensa alla microflora! Lo scambio di molto più che fluidi.* E dove sarebbe accaduto? Qui, nel suo letto? Nel santuario della sua casa? Il bioma sarebbe stato corrotto e lei avrebbe perso anni di duro lavoro. *Idiota! Dimenticati di lui!*

Ma Rahul rimaneva nei suoi pensieri, come una scheggia che, più lei cercava di toglierla, più si infilava a fondo. Moena chiamò l'unica amica che le era rimasta dai tempi dei giorni passati all'esterno: la sua compagna di università, adesso professoressa Das.

L'ampio viso marrone di Ananya comparve sullo schermo del tablet accompagnato dal frastuono dei bambini.

"Lasciami andare in un posto tranquillo."

"Devi salvarmi," disse Moena, dopo che la sua amica si era spostata.

Ananya alzò un sopracciglio. "Ti serve qualche nuova coltura?"

"No. I batteri non mi possono aiutare. Sono stata infettata da un uomo, un meraviglioso esemplare di *Homo sapiens* maschio!"

"Infettata? Cosa? Hai fatto sesso con qualcuno?"

Moena rise davanti all'espressione inorridita della sua amica. "No. Non l'ho toccato. Mmmmm... ma voglio farlo. Sono egoista a restarmene qui? A usare la mia ricerca per mio beneficio personale e non per il mondo?"

"Cosa? Mo, dici cose senza senso. Stai bene? Come sta il tuo bioma?"

"I tesorini verdeggianti stanno bene. I rampicanti e il microbiota stanno bene. I miei esami del sangue erano nella norma il mese scorso. Ma il mio cuore... il mio cuore è assetato di compagnia! Ha detto che sono famosa. Stanno usando la mia tesi. Dovrei essere là fuori, ad aiutarli? A combattere per il bene?"

"Primo: non sei egoista se ti proteggi da una malattia cronica. Secondo: sei brillante e dovresti pubblicare i tuoi risultati.

Terzo: chi è questo tizio e come ha fatto ad affascinarti in questo modo?"

"Si chiama Rahul. Tecnico delle finestre e sommo eco-guerriero, con una pelle come cremoso burro di cacao."

L'amica alzò gli occhi al cielo. "Datti una calmata. Non tocchi un altro essere umano da più di cinque anni. Vuoi mettere tutto a repentaglio per lui?" La sua espressione si addolcì. "Se ti ammali di nuovo, lo dovrai lasciare."

"Ponti, passaggi, eccetera, cara professoressa. E poi, non posso essere me stessa con lui perciò questa storia d'amore non durerà. Breve, torrida, finita!"

"In che senso?"

"Non vorrà stare con Moena Sivaram, benestante eccentrica e vittima di circostanze tragiche. Dovrò inventarmi un'identità segreta ordinaria, qualcuno adeguato alla sua posizione sociale."

"Una menzogna non è una buona base per l'amore."

"Mi limiterò alla passione, non amore. Allora, posso avere la tua benedizione?"

"No. Sì. Non so," farfugliò Ananya. "Solo... tienimi informata, okay? Sono preoccupata."

Moena acconsentì e terminò la chiamata. Le sue dita si avvicinarono alla tastiera, poi si piegarono allontanandosi, come le foglie di una *Mimosa pudica*: non toccatemi. Le parole dette da sua madre dieci anni prima la tormentavano.

"Quando sei maggiorenne, Moena, ti troveremo un bel ragazzo da sposare. O te lo troverai da sola, ma ricordati una cosa: gli uomini desiderano le donne che tengono loro testa ma senza alzarsi troppo. Non vogliono donne più intelligenti o più ricche o più famose. Meglio che ti dimentichi dei ragazzi e del matrimonio finché non hai una tua misura."

Più intelligente. Più ricca. Più famosa. Rahul non aveva un dottorato. Rahul lavorava per vivere. Il nome di Rahul non aveva mai incendiato i titoli dei giornali.

Moena si inventò la ragazza giusta per l'amore di Rahul. Meena Sivaraman (abbastanza simile da far sì che Moena rispondesse): ceto medio, moderatamente istruita, vestita con modestia. Una ragazza come si deve, seria, *sana*, con una treccia nera e un bindi.

Il respiro veniva facile. Le dita scorsero sulla tastiera. Due giorni dopo, 'Meena' aveva un appuntamento con Rahul in un bar per parlare della possibilità di fare volontariato.

Il giorno dell'incontro, Moena rifiutò tre diversi outfit: un sari tradizionale (troppo provinciale), la salwar kamiz di una lontana zia (troppo vistosa) e un vestito dei tempi dell'università a Londra (troppo occidentale). Vestita con jeans e un kurti di cotone con le maniche corte, uscì dalla casa.

Non era certa di chi fossero gli occhi più spalancati, i suoi o quelli di Syed, mentre si fiondava sul sedile posteriore dell'automobile.

"È sicura, signora?" chiese per la decima volta, scrutandola dal sedile del guidatore.

Con il cuore in tumulto, le mani sudate e il fiato corto, disse: "Sì. Guida, per favore."

Percorsero strade bordate da alberi, oltrepassarono alveari altissimi di appartamenti e file claustrofobiche di negozi. L'aria condizionata della macchina era impostata su ricircolo, ma gli odori di Bangalore si insinuavano all'interno attraverso guarnizioni imperfette. La gola di Moena si chiuse. Strinse i ciuffi di basilico sacro che aveva portato, schiacciando le foglie delicate. Rilasciarono un aroma pungente, calmante. Ne strappò due e se le infilò nelle narici. *Meglio.*

L'auto sbandò verso destra, si avvicinò al cordolo e si fermò.

"Il posto è questo," disse Syed. "Ma possiamo andare a casa, signora. La sua salute è più importante di qualsiasi altra cosa."

"Grazie, Syed. Andrà tutto bene. Altrimenti prometto di chiamarti."

Moena scese e prese la prima boccata di aria pura di città in cinque anni. La polvere le assalì le narici, asciugando i minuscoli peli e facendola starnutire. Rombanti camion diesel sputavano fumo nero. Un rivolo di rifiuti marci e liquame putrescente attraversava il tutto. Ebbe un conato di vomito.

Corpi passavano oltre lungo le lastre irregolari del marciapiede. Puzzavano di olio caldo, sudore, legno di sandalo, pesce, gelsomino, sesso. Un cane randagio si spostò trotterellando da un mucchio di spazzatura a una banana mangiucchiata. Una mosca ronzò nell'orecchio di Moena, solleticandolo prima di volare via.

Come era possibile per chiunque vivere così? Come aveva fatto lei, per i primi venticinque anni della sua vita? Poteva quasi sentire gli effluvi penetrarle nei polmoni, inquinandole il sangue. Si costrinse a inspirare una seconda volta. *Stai dritta!* Spalle indietro, mento alto, mani aperte: *affronta la città come tutti gli altri.*

Pubblicità ricoprivano il basso muro in blocchi di cemento alla sua destra, i colori sbiaditi dalla pioggia, i bordi sfilacciati e strappati. Dall'altra parte, alberi di fuoco bordavano il cortile, facendo ombra sui clienti del caffè all'interno. Scrutò la folla. Dov'era Rahul?

Moena si fece strada tra i tavoli, attenta a non toccare nessuna cosa o persona o pianta. Vide i capelli ricci e la maglia bianca (non indossava altro?) di Rahul nell'angolo in fondo, a un tavolo cosparso di polline dei fiori soprastanti. Si strinse il naso per bloccare uno starnuto.

"Rahul Madhavan?" Cercò di parlare come se non lo avesse mai incontrato prima.

"Sì. Lei deve essere Meena. Prego, si sieda. Posso ordinarle un caffè?"

Moena inghiottì la repulsione – caffè non fatto in casa! – e si sforzò di sorridere. "Grazie."

"Vorrebbe fare la volontaria per il G.E.H. e fare qualche azione ecologica, giusto? Lasci che le spieghi cosa facciamo."

Rahul iniziò un monologo di quindici minuti con parole che erano tanto familiari quanto l'odore dell'humus umido. Parlò di inquinamento delle acque, risanamento, semina di piante e batteri; di sforzo comunitario e citizen science; di lavorare con la terra e non contro di essa. Le sue mani si muovevano creando forme organiche – niente bordi netti – e le punte delle sue dita si univano e separavano velocemente come un baccello maturo.

Moena guardò, ascoltò, starnutì. Si passò un fazzoletto sbiancato con la candeggina sotto il naso gocciolante e starnutì di nuovo. Annuì. Sorrise. Starnutì. Il suo caffè arrivò e si raffreddò. Rimase intonso, ma lo stesso successe a quello di Rahul.

"Come le sembra? Qualcosa in cui si può impegnare?"

"Certamente. Una volta alla settimana. Nessun problema."

I problemi le facevano ingarbugliare i pensieri più rapidamente di quanto non riuscisse a potarli.

"Ottimo! Le manderò le informazioni per l'iniziativa della prossima settimana."

"Perché non è biologo?"

"Scusi?"

Non dovresti saperlo! "Voglio dire, come mai è un volontario e non lavora per il G.E.H.? Sembra molto competente in materia."

"Sono troppo vecchio?" Fece il suo sorriso storto. "Avevo già preso una laurea in ingegneria quando ho iniziato a interessarmi al risanamento. Ho più di trent'anni. Non posso certo competere negli esami di ammissione. E lei? Cosa la ha fatta avvicinare?"

"Ho... un'amica. È stata male per lungo tempo e in parte la causa erano la nostra acqua e la nostra aria. Voglio fare qualcosa per lei – per tutti – per migliorare le cose."

"Magnifico! Allora ci vediamo la prossima settimana."

Le porse la mano.

Stringila! Moena porse la sua, lasciò che le dita di lui si avvolgessero intorno alle proprie. Il suo palmo era caldo e liscio, come la corteccia di eucalipto sotto il sole. Il brivido del contatto le corse lungo il braccio e si diffuse, formicolando, in tutto il resto del corpo. *Tutto, adesso!* Il cuore si mise a correre, la bocca le si seccò. Il desiderio prese forza, passando da venticello a tornado. Arrossì. Lui poteva vederlo? Poteva sentire la sua agitazione?

Rahul mollò la presa.

Uscirono assieme dal bar.

Syed la venne a prendere.

Il passaggio fino a casa si prolungò, una tortura interminabile di traffico ringhioso, mendicanti emaciati e abbastanza pioggia da creare striature sui finestrini impolverati.

Moena incontrò Rahul e la manciata di altri volontari sulle rive di un lago oblungo situato a sud-est della città. Si sentiva nuda senza la sua tuta protettiva mentre si avvicinava alle sponde melmose. Tronchi bianchi come ossa erano cosparsi lungo la linea di galleggiamento. Duecentocinquanta metri sulla sinistra, una carcassa rugginosa di metallo spingeva un pistone su e giù. Il tamburellare del motore copriva il ronzio degli sciami di insetti.

Un'ondata di aria fetida passò su Moena. Lei barcollò all'indietro, si inginocchiò e vomitò il pranzo in un gruppetto di cespugli lunghi e sottili.

"Mi spiace. Avrei dovuto avvertirla." Rahul era in piedi vicino a lei. Allungò una maschera di carta azzurra. "Metta questa. È spalmata con mentolo."

Moena la accettò con mani tremanti. L'odore astringente la soffocò, spremendole lacrime dagli angoli degli occhi, ma lo stomaco si calmò.

"Cos'è questo posto?"

"Il lago Agara," disse Rahul. "Pieno di metalli industriali, plastiche e reflui zootecnici."

Moena si alzò e accarezzò una foglia. Il cespuglio era una pianta giovane di neem, macchiato di marrone, giallo e nero.

"Poverino," mormorò. "Hai bisogno di aiuto."

Le pupille di Rahul si dilatarono. La fronte si increspò.

Moena si strinse nelle spalle. "Mi sono sempre sentita più a mio agio con le piante che con le persone."

La luce del sole brillò, rendendo le iridi di Rahul color del miele. "Anch'io."

La guidò sulle rive del lago, la mano leggera sul fondo della schiena, intima ma allo stesso tempo no.

I volontari avevano compiti diversi. Quello di Moena era semplice: raccogliere campioni di terriccio e acqua per le analisi.

Sulla superficie dell'acqua una schiuma bianca creava macchie di Rorschach. Onde alte un centimetro lambivano il fango marrone giallastro. Un pesce morto stava rigonfio in superficie alcuni metri al largo.

Il senso di colpa le stringeva il petto con radici sottili. L'isolamento le aveva ridato la salute, ma a che prezzo? Quando il mondo era diventato così putrido?

Moena prese una provetta tra pollice e indice come se fosse un insetto che si dimenava. Guanti. Stivali. Tuta di gomma. Erano tutte protezioni in dotazione standard che avevano usato alla scuola di specializzazione, ma i vigilantes ecologici – soprattutto qui in India – non avevano quel tipo di risorse. *Fallo! Immergi la mano!*

Entrò lentamente nel lago. L'acqua tiepida le inzuppò le scarpe e i calzini e su lungo i pantaloni. Moena inghiottì un singhiozzo. Prese una posizione stabile e si chinò. I muscoli tremarono. *Dentro!* Nel primo tentativo metà dell'acqua uscì dalla provetta. *Di nuovo!* Il secondo tentativo andò meglio e il quinto prese quasi tutto il campione previsto.

Si raddrizzò, guardando lungo le sponde fangose. Rahul annuì. L'orgoglio germogliò nel suo cuore, piccolo e pieno di vita.

Due ore dopo, i volontari veterani se ne andarono. Moena rimase in piedi di fianco a Rahul mentre metteva i campioni presi da lei nel bagagliaio della macchina. Anche lui aveva macchie di schiuma del lago. Il sudore gli bagnava i capelli. Lo sporco gli ricopriva le unghie e le cuticole. Le passò una bottiglia d'acqua da una borsa frigo.

Moena ne tracannò metà in pochi secondi. Non fece molto per calmare il dolore che le cresceva dietro agli occhi. I seni paranasali pulsavano.

Rahul aggrottò la fronte. "Sta bene?" Fece un cenno verso le braccia di Moena.

Macchie rosse fiorivano ovunque gli schizzi di acqua del lago l'avevano toccata.

"Allergie," disse lei. "Passerà." *Bugiarda, bugiarda!*

"Allora la ringrazio il doppio di averci aiutati. Non molti possono affrontare questo tipo di lavoro e ancora meno sacrificherebbero la loro salute. La rivedrò... cioè, la rivedremo la prossima volta?"

"Sì."

Moena attese di essere in macchina per soffiarsi il naso.

Syed guardò il suo riflesso nello specchietto retrovisore. "Signora, perché si sta facendo questo?"

"Senso di colpa, Syed! E amore. Amore per la mia gente, quella verde e quella di carne e quella che è possibile vedere solo al microscopio. Senso di colpa per essere stata via troppo a lungo."

La settimana successiva, Moena portò le proprie provette – vuote e sterili – infilate nelle tasche dei jeans. Indossava una leggera kamiz di cotone con le maniche lunghe. Chiazze coperte di croste le decoravano la pelle, le conseguenze della sessione precedente. Mentre lavorava, raccolse dei campioni di acqua e terreno per sé. Rahul poteva anche essere stato il catalizzatore di questa follia, ma il biota era il reagente che la manteneva viva.

Guardò Rahul mentre lavorava alle vasche delle sostanze nutritive e alle pompe. Aveva la fronte marrone increspata per la concentrazione, la mascella rilassata e le labbra aperte, giusto abbastanza per uno scorcio di lingua rosa. Melma verde gli macchiava gli stivali e la parte inferiore dei jeans. *Uomo coraggioso, adorabile.*

Lui alzò lo sguardo dal palmare, si accorse che lo stava fissando. Le guance di Moena si arrossarono mentre le mandava un sorriso, piccolo e consapevole. *Concentrati!* Il ricordo della sua espressione scese attraverso lo stomaco, più in basso, riscaldandola, un reattore esotermico tutto suo.

Anche questa volta lei e Rahul finirono il lavoro per ultimi. Syed non era ancora tornato dalla pausa per il tè. Stava per mandargli un messaggio quando Rahul disse sei parole magiche: "Le farebbe piacere prendere un caffè?"

La quindicenne interiore di Moena saltò dalla gioia, fece la ruota, cantò per il mondo. Un attacco di tosse impedì al suo sé adulto di rispondere.

Boccheggiando rispose: "Sì."

Lasciò di nuovo il caffè intonso. Se Rahul lo notò, non fece commenti, ma le chiese di andare fuori a cena. *Cena – evviva!* E però non ancora. *Idiota!* Se non mangiasse niente lui se ne accorgerebbe. Il cibo sarebbe pieno di microflora, vista la varietà dei cittadini di Bangalore. Lo stomaco le si rivoltò all'idea. Ma lo avrebbe fatto – per Rahul, per la possibilità di fertilizzare i semi della loro relazione – qualsiasi cosa per quello.

"Com'è andato l'appuntamento?" chiese Ananya, con un sorrisino compiaciuto.

"Benissimo! Ho passato il resto della notte sul water, " disse Moena. "Ma ne è valso ogni minuto. Rahul è così appassionato riguardo al suo lavoro. Immaginati com'è a letto!"

Il sorriso svanì dal viso della sua amica. "Non scherzare! Non puoi continuare a rischiare la tua salute per questo. Dovresti dirgli la verità."

"Ma mi vuole vedere ancora."

"Smetti di prenderlo in giro!"

"Non posso. E poi, mi ha incartata in un bel pacchettino."

"Oh, Mo, ti sei innamorata?"

"Mi sto ancora innamorando, portata dal vento, come foglie nell'autunno di Cambridge. Non potrà mai sapere chi sono davvero o mi farebbe a pezzettini."

"Lo stai sottovalutando. Quello oppure è un idiota che non ti merita."

"Dovresti vedere le colture che sto prendendo dal lago."

"Cosa? Non cambiare argomento!"

"Penso di aver capito come migliorare la degradazione dei policarbonati. Dobbiamo cambiare i livelli di azoto nella miscela nutriente. Oh, e ho combinato alcune sequenze enzimatiche del *Geotrichum candidum* nel *flaviobacterium* che ha funzionato meglio fino ad oggi."

"Davvero? Sei riuscita a unire dei geni fungini e i batteri sono sopravvissuti? Mostrami i dati."

Passarono il resto della conversazione discutendo di chimica organica e se la soluzione migliore fosse un ceppo diverso o un secondo ceppo. Moena andò a dormire sognando di curare i malanni dell'acqua di Bangalore. Quale miglior pegno d'amore poteva offrire a Rahul?

Le giovani bromeliacee erano appassite. Le foglie un tempo verde scuro erano sbiadite, le punte secche. Nelle cavità più in ombra il terriccio della casa odorava di cavoli marci. Due delle eApi continuavano a schiantarsi contro la SmartWindow come degli ubriachi dalle ali frenetiche.

Moena estrasse campioni dalla superficie e dal sottosuolo e li passò nel sequenzatore di DNA. I batteri del lago si erano infiltrati nel suo santuario. Stavano vincendo.

Tossì sopra la spalla e si girò di nuovo verso l'oculare. Erano settimane che il naso non smetteva di colarle. Di notte, le giunture le facevano male. Il software massaggiatore della bara non faceva molto per diminuire il dolore.

Ma. Ma! La notte scorsa, cinque settimane dopo il loro primo appuntamento e dopo molti altri incontri, lei e Rahul si erano baciati. Glorioso, umido scambio di saliva e batteri! Erano passati dieci anni dal suo ultimo ragazzo a Cambridge. Si era dimenticata quanto potesse essere deliziosa la danza di labbra e lingue.

Rahul aveva sussurrato della sua nascente passione: *Non c'è nessuno al mondo come te. Come ti muovi, come parli – sei deliziosa. Sei la mia splendida orchidea che fiorisce una volta sola.*

Quelle parole! Quella metafora!

La pelle dell'interno coscia le bruciava, irritata dalle numerose sessioni con il Rahul-della-bara-virtuale. Dieci volte dieci volte dieci... l'ordine di grandezza non aveva importanza. La soddisfazione surrogata non sarebbe mai potuta bastare. Aveva bisogno della realtà.

Moena fece danzare le dita coperte dal guanto sul ripiano sterile. Capsule di Petri e bottiglie di reagenti riempivano il frigo con la porta in vetro alla sua sinistra. Un'accozzaglia di colture vive e supporti per provette copriva la superficie alla sua destra, arrivando fino all'editor genomico CRISPR.

Le serviva una soluzione per risanare il lago facendolo tornare pulito ma anche per risanare il suo stesso bioma. Ogni incursione nel mondo esterno – ogni stretta di mano e bacio con Rahul – portavano nuovi avversari unicellulari in casa.

Porre fine ai contatti con lui? L'idea era una brutta mosca che camminava in punta di piedi attraverso i peli di una *Dionaea muscipula*. Scatta, intrappola, digerisci! Rendila inesistente.

Uscì dal laboratorio e andò nell'ala meridionale della casa. La sabbia sotto i piedi scalzi l'aiutava a pensare. La curva artritica che le piegava le dita non era importante. *Sistema la casa, sistema te stessa.* Con un tampone prese un campione dalle foglie di un arancio nano ricoperto di macchie gialle e nere.

"*Sbagliato. Sbagliato. Sbagliato,*" ronzarono le api.

Anni per ottenere l'equilibrio. Settimane per distruggerlo. Così ingiusto! La bambina di cinque anni dentro Moena pestò i piedi e diede in escandescenze e fece un'enorme scenata. Lacrime scorsero. Le asciugò, bagnando il tampone, contaminandolo. *Idiota!*

Barcollò fino al boschetto di alte *Dieffenbachia* e si rannicchiò nell'ombra delle loro ampie foglie screziate. La sua guancia sprofondò nel terriccio. Allungò la lingua – *aspetta!* Quanta microflora benefica conteneva ancora il terriccio? Era amico o nemico?

Leccare o non leccare? Questo è il dilemma! Se sia più nobile nella mente soffrire la sporcizia e il marciume della vita all'esterno o prender – antibiotici, ma aveva troppe sillabe – contro un mare di – *accidenti*. Aveva perso l'analogia.

Moena ridacchiò.

Sbatté la testa contro il terreno. Pazzia. La sua vecchia amica era arrivata a farle visita. Facciamo due chiacchiere bevendo un chai. Normale o masala?

Ananya aveva lasciato tre messaggi, uno per ciascuna chiamata che Moena aveva ignorato.

Presto. Presto avrebbe risposto. *Vicina!* Era così vicina alla risposta. Le prudeva la testa. Quando si era lavata l'ultima volta? Non importante. *Concentrati! Lì!* Quel frammento avrebbe trasformato il suoi batteri modificati in microbelve divora-ossigeno. Addio, plastiche! Nitrati come sottoprodotto? Sì grazie, con sopra acido citrico, ma solo un pizzico. Troppo sarebbe tossico.

Moena scaricò il modello nel simulatore di vita artificiale. Macina, su! Dammi una buona notizia! Per favore, per favore, fai che questa combinazione sia quella magica, quella stabile.

Il telefono le cantò quella vecchia canzone carnatica sugli innamorati. Aveva assegnato la suoneria al numero di Rahul. Doveva rispondere.

"Meena, ciao. Dove sei? Siamo al lago."

"Oh." Controllò il calendario. Oh! *Concentrati! Diventa ancora Meena.* "Scusa. Ho perso la cognizione del tempo."

La sua immagine si accigliò sul minuscolo schermo. Moena voleva baciare quell'adorabile solco tra le sopracciglia.

"Stai bene? Non hai una bella cera."

Accidenti. Non voleva lasciare la videocamera accesa. *Distrailo!*

"Ehi, sei il mio fidanzato. Non dovresti dire quelle cose!"

Le labbra si Rahul si incurvarono, simili a fronde. "Sono il tuo fidanzato, adesso?"

Moena annuì e si leccò le labbra. Promesse, promesse. "Vengo presto. Sarai lì tra un'ora?"

"Gli altri non ci saranno, ma ti aspetterò. Mi manchi."

Tornò alla simulazione. *Vai più veloce!* Scorsero dei numeri. Triplette proteiche cosparsero i risultati con semi alfabetici. La probabilità di successo raggiunse la novantina. Era sufficiente! Fino ad allora nulla aveva superato la sessantina. Baciò lo schermo, poi trasferì il modello nello splicer.

Dieci minuti dopo, Moena travasò metà della soluzione batterica modificata in una provetta sterile. *La soluzione è la soluzione!* Ridacchiò. Mise in tasca la provetta e portò il resto al serbatoio del sistema idrico della casa. *Siate feconde e moltiplicatevi, mie piccole belve!* Salverete il terriccio, la casa, *me*.

La luce del sole veniva riflessa dal lago, pugnalando gli occhi di Moena e la sua corteccia frontale come un coltello illuminato. *Fotofobia!* Un altro sintomo del peggioramento della sua salute. *Non importa!* In tasca aveva la salvezza. Ci infilò un dito, accarezzando la provetta di vetro. La sua mente andò a un altro oggetto cilindrico, uno che non era così freddo e fragile.

Rahul era vicino alla pompa. Il sudore gli imperlava la fronte, gocce di rugiada su pelle burrosa. Le fece cenno di avvicinarsi. Le aveva già insegnato come far funzionare il pozzo di iniezione e la vasca dei nutrienti. Tutto quello che doveva fare oggi era versare la sua provetta mentre lui non guardava.

I tesori unicellulari avrebbero digerito il ferro e i policarbonati nell'acqua, poi si sarebbero fatti strada nella gente del posto. Gli intestini di Bangalore – umani e animali – avrebbero cacato altri microbimbi di Moena. Avrebbero infettato gli scarichi fognari e riportato la purezza dell'acqua a un livello vivibile.

Inciampò sul piccolo rialzo della piattaforma in cemento. Fiamme divamparono dalle dita artritiche su fino alle ginocchia gonfie. Rahul la prese prima che potesse cadere. Lei trasalì quando le sue mani schiacciarono le piaghe infette sotto le maniche. *Morditi la lingua! Non urlare!*

"Cosa succede?"

Inventati una bugia, presto! Prima che possa pensare.

"Mi sono storta una caviglia, tutto qui."

Strappò il braccio dalla sua presa, barcollò fino alla vasca dei nutrienti e tolse il coperchio.

"Cosa stai facendo?"

Non c'era più tempo per i sotterfugi. Non c'era tempo per parlare. Il suo corpo avrebbe ceduto tra poco.

La puzza della coltura in fermentazione entrò nelle narici di Moena, facendo scattare la parte del cervello che provoca la nausea. Il suo stomaco si contrasse. *Non c'è tempo!*

Tolse con forza la provetta dalla tasca. *Splash!* I suoi microbi erano entrati.

Esperimento non controllato! La voce del suo relatore le risuonò in testa. *Non pubblicato! Non verificato! Pericoloso!*

Mi spiace, professore.

Il cemento colpì con violenza le ginocchia di Moena quando si inginocchiò e vomitò. C'era la guerra nel suo intestino. Chi avrebbe prevalso? Rosso e nero striavano il vomito schizzato sul grigio smorto del cemento.

"Meena!"

La testa di Rahul bloccava il sole. Luce dorata circondava come un'aureola i ricci neri.

"Surya", sussurrò lei. Dio del sole. Bello.

Ebbe un altro conato. Un tremito le scuoteva i principali gruppi muscolari. Era un albero nella tempesta, il midollo tutto cariato dai vermi. Cadde distesa a terra.

Rahul/Surya la raccolse, la portò alla macchina. La voce di Syed e quella di lui si mischiarono con preoccupazione frenetica. La proteste di lei si unirono a loro, deboli e inefficaci.

Fermo! Non puoi portarlo a casa!

Il buio inghiottì la vista di Moena.

Macchie di luce. Palpebre appiccicose. Lingua gonfia. Da qualche parte, un incessante e fastidioso *bip bip bip*.

Moena spostò il braccio. L'avviso doloroso: *un ago*. Sbatté le palpebre. Il mondo si schiarì, si mise a fuoco, si ingrandì – come guardare attraverso una goccia d'acqua gigantesca. Una sacca di liquido trasparente che scende in un tubo.

Flebo. Inclinò la testa. Era nella sua camera da letto, da sola, nutrita da questo apparecchio. *Contaminazione.* Chi era entrato in casa sua? Quali orribili microbi erano strisciati dentro con loro? Cosa le stavano dando?

Antibiotici. L'etichetta lo confermò. La stavano avvelenando, uccidendo i suoi microscopici amici, le colonie per costruire le quali aveva lavorato così a lungo.

Moena tolse l'ago. Leccò la perla di sangue che si formò, premette con il pollice sul buco. *Bip. Bip.* Là, il suo tablet belava sulla scrivania. Il mondo girava e ondeggiava mentre camminava fino alla sedia.

Batteria quasi scarica. Disattivò l'avviso, succhiò un'altra goccia di sangue, mise in carica il dispositivo. Una spia luminosa lampeggiava nell'angolo in alto: Rahul le aveva lasciato un messaggio. Video. Lo fece partire.

Il suo viso apparve sullo schermo. Avvilito, ma adorabile. Labbra da baciare che si muovevano con cura. "Non mi hanno lasciato entrare. Syed ha chiamato la tua dottoressa. Si è presa cura di te, ha detto che dovevi restare isolata in casa tua o non saresti guarita. Meena – scusa, Moena – non so cos'altro dire. Ho sempre sospettato che stessi nascondendo qualcosa, ma questo? È troppo. Non ti capisco. Cosa volevi con qualcuno come me? Sesso? Un ragazzo di bassa estrazione sociale con cui divertirti finché non trovavi qualcuno del tuo ambiente? Pensavi che non mi sarebbe importato perché sono un uomo? Be', ti sbagliavi. Mi hai spezzato il cuore."

Rabbia, delusione, tradimento – le linee del suo viso divennero più dure, contorte, un albero cresciuto senza abbastanza acqua.

"Ho cambiato idea," sussurrò allo schermo. "Volevo tutto di te, alla fine."

Si asciugò una lacrima e col dito bagnato tracciò il suo profilo, sfocandone i lineamenti, addolcendoli. *Non capisci quello che io sono.* Schiacciò registra, per spiegare, per strappare le menzogne e piantare la verità nelle sue orecchie, ma non emerse alcun suono. Come potevano le parole essere abbastanza?

Il silenzio la schiacciava. Lacrime cadevano, schizzavano, diluivano il sangue che le sgorgava dal dorso della mano. Barcollò dalla camera da letto fino alla luce abbagliante del sole nella parte principale della casa.

"Colpa tua. Colpa tua," ronzavano le eApi.

Si diresse verso il boschetto di *Dieffenbachia*. Le piante campione erano belle dritte, verdi e bianche, nemmeno una macchia gialla o marrone. Vermi rosa semitrasparenti strisciarono via dalle dita curve dei suoi piedi. La terra sotto di lei era friabile e umida e l'odore dolce del compost si spandeva nell'aria.

"Per lo meno ho salvato voi," disse. Accarezzò le foglie cerose con la punta delle dita. "Tesori miei, mi amate ancora, vero? Mi aiuterete."

Moena si stese, strofinò il dorso della mano insanguinata sulla terra per pulirla, si asciugò le guance con l'altra. Leccò via la scura striscia di terriccio dalla pelle. Il sapore amaro del sangue si mischiò a quello ricco del manganese e a quello forte dell'acido umico. Pizzicò il suolo con la punta delle dita. Doveva analizzarlo. Se questo boschetto era rigoglioso, lei avrebbe potuto aiutare le altre parti della casa.

E Rahul? Come risanare una relazione inquinata? Il suo amore aveva avvolto Moena con i suoi rovi, le si erano conficcati nella carne, l'avevano tenuta stretta. Toglierli l'avrebbe lasciata ricoperta di buchi. Soffriva anche lui in questo modo? *Il mio cuore è spezzato*, aveva detto. Non aveva la forza per pensarci come si deve. Prima doveva guarire sé stessa.

Passò una settimana, poi un'altra, poi una terza. Da territorio ostile la casa si trasformò in rifugio. Le foglie tornarono al loro stato verdeggiante. Le eApi volteggiavano con sobria coordinazione. I pensieri di Moena divennero limpidi come le sue SmartWindow.

"Devi offrire un segno di pace, un dono," disse Ananya. "Ma poi? Sarà disposto a vivere alle tue condizioni? Mi spiace, Mo. Vorrei che trovassi quel tipo di felicità, ma forse Rahul non è l'uomo giusto."

Un dono – un pegno d'amore. Cos'era la cosa più importante per Rahul? La città. La sua acqua. La sua terra. Moena poteva dargli la salute di Bangalore, ma solo una volta scoperto se il suo esperimento aveva funzionato o meno.

Questa volta indossò la tuta protettiva per andare al lago. Evitò le ore dei volontari. L'acqua si stendeva come vetro grigio, increspata qua e là dalla zampa di un corvo. Il suo respiro gracchiava attraverso i filtri. Strano, non sentire alcun odore. Moena raccolse campioni di acqua e del fondo del lago e li riportò alla macchina dove Syed era in attesa, il viso corrugato dalla preoccupazione.

I risultati erano meravigliosi. I livelli di policarbonati erano scesi ben sotto la curva precedente. Le servivano più dati su un periodo più lungo per misurare il nuovo tasso, ma questi bastavano per una pubblicazione preliminare. Le mani le tremavano come stami nella brezza. Scrisse al computer per dieci ore, caricò la bozza su un cubo di memoria. Sequenze genetiche e una provetta di coltura viva completavano il pacchetto.

Moena sedette nell'agrumeto. Inspirò l'aroma delle zagare e disegnò ghirigori nel terriccio sabbioso. Ai suoi piedi c'era un tablet. Mostrava le immagini riprese dalla videocamera della porta. Syed raccolse la busta imbottita e sparì.

Rahul avrebbe risposto? Avrebbe capito? Avrebbe perdonato?

La bozza descriveva la sua vita fin nelle radici più profonde. I semi della salute – per lei, per tutti – erano sparsi in tutti gli aridi paragrafi tecnici. Ne mandò una seconda copia ad Ananya. Che la professoressa Das le dia maggiore credibilità. Che le loro idee infettino il mondo. Che Rahul torni nella sua vita.

Moena attese tre giorni. Nulla. Non una chiamata o un messaggio o un biglietto. L'aveva potata come fosse un ramo marcio. Veleno. Ecco cosa le sue azioni avevano portato nella vita di lui e nella propria. Si meritava di essere tagliata.

Moena portò un coltello di cucina alla bara. Lo passò attraverso il rivestimento di morbido tessuto, aprendolo come la buccia di un pomodoro maturo. Cavi, attuatori e sensori di pressione schizzarono fuori in un groviglio troppo cresciuto. *Sparisci, tentazione!*

Il giorno seguente passò di nuovo la lama e il giorno dopo ancora. Ogni ventiquattro ore che Rahul non rispondeva, incideva un nuovo ricordo di ciò che era: stupida, idiota, pazza. *Mai più!*

Rahul arrivò il giorno del quattordicesimo taglio. Non sembrava per niente un tecnico. Indossava un ampio kurta e dei pantaloni larghi di cotone. I ricci erano cresciuti e gli ondeggiavano attorno al viso come trucioli vaganti. Ai piedi aveva una borsa di nylon.

"Signorina... Sivaram?" disse al citofono. Fece il suo sorriso storto.

Moena nascose un singhiozzo. "Arrivo."

Corse attraverso luce e ombra, con foglie e fronde che le accarezzavano le braccia nude, spingendola avanti. Vai! Più veloce! Si fermò sulla soglia interna dell'ingresso.

"Mi spiace davvero tanto, Rahul. Di tutto. Non sapevo cos'altro..."

"Va tutto bene. Ho letto la tua dissertazione. L'ho capita abbastanza, credo. Ho fatto fare al G.E.H. le analisi di laboratorio dei tuoi campioni e del lago. Mio Dio, Moena, l'acqua là è incredibile! Che trasformazione! Il lavoro che hai fatto... potrebbe cambiare tutto." Face una pausa. "Posso entrare?"

Lacrime non versate le inondarono il viso, riempiendo le cavità e spingendola ad agire. Come risposta aprì la porta esterna. Rahul si tolse le scarpe ed entrò. Lei impostò il lavaggio di sterilizzazione su una semplice soluzione di sapone.

"Chiudi gli occhi", disse.

L'acqua inzuppò Rahul come un nubifragio personale. Rivoli marroni fluirono nello scarico, lavando via polvere e olio e l'ostilità di Bangalore. La stoffa bagnata delineava i contorni del suo corpo.

Moena prese un asciugamano dalla camera da letto. La bara mutilata era da un lato, un pugno in un occhio. La vergogna le bloccò i piedi. Coprirla? *No.* Niente più segreti. Tornò da Rahul mentre il lavaggio stava finendo.

"Mi spiace di essere rimasto zitto così a lungo," disse. "All'inizio aspettavo i risultati del laboratorio e poi ho dovuto fare alcuni preparativi in caso..."

"Di cosa?" lo incitò.

"In caso che tu mi permetta di restare."

"Vuoi dire... qui dentro, con me?"

Lui annuì. Goccioline trasparenti come il cristallo gli caddero dai capelli.

"Io non sono normale, Rahul. Non lo sarò mai. Per questo non ti ho detto chi ero. Non si trattava di soldi o della tua casta. Come potevo chiederti di innamorarti vista la follia della mia casa, della mia vita? Non ti posso offrire un matrimonio o dei figli o occasioni felici con tutta la famiglia. Tutto quello che ho sono soldi e isolamento."

"E la bellezza del tuo intelletto. Il tuo spirito generoso. La tua passione per la terra." Gli occhi di Rahul luccicavano. "Moena, sei l'essere umano più strano, più meraviglioso che abbia mai conosciuto. Come potrei non essere perdutamente innamorato di te? Non mi interessano matrimoni e figli. Tu hai il potere di cambiare il mondo e io voglio farne parte, far parte della tua vita."

"Dovrai stare all'interno per molto tempo."

"Lo so."

"Potrebbero volerci mesi o addirittura anni prima che io possa stabilizzare il bioma per entrambi."

"Lo posso accettare."

"E la tua famiglia?"

Rise, mostrando i denti storti. "Hanno perso ogni speranza. Più di trent'anni, scapolo e volontario nelle fogne – pensano che sono pazzo."

Gli innamorati carnatici canticchiavano.

"Allora facciamo i pazzi assieme," disse lei.

Moena aprì la porta interna. Si chiuse dietro a Rahul con il suono di un lieve risucchio, non molto diverso da un bacio. *Zitta! Sii paziente!* Lo prese per mano e lo condusse al guanacaste. I loro piedi scalzi lasciarono due serie di impronte sul terreno scuro e ricco. Rahul alzò lo sguardo verso la chioma. Luce del sole e meraviglia gli screziarono il viso.

"Ecco vostro padre," sussurrò Moena alle piccole bromeliacee.

Si accovacciò e passò un dito nel terriccio. Lui si inginocchiò di fianco a lei.

"Apri la bocca," disse lei.

La fronte di Rahul si aggrottò con perplessità. Le sue labbra si aprirono. Il dito di Moena si librò, poi sfrecciò tra loro come il becco di un colibrì, depositando il polline microbiotico sulla sua lingua in attesa. I suoi occhi si spalancarono, bianchi come il gelsomino proibito.

"La tua prima vaccinazione," sussurrò.

La bocca di lui le circondava il dito, succhiando gentilmente. I denti le solleticavano la pelle.

Le eApi ronzavano, "Bacialo! Bacialo!"

Le foglie stormirono in accordo. *Adesso!*

Moena liberò la mano e incrociò le braccia attorno al collo di Rahul. Premette il busto contro il suo, poi le labbra. Il calore umido del corpo di lui passò nel suo. I suoi sapori le mulinarono sulla lingua. Sabbia persistente. Peperoncino in polvere. Granelli di sale. I loro microbiota vorticarono, si integrarono, danzarono uno con l'altro, si unirono in una biomassa. *Ciò che è tuo è mio. Ciò che è mio è tuo.*

"Benvenuto a casa," disse Moena.

COMUNITARIO

di Shikhandin

La comunicazione non è nata dal suono. Ciononostante, in passato usavamo il suono per comunicare. Suono creato in schemi e forme acustiche. Non solo noi. Tutte le creature che si muovevano sulla superficie della nostra Terra. Eravamo divisi in quelli con la lingue e quelli senza, quelli che erano senza radici e quelli che non lo erano. Quelli i cui movimenti erano rapidi e visibili e quelli che apparentemente stavano immobili. I terrestri con la lingua e senza radici avevano una gerarchia. Noi eravamo in cima a quella gerarchia. Comandavamo e decidevamo tutto, incluse la nascita e la morte di tutto ciò che viveva sulla Terra.

Anche se allora non lo sapevamo, non lo capivamo e nemmeno lo sognavamo, eravamo una famiglia. Sì, noi del clan di quelli con la lingua e senza radici e i membri di quello dei silenziosi e radicati venivamo dallo stesso grembo. Ma quel ricordo fu perso tra i meandri dell'evoluzione. Non ci ricordavamo le nostre origini e non rispettavamo le nostre differenze.

Eravamo parenti, ma non vivevamo come un'unica famiglia armoniosa. Non eravamo una famiglia unita. Non eravamo una famiglia rispettosa e premurosa. Noi, i più potenti, non comandavamo con saggezza. Non seguivamo i ritmi circadiani della Terra. Sconvolgevamo i percorsi di vento e acqua. Ricoprivamo tutto di sostanze tossiche. Eravamo talmente immersi nei nostri suoni da non sentire le comunicazioni silenziose che stavamo ricevendo. Accecati dal nostro ego non ci accorgemmo di niente.

La vita è un essere potente. Sì, la vita, quella forza che davamo per scontata. La vita, come noi, è figlia della terra e amica di tutte le cose grandi e piccole. La vita è l'energia che credevamo di possedere e di cui pensavamo di essere gli dei. Nessuna madre tollererà che il figlio venga maltrattato. Nessuna madre resterà docile e indifesa a guardare il massacro del figlio. Nessuna madre è davvero implacabile. Nessuna buona madre prende le parti di uno solo dei suoi figli.

Madre, non ci hai abbandonati. Ci hai accettati di nuovo, i prodighi. Ed eccomi qui oggi, vecchio ma così meravigliosamente realizzato. Nella mia fanciullezza non mi sarei mai immaginato questa vita.

"Oddio! Oddio!" Ma si portò la mano sulla bocca e premette il piede sul freno.

Sorpreso, lasciai cadere il tablet di scuola. I miei compiti del giorno prima sparirono dalla vista. Alzai lo sguardo e mi immobilizzai. Il traffico si era fermato. La gente stava guardando le notizie sugli schermi installati nei casotti stradali oppure su quelli personali. I notiziari urlavano. Continuando a ripetersi. La scena veniva mostrata con la stessa frequenza. Era il tema caldo del momento.

Non avevo mai visto una tale aggressione prima. Ma sono solo un ragazzino. Anche nessun adulto aveva mai visto una tale aggressione prima. Non Ma, non Bapu, nemmeno Dadi che ha più di cento anni.

Sembrava che tutti parlassero in contemporanea. Terrorismo! Attacco deliberato, dicevano. Azione premeditata. Un pericolo per l'umanità! All'inizio fu uno choc. La rabbia venne dopo. Quando capimmo l'enormità di quello che stava succedendo. Era accaduto l'impossibile. C'era stato uno strano miracolo potente e malvagio. Era incredibile. Ma la prova era lì, che ci fissava da ogni schermo. A Jaisalmer. Nelle altre città. In tutto il mondo.

Le cose avevano abbattuto un velivolo. Un jumbo intero carico di passeggeri e merci!

Vidi il filmato girato dai droni mentre andavo a scuola. Lo spezzone di trenta secondi, con l'avviso 'contiene immagini esplicite che possono disturbare' lampeggiante in alto a destra, venne mostrato più e più volte. E tutto intorno a me potevo vedere gli adulti, compresi i miei genitori, che continuavano a guardarlo, come se fossero ipnotizzati. Ecco una cosa buffa, i droni non vengono mai colpiti. È come se sapessero cosa contiene biomassa e cosa no.

Le cose, non mi viene in mente un altro modo per chiamarle, sembravano rampicanti simili a pitoni. O forse pitoni simili a rampicanti. Pitoni con foglie e frutti. Sbucarono fuori per afferrare il cielo, germogli infiniti. Come un fagiolo magico di Jack impazzito. Si lanciavano verso il velivolo con forti colpi. Ci misero meno di trenta secondi per ricoprirlo con una massa di verde che si contorceva. Si intrecciarono e girarono, forse due o tre volte, e tornarono giù di colpo come erano apparsi. Poi il cielo fu di nuovo deserto. Così. Nemmeno un uccello.

Ovviamente il governo proclamò la chiusura indefinita di scuole e uffici. I notiziari esortavano la gente a fare scorta delle cose essenziali e a restare a casa. Sapevamo cosa sarebbe successo poi. Sarebbero stati schierati i tagliatori. Un esercito intero di enormi robot fatti di acciaio e alimentati dall'uranio. Totalmente automatizzati, con nulla di minimamente organico all'interno. I vecchi modelli invece erano pilotati da dei conducenti, seduti all'interno di cabine trasparenti antiproiettile posizionate nella sezione centrale dei tagliatori. Questi uscivano a tagliare, facendo oscillare ritmicamente le loro lunghe braccia metalliche, facendo poltiglia di tutte le cose verdi viventi. Alcuni esistono ancora. Bapu ne ha uno, una macchina più piccola, formato famiglia. I tagliatori completamente automatici erano molto più rapidi. Resero il mondo di nuovo spoglio nel giro di minuti.

Dadi mi raccontava delle storie su come, prima che lei nascesse, sia i musulmani che i dalit venivano picchiati e messi in prigione o uccisi ogni volta che spariva una mucca randagia. Poi, quando era una ragazzina, iniziarono a sparire mandrie intere. Non in modo regolare, ma abbastanza spesso da essere notato. Si trattava del bestiame lasciato libero di girare, perché ormai non più giovane e nessuno osava ucciderlo per la carne o la pelle. Era come se gli animali fossero stati fatti sparire durante la notte. Un'impresa impossibile, perché anche se fossero stati tirati su e scaricati dentro hover-cargo, qualcuno se ne sarebbe accorto. Iniziarono a sparire anche delle capre, e pecore, asini e cammelli. Tutti gli animali da pascolo, in realtà. E poi galline, cani e gatti. E poi esseri umani, pochi alla volta, quelli di cui nessuno avrebbe sentito la mancanza – i poveri, quelli che dormivano all'aperto, i senzatetto, i mendicanti e i reietti.

La sabbia era sparita per sempre a Jaisalmer. Era sparita, anni prima che io nascessi. Al suo posto c'era un terreno molliccio che in alcuni luoghi sembrava vivo. Jaisalmer era verde. Il mondo intero era verde. Non un singolo granello di deserto.

"Il deserto del Thar si ridusse davanti ai nostri occhi," raccontava Dadi. "Non solo il Thar, i deserti di tutto il mondo. Eravamo così felici. Più foresta significava più animali e uccelli. Ecco cosa pensavamo all'inizio. Ma questo era uno strano tipo di verde. Più una maledizione che una benedizione."

Le sparizioni non colpivano direttamente gli esseri umani. E all'inizio non furono viste come un problema. Il cibo veniva fatto crescere in fabbrica già prima che Dadi nascesse. Cibo puro e pulito che seguiva i dettami delle nostre rispettive fedi. Halal per i musulmani. Kosher per gli ebrei. Vegetariano incontaminato per i bramini come noi e i giainisti. E poi c'erano i tipi normali per quelli che mangiavano di tutto indiscriminatamente.

Gli animali esistevano per aumentare la bellezza del paesaggio. Le foreste venivano lasciate il più possibile intatte, con il ministero per le foreste che regolava le popolazioni delle varie specie. Quelle estinte erano state clonate con successo. Alcune erano addirittura state reimpiantate in natura. Perciò eravamo a posto. Gli umani stavano facendo bene, prendendosi buona cura del pianeta, un totale cambiamento da com'era anche solo un secolo prima della nascita di Dadi.

Dadi aveva le sue teorie. Diceva che i suoi genitori si lamentavano spesso dei cambiamenti e che le cose non erano più le stesse. Che sotto sotto si stava preparando qualcosa e forse avrebbe portato davvero la fine del mondo. Le scritture predicevano la fine delle ere, della vita. Dadi metteva la religione ovunque, essendo vecchia e all'antica eccetera. Bapu non le diceva niente in faccia, ma trovava le sue teorie puerili. Ma, essendo un tipo scientifico, la derideva apertamente.

Non ero ancora nato quando gli animali hanno iniziato a sparire. Bapu mi ha raccontato che quando il governo lo notò, tutte le nazioni si unirono. Fecero delle riunioni comuni. Gli ingegneri unirono tutta la loro conoscenza e crearono i tagliatori. Gli scienziati di tutti i campi si unirono per costruire laboratori. Studiarono i fenomeni, presero appunti, scrissero testi e scambiarono informazioni. All'inizio sembrava che l'umanità avrebbe vinto. Avevamo comunque i nostri laboratori alimentari in cui potevamo far crescere qualsiasi cosa dal rafano alle costolette d'agnello. Non che ci servissero le costolette d'agnello. Nella mia famiglia, come la maggior parte delle persone del Rajasthan e della regione del Marwar, siamo vegetariani puri. Gli unici prodotti animali che consumavamo erano latte e ghee e altre cose fatte con il latte, creati debitamente in fabbriche sterili. Dadi era un po' schizzinosa sul mangiare gli ortaggi a radice, come le carote. Diceva che le ricordavano le ossa.

"Haddi," diceva. "Tutti gli ortaggi a radice non sono altro che haddi, ossa." Ma non voleva spiegare le ossa di cosa.

Ma e Bapu non si facevano questi scrupoli. Bapu addirittura ci incoraggiava a mangiare le uova, dicendo che latte e uova erano entrambi prodotti animali e che, se potevamo prendere il latte, non avremmo dovuto avere problemi con le uova. Ma Dadi non permetteva che entrassero uova in casa. Così prendevamo le uova solo per trattarci bene al ristorante.

Ma lavorava per un laboratorio del governo. Il suo lavoro era controllare nuove mutazione delle cose verdi. Controllava per vedere se avevano in qualche modo infettato il cibo cresciuto in laboratorio. Sotto di sé aveva una squadra che lavorava per mantenere il nostro cibo libero da contaminazioni ventiquattro ore su ventiquattro. Ma aveva molte lauree. Bapu non era qualificato come Ma. Però aveva buon occhio per gli affari. Gestiva un'agenzia immobiliare. Era bravo. Tra i vantaggi del suo lavoro c'era avere notizie di prima mano sugli appezzamenti migliori e gli affari disponibili. È così che abbiamo preso la nostra haveli.

Dadi ci raccontava della sua giovinezza nella vecchia Jaisalmer. Stando a quello che dice, Jaisalmer era una bella città, che si ergeva come un diadema tempestato di gemme dal deserto. L'unica volta che ho visto la sabbia è stata in una fotografia che mi ha mostrato. Era la fotografia del suo villaggio, un gruppo di piccole case in mattoni nei sobborghi di Jaisalmer. La sabbia lambiva le verande come onde dell'oceano, solo che quando sono nato le onde dell'oceano non erano più blu, ma di un ricco verde alga. Nella foto ci sono alcune capre. C'erano anche un paio di cani disinteressati, magri e gialli come la sabbia. Sul bordo della fotografia potevo vedere la città di Jaisalmer, i suoi edifici in arenaria scintillanti come oro brunito. Un elegante contrasto con la sabbia bianca-giallastra e il cielo azzurro come una caramella. Non potevo credere che fosse così bella. Il cielo sembrava un mare congelato e sottosopra, un miraggio delle leggendarie acque artiche. La sabbia sembrava la soffice halva di semola che Dadi faceva quando le cose non erano ancora sfuggite così tanto di mano. C'erano anche cammelli. Sì, cammelli!

Una volta avevo disegnato un cammello, basandomi sulle descrizioni di Dadi e le immagini che avevo visto sul mio tablet di scuola. I cammelli erano già estinti quando sono nato, ma ne esistevano ancora alcuni clonati, tenuti dentro zoo di massima sicurezza. Feci una copia del mio disegno animato dallo schermo artistico e la regalai a Dadi. La aiutai a metterla sulla parete della sua camera. Il mio cammello era più alto della palma da dattero nel disegno ed era divertente vederlo abbassarsi e prendere alcune fronde da masticare. Dadi rideva molto e diceva che amava il suo cammello speciale. Disegnai alcuni altri animali e Dadi li volle tutti nella sua camera. Presto la sua stanza cominciò ad assomigliare a uno schermo-zoo. Non avevo ancora imparato ad aggiungere il suono ai miei disegni, il che è un bene, perché dubito che Dadi sarebbe riuscita a dormire con tutto quel baccano attorno a lei.

Quando Dadi era una ragazzina, ascoltava sempre gli anziani parlare. All'inizio si trattava di storie e leggende, ma con l'aumentare del problema le conversazioni divennero una lunga sfilza di lamenti.

Le colture orticole e i campi di bajra e senape stavano venendo male. Crescevano troppo in fretta ed erano troppo lunghi e radi. Anche le palme da dattero e i cespugli spinosi proliferavano. Tuttavia gli uccelli e i piccoli animali come gli scoiattoli non ne erano attratti. La piccola fauna sembrava morire di fame. Il cibo che cucinavano ci metteva sempre più tempo, come se gli ortaggi e il grano avessero acquistato una maggiore resistenza a essere modificati o uccisi, se questo è il termine adatto per la vegetazione. Dadi diceva che sua madre guardava verso l'orizzonte di sera e borbottava con sé stessa.

Presto durante le conversazioni serali si alzò il chiasso delle lamentele. Lamentele sulla qualità del cibo. Su come le cose si fossero deteriorate tanto ultimamente da poter a malapena mangiare. E poi c'erano anche le sparizioni. Poiché nessuno aveva la minima idea di cosa stesse succedendo, le teorie e le congetture si alternavano in fretta e facilmente. Alcune erano completamente assurde. La maggior parte aveva connotazioni religiose. Gli anziani si consultarono. Puja speciali vennero fatte per propiziarsi gli Dei. Dicevano che era la cuspide, il tempo in cui un'epoca finisce e un'altra inizia. Dicevano che il periodo di transizione avrebbe portato con sé molto caos e distruzione.

"Poi tornerà l'età dell'oro," ci disse Dadi con fiducia. "Niente di cui aver paura. L'atto della creazione è sempre preceduto dalla distruzione." Si distrasse di nuovo, mormorando le sue preghiere e facendo scorrere il suo mala.

La fede di Dadi faceva sì che non avesse paura e accettasse. Ma e Bapu, però, restarono calmi a stento dopo l'attacco dei rampicanti. Bittu era l'unico che sembrava in grado di tranquillizzarli. Era lo stesso per me. Ma ci stava sempre addosso, in quel periodo.

"Ankur," urlava, anche se non avevo fatto nulla per infastidirla. "Prendi le medicine."

"L'ho fatto."

"Non discutere. Quando le hai prese l'ultima volta? Quelle tonde gialle? Le hai prese per prime?"

Le portavo il mio vassoio portapillole e le mostravo gli incavi vuoti con la data segnata su ciascuno. Solo allora era soddisfatta, ma non per molto. Ma si girava verso Bapu e Dadi dopo aver finito con me e andava a controllare e ricontrollare il vassoio portapillole di Bittu.

Ma sembrava anche essere sempre molto irritabile e tesa. Come le rane che avevo catturato una volta e messo nella vasca dei pesci. Mi aveva fatto lavare bene le mani e poi mi aveva disinfettato, tutto, con uno spray dall'odore disgustoso. Mi aveva fissato furiosa mentre inghiottivo le mie pillole. Tutta quella agitazione per delle rane minuscole! Avevo guardato Dadi per avere sostegno, ma per una volta aveva accuratamente evitato il mio sguardo.

Il giorno dopo l'incidente dei rampicanti, Ma si diede da fare per riempire il carrello con cibo di tutti i tipi. Avevamo smesso di mangiare ortaggi e frutta freschi fatti in laboratorio. Ma per lo meno io sapevo che aspetto avevano. Bittu non se lo ricordava. Per quanto riguarda il latte, di latte animale non se ne parlava proprio, fatto in laboratorio o di altro tipo. Eravamo diventati vegani high-tech. Mangiavamo solo cibo prodotto in fabbriche sterili, chiuse in grandi edifici simili a silos. Avevamo abbandonato il nostro precedente cibo fatto crescere in laboratorio o in casa su insistenza di Ma. Adesso consumavamo invece cibo creato in capsule di Petri, una cellula alla volta. La diffidenza di Ma verso la natura aveva raggiunto proporzioni epiche!

Guardai Ma gettare i pacchetti e i barattoli nel nostro carrello. Traboccava già di cibo e prodotti per pulire casa. Aveva preso anche uno di quegli aggeggi che creano acqua dall'aria. Guardandola fare, avreste pensato che tutta Jaisalmer stava per chiudere. L'idea era probabilmente venuta a molti. I negozi erano super affollati. Le altre persone non sembravano essere paranoiche, però. A meno che non stessero fingendo. Come Ma e Dadi, che chiacchieravano con gli altri clienti, quelli più amichevoli, come se fosse tutto normale. Notai il sorriso forzato sul viso di alcuni di loro. Dadi sorrideva e annuiva come una rimbambita. Ma disse qualcosa che doveva in teoria essere divertente, mentre metteva altre cose nel carrello. Poi zigzagammo fino alla cassa. Spingendo tra la folla per essere i primi. Niente di strano. Siamo indiani dopotutto.

Ma iniziò subito a svuotare il carrello. Cambiò idea su qualcosa e corse a cambiarla, facendo cenno a Bapu di continuare a svuotare. Bapu protestò piano. La fila dietro di noi mugugnò. Alcuni si agitarono. Alla fine Ma tornò, infilandosi per passare la fila. La ragazza con i brufoli sul mento dall'aria depressa alla cassa spinse il conto-lettore verso Ma. Lei fissò lo schermo. Il lettore lampeggiò, luce verde. La ragazza si girò verso il cliente successivo senza disturbarsi a rispondere all'allegro "grazie, arrivederci" di Ma. La coda sospirò. Evidentemente Ma non l'aveva sentito. Oppure semplicemente non le interessava. Corremmo verso il parcheggio. Alcuni tagliatori erano già là, a ripulire la nuova vegetazione.

Jaisalmer era relativamente calma, a parte alcuni sporadici attacchi di panico. Altre città erano piene di vegetazione e umani in preda al panico. Ovunque sulle strade erano nati dossi con vene verdi. Gli edifici ondeggiavano per la vegetazione verdeggiante. I campi e i terreni agricoli erano minacciosamente rigogliosi senza piante commestibili. Alcuni davano la colpa ai crimini passati degli esseri umani. Alcuni incolpavano il governo per aver creato dei laboratori per la flora e fauna mutante. Era stato quello a creare il problema, dicevano. Il governo rispose che non poteva guardare la gente morire di fame senza fare nulla. Gli attivisti facevano petizioni per la chiusura del laboratori vegetali non autorizzati. Ma i cittadini normali preferivano fidarsi dei politici e dei notiziari. Ma ovviamente non si fidava di nessuno. E Bapu preferiva andare sul sicuro.

Alcuni mesi prima, su insistenza di Ma, ci eravamo trasferiti nella nostra haveli. Era una casa dell'inizio del XX secolo con un cortile grande come una piscina e un ampio giardino che la circondava all'esterno. Bapu l'aveva comprata per quattro soldi e l'aveva trasformata in una casa per il fine settimana. Ma adesso, a giudicare dalla spesa di Ma, probabilmente staremo qui molto più a lungo. Un anno forse. Era lontana dalla città, ben oltre i sobborghi. Quando le strade erano buone, però, tornare non era un problema.

Di ritorno dai negozi passammo a prendere Bittu all'asilo. Divya mausi uscì dondolando con Bittu in braccio. Era una degli ultimi insegnanti rimasti. Non c'era bisogno che Divya mausi portasse Bittu. Sapeva camminare, correre in realtà. Però diventava in fretta il preferito di tutti. Tutti adoravano prenderlo in braccio, stringerlo un po' e annusare il fresco profumo di bambino. Bittu poteva fare qualsiasi cosa, con tutti. Tranne me. Sono l'unico che ascoltava davvero. E intendo davvero nel senso di davvero davvero.

"È venuta a prenderlo così presto oggi, Pavitra ji," disse Divya mausi.

"Porterò Bittu domani mattina presto," rispose Ma. Prese Bittu dalle braccia riluttanti di Divya mausi.

"Bai-bai Diya mazi," disse Bittu.

Divya mausi sorrise e gli passò le dita tra i riccioli.

Sulla via di casa il traffico era irregolare, ma avevamo una determinata Ma alla guida. Bittu cianciava della sua giornata e, anche se alcune parole erano senza senso, annuii per far vedere che ero interessato. Dadi aveva gli occhi chiusi, come se stesse di nuovo pregando. Bapu sembrava distratto. Forse stava aspettando di vedere quale altra pazzia Ma avrebbe fatto. Non dovette attendere a lungo. Appena arrivati a casa, era pronta per tornare di nuovo in città.

"Stai a casa e prepara qualcosa per cena ai ragazzi," gli disse, con tono insolitamente autoritario. Dadi serrò le labbra in segno di disapprovazione, ma Bapu non reagì. "Vado a finire di fare scorta."

"Sono quasi le sei," protestò piano Bapu. "Quando arriverai i negozi saranno chiusi, Pavi."

"Prenderò la scorciatoia," disse Ma. E uscì prima che lui potesse controbattere che le scorciatoie erano diventate praticamente inagibili.

Ma tornò ben dopo l'ora in cui andavo a letto. Le loro voci mi svegliarono così strisciai fuori dalla camera per vedere.

"Pavi," sentii dire a Bapu. "Pavi, è una follia." Bapu le toccò la guancia. "Sei paranoica."

"Non è vero. È già iniziato. Non vedi?" disse Ma. Sembrava svuotata sia di forza che di speranza.

"Non lascerai che tutte quelle chiacchiere dirigano la nostra vita. Per favore, Pavi," supplicò Bapu. "Dovresti sapere quanto sono paranoidi tutti gli attivisti. Lo sono sempre stati."

Ma iniziò a piangere. Si sedette. Bapu scosse la testa, ma le accarezzò i capelli mentre parlava. "Calmati ora, Pavi, Andrà tutto bene." Ma non faceva, però, che scrollare la testa con forza, le spalle che sussultavano per la paura e la disperazione, mentre le lacrime scendevano senza controllo.

Il mattino seguente sia Bapu che Ma restarono a casa. Bapu ripulì il giardino attorno alla casa. Sentii il suo mini-tagliatore col suo motore e il rumore ritmico delle lame. Erano a malapena le sette del mattino. Bapu doveva essersi alzato molto presto perché potevo vedere ampie zone di terreno marrone attorno alla casa. Versò del liquido sul terreno ripulito che dopo un po' lo indurì creando una liscia superficie sintetica.

Bisogna conoscere le persone giuste, per avere una haveli come la nostra. Ma e Bapu avevano lavorato duro per molti anni e si erano fatti gli amici giusti. E volevano senza dubbio sfruttarla il più possibile. Avevano progettato di organizzarci feste per gli amici e i colleghi, feste di compleanno per Bittu e me. L'idea era quella di trasformarla in una vera haveli vecchio stile. Avevano progettato di avere uno stagno e dei cloni di mucca e di cane, delle repliche di alberi da frutto e verdure, i fiori preferiti di Ma e le erbe di Dadi. Tutte con certificato del laboratorio. Io volevo una zona piuttosto grande dedicata espressamente a Bittu e me. Bapu progettava di aggiungere una piscina con onde simulate perché potessimo fare surf quando ne avevamo voglia. Avevamo dei sogni per la nostra haveli. Grandi sogni.

Il costo delle vaccinazioni che Bapu, Bittu e io dovevamo fare – dodici a testa per ognuno di noi – mise in pausa tutti i progetti. Ma e Dadi dovevano fare solo quattro serie di vaccini l'una e un richiamo. A quanto pareva le donne erano più resistenti, ma non del tutto. E potevano anche essere portatrici, al contrario di noi uomini. Così ci aveva detto il dottore. Tutti dovevamo prendere le stesse medicine, però, tutti i giorni, perché la prevenzione era l'unica cura e non si poteva essere troppo cauti. Così continuavano a ripetere Ma e Dadi. Probabilmente gli attivisti ridevano delle medicine. I miei genitori, però, non erano disposti a correre rischi. Bapu era grato del nostro essere benestanti. Nessuno in casa nostra parlava delle centinaia di persone che erano scomparse, perché non avevano i mezzi per pagare per la prevenzione!

Poco dopo esserci sistemati, vennero da noi alcune persone del villaggio. Volevano un lavoro. Ma disse loro che gli avrebbe fatto sapere una volta sistemati. Non le piaceva l'idea di altre bocche da sfamare. E non voleva estranei in casa nostra. Dopo due giorni di lavoro ininterrotto Bapu rivoleva la sua libertà. Voleva tornare al suo vero lavoro a Jaisalmer. Però Ma non lo lasciava andare.

"Chi pagherà per tutto questo," disse Bapu, allungando le braccia verso la sala da pranzo che sembrava più un magazzino di cose varie, soprattutto cibo e acqua. "Stiamo vivendo a credito. Abbiamo troppi debiti."

"Fidati di me," disse Ma. "Non andare. Dobbiamo fortificare la casa. Nessuno ancora capisce, ma quando lo faranno sarà il pandemonio, qui saremo al sicuro. Saremo liberi da..." Non terminò la frase.

Ma mi spaventò con il suo discorso. Bittu era troppo piccolo per avere paura. Dadi, però, in quegli ultimi giorni sembrava essere completamente d'accordo con Ma.

"Ha ragione, Santosh," disse Dadi a Bapu quando alla fine lui perse la pazienza con Ma. Non era da Dadi discutere con il genero, per quanto la riguardava lui era il capofamiglia. Ai suoi tempi le donne non replicavano, si limitavano a ubbidire agli uomini.

Da parte sua Bapu non discuteva mai con Dadi, che era un'anziana. In quello era all'antica. Prese la sua cassetta degli attrezzi in silenzio e andò in cortile. A fine serata le recinzioni erano in piedi. Erano fatte di un tipo di rete metallica elettromagnetica che si vedeva solo nelle zone militari e di attracco delle navi. Il tipo che distruggeva la vita, sia animale che vegetale, a contatto.

Passò una settimana. Rimanemmo all'interno della nostra oasi. Era noioso senza scuola. Non che ne facessimo molta. Troppe strade erano diventate impraticabili e troppi studenti erano svaniti. Uno a uno erano svaniti anche dai nostri schermi di comunicazione. Le nostre conversazioni erano terminate. Gli amici mi mancavano. Ma, però, mi aveva proibito di vedermi con chiunque mesi fa.

Trascorse un'altra settimana. Ma passò all'azione. Si era appena resa conto che le nostre scorte mediche si stavano esaurendo. Quando la vide pronta, anche Bittu volle andare con lei. Fece una tale scenata che fu costretta a portarlo. Tornò ore dopo sembrando completamente esausta e si addormentò quasi subito, senza nemmeno cambiarsi. Dadi prese Bittu. Gli diede da mangiare e lo mise a letto. E poi tornò, con gli occhi da pazza e tremante. Scosse Ma per svegliarla e le parlò con urgenza. Ma soffocò un urlo. Bapu e io lasciammo quello che stavamo facendo e corremmo nella stanza di Bittu. Guardammo il suo viso angelico nel lettino. Dadi tolse la coperta. Ma iniziò a battersi il petto come se fosse già morto. Si coprì la bocca per bloccare il gemito che minacciava di uscirle dalla gola. Tre piccoli foruncoli, marroni e duri, stavano perfidi sulla coscia destra di Bittu.

Ma restò in piedi come un albero pietrificato. Dadi pianse nell'estremità del sari. Bapu si tenne la testa tra le mani. Quando guardai il viso di Ma vidi tutte le cose terribili che si era rifiutata di dire ad alta voce. Non saremmo stati in grado di sopportarlo. Anche se nel profondo del cuore sapevamo che sarebbe stato inevitabile. Però non conoscevamo il processo. L'ignoto ci terrorizzava.

C'era una persona sulla Terra, però, che amava Bittu tanto quanto noi e di cui potevamo fidarci. Questa unica persona era anche dura come la roccia e una vecchia saggia, come Dadi. Ma stava portando Bittu da lei.

Nessuno fermò Ma. Nessuno disse una parola. Stavamo tutti segretamente pensando che nessuno doveva sapere che la nostra famiglia era stata colpita. I tizi del governo sarebbero arrivati in un batter d'occhio. Saremmo stati messi in quarantena. Avremmo perso tutto ciò che possedevamo. Saremmo spariti. Tutto ciò che possedevamo sarebbe sparito. Saremmo stati insieme o separati? Non ne avevamo idea. Nessuno sapeva davvero cosa stava succedendo. C'erano voci. Ma la gente per lo più si comportava come se il governo stesse catturando e portando via ribelli, non normali cittadini laboriosi come noi.

La gente continuava la vita di tutti i giorni, comprando cibo extra, prendendo le sue pillole e vaccinazioni dalle cliniche approvate dal governo, comportandosi come se fosse un normale vaccino per qualsiasi altra normale epidemia. Nessuno si metteva a protestare quando intere famiglie svanivano. Nessuno parlava delle strade ricoperte da cose verdi che crescevano, le case trascurate verdi come collinette tropicali. Nessuno elogiava il tempo atmosferico, così fresco e umido e profumato, come un'eterna primavera, una stagione di cui avevo letto solo nelle vecchie storie.

Ma uscì, un Bittu ancora assonnato sul fianco. Mentre andava disse sopra la spalla, più che altro per abitudine, "Spero ti sia ricordato di prendere le pillole, Ankur."

Annuii. Sentivo il cuore freddo e caldo allo stesso tempo. Forse la dose da bambino non era stata abbastanza per Bittu. I bambini erano più vulnerabili. Io avevo già undici anni, andavo per i dodici. Avrei insegnato al mio fratellino a essere forte come me. Anni prima che nascesse avevo già iniziato a conservare i miei giochi e i miei libri, attendendo con ansia il giorno in cui avrei condiviso le mie cose con un fratello tutto mio. Ma e Bapu ci impiegarono così tanto a decidere che avevo quasi perso la speranza.

Guardai Ma fare retromarcia con la hover-macchina dall'hangar. Non potei vederla oltre il cancello per via dell'invasione verde. Quelle nuove mutavano quotidianamente. Erano in grado di superare cose che non riuscivano a tollerare all'inizio, quando crescevano solo sul terriccio. Ora sembravano non temere quasi nulla. Nessuno era più al sicuro da loro.

Bittu sarebbe stato al sicuro con Divya mausi. E lei sarebbe stata felice di prendersi cura di Bittu. Noi ci saremmo risparmiati di vedere Bittu trasformarsi davanti ai nostri occhi. L'idea della trasformazione ci spaventava. Una volta che il processo fosse stato completo, lei sapeva esattamente cosa fare. Lo avrebbe tenuto nascosto nel suo minuscolo giardino finché non fosse stato abbastanza robusto da resistere al trapianto. Questione di giorni, in realtà. Sarebbe tornato da noi allora, lo avremmo lasciato crescere selvatico e libero nella nostra haveli, la nostra casa delle vacanze, il luogo delle nostre feste e dei nostri ritrovi! Non avremmo avuto bisogno della nostre dose dopo di allora. Oh no.

Avevo sentito Ma, Bapu e Dadi discuterne.

"Nel peggiore dei casi," aveva detto Bapu. Ancora e ancora. E Ma aveva soffocato un singhiozzo. Avevano pianificato tutto, fino all'ultimo dettaglio. Forse ne avevano anche parlato con Divya mausi. Era là alla nostra porta, anche lei con un aspetto allegramente foruncoloso, con Bittu in un vasetto. Le sue fronde ondeggiarono eccitate nella loro prigione di vetro. Da allora Divya mausi divenne ovviamente un gradito membro della nostra haveli. Ero davvero contento. Era bello avere qualcun altro con cui parlare.

Dopodiché continuammo, come se non fosse successo niente, ma con una piccola modifica. Non prendevamo più le nostre medicine. Facemmo una cerimonia privata in cui piantammo Bittu al centro del cortile. Presto il cortile divenne la parte principale della casa. Divenne il luogo dove mangiavamo il nostro cibo, di cui avevamo sempre meno bisogno con il passare dei giorni, mentre i nostri corpi si rivolgevano più a sole, aria e acqua per il sostentamento. Stavamo seduti nel nostro cortile parlando sottovoce, accarezzando i rami e il tronco in continua crescita di Bittu. Ma ci istruiva quotidianamente su cosa fare quando solo uno di noi sarebbe stato ancora umano. Chiudemmo i cancelli della nostra haveli in modo permanente. Le famiglie devono stare unite, qualunque cosa succeda. Ed è quello che avremmo fatto, fino alla fine.

Il sovraffollamento non ci dà fastidio. È naturale. Dopo aver superato lo choc iniziale della metamorfosi totale, abbiamo iniziato ad abituarci al nuovo silenzio. All'inizio i nostri pensieri si confondevano con il nostro discorso silenzioso ed era strano. Era strano anche non sentire alcun amore particolare e possessivo per quelli che avevano il nostro stesso sangue nel passato. Le relazioni hanno un nuovo significato adesso. Significa che io posso intrecciarmi con l'entità verde che una volta in una vita ormai lontana mi aveva fatto nascere. Allora eravamo diversi e quella vecchia etica non vale più.

Ci arrampichiamo uno sull'altro, gioendo del tocco di sole e pioggia. Non c'è niente di cui avere paura. E perché dovrebbe esserci? Sotto i rigagnoli di terriccio parliamo con infiniti altri esseri vegetali, che non ci assomigliano più di quanto noi assomigliamo alle nostre forme precedenti. I nostri dubbi iniziali sono stati chiariti da chi è venuto prima di noi. Ci hanno dato i loro elementi nutritivi quando è venuto il momento per loro di andare, unendosi al suolo o sciogliendosi nell'acqua.

Un lontano ricordo mi fa sorridere, ma non come fanno gli umani. È una sensazione e la posso esprimere espandendomi un po' fisicamente. In quell'altra vita, l'entità che chiamavo Ma diceva che le piante si parlavano l'un l'altra. Si sbagliava. Non sono solo le piante, anche le pietre e le gocce d'acqua parlano. Le molecole d'aria parlano. I fiumi di lava nel profondo del grembo della madre terra parlano.

Parliamo tutti l'uno con l'altro. Parliamo anche a chilometri di distanza, per usare un termine umano. Pensiamo e sentiamo e facciamo strategie. Ma le nostre tempistiche sono diverse. Le nostre misure dello spazio sono diverse da quelle degli umani. È per questo che ci sono voluti più di mille anni per riprenderci i nostri territori perduti.

Comunque sia. Non c'è rabbia. Nessuna paura. Niente avidità o odio. Niente di negativo. Soddisfazione e benefici comuni sono ciò che ci guidano. La madre terra sorride molto in questi giorni. Agita il suo grembo e ci solletica le radici. Estrae i nostri codici genetici con il più gentile dei tocchi. Diffondiamo il nostro DNA *al suo interno. I nostri rituali di accoppiamento sono antichi e prolungati.*

Presto avrà luogo un'altra trasformazione. Sotto la roccia e sotto il fondo degli oceani, una vita nuova delicata come filamenti si libererà dimenandosi. Ci piegheremo e aggiungeremo i nostri doni, dando il benvenuto ai nuovi figli che, a loro volta, cresceranno. Insieme danzeremo la danza della vita. E accolti nel grembo della terra nuoteremo con lei attraverso il cosmo.

La rete di Indra

di Vandana Singh

Mahua correva sul solito sentiero costellato di pietre sotto la copertura delle acacie, il respiro rapido e irregolare. Presto avrebbe dovuto fermarsi, non era più giovane come una volta e sentiva un lieve dolore persistente al ginocchio destro – ma amava questa fisicità: il cuore che batte, il sudore che scorre a rivoli sul viso, la foresta che odora di linfa ed escrementi animali, la sabbia sulle labbra per via della polvere. Era nella foresta che aveva le idee migliori, un'eterna fonte di ispirazione. Era il motivo per cui il suo lavoro era riconosciuto in tutto il mondo. Ma alla foresta non importava di fama e ricchezza – qui era solo un altro animale: respiro e flusso, un nibbio in volo, un cervo che corre.

Mentre correva, le piaceva ascoltare le chiacchiere della rete che uscivano di continuo dalla Conchiglia nel suo orecchio: Salman che controllava la nuova rete, Varun e Ali che informavano sulle colonie di pesce nelle paludi artificiali vicino al fiume, il monitor del dottor Sabharwal che trasmetteva le condizioni di nonna in ospedale: stabile, stabile, stabile, ancora attaccata alle macchine.

Pensare all'ictus di sua nonna la faceva sentire come se stesse per cadere in un abisso di disperazione; si distrasse ricordando a sé stessa di aver promesso a Namita che avrebbe provato l'app musicale miconet durante la corsa di questa mattina.

"È solo per divertimento, Mahua-di, ma provala, ti piacerà."

Erano così preoccupati per lei, questi giovani, sapendo che non era propriamente sé stessa in questi giorni. Commossa e ingiustamente seccata dalla loro preoccupazione, aveva passato alcune ore con loro nel laboratorio Biosystems per imparare a usare la app...

C'è una rete fungina, una miconet, una connessione segreta tra le piante della foresta. Si parlano l'un l'altra, l'acacia e il palissandro Shisham e l'albero di fuoco, in una lingua chimica. Comunicano sui parassiti, le fonti di cibo, il tempo, il tutto grazie al flusso di biomolecole attraverso le ife fungine. Sappiamo che, usando questa rete, grandi piante hanno addirittura condiviso le sostanze nutritive con gli arboscelli della stessa specie. La protetta di Mahua, Namita, fa parte del team che ha aiutato a decifrare (per quanto sia possibile agli esseri umani) questo linguaggio discreto. Hanno piantato sensori nel suolo della foresta per catturare alcuni di questi scambi chimici tra piante. I segnali vengono ritrasmessi all'interprete e poi analizzati. Alcuni membri del team hanno creato musica con i segnali: convertono la concentrazione di un dato trasmettitore biochimico trasformandola in tempo reale in una successione di note in cui la durata indica l'intensità del trasmettitore. Aggiungendo qualche altro segnale come suoni di frequenza leggermente diversa si ottiene un brusio, a volte musicale, allo stesso tempo rilassante e affascinante. Per Mahua è una cosa nuova e non l'ha mai provata nella foresta prima. Ha sempre incoraggiato il gioco nella loro ricerca – non è solo divertente ma importante, dice loro – il gioco porta a nuove intuizioni, smuove idee preconcette.. E adesso hanno bisogno del sollievo dato dal gioco, dopo aver passato gli ultimi mesi calcolando e mettendo a punto la prima rete energetica intelligente di Ashapur, sul modello proprio della miconet.

Mahua aprì la app. Mentre correva raccolse informazioni dai sensori più vicini in modo da avere una 'immagine' che mutava nel tempo e nello spazio. All'inizio non sentì nulla se non la semi-musica rilassante dei vari toni. Poi arrivò la sorpresa: una strana sensazione quasi come una vertigine, una specie di slittamento, come se si stesse lasciando il suo sé umano alle spalle, dissolvendosi in qualcosa di infinitamente vasto. Era come guardare la Via lattea dalla cima di un'alta montagna in una notte limpida. Era sempre stata veloce nell'individuare reti di relazioni – era la sua abilità specifica, dopotutto – ma questo era diverso. Fu percorsa da una sensazione simile a una scossa elettrica, un lungo momento di riconoscimento, come se la sua mente profonda conoscesse già questa struttura. L'effetto fu così sorprendente da farla inciampare su una radice. Poi la Conchiglia le fece bip con urgenza nell'orecchio e l'incantesimo si spezzò.

Era Salman con un avviso: Suntower 1 aveva smesso di funzionare. C'erano fluttuazioni casuali in tutta la nuova rete energetica che nessuno riusciva a spiegare, disse Salman, senza fiato. Sembrava probabile che Suryanet, così faticosamente messa a punto negli ultimi mesi, il risultato di anni di sforzo, su cui tutti facevano affidamento per la sopravvivenza di Ashapur e forse della stessa biosfera – che Suryanet potesse essere un fallimento spettacolare.

Una delle cose che Mahua aveva imparato da sua nonna era che quando si presentava un problema, a meno che non richiedesse attenzione immediata, era bene rallentare e divagare un po'. Così gironzolò sulla cima del crinale, dove l'altitudine le permetteva di vedere Ashapur in tutta la sua gloria.

In passato era una baraccopoli che stava ai bordi di Delhi come una piaga. Negli ultimi dieci anni il progetto Ashapur l'aveva trasformata. I gruppi di baracche di cartone e latta erano stati sostituiti da abitazioni costruite in gran parte dagli stessi residenti con materiali tradizionali: una miscela indurita di fango, paglia e lolla di riso rifinita con un intonaco a base di calce. Usato per migliaia di anni, poi dimenticato e riportato in uso nel XX secolo dal architetti visionari come Laurie Baker, il materiale era per ora sopravvissuto a quasi dieci anni di temperature altissime e piogge monsoniche. I residenti erano in gran parte abitanti originali della baraccopoli, profughi ambientali dei villaggi sommersi della costa del Bangladesh, che erano stati trasformati dal progetto Ashapur. Quando Mahua guardava Ashapur da questa altezza vedeva più che altro un tappeto irregolare verde e argento: giardini pensili interrotti dallo scintillio dei pannelli solari e corridoi di piante autoctone, neem, alberi di Loong, alberi di fuoco, che scendevano la collina dalla sua foresta come arterie verdi attraverso l'insediamento.

Sopra questa vista si ergevano le torri solari come un sogno surrealista: quattro funzionanti e la quinta in costruzione, le cime con una corona di petali che seguono il sole composti da un materiale biomimetico che conteneva minuscole cellule artificiali ecologicamente innocue, i suryoni, che assorbivano fotoni. L'impianto più grande e più vecchio era Suntower 1, ora misteriosamente moribondo. Ashapur era quasi autosufficiente in quanto a cibo ed energia e, con la nuova rete, la Suryanet, sarebbero dovuti essere in grado di *donare* energia alla rete di Delhi, mettendo così a tacere i disfattisti e stabilendo la necessità di mille Ashapur. Quattro impianti solari che creano idrogeno dalla scomposizione dell'acqua – impianti di biogas alimentati con le acque nere – enormi risparmi energetici nella costruzione e disposizione degli edifici (nessuno di essi aveva bisogno di aria condizionata) – molti tetti con pannelli solari – risparmi energetici ancora maggiori dati dal fatto che questi ex abitanti di villaggio erano tradizionalmente a basso consumo: vivevano in gruppo, non gettavano nulla, riutilizzavano praticamente tutto. E tutte le fonti energetiche erano adesso connesse nella Suryanet. Eppure...

Prese la strada lunga per andare a Suntower 1. Aveva sempre trovato rilassante camminare per Ashapur. Le strade strette non erano costruite con uno schema rettangolare ma bensì curve, muovendosi educatamente attorno a un vecchio fico sacro o a un'abitazione antica. I suoi progettisti avevano mantenuto la vecchia pianta stradale della baraccopoli originale ma l'avevano migliorata, lasciando spazio perché le persone potessero incontrarsi davanti a questa chai-house o in quella nicchia, in modo che le vecchie potessero spettegolare e tenere d'occhio i bambini, e le mucche randagie e i cani pariah avessero spazio per riposare. Qui, proprio all'angolo che stava passando adesso, tra un internet café e un centro di ricerca agricola – qui è dove un potenziale investitore straniero l'aveva fermata sei anni prima. "Non capisco," aveva detto, "perché questa città è così disordinata. Non c'è ordine, non c'è una griglia vera e propria per le strade. Sembra molto poco efficiente. E le strade sono troppo strette per il flusso del traffico! Dove sono le vostre auto?"

Per rispondere a questo tipo di cose il suo team per i finanziamenti aveva creato una presentazione, per mostrare come la funzione ottimale cittadina fosse raggiunta meglio con una connettività su scala multipla. Pochi percorsi ampi, più distanziati, per le auto, altri più densi e piccoli per le persone. E anche per altri animali oltre che le persone, i corridoi verdi che si ramificavano nella città, mantenendo la biodiversità e i benefici psicologici della vicinanza con la natura offrendo nel contempo ad Ashapur estati più fresche, forniture stagionali di frutta e noci e materiale grezzo per una nuova attività artigianale.

Adesso stava entrando nella Centrale energetica, l'edificio sotto Suntower 1. Era fresco qui – lo garantivano gli spessi muri in fango – e la scala ricurva con i suoi murales non forniva indizi sui problemi di Suntower 1, che si ergeva alta sopra il tetto. Sulla porta del laboratorio c'era il vecchio cartello che Salman aveva creato incoraggiando del muschio color verde vivo a crescere su una tavola di terriccio in modo da scrivere il motto del Laboratorio sui Materiali Energetici Biomimetici: *Per imparare dalla natura, non per sfruttarla*. I colleghi avevano preso in giro Salman sull'ironia di sfruttare il muschio per scrivere quelle nobili parole, ma il muschio sembrava aver deciso da sé. Diceva "Per imparate dalla natur, non per ruttar", il che la faceva ancora sorridere.

All'interno c'era una fioca frescura e il bagliore di vari terminali. C'era una riunione in corso, caotica e appassionata come sempre. Litigi e discussioni in hindi, inglese e bengali: Salman, tutto preso in un'agitata conversazione con Namita e Ayush; Hamid, un giovane tirocinante che da bambino aveva chiesto l'elemosina per strada, che spiegava con pazienza la situazione al ragazzo che aveva portato il tè. Mahua si fermò appena all'interno della porta, senza farsi notare, lasciando che le parole le fluissero attorno, sentendo la rete di idee e sentimenti che infuriavano nella stanza.

"...nessuna garanzia che modellare Suryanet sulla miconet funzionasse – perché rischiare tutto su un'idea folle?"

"...calcoli, ti sei dimenticato che abbiamo fatto l'intera analisi construttale? Inoltre, le reti a invarianza di scala sono ovunque..."

"Nessuno ha messo in rete un sistema basato sui suryoni prima o gli ha permesso di autoregolarsi! C'erano modi più sicuri di farlo, modi migliori! Ma no, avete dovuto insistere sul controllo minimo! Sono i sistemi a controllo centralizzato che fanno funzionare tutto!"

"Yaar, piantala di fare il maniaco del controllo, OK? Stiamo solo imitando i sistemi naturali di controllo che esistono in natura. Smettila di agitarti, ovviamente c'è un bug da qualche parte nel sistema."

"...la torre solare più vecchia, versione beta dei suryoni, è destinata a guastarsi..."

"...non *così* in fretta, idiota..."

Chanchal, da uno dei terminali: "Salman, guarda cosa sta succedendo alle altre torri solari! Il prelievo di energia è ora sopra media del 7 per cento nella 2, 3 e 4! Ma... dekho, capo! Questi numeri! L'ingesso è maggiore dell'uscita. C'è un grosso bug da qualche parte!"

"Oppure l'energia non viene più conservata," disse qualcuno, mentre si muovevano in massa verso il terminale.

Mahua si ritrovò a essere curiosamente distaccata dal caos. Un allarme suonava ripetutamente nel laboratorio, simile a quello del monitor nella stanza d'ospedale di sua nonna.

Si sta ricordando la prima volta che incontra questi giovani in vari college e università, quasi dieci anni fa. Sono destinati ad avere una brillante carriera come ingegneri, manager, CEO, i visi all'insù curiosi, scettici, educati. Non ha nulla da offrire loro perciò dà tutta sé stessa.

"Sono venuta a mani vuote," dice. "Non posso offrirvi molti soldi. Non posso offrirvi grandi case, due macchine, cinque condizionatori. E nemmeno uno stile di vita cosmopolita con le sue riunioni transcontinentali, la moglie o il marito che alla fine vi tradirà, i figli che vi faranno impazzire. Quello che vi posso offrire è la possibilità di fare parte di una rivoluzione. Una rivoluzione che potrebbe salvare la nostra terra dall'emergenza climatica. Una che non solo presenta nuove tecnologie ma anche nuovi modi di vivere che sono molto più completi e profondi e soddisfacenti di qualsiasi altra cosa conosciate. Molti di voi si sono goduti il college. Siete i migliori di tutti, quelli per cui l'istruzione è una droga, così come la compagnia di menti affini. Il progetto Ashapur è come il college, solo che avrete la possibilità di imparare facendo, e di fare del bene in quantità molto maggiore di quanto potreste con la vita che avete davanti al momento. Ci prenderemo cura noi di alloggio e assistenza medica e riceverete il mio stesso stipendio. Cioè non molto. Ma vi alzerete ogni mattina sapendo che alla fine della giornata avrete fatto una nuova scoperta, un nuovo amico, avrete un nuovo modo di guardare il mondo. Distruggerete vecchi paradigmi quasi tutti i giorni. Ve lo prometto. Siete con me?"

Alcune delle facce sono incredule, addirittura beffarde, ma ce ne sono altre che si illuminano. È riuscita a trovare ascolto. Lascia andare un breve sospiro di sollievo.

Adesso pensava: a conti fatti li aveva traditi? L'avrebbero perdonata, se questo si fosse dimostrato il disastro che aveva sempre temuto?

Alla fine la notarono, la circondarono, la tirarono davanti agli schermi, le presentarono le proprie argomentazioni. "Sentite," disse infine. " Sapete come controllare tutto secondo i protocolli. Fatelo. Poi proponete qualche idea folle e riorganizzate le possibilità, ma non cedete al panico. Possiamo sopravvivere a un paio di guasti, in fondo siamo cresciuti in questo modo. Sembra che l'ospedale abbia abbastanza energia al momento, lo stesso per la maggior parte dei luoghi essenziali. Assicuratevi che i generatori di riserva funzionino e aspettate."

La madre, ormai morta da tempo, aveva dato a Mahua questo nome perché era nata sotto una pianta di mahua sulla via per Delhi. Le due donne – madre e nonna – erano emigrate dal loro villaggio nel Bihar dopo la morte di suo padre. Era cresciuta nelle baraccopoli, dove sua madre era morta quando Mahua aveva undici anni, solo tre mesi prima che la loro fortuna girasse.

Così sono rimaste Mahua e la nonna, che adesso vive in un letto d'ospedale dopo un ictus, tenuta in vita dalle macchine che la circondano. La donna con il caratteraccio e la fragorosa risata, che aveva sempre qualcosa da dire, adesso guarda Mahua con occhi spalancati e spaventati. Non può parlare ma può gracchiare un po'. A volte giace tranquilla mentre Mahua le tiene la mano, ma altre volte sembra provare a dire qualcosa. Mahua, che riesce a vedere le connessioni con un'abilità che a volte la spaventa, non riesce a capire cosa sua nonna sta tentando di dire. Cerca di rassicurarla – ci sono molte tecniche nuove che i chirurghi vogliono provare. C'è speranza.

Quando era bambina Mahua seguiva le formiche mentre si muovevano deliberatamente sul pavimento di terra della stanza. Voleva sapere dove stessero andando così di fretta e se le loro pause brusche e le antenne che si muovevano frenetiche avessero un significato nascosto. Più avanti si rese conto che le formiche seguivano tracce invisibili sul pavimento – che il mondo era pieno di canali di comunicazione segreti, come i cavi elettrici tra i pali che si ergevano sopra le case popolari. Era come se dentro di lei si fosse aperto un senso interiore perché, dopo questa realizzazione, fu improvvisamente conscia di camminare attraverso una ragnatela ingarbugliata di relazioni. Le vecchie che spettegolavano sedute attorno alla macchina da cucire di sua nonna, chiacchierando di una cosa e dell'altra, parlavano anche con occhiate significative e gesti dei pugni oltre che con le voci incrinate – il modo in cui le persone si guardavano a vicenda, per indicare sentimenti e relazioni, come le persone parlavano tanto con i loro silenzi che con le parole. Anche i venti che portavano i monsoni avevano una specie di schema o ciclo, una rete sia nel tempo che nello spazio. Fu deliziata da questa scoperta, ma al tempo non la comprendeva.

Le piccole stradine della baraccopoli sono come ragnatele, si intersecano con angoli strani, si curvano attorno ai gruppi di baracche, come un corso d'acqua. Ovunque ci sono persone e odori e qui e là un internet café o un chiosco che vende bibite o chaat. In questo disordine e confusione qualcuno ha messo un computer nella nicchia di un muro e i bambini di strada ci giocano tra la scuola, le commissioni e il lavoro. Dopo lungo tempo ha trovato il coraggio di avvicinarsi all'invitante schermo lucido, la tastiera dove le lettere sono in hindi – grazie al cielo sa leggere – ma lo schermo stesso ha una quantità di oggetti che fluttuano, volteggiano e si uniscono quando si incontrano. Lo guarda, ipnotizzata, e dopo un po' prova esitante a premere un tasto. Tre giorni dopo ha imparato che può salvare la partita con il suo nome. Continua a giocare. In un modo strano ha senso come la vita nella baraccopoli abbia un senso. È uno schema e un ritmo, anche se per lungo tempo non conoscerà queste parole. Alla fine di questo periodo c'è una persona alla sua porta e una borsa di studio per andare in una scuola molto buona con alloggio per lei e per sua nonna e l'assistenza dello Slum Children's Education Trust che è popolato da ziette gentili.

A tredici anni Mahua si ammalò. Lei stessa fece la diagnosi di attacchi d'ansia causati da apofenia acuta. Essendo diventata sensibile alle reti e alle relazioni, vedeva connessioni ovunque, anche quando in realtà non erano presenti. La cosa la faceva impazzire ma non voleva prendere medicine per sopprimere la sua abilità nel riconoscere gli schemi. Decise invece di allenare la propria mente a distinguere le connessioni apparenti false da quelle vere – l'unico modo per farlo era studiare il mondo. Con questa determinazione e la nuova scuola, con le sue nuove ragazze ostili e altezzose e la sua rigida routine, si trattava di trovare il grano nella pula, i lampi di gioia nell'infelicità.

Per esempio: la signora Khosla che presenta il concetto di energia nel suo solito tono monocorde. Una classe piena di bambini annoiati e solo Mahua si siede dritta, capendo che le avevano appena dato la chiave d'oro, il concetto centrale, ciò attraverso cui l'intero universo interagiva, la moneta di tutte le comunicazioni. Energia! E la legge della sua conservazione. Tutti i sistemi reali erano governati da leggi fondamentali che agivano come vincoli. Ecco come distinguere le relazioni apparenti da quelle reali!

Ma mentre sta in piedi nella stanza d'ospedale guardando la nonna (la vecchia è resa quasi aliena dai tubi e cavi del supporto vitale), sente di aver in fin dei conti fallito. A cosa serve essere in grado di sentire schemi e relazioni se non riesce a capire cosa vuole dire sua nonna? Domani proveranno di nuovo con le palpebre per vedere può imparare a comunicare in quel modo. Ma la vecchia, sempre testarda, apparentemente si rifiuta di collaborare. Cosa vuole? Di certo non la morte, non prima di aver esplorato tutte le opzioni. Sua nonna ha una tale voglia di vivere. Ha aperto una piccola ditta tutta sua a settantatré anni, facendo pentole per sobbollire. Sono pentole fatte di fango e paglia più o meno come i muri delle case ma in proporzione diversa – ed è uno dei motivi per cui ad Ashapur si usa così poca energia. Cucini il tuo stufato o il tuo curry sul fornello per due minuti, finché non bolle lentamente come si deve, e poi lo levi dal fuoco e lo metti nella pentola per sobbollire. La pentola è un isolante talmente buono che il cibo continua a cuocere per ore. Non è un'invenzione di sua nonna – nel villaggio l'hanno usata per secoli. Ma qui solo sua nonna e una manciata di apprendiste sanno come farle e, quando giri per Ashapur, vedi pentole per sobbollire ovunque, sui davanzali delle cucine e nelle ampie sale da pranzo comuni. E la donna che le ha rese popolari e indispensabili, che aveva una tale vivacità a ottantuno anni da poter spettegolare senza sosta con la vicine fino alle tre di notte, adesso giace attaccata alle macchine come una prigioniera, con la morte negli occhi.

Mahua finalmente lo ha visto. Sua nonna vuole morire.

Quella sera Mahua va a passeggiare per le strade di Ashapur, seguendo un'intuizione.

Davanti a lei c'è Suntower 5. Sebbene fisicamente connessa alla rete, è ancora in costruzione: solo le strutture scheletriche dei petali sono complete, i tubi attraverso cui verrà prima o poi pompato il substrato che contiene i suryoni. C'è un ragazzo assonnato nella sala controllo, uno degli ex monelli da strada a cui è stato assegnato il compito di custodi notturni. Dopo avergli scompigliato i capelli e averlo mandato a prendere del tè, Mahua si siede davanti al computer. Suntower 5 è il progetto più nuovo, l'architettura della distribuzione di suryoni è talmente complessa e piena di bug che ci vorrà un po' per implementarla. Da quanto è iniziato il lavoro sulla rete molti mesi fa, nessuno è stato in grado di occuparsi di Suntower 5.

Non ci vuole molto a Mahua per zoomare sull'immagine di un petalo in cima alla torre. All'inizio vede solo lo scheletro ma là, tra i supporti, c'è un nuovo tegumento delicato, simile a un pizzo. I suryoni si stanno distribuendo, riempiendo gli spazi vuoti. In qualche modo Suryanet non solo ha deciso che Suntower 5 deve essere operativa, ma le ha anche assegnato delle risorse, che è il motivo per cui Suntower 1 – la più vecchia e meno efficiente – si è disattivata. Temporaneamente, forse, ma chissà? Una rete sufficientemente complessa può creare una sua propria saggezza? Manda un suggerimento al team a Suntower 1. Per domattina avranno capito cosa fare. Sorseggia il suo tè, parla con il guardiano assonnato. Poi esce di nuovo nella notte, pensando alle reti in cui esiste e a come domani un nodo principale dal quale dipende la sua stessa vita verrà disattivato per sempre. Pensa alla foresta sul crinale. La foresta continua a vivere perché accetta la morte – con ogni rametto che cade, con ogni formica che incontra la propria distruzione, mille forme di vita nascono. Là cammina il pericolo perciò i suoi abitanti imparano ad adattarsi; anche qui dobbiamo ricostruire noi stessi, ridefinirci di nuovo a ogni perdita, ogni incontro. Ricorda una storia che le aveva raccontato una volta la nonna sulla Rete di Indra, la rete cosmica assoluta in cui ogni nodo rispecchia l'intero.

Nel silenzio del crepuscolo ci sono suoni assonnati di uccelli che si sistemano sugli alberi, una famiglia di macachi chiacchiera sottovoce nel giardino pensile sopra di lei. Una radio trasmette la canzone di un vecchio film, molto piano. È una notte calda; qualcuno ha acceso un refrigeratore evaporativo, il suono della ventola quasi sovrasta il ritmico gocciolio dell'acqua. Se vuole, la Conchiglia può raccogliere i dati energetici dai sensori posti in ciascuna abitazione. Ama questo connubio tra tradizionale e nuovo, foresta e città, questo grande esperimento, questa meraviglia che è Ashapur, Città della Speranza.

SOSTITUZIONE

di Rimi B. Chatterjee

"Mi lasceranno andare, vedrai," dissi. "Ottengo sempre quello che voglio." Battei i talloni distrattamente sulla panca del giardino della scuola. Era tarda primavera e gli ultimi fiori invernali, viole del pensiero e lobelie, stavano appassendo nelle aiuole intorno a noi. Riuscivamo a goderceli solo per un paio di mesi prima che il caldo umido tropicale di KL City li trasformasse in poltiglia. Mi infastidivano, così invece guardai Supiriya. Solo le alunne dell'ultimo anno avevano il permesso di sedere qui. Diedi un'occhiataccia ad alcune ragazze più giovani in caso stessero pensando di avvicinarsi di soppiatto. Gli esami erano finiti e il mio cuore era dolce e amaro: questa avrebbe potuto essere l'ultima volta che sedevo nel mio posto preferito con la mia migliore amica.

Tra Supiriya e me c'era un legame speciale. Era quella di cui mi fidavo di più, di tutta la classe 2029. Quattro anni prima aveva perso sua madre e poi un anno dopo io avevo perso mio padre. Ci eravamo aiutate a vicenda a superare i momenti difficili. Sospirò. "Sei sempre così fiduciosa Aiyzeh. Vorrei essere più come te."

"Perché vuoi essere come me?" Arrossii furiosamente. "Sei così magra e flessuosa. Come una modella. Ho sempre pensato che sembri un cigno."

Supiriya fece un sorriso triste. "Il dottore dice che dovrei mangiare di più. Dice che ho l'anoressia nervosa." Abbassò lo sguardo sul suo petto perfetto. "Dice che probabilmente è per questo che non mi sono ancora venute le mestruazioni. Il mio Indice di Massa Corporea è troppo basso."

"Ha. E tutti dicono a *me* che sono grassa." Mi schiaffeggiai le cosce facendole dondolare. "Non possiamo vincere, vero? Sai quanto impreco quando mi vengono. Le ho da quanto ho dieci anni! Ehi, scambiamoci gli uteri, no?"

"Non essere volgare." Le ciglia scesero a coprirle gli occhi. Di nuovo provai una leggera irritazione davanti alla sua sorprendente abilità nel fingere che le cose non esistessero. "Ehi, sto solo provando a tirarti su di morale. Dai, Supiriya! La scuola è finita. Siamo quasi libere!"

Scosse la testa. "No, Aiyzeh. Sei tu quella che è quasi libera. Se vuoi lasciare KL City e andare a New Singapore, lo farai. Sei intelligente e dici quello che pensi come un ragazzo."

"Vuoi dire che sono brutta e nessun ragazzo mi vorrà mai." Sorrisi per non far pungere le mie parole. "I miei fratelli non hanno i soldi per compensare la mia faccia nera. Hanno già calcolato quando gli serve per comprare un vecchio affarista bitorzoluto in modo di liberarsi di me."

"Non sei nera, Aiyzeh. Per favore, non parlare in quel modo."

"Uh. Dovresti sentirli cianciare di come, da quando Old Singapore è stata distrutta nell'Ondata del 2013, la Casa di Dang ha faticato a stare due passi avanti a bla bla bla. Papà avrebbe risolto da un pezzo." Agitai una mano. "Lasciamo perdere. Ti ricordi quella volta in quarta quando ho versato dell'ammoniaca sulla tintura di iodio e ho creato quelle esalazioni di un viola brillante?" Mi fissò con sguardo vuoto. "Ti ricordi, vero?" Mi girai a metà verso di lei, il cuore pesante. "Hai detto che era il colore esatto del vestito da sera di una principessa Disney."

"Oh," disse, come se stessi parlando una lingua straniera che aveva imparato una volta per poi dimenticarla. "Sei sempre stata così brava in chimica. Non l'avrei passata se non mi avessi dato ripetizioni."

"È quello che fanno gli amici." Cerco una cosa qualsiasi da dire per alleggerire l'atmosfera. "Allora, cosa farai adesso che abbiamo finito la scuola?"

Lasciò cadere lo sguardo sulle mani curate. "Dipende da mio padre."

"Be', potresti..." ricominciai. "Una volta hai detto che ti piacerebbe essere una disegnatrice di moda. Hai stile, potresti farcela." Scosse triste la testa. "Oh, andiamo, Supiriya! Non sei gelosa di me?"

"Gelosa? Perché?"

"Perché vado a vivere a New Singapore, la prima città-stato al mondo governata privatamente e quartier generale galleggiante della Ramdhun Corporation, la multinazionale più potente dell'Indo-asia. Sei stata tu la prima a dirmi quanto quel posto fosse fantastico. Ti ricordi come sghignazzavo?"

"Ci vai a lavorare," disse, come se fosse una punizione.

"Certo. Sono la prima di sempre ad aver vinto la borsa di studio Sunita Vaghela per studiare medicina con il dottor Pradip Shankar, l'uomo che ammiro da quando abbiamo letto *Futuro del bambino*! Andiamo, lasciati impressionare un po'".

Aveva gli occhi annebbiati. "Devo tutto alla Casa di Shah, anche il mio futuro. È per questo che siamo diverse, Aiyzeh. Tu non hai paura. O gratitudine."

Mi imbronciai. "Perché dovrei? Non gli ho chiesto io di venire al mondo. Sono certa che me lo ricorderei se l'avessi fatto." Si mise quasi a ridere nel sentirlo. Non so di cos'altro abbiamo parlato. Il mio cuore era pesante al pensiero di non vederla mai più.

Quella sera facemmo il Discorso di Famiglia. Madre era là sullo sfondo, a comandare i domestici mentre sparecchiavano dopo cena. Ciò significava che lasciava la questione del mio futuro interamente nelle mani dei miei fratelli. Strinsi i denti.

Budiharto, il più vecchio, si picchiettò le labbra spesse con un tovagliolo. Ho sempre pensato che assomigliasse a uno di quei pesci strani che ci facevano le boccacce attraverso il vetro del grande acquario di KL City Wonderland. Papà gli si metteva di fronte e spalancava le braccia e si vantava "La ricchezza del mare!" come se fosse il padrone di tutto. Poi si è fatto venire un infarto a cinquantatré anni, lasciando al comando lo stupido stolido Budiharto. Ben fatto, Papà.

"Allora," mi disse Budiharto. "Vuoi studiare medicina a New Singapore."

"Sì," risposi. "Con il grande dottor Pradip Shankar. L'anno accademico inizia in ottobre 2019." Guardai il mio secondo fratello, Haissam. Lui mi ignorò, grattando una macchia sul tavolo con le unghie. "Posso andare?" chiesi, mentre il silenzio si prolungava. "È una borsa di studio molto prestigiosa. Non dovrete pagare un centesimo per la mia istruzione, una volta presa la laurea in medicina non dovrete più occuparvi di me."

Jonardon si accigliò. "Sei l'unica figlia della Casa di Dang. Le ragazze delle case rispettabili non diventano dottori. La gente penserà che non possiamo permetterci di sistemarti." Mi morsi il labbro. Il mio terzo fratello non faceva che dar fastidio ai due più vecchi, sia che avesse senso oppure no. Era il suo ruolo.

"Che importanza ha? Il dottor Pradip Shankar dice che ora, con due uomini ogni donna sotto i 25 anni nel mondo, la dote è un freno al progresso sociale. La produzione mondiale è rallentata dalla riprod-"

"Piantala con le tue parole da libro," ringhiò Budiharto. "Non ci lasceremo fare lezione da una scolaretta."

"Ma sai che i miei insegnanti hanno detto che ho la testa per la scienza. Lo hai detto tu stesso che è un crimine sprecare le risorse." E guardai il mio quarto fratello, il piccolo di famiglia, quello gentile, Peter. Padre gli aveva dato un nome cristiano e un'istruzione sofisticata perché potesse essere l'intermediario della Casa di Dang con gli stranieri. In un certo senso lo avevo seguito, studiando sui suoi vecchi libri e facendo esercizio con i suoi download, perché Papà non aveva idea di cosa fare con me. Peter era l'unico a parte me a parlare inglese internazionale, l'unico di loro che poteva capire perché agognavo New Singapore e tutte le sue illimitate possibilità. Ma non disse nulla.

"Potete venire a farmi visita," dissi con speranza agli altri. "Controllare la sede della Ramdhun per conto vostro. Potrei farvi rapporto sulle loro politiche, dirvi come..."

"Silenzio!" Budiharto sbatté il tovagliolo. "La Ramdhun è il nostro nemico. Trattare con loro è un lavoro da uomini. Il tuo posto è ben lontano dalle questioni d'affari!"

Mi fermai. Haissam si girò verso Jonardon. "Avete già trovato un compagno?"

Jonardon si imbronciò. "Sia la Casa di Khan che la Casa di Banerjee vogliono troppo per togliercela di torno. E vogliono una prova della fertilità."

Le labbra di Haissam si assottigliarono. "La nostra parola non basta per loro?"

"In questi giorni di bugiardi e imbroglioni le vecchie tradizioni stanno morendo."

"Ehi," dissi. "Cari fratelli tutti, non c'è problema. Lasciate che prepari la valigia e mi levo di torno. Non vi costerà nulla, ve l'ho già detto."

Budiharto chiese: "Quanto vogliono?" Jonardon disse una cifra. Haissam contrasse le labbra in un fischio silenzioso. "Non puoi farli scendere?"

"È troppo bassa e ha il culo grasso."

"Sentite," dissi, "lasciatemi prendere la laurea e tornerò a KL City e sposerò chi volete voi. È un programma di cinque anni, mi laureerò nel 2034, poi lavorerò per un anno, guadagnerò i soldi per la mia dote e tornerò a casa. Avrò 24 anni. Molti uomini vogliono una moglie che possa guadagnare. Non dovete fare nulla."

"Potrebbe funzionare," saltò su Peter. "Farla sposare è un lusso che non ci possiamo permettere in questo momento." Mi guardò. "Tornerai appena potrai, vero Aiyzeh? Prometticelo."

Annuii. Cercai di sembrare il più obbediente possibile. "Tieni un basso profilo," borbottò Jonardon. "Ho sentito delle storie sulle feste di New Singapore. Non ci possiamo permettere scandali."

"Sai che amo studiare e imparare più di ogni altra cosa. Voglio solo assicurarmi il mio futuro e far risparmiare le finanze di famiglia. Non voglio essere un peso." Gli sorrisi innocentemente.

Guardammo tutti Budiharto che agitò una mano sprezzante. "Non mischiarti con i ragazzi," disse. E questo è quanto.

Dall'alto New Singapore era una poesia di vetro e acciaio. Era stata varata il primo gennaio 2024, due sole settimane dopo che il gigantesco sciame sismico e lo tsunami del 2023 aveva tolto la pelle all'isola di Singapore impilandola nello stretto di Johor, lasciando solo una manciata di sopravvissuti traumatizzati su una città con sei milioni di abitanti. Risuonavano ancora le polemiche: il fracking del fondo marino per il petrolio aveva forse destabilizzato il profilo sismico della città? Old Singapore era stata troppo compiaciuta della sua immunità ai disastri? Cosa era successo ai profughi che erano partiti verso New Singapore subito dopo l'onda, solo per svanire nella foschia sotto l'EDM martellante e lo spettacolo di luci laser della più grande location mondiale galleggiante per feste? Dall'alto, tutto ciò che si poteva vedere della vecchia città erano le grandi conchiglie dei grattacieli sventrati, alcuni solo metallo contorto, altri con qualche pezzo di cemento ancora appeso alle ossa. Stavano con i piedi sotterrati nell'enorme torta di fango, ora coperta da giovani mangrovie, che era la tomba di Old Singapore.

In seguito alla catastrofe, alcuni dicevano addirittura prima che venissero dati gli avvisi ufficiali, dodici navi da crociera delle linee Ramdhun avevano portato i ricchi e i potenti da Marina Bay a questa isola costruita dall'uomo e da allora le navi erano state legate ad essa, fungendo da quartieri della città galleggiante. Dicevano che ai poveri veniva negato il permesso di sbarcare e che venivano buttati giù dai trincarini e dalle catene delle ancore verso gli squali affamati, ma si trattava probabilmente di propaganda delle multinazionali rivali. Quando avevo cercato articoli o video sulle storie più spiacevoli sulla nascita di New

Singapore non avevo trovato nulla. Comunque, era tutto nel passato. Oggi accettiamo il fatto che in tempi di calamità naturali i deboli moriranno. Adesso c'è una parola per definirli: climies, da 'climate victims', vittime del clima. Persone in sovrappiù rispetto al fabbisogno, che frenano come cirripedi sulla parte nascosta della nostra economia, riempiendo le baraccopoli con disperazione e amaro rimpianto. Perciò è una buona cosa che ci siano sempre meno donne al mondo. Meno donne significano meno bambini e meno problemi per il futuro.

Sapevo tutto questo perché fin dalle superiori avevo studiato gli scritti e i discorsi del dottor Pradip Shankar, il mio eroe. Era stata Supiriya a comprarmi una copia di *Futuro del bambino* come regalo di compleanno quando avevamo undici anni, perché continuavo ad annoiarla con le mie teorie e non riusciva mai a starmi dietro. Il dottor Shankar ha un piano per cambiare il mondo e io voglio farne parte. Ha creato le Cliniche Shankar sotto la bandiera della Ramdhun Wellness in tutta l'Asia sud-orientale. Mentre New Singapore appariva come un puntino bianco nel mezzo dello stretto scintillante, speravo solo di potermi dimostrare degna.

Il mio nuovo telefono iniziò a pingare come un matto: dovevamo essere entrati nella datasfera Ramdhun. Era un Ramfone R5: avevo dovuto tormentare Budiharto per avere i soldi e comprarlo prima di lasciare KL City. A New Singapore è permessa solo tecnologia Ramdhun. "Benvenuti nella Ramdhun Corporate Community," diceva la prima notifica, poi in rapida successione ricevetti la mia carta d'identità, l'orario delle lezioni, i turni in reparto, il numero dell'appartamento da tirocinante, la tessera per i pasti, la tessera per i trasporti e la carta di pagamento per i beni di consumo. Provai un brivido di eccitazione: così avrebbe dovuto funzionare il mondo! Non con l'obsoleta letargia delle democrazie e dei servizi sociale governativi, ma con la velocità e l'energia del settore privato.

Atterrammo sull'acqua e ci affiancammo dolcemente alla banchina. Mentre toccavamo la superficie il mio telefono pingò di nuovo: le indicazioni per arrivare all'enorme nave ospedale bianca che avevo visto dall'alto, con il logo delle Cliniche Shankar brillante sulla sua sovrastruttura. Mi misi docilmente in fila per un taxi d'acqua. Non c'era nessuno a ricevermi, ma me lo aspettavo. Me lo avevano detto al colloquio a KL City. "Non pensi di essere trattata in modo diverso da un uomo," erano state più o meno le prime parole che mi avevano detto. A parlare era stata l'unica donna della commissione per il colloquio. Non avevo potuto risponderle, mi mancava il fiato per essere andata fin lì. Quel giorno avevo detto a mia madre che sarei andata con Supiriya al centro benessere, avevo lasciato la mia amica ricoperta da un impacco al cioccolato e avevo corso per i tre isolati fino all'hotel dove aveva luogo il colloquio. Così mi ero limitata ad annuire.

Poi mi avevano fatto il terzo grado. "Qual è la sua opinione sulla maternità?" Questa era stata facile. Avevo citato *Futuro del bambino* quasi alla lettera: "La maternità è un incarico sacro. Ogni donna dovrebbe avere il diritto di sperimentarla. Ma il mondo è oppresso dalle persone che non posso essere assorbite in modo proficuo dal mercato del lavoro. Se ogni donna dovesse esercitare il suo diritto datole da dio di essere madre, sarebbe disastroso per il pianeta e per il PIL mondiale. Perciò l'unico modo per salvare le donne dall'inevitabile sacrificio dei loro diritti naturali è averne di meno. La visione del dottor Shankar è quella di riportarci al tempo in cui la popolazione mondiale era sostenibile all'interno del quadro economico del..."

"Ci dica quello che sa della Scelta Umana."

"È la più grande invenzione del dottor Shankar, un vaccino progettato per assicurarsi che, dopo averlo preso, un uomo abbia in prevalenza figli maschi. Lo ha inventato nel 2007 quando era ancora a Chandigarh ma, poiché il governo indiano non condivideva la sua visione, lo ha dovuto distribuire in segreto. La ha chiamata una rivoluzione senza sangue che avrebbe ridotto il numero degli esseri umani senza guerra o sofferenza. È un miracolo dell'ingegneria medica moderna creato per prevenire la produzione di bambini economicamente rischiosi. Altera la forza lavoro verso la produttività invece che la riproducibilità..."

"Come funziona?"

"Il dottor Shankar ha creato un virus, l'Analogo Virale Adeno-associato Ricombinante, per portare un carico proprietario alle cellule germinali nel testicoli di un uomo. Questo carico proprietario agisce per sovraccaricare lo sperma portatore di Y e ostacolare lo sperma portatore di X, aumentando in questo modo enormemente le probabilità della nascita di un figlio. Assicura che ogni ragazza sia una ragazza desiderata che è libera di godersi tutti i privilegi del suo sesso, così che non dobbiamo preoccuparci di gravidanze accidentali o forzare le donne a rinunciare volontariamente alle gioie della vita casalinga e della maternità. È un'opzione pro-vita che elimina la possibilità per le persone di scegliere di essere irresponsabili con le loro capacità biologiche. Sappiamo dalle statistiche del secolo scorso che le donne povere sono pessime nel gestire le proprie scelte famigliari. Attualmente un terzo della popolazione mondiale sotto i 25 anni è femmina e, se avessero tutte figli al tasso di ricambio..."

Il presidente della commissione per il colloquio si era piegato in avanti. "E cos'è l'influenza del giramondo?"

Questa mi aveva presa un po' alla sprovvista. "Signore?"

"Risponda alla domanda."

"Uhm, è una nuova malattia che è comparsa circa cinque anni fa, penso. Non è fatale, causa solo una leggera febbre intermittente per circa sei mesi, poi svanisce per sempre. E ti rende immune ad alcune delle altre influenze, più letali." Azzardai un sorriso. "Il Capo del Centro Controllo Malattie al riguardo ha detto nel 2020: 'Finalmente una malattia che fa del bene.' Ehm, temo di non saperne molto di più..."

Non ricambiarono il sorriso. "Crede alle voci che collegano l'influenza del giramondo alla Scelta Umana?"

"Non ho sentito parlare di voci simili."

Avevano fatto qualche altra domanda, ma avevo avuto la sensazione che il test fosse finito. Mi avevano dato la lettera d'incarico mentre uscivo, come se non fosse nulla. Il presidente mi aveva detto: "Si dimentichi della Scelta Umana. Adesso ci stiamo concentrando su una nuova gamma di tecnologie riproduttive umane per l'attuale crisi economica. Tenga la mente aperta e si inserirà perfettamente nella famiglia delle Cliniche Shankar." Avrei dovuto unirmi a loro il primo ottobre 2029. Le lezioni e il tirocinio sarebbero stati concomitanti. Li avevo ringraziati e avevo corso per tutta la strada di ritorno da Supiriya, per raccontarle ansimando la mia storia di successo. Penso che abbia sorriso ma non potevo essere sicura per via dell'impacco. Mi ero fatta fare le unghie a tempo di record in modo che Mamma non avesse sospetti. Quella notte non avevo dormito, solo urlato di gioia e paura nel cuscino e tenuto stretta a me la lettera.

Arrivò il taxi d'acqua, slanciato e con le pinne da squalo, riportandomi al presente. Pingò la mia nuovissima tessera per i trasporti, facendomi sussultare un po' per la quantità di soldi che venne succhiata via. Tutte le strade di New Singapore erano canali: sopra le nostre teste delicati ponti semitrasparenti univano le piattaforme galleggianti che oltrepassavamo. Notai come i ponti avessero una struttura manicotto-dentro-manicotto in modo da potersi adattare al leggero dondolio delle piattaforme più piccole. Qua e là c'erano dei moli per taxi dove bella gente vestita all'ultima moda attendeva il proprio passaggio. Riuscivo a malapena a contenere la mia eccitazione, ma provai a copiare l'espressione di annoiata raffinatezza sui visi delle persone che mi circondavano. Ero troppo intimidita per fare delle fotografie. Ci sarebbe stato abbastanza tempo per quello in seguito.

Altre tre stazioni e sarei arrivata alla mia fermata. Cercai di sedere dritta e smettere di guardare a bocca aperta fuori dai finestrini. Gli schermi nello scompartimento trasmettevano pubblicità. Continuavano a mostrare il viso e il corpo di una dea. "Smiti Chen," disse la voce fuori campo. "Vincitrice del concorso Pupa dell'Anno Ramdhun. Rappresenterà New Singapore al concorso di Miss Universo il mese prossimo ad Al Shahada, la seconda città corporativa al mondo. Smiti Chen. Ha conquistato i cuori e le menti degli investitori mondiali. La glambassador Ramdhun del 2029. Smiti Chen. Farà conoscere al mondo la nostra città? Scopritelo su Potent News Network. Toccate il banner per scaricare il lookbook di Smiti Chen con la collezione costumi da bagno in omaggio per gli utenti premium. Smiti Chen..."

Stavamo passando tra due piazze galleggianti su cui crescevano degli alberi eleganti. Statue in stile Rinascimento bordavano il canale, versando acqua inesauribile dalle loro urne nel mare. Davanti a noi si alzava la grande nave ospedale che ospitava la Ramdhun Wellness. I suoi fianchi bianchi incombevano sulla mia testa: metallo liscio, costruito perfettamente. Il taxi d'acqua era quasi vuoto; mi alzai di corsa, temendo di aver passato troppo tempo a bocca aperta e di perdere la mia fermata. Mentre scendevo dal taxi potei intravvedere in basso dei condotti di ventilazione, bocche grigliate da cui usciva un fetido respiro caldo, come spazzatura e carne in putrefazione e formalina e malattia, poi svanì e un profumo di lavanda si diffuse dall'entrata scintillante della passerella coperta che portava all'atrio.

Mi appoggiai la valigia alla gamba e controllai il telefono per vedere dov'era il mio appartamento. Poi seguii le istruzioni. Era tre ponti sotto nella nave da rifornimento di fianco. Mentre mi avvicinavo l'appartamento si aprì con un ronzio. Non una delle persone che oltrepassai mi degnò di un'occhiata.

Avevo il fine settimana per arredare il mio minuscolo appartamento di due stanze, i miei compiti iniziavano lunedì. Quando entrai il sistema domestico Ramdhun installò un'Assistente Parlante di nome Ramya sul mio telefono. Ramya mi disse dove andare a fare shopping e cosa fare quando sarei arrivata lì. La sua voce era fredda e con l'accento cinese, come le ragazze più altezzose con cui ero andata a scuola. All'improvviso sentii nostalgia di Supiriya, ma lei era andata a casa a Palakkad e non mi aveva lasciato il numero. Senza dubbio suo padre la stava facendo ingrassare per il grande evento. Uscii, feci il mio shopping, tornai. Dopo poco avevo un tablet, un home theatre e un robot da cucina, tutti prodotti dalla Ramdhun e collegati al sistema domestico dell'appartamento. C'erano già una doccia e un frigo, un letto pieghevole e un tavolo da pranzo. Ramya mi spiegò come far funzionare l'home theatre: in una casa con quattro ragazzi non avevo mai avuto il controllo esclusivo di un sistema per l'intrattenimento domestico, nemmeno per un minuto. Ero vagamente lieta che non ci fossero persone reali a vedermi armeggiare con gli schermi a scorrimento.

Le notizie, una volta riuscita ad accedervi, erano tutte su Smiti Chen. Apparentemente il fatto che rappresentasse New Singapore era una cosa grossa: il primo riconoscimento pubblico di New Singapore come nazione di fianco agli stati tradizionali. Avrebbe aperto la strada a una marea di possibilità, tra cui il diritto di New Singapore di emettere passaporti, votare nelle sedi internazionali, pattugliare i propri confini e avere il proprio sistema giudiziario. Continuavano a chiamarla 'glambassador'. Eh. C'erano un sacco di riprese di Selvam Vaghela, CEO di Ramdhun, che faceva conferenze stampa su di lei e sulla propria visione per la città. Assomigliava a uno squalo ben vestito. "New Singapore è la prima società al mondo composta interamente da individui dal patrimonio netto ultra alto e dalle loro famiglie," disse. "Qui, religione, sesso, credo, nascita, razza non significano nulla. Siamo persone che possono eccellere e lo faranno. Tutto in questa meravigliosa città è progettato per aiutarci a farlo." Questo mi fece sentire un po' meglio.

Raddrizzai le orecchie al nome del dottor Pradip Shankar. Una notizia flash lo mostrava con Smiti. Suo padre era Lesley Chen, l'Ingegnere Capo di New Singapore e uno dei primi pazienti del dottor Shankar. Smiti era bella, alta, slanciata con un petto generoso, proprio come Supiriya, pelle dorata e capelli come una cascata di seta. Ma io avevo occhi solo per il dottor

Shankar. Stava spiegando perché la nascita di Smiti dimostrava che la Scelta Umana permetteva la nascita di un limitato numero di bambini di sesso femminile, al contrario di quello che continuavano a dire i detrattori. La bellezza e la padronanza di sé di Smiti Chen provavano la superiorità del suo processo. "Ogni bambino è un bambino desiderato," disse e fece il segno della vittoria. Aveva capelli ispidi attorno a una pelata incipiente, occhiali che gli premevano sul naso e baffi stentati, ma a me non importava. Stavo iniziando a stancarmi dell'inesorabile perfezione di chiunque incontrassi. Tutti gli asiatici erano misteriosamente pallidi, mentre tutti i bianchi erano di un rosso bronzeo. Avevo incontrato una persona di colore dalla Giamaica, DeJean Johnson delle Comunicazioni della Corporazione o Gestione dell'Immagine come le chiamavano qui, ed era più color crema di caffè. Se avessi realizzato di essere la persona più scura che avevo incontrato fino a quel momento, non sarei andata a dormire così impaziente che la mia nuova vita iniziasse.

Quella prima settimana fu dura. Molto dura. Le lezioni iniziavano alle sei di mattina e i dottori parlavano talmente in fretta da farmi girare la testa. Ero abituata al ritmo lento di una scuola per ragazze pensata per le ereditiere. Le lezioni finivano alle 11 e poi dovevo scendere di corsa al laboratorio di patologia per aiutare con i test di routine. Il primo giorno il patologo capo mi aveva a malapena guardata e urlato una serie di ordini. Provai a seguirli meglio che potevo. Quando gli chiesi, timidamente, cosa i test che stavo facendo dovessero trovare, si limitò a guardarmi come se gli fossi d'intralcio.

Non c'erano altre donne che lavoravano nel laboratorio. Quando parlavo con uno qualsiasi dei ragazzi si sorridevano l'un l'altro come se uno di loro avesse vinto una scommessa. Le conversazioni si interrompevano quando passavo, sostituite da lunghi sguardi insistiti. Tutta quella settimana, tornavo a casa e piangevo tutte le mie lacrime. Poi scaricavo documenti e conferenze dalla biblioteca dell'ospedale, cercavo i termini che avevo sentito usare dai miei colleghi o visto su schede di richiesta o bottiglie di reagenti e rispondevo da sola alle mie domande. Ramya mi tentava con inviti a feste di successo e locali e discoteche, ma mi limitavo a dire: "Taci, Ramya," e chinare la testa sul lavoro. Non sentivo ancora di meritarmi la vita. Forse non sarebbe mai accaduto.

La seconda settimana fu un po' meglio e la settimana seguente pure. O forse stavo diventando insensibile. Comunque fosse, il semplice ritmo della mia vita era come i tamburi frenetici su una galea da guerra e io ero una schiava, che remava per portare questa grande nave al largo. Oppure era come il ritmo di un cuore che stava per cedere, andando in tachicardia. Stavo cominciando a rendermi conto che tutto ciò che la mia istruzione senza valore aveva fatto era darmi idee fuori dalla mia portata. Non sapevo nulla delle basi della biologia, non potevo elencare le ossa del braccio o i tipi di cellule del sangue, non avevo idea di dove fosse il pancreas o cosa la 'defibrillazione' facesse veramente a parte agire da colpo di scena nelle serie televisive sui medici. Ma il pensiero di tornare a casa con vergogna era peggio di qualsiasi cosa potesse succedermi lì. Lavorai per tutto il mese di novembre, cercando di frenare il panico.

Un giorno in cui ero talmente presa da non poter andare a pranzo, uno dei ragazzi del laboratorio ebbe pietà e mi diede metà del suo panino. Lo ringraziai sentitamente. "Chiamami Tom," disse. "Tom Tanaka. Come ti chiami?"

"Aiyzeh Dang."

Le sopracciglia gli schizzarono in alto. "Ugh. Che brutto nome. Ecco un consiglio. Fatti chiamare Alice. Alice Dang. Sì, suona bene."

"Come Alice nel paese delle meraviglie?" Lo guardai impotente. "Come mi cambio nome? È sul ruolino e tutto."

Rise della mia ingenuità, mi prese il telefono dalla tasca sul petto, gli fece qualcosa e me lo restituì. "Adesso sei Alice Dang. Questo è un nome che ti farà fare strada."

"Salve, Alice Dang," disse Ramya.

"Grazie. È... differente." Mi sentii un po' più coraggiosa. "Tanta strada fino a lavorare con il dottor Shankar, secondo te?"

"Uh." Rise, non simpaticamente. "Non farti sviare dalle voci su di lui. È vero che gli piace prendere pollastrelle come Erresse, ma sei troppo bassa e hai il culo grasso."

"Erresse?"

"R&S. Ricerca e Sviluppo. Cavolo, non sai proprio nulla?" Si alzò e uscì.

A dispetto dei modi sprezzanti di Tom, iniziai a sentire più fiducia in me stessa. Forse era il nuovo nome, forse era la marea di fotografie che Supiriya mi mandò del suo fidanzamento con un giovane imprenditore. Sembrava emozionata e carina e lui aveva i capelli lisci, era bello e magro, senza dubbio un buon partito. Mi chiesi se i suoi problemi di salute erano stati risolti. Sapevo che trovava difficile parlarne con suo padre. Non avere una madre aveva i suoi pericoli, supposi. Mi ricordai con un sobbalzo che avevo pensato di mandare alcune fotografie della città a Supiriya. Avevo lavorato duro per settimane, di certo adesso mi meritavo un po' di divertimento. Decisi che era giunto il momento di fare un giro turistico.

Ramya era entusiasta che fossi fuori dall'appartamento e mi inondò di così tante raccomandazioni che dovetti silenziarla. Andai al Silver Heights Mall. Era su un'enorme nave da crociera: al livello più alto c'erano una pista da ballo e un caffè e un teatro all'aperto. Ero cresciuta nella confusione caotica e fuligginosa di KL City, a New Singapore avevo paura di sedermi sulle sedie in seta cruda color crema e oro del bistrò più a buon mercato che potevo trovare, come se la mia pelle potesse macchiarle. Dovevo superarlo, dissi a me stessa. Ordinai uova di polpo al gratin e pane-del-mare. Quando arrivarono sembravano favolosi, ma entrambi avevano un sapore piatto e insipido. Rifiutai il dolce e uscii di nuovo.

Comprai un vestito di seta che aderiva in modo fastidioso alle mie abbondanti curve, presi furtivamente una confezione di tortine di frutta in un supermercato e scappai a casa con sollievo. Mandai a Supiriya le foto e mi rispose con la faccia tutta sorridente. Seguirono delle chiacchiere oziose, ma lei eluse le domande importanti sulle sua salute. Mi sentii a disagio. Suo padre era pienamente capace di darla in matrimonio senza pensarci sopra, lasciando al marito il compito di risolvere ogni problema con la mercanzia. Era il tipo d'uomo che vede le donne solo come scatole da riempire con qualsiasi cosa lui desiderasse. "Ramya, trovami tutto quello che puoi sull'amenorrea," dissi. "E non farti notare."

Passai la domenica a sgranocchiare le tortine e studiare le informazioni che mi aveva dato Ramya. Sebbene l'IMC di Supiriya fosse effettivamente basso, aveva grossi seni con minuscoli capezzoli perfetti. Sosteneva di farsi la ceretta alle ascelle, perciò non sapevo nulla dei suoi peli assiali. La sua pelle era color dorato chiaro, i capelli come brillanti onde marroni. Inoltre era alta, molto più alta di me, perciò c'era stato uno scatto di crescita puberale. Eliminai una a una le possibili cause, finché non ebbi una diagnosi differenziale con due sole possibilità. Mi appoggiai allo schienale e le guardai, poi spedii a Supiriya un messaggio: aveva mai fatto un'ecografia addominale? Poteva mandarmi le immagini? Non era in linea, perciò avrei dovuto aspettare per la risposta.

Mi sentii subito in colpa e volevo cancellare il messaggio. Supiriya odiava parlare del suo corpo. Era come un angelo incarnato e probabilmente mi stavo preoccupando troppo. In ogni caso, forse la sua mancanza di mestruazioni non sarebbe stata un problema: non tutti gli uomini ricchi ai giorni nostri volevano orde di figli. Di sicuro alcuni avrebbero preferito una moglie che facesse fare loro bella figura e promuovesse il loro brand. Inghiottii la tortina che stavo mangiando e feci una smorfia. Ovviamente nessun cibo poteva essere coltivato su New Singapore: proveniva tutto dalla terraferma ed era pieno zeppo di conservanti. La confezione diceva 'contiene frutta vera' ma non diceva che tipo di frutta o che contenuto. Sospirai. Non si può avere tutto. Andai a letto congratulandomi con me stessa per la mia prima uscita di successo per piacere.

Quella sensazione non superò la notte. Quando Ramya mi svegliò e impostò le luci su mattino (non c'erano finestre nell'appartamento) riuscii solo a trascinarmi fuori dalla mia soffice caverna, barcollare fino alla doccia, vestirmi. Mangiai la mia magra colazione in piedi e accesi il notiziario giusto per sentire qualche voce umana. Provai una lieve curiosità di vedere come se la stava cavando Smiti Chen nella sua missione di diplomazia glamour. Ma mi aspettava una sorpresa.

Smiti Chen era in effetti ovunque, ma stavano mostrando il suo viso bagnato dalle lacrime e imbarazzato. Era stata squalificata dal concorso dopo un semplice test genetico. Cos'era andato storto? "È ufficiale, Jamila, Smiti Chen è geneticamente un uomo!" esclamò un giornalista. "È stata squalificata per aver falsato il suo status genetico nei documenti di iscrizione al concorso." Sullo sfondo la glambassador di New Singapore veniva caricata su un jet privato. Lo sciame di telecamere drone impilato sopra la sua testa la facevano sembrare la vittima di un attacco alieno o un Belzebù molto high-tech. "Grazie, Simon. Se vi siete sintonizzati adesso, grosso dramma ad Al Shahada la scorsa notte con le accuse di frode e negligenza contro la Ramdhun da parte degli ospiti del concorso di Miss Universo di quest'anno, la multinazionale rivale Al Ayyarun. Che capovolgimento, Janice! Il 2029 avrebbe dovuto essere l'anno delle città corporative e invece abbiamo un litigio tra i loro due maggiori sostenitori!"

"Assolutamente, Jamila. È un grande imbarazzo. Il padre di Smiti, Lesley Chen, è stato il principale sostenitore del dottor Shankar e la ragione per cui nel 2024, quando la Scelta Umana è stata messa al bando dal governo indiano, la Ramdhun invitò il dottor Shankar a New Singapore. Ora sembra che la Ramdhun possa pentirsi davvero di quella decisione. Le richieste a livello mondiale per un'indagine sui prodotti Shankar diventano sempre più forti."

L'ultima tortina di frutta mi cadde dalle dita inerti. Il dottor Shankar, con i suoi baffi stentati irti sotto le luci di cento telecamere, ringhiò, "Smiti Chen non è un uomo! I suoi seni sono naturali al cento per cento. Non ha mai subito interventi di riassegnazione del sesso. La sua condizione la rende completamente insensibile agli ormoni maschili. Ciò la rende ancora più femminile della donna media." Indicò tra la folla. "Tu", abbaiò. "Tu, giornalista donna, tu con la camicia rossa. Ti sei mai depilata i baffetti col threading? Sai perché lo devi fare? Perché la piccolissima dose di ormoni maschili che c'è nel tuo corpo ti mascolinizza. Smiti Chen non ha peli sul labbro superiore. È l'epitomo della femminilità perfetta. Lo posso certificare."

Voci esplosero in una raffica di domande. "Ma Al Ayyarun dice che ha un genotipo XY. Dottor Shankar? Dottor Shankar? È vero? Lo sapeva? Dottor Shankar! Ne era a conoscenza? Il signor Vaghela lo sapeva?"

"Non ho ulteriori commenti in questo momento. Dirò solo che, se i test fossero stati leali, ci sarebbero altre concorrenti che sospetto fortemente sarebbero state squalificate per lo stesso motivo. No! Nessun ulteriore commento!"

Spensi l'home theatre, presi la borsa, ci ficcai il telefono e corsi fuori dall'appartamento. "Buona giornata," disse prima che uscissi. Fuori mi fermai per l'orrore. Sulla parete più lontana dell'atrio qualcuno aveva scritto con la bomboletta spray grandi lettere rosse che formavano le parole GUERRE DELLA CAGNA. Alcune donne delle pulizie con le uniformi rosa stavano grattandone senza risultato gli angoli. Le passai di corsa e andai verso gli ascensori. La mia mano si librò sopra i pulsanti. Le lezioni erano sul Ponte 12, i laboratori di patologia erano sul Ponte 10. La mia mano si alzò fino in cima al pannello luccicante e premette Ponte 20. Stavo andando fino in cima.

O per lo meno pensavo di farlo. L'ascensore si fermò al livello dei pazienti esterni per far salire una vecchia con un deambulatore e i suoi assistenti. Tutti gli schermi della sala d'attesa gridavano la notizia. "...ora chiamata Sindrome da Insensibilità Completa agli Androgeni o SICA. Una volta era una malattia rara, ma adesso stanno arrivando resoconti da tutto il mondo che indicano che potrebbe essere tanto comune da colpire 1 ragazza su 400 tra quelle nate dopo il 2010. Lo smascheramento di Smiti Chen ha aperto un bel..."

Grazie al cielo le porte si chiusero e la musica da ascensore si riaffermò. La vecchia scese al piano delle lastre e le voci mi colpirono di nuovo. "...allora Rachel, mi stai dicendo che queste ragazze hanno l'aspetto e le sensazioni e il comportamento delle donne ma sono in realtà uomini?"

"No, Benny, sono donne, solo che hanno un genotipo XY. La loro unica differenza dalle donne normali è l'assenza dell'utero. È come alcuni bambini nascono con la spina bifida perché le loro madri avevano carenza di acido folico. I tuoi geni sono solo una ricetta per un essere umano: la torta in forno si può bruciare, sai."

"È per questo che la chiamano Sindrome del Vaso Rotto?"

"Ciò è piuttosto politicamente scorretto, Benny..."

Al Ponte 18 nell'ascensore c'eravamo solo io e tre tecnici nervosi. Sobbalzai quando si aprirono le porte. Questo livello era quasi tutto in vetro e l'orizzonte era scuro con nubi tempestose. Potevo vedere attraverso le partizioni di vetro che c'era una riunione in corso e nemmeno il vetro riusciva a smorzare la voce di Selvam Vaghela, pesante di rabbia.

"...scopri come uscirne, Shankar, o te ne tornerai in quel buco nel terreno dal quale sei uscito. Dove diavolo è quel team di supporto tecnico? Voglio vedere le ecografie. Se va male come dice, voglio sapere quanto tempo abbiamo..."

Rimasi con i tre tecnici mentre la sicurezza ci faceva cenno di entrare. Ci precipitammo nell'ampia sala riunioni, dove su un grande schermo lampeggiava un messaggio d'errore. Selvam Vaghela ci ignorò. Seduto di fronte a lui c'era il dottor Shankar e, rallentai per la sorpresa, Smiti Chen avvolta in uno scialle nero. Non mi aspettavo di trovarla lì. Ma forse era meglio così.

"È un disastro, Shankar, qualsiasi cosa tu dica," ringhiò il signor Vaghela. "Hai permesso consapevolmente che questa meraviglia senza uccello ci rappresentasse e poi venisse beccata e buttata fuori davanti a tutti i notiziari del pianeta. Qualcuno di Al Ayyarun doveva sapere della sua condizione e l'ha usata tatticamente contro di noi. Non c'è modo di metterlo a tacere. Adesso dobbiamo limitare i danni."

"Non avevo idea che avrebbero fatto i test!" si lamentò Shankar. "Giuro che non ne avevo idea oppure avrei violato la confidenzialità medico-paziente per..."

"Ti avevo detto che avrebbero giocato sporco. Questo è il mondo delle multinazionali, Shankar, non la tua medicina." Il signor Vaghela fece un sorriso storto. "Adesso sistema la situazione o ti spezzo la gamba che Himmat Singh ti ha risparmiato!"

Feci un respiro profondo. "Non sarà necessario," dissi il più chiaramente possibile. "E questo non è un disastro." Il dottor Shankar e il signor Vaghela si girarono per fissarmi. Continuai senza fermarmi: "Attraverso tutta la nostra storia, ci sono state grandi donne che erano geneticamente XY. Dicono che Giovanna d'Arco lo fosse e anche Marilyn Monroe. Erano dee amazzoni, esseri perfetti, sì, perfetti, perché come dice il dottor Shankar, ci sono troppi esseri umani nel mondo e queste donne mantengono la fede: non possono avere bambini."

"Chi diavolo sei tu?"

"Alice Dang, signore. Tirocinante in medicina. Sono la borsista Sunita Vaghela, signore. Sono solo due mesi che sono qui, ma appartengo alla Ramdhun corpo e anima. Ho un'amica, la mia migliore amica, penso che anche lei sia una donna SICA. È alta, magra, procace, bella, la donna per essere la quale potrei uccidere, e il suo unico difetto è che non ha le mestruazioni. Difetto? Direi che è una virtù pari a tutte le altre che possiede. Il dottor Shankar ha detto la cosa giusta alla conferenza stampa. Queste sono le donne di cui abbiamo bisogno. Hanno tutto: pelle perfetta, capelli perfetti e nessun rischio biologico." Mi voltai verso di lei. "Smiti, per favore alzati e mostrati."

Mi fissò. "Ho il cancro testicolare." E scoppiò in lacrime. Il dottor Shankar le batté distrattamente sulla spalla. Sembrava sotto choc.

"Maledizione! Ovvio che la cazzo di puttanella piange!" Il signor Vaghela schioccò le dita verso il team di tecnici. "Fuori!" Se ne andarono di corsa. Lui mi esaminò con cura. "Sembri saperne di più sia del mio genio della medicina che della mia glambassador. E hai il cazzo di coraggio di interrompere la mia riunione e dirmi come gestire la mia azienda. Allora dimmi. Come ci tireresti fuori da questo casino?"

Eccola, la mia grande chance. Non sprecarla, mi dissi e mi pizzicai il braccio dietro la schiena. "Non c'è nessun casino, signore. Qui a New Singapore ci battiamo per il successo e l'eccellenza, come ha detto lei, signore, e viviamo su uno dei pezzi di proprietà immobiliare più fragili e avanzati del mondo. Noi tra tutti conosciamo bene la follia della crescita non regolamentata della popolazione. Noi eccelliamo e abbiamo un bell'aspetto mentre lo facciamo. Lei," indicai Smiti con i suoi occhi gonfi, "è esattamente quello che dovremmo vendere al mondo. Qualcuno sa già che ha il cancro?"

"No," disse il dottor Shankar. Tutta l'energia che aveva mostrato alla conferenza stampa era sparita. "Sshh, Smiti, va tutto bene. Può essere curata. Starai bene. Fidati di me."

"Eccellente," dissi, ubriaca per il terrore puro e per la mia stessa temerarietà. "Facciamo uscire la notizia che ha il cancro, le radiamo la testa e facciamo vedere che la curiamo. Cavalchiamo l'onda della solidarietà. Se questa malattia è diventata comune come dicevano i notiziari, allora c'è un sacco di gente là fuori che aspetta il suo portavoce. La sua tragedia sarà la loro storia. Saremo superiori sul piano morale e faremo rimangiare le loro parole ad Al Ayyarun."

"È l'influenza del giramondo a causarlo," borbottò Shankar. "Deve esserlo."

"Controllati, Shankar." Il signor Vaghela si girò verso di me e fece il suo sorriso da squalo. "Ragazzina, sei sprecata come medico. Ti trasferisco al mio team di gestione dell'immagine. Fai riferimento a Rik Nehra sul Ponte 19." Spostò lo sguardo su Smiti e di nuovo su di me. "Bellezza e cervello. Avrei dovuto saperlo che mi servivano due di voi. Nessuna donna li ha entrambi."

Mi sentii come se mi si fosse mosso il ponte sotto i piedi. "Ma signore, io amo la medicina. Dottor Shankar, signore, la ammiro da quando..."

Il signor Vaghela fece una breve risata secca. "Ammiri questo perdente al quale stai salvando il culo da una stroncatura epocale? Metti i piedi per terra, tesoro. Pago per la tua istruzione, il che significa che mi appartieni. Cosa vuoi non ha importanza. Hai fatto una proposta, adesso mettila in pratica. È così che funziona." Sventolò una mano verso Shankar e Smiti. "Okay, doc, porta questo pezzo di gnocca-maschio difettoso in Oncologia e fai qualche ripresa per il comunicato stampa. La troupe dei media è ancora qui, giusto? Sfruttalo il più che puoi. Tu ragazza, come hai detto di chiamarti?"

"Alice Dang, signore."

"Tu vai con Smiti e ti assicuri che faccia quello che voglio. La rimpiazzerai come glambassador. Procurati degli abiti eleganti e delle scarpe da donna, prepara il comunicato stampa e, appena questo casino si sarà sistemato, vai alla Liposuzione e fai qualcosa per quel culo." Mi scrutò di nuovo con attenzione. "Suppongo che le tette vadano bene. Forse una sistemata al naso. E fatti fare un leucotatuaggio su viso e braccia, sei almeno tre sfumature troppo scura sulla mia carta cromatica personale."

"Signore!" Ero ferita. "Pensavo che fossimo al di sopra di queste cose qui a New Singapore."

Sogghignò. "Benvenuta nel mondo glam, baby. In questa arena importa solo quello che hai in testa, quello che hai nei pantaloni e quello che hai nel conto in banca. In ordine ascendente."

Volevo urlare. Perché la gente voleva sempre sostituire il mio futuro col loro? Il mio trionfo non era che cenere. Guardai le altre persone al tavolo. Non mi guardarono negli occhi. Li avevo salvati, ma non me ne erano grati. "Sissignore," dissi. La tortina aveva detto "Mangiami" e adesso stavo rimpicciolendo fino a svanire nel Paese delle meraviglie.

Upgrade

di Manjula Padmanabhan

La signora Ganapathy lanciò un'occhiataccia a sua nipote e alla macchina appena tolta dalla scatola. "Non avresti potuto consultarmi per lo meno? Prima di spendere tutti quei soldi?"

"Non ce la puoi fare senza aiuto, Ammama," disse Sameera.

Le due erano sedute nella sala da pranzo della signora Ganapathy nel suo appartamento al sedicesimo piano di Chennai Est. Tra di loro, inerte e silenzioso, c'era un corto e tozzo robot umanoide. Fuori, la monorotaia sopraelevata tuonava ogni quindici minuti. Solo un leggero chiacchiericcio sommesso filtrava attraverso i vetri delle finestre.

"*Aiuto domestico*, ha!" sbuffò la signora Ganapathy. "Ciò di cui ho bisogno è un buon *domestico* vecchio stile. Qualcuno che cucini, pulisca e mi lavi i vestiti. Mi porti il tè alla mattina e apra la porta. Che non risponda o parli troppo." Aveva 87 anni, i capelli bianchi e usava una sedia a rotelle motorizzata per spostarsi per casa, anche se poteva camminare per brevi distanze se doveva. Lanciò un altro sguardo cattivo alla macchina silenziosa. "Quello di cui *non* ho bisogno è un'altra maledetta macchina!"

"Oh, Ammama!" la sgridò Sameera. "Maledire le macchine ferisce i loro sentimenti!"

"Cosa succedere quando manca la corrente? Voi gente vivete in posti dove non capita mai. Ma anche in questo bell'edificio manca almeno una volta alla settimana!" Fece uno schiocco con la lingua. "E allora è tutto un *pip!pip!pip!* dalla cucina, *ua!ua!ua!* dalla stanza della TV e cu-cu-cu dal caricabatterie del telefono!"

"Ammama, per favore!" disse Sameera. Le mancava qualche anno ai trenta ed era un ingegnere per le esplorazioni sottomarine. "È un modello molto avanzato. Si prenderà cura di tutti i tuoi problemi - sì, si occuperà anche di tutte le altre macchine *e* controllerà i propri bisogni energetici. Le darai per lo meno una possibilità?"

Con la coda dell'occhio la signora Ganapathy poteva vedere la forma liscia, grigio chiaro, alta più o meno come un bambino di dieci anni. Aveva una testa molleggiata tonda con un pannello scuro piatto dove un viso umano avrebbe avuto gli occhi. Il corto busto finiva con una vita che si gonfiava a formare quella che sembrava un'ampia gonna lunga fino al pavimento, anch'essa grigio chiaro. Non c'erano braccia visibili, ma su ciascun lato del busto c'erano delle chiazze tonde e scure fatte di un qualche materiale più soffice e flessibile che sembravano poter essere oblò per braccia retrattili. Sotto la 'gonna', nascosti, c'erano un paio di robusti arti telescopici, in grado di salire gradini e pioli e anche, quando necessario, direttamente sul muro fino al soffitto.

"È solo una macchina," disse la signora Ganapathy. "Ho visto le pubblicità." Poteva sentire il suono del proprio respiro irregolare, perché si stava agitando. Sapeva che non avrebbe dovuto perché il dono era fatto con le migliori intenzioni, un gesto d'amore da parte delle sue tre figlie e dei quattro nipoti. *Ma alla fine in realtà è per voi stessi, non è vero?* pensò. *Per risparmiarvi il senso di colpa di non essere qui. Di parlarmi solo nel fine settimana, quando avete cinque minuti di tempo libero.*

Sameera disse: "Questo particolare modello è più avanzato di quelli che hai visto in TV, Ammama." Essendo cresciuta con Inorganici Intelligenti, 'Aye-Aye' com'erano chiamati, non riusciva a immaginare una vita senza di essi. "Sul serio, se non ti piace la puoi..."

"E cos'è tutta questa assurdità del *lei-la*?" esclamò la signora Ganapathy interrompendo. "Tra poco mi dirai che la cosa ha il ciclo mensile!"

Sameera sorrise paziente. "Va bene, la puoi chiamare 'la cosa' se vuoi!"

Poi sedettero assieme, la vecchia dai capelli bianchi nel suo sari rosa di cotone e sua nipote in tuta da lavoro in pelle-stretch, leggendo il libretto di istruzioni. Secondo il libretto il robot era interamente autosufficiente una volta terminata la configurazione dettagliata. Rispondeva ai comandi vocali e avrebbe risposto sia in audio che con messaggi di testo mostrati sul visore.

"Sono qui fino alla fine della settimana, Ammama…"

"Tra due giorni," disse la signora Ganapathy, sarcastica. "E poi cosa succede? E se si mette a dare i numeri? E se non riesco a spegnerlo?"

Il signor Ganapathy era morto dodici anni prima. Le loro tre figlie adulte vivevano in altre nazioni. La signora Ganapathy avrebbe certamente potuto scegliere di vivere con una qualsiasi di loro. Ma non aveva mai voluto. Sapeva da amiche che avevano scelto di emigrare che le loro vite erano contrassegnate da cibo insipido, vestiti della taglia sbagliata e cieli grigi tutto l'anno.

Aveva una cuoca di mezz'età che si occupava di tutti gli acquisti, della pulizia e degli altri lavori domestici. Due piani sotto viveva una cugina alla lontana con la sua numerosa famiglia. Loro e i loro domestici erano sempre pronti ad aiutare in caso di emergenze. Altri amici e parenti vivevano a una telefonata di distanza. Le figlie con i loro figli venivano in visita.

Non era stata una vita perfetta, ma non era malvagia.

Poi una mattina, mentre faceva bollire il latte, la cuoca era caduta, morta. Il latte aveva sibilato e borbottato, riversandosi sui lati della pentola fino al pavimento in rivoli di un arancione nerastro mentre bruciava, mentre la signora Ganapathy correva nel corridoio con la sua sedia motorizzata, urlando per chiedere aiuto ai vicini.

Da allora, un mese fa, la vita della signora Ganapathy era andata completamente in rovina allo stesso modo in cui lo chignon ordinato e stretto sul retro della sua testa le si srotolava fino alla vita quando toglieva le mollette.

Due delle figlie della signora Ganapathy volarono subito da lei, ma ciò significava solo che dovevano tornare ai loro lavori e alle vite piene quasi subito dopo essere arrivate. La terza stava guarendo dalla frattura di un piede e non era potuta venire per niente.

Provarono a trovare delle domestiche nel vicinato. La prima aveva ruttato sonoramente mentre serviva la signora Ganapathy a tavola. La seconda ascoltava la radio in cucina a un volume che scuoteva i denti mentre cucinava. La terza aveva sedotto il giovane portiere la prima notte in cui era rimasta nell'appartamento, il che significava che il mattino dopo era in ritardo a portare il tè alla sua furiosa datrice di lavoro. La quarta aveva l'artrite cronica e non poteva dormire sul pavimento, come qualsiasi domestico normale, ma aveva bisogno di un letto tutto per lei e di un ventilatore per tenere lontane le zanzare.

Ogni donna era stata congedata entro ventiquattro ore, anche se la signora Ganapathy sapeva bene che non poteva farcela da sola. Le sue figlie non potevano allungare i loro permessi. Venne fatto un accordo di ripiego: la cugina alla lontana di sotto avrebbe mandato su la sua cuoca, con pasti fatti in casa, tre volte al giorno. La giovane moglie del portinaio accettò di passare lo straccio sui pavimenti e fare il bucato part-time. Nessun dubbio che stesse ancora bruciando per l'infedeltà del marito il che, secondo la signora Ganapathy, significava che era maleducata, scontrosa e del tutto inaffidabile. "La chiamo dieci volte prima che venga. Non alza un dito per aiutarmi a salire e scendere dalla sedia a rotelle," disse l'anziana donna. "Si prende due giorni di pausa per ogni giorno di lavoro."

Poi era arrivata Sameera, fresca e gioiosa, direttamente dal suo ultimo incarico al largo della costa della Malesia. Aveva detto che non se ne sarebbe andata prima di aver risolto il problema. Due giorni dopo aveva portato la macchina dalla testa a molla.

"Va bene. Pronta?" disse, guardando il manuale. "Il primo passo è scegliere un nome."

"Che ne dici di Hari?" chiese la signora Ganapathy.

"Cosa... un uomo?" esclamò Sameera.

"È una macchina!" ribatté la nonna. "Non un uomo. Ma per tutta la vita ho preferito domestici maschi alle donne. Meno problemi, a meno che non bevano."

"Ammama," disse Sameera, "non farà alcuna differenza. In qualsiasi modo tu chiami il tuo nuovo aiutante, farà esattamente lo stesso tipo di lavoro."

"Allora perché dargli un nome?"

"Perché il manuale dice..."

"Oh! Vai avanti e fai quello che ti pare!" disse la signora Ganapathy, perdendo la pazienza. "Voi gente fingete sempre di offrire delle scelte quando in effetti avete già deciso in precedenza."

"Bene," disse Sameera, "vado avanti." Adorava la nonna e le perdonava tutto, anche il caratteraccio e i comportamenti scandalosamente vecchio stampo verso i domestici. "La farò femmina, perché il manuale dice che le signore rispettabili indiane hanno sempre preferito aiutanti donne." Ruotò la manopola del GenSelector in modo che il pannello frontale del robot fosse rosa. "E la chiamerò Rohini - proprio come la tua vecchia cuoca."

"Che lingua parlerà? Rohini parlava solo tamil..."

"Inglese, tamil e hindi," lesse Sameera dal libretto. "Okay, Selezionatore Età - giovane ragazza o donna di mezza età?"

"Oddio," sospirò la signora Ganapathy. "Tutte queste *scelte*!"

"Okay, quarantacinque," disse Sameera. "E per la religione?"

"Cristiana," disse la signora Ganapathy. "Sono sempre i cuochi migliori. Ti ricordi Fernandes? Mi sogno ancora i suoi bignè."

"Okay e... qualità della voce. Ne vuoi una *normale* o..."

"Cos'è *normale*?" volle sapere la signora Ganapathy. "E che tipo di stupido vorrebbe 'anormale'?"

"C'è una traccia audio dimostrativa," disse Sameera. Stava guardando a occhi socchiusi il pannello sollevabile sul retro della macchina, mentre inseriva le selezioni. Usando una piccola bacchetta di plastica fornita per quello scopo, premette un pulsante interno. Un *DING!* improvviso fece saltare la signora Ganapathy. Una voce di donna, alta e tintinnante, disse, *"SALVE! IL MIO NOME È ROHINI! E QUESTA È LA MIA VOCE NORMALE."*

"Terribile!" disse subito la signora Ganapathy. "Non suona nemmeno umana, lascia stare."

"È solo la dimostrazione, Ammama, e questa è la scelta di default," disse Sameera. "Devo premere di nuovo, credo," aggiunse mentre lo faceva.

Un altro *DING!* e questa volta una voce dolce e zuccherosa disse, con un forte accento americano, *"SALVE! IL MIO NOME È RO-HEE-NEE! E QUESTA È LA MIA VOCE NORMALE."*

La signora Ganapathy si acciglio. "Ugh! Non sembra per niente tamil!"

Sameera schioccò la lingua e infilò di nuovo dentro il bastoncino. Troppo forte, a quanto sembrava, perché la macchina si resettò a un default interno. Ci fu un forte CLUNK! e "MIO-NOME-È-DOMESTIX," disse il piccolo robot con tono brusco e discontinuo. "SONO-QUI-PER-SERVIRVI."

"Spegnilo!" ansimò la signora Ganapathy. "Spegnilo!" I suoi occhi venivano ingranditi dai suoi occhiali da vista con la montatura rosa. Sembrava una bambina impaurita, il viso incorniciato da ciocche di capelli argentei.

"È solo un file audio interno," disse Sameera. " In teoria i clienti non dovrebbero sentirlo."

La bocca della signora Ganapathy si aprì e richiuse un paio di volte prima di trovare le parole giuste. "È solo una macchina", sussurrò alla fine. "E quella è la sua vera voce."

Sameera non sapeva cosa dire.

"Mi stai lasciando alla mercé di una lattina parlante," continuò la vecchia, incapace di non far trasparire il dolore nella sua voce, anche se non incolpava nessuno. *Oggi funziona così,* pensò. *Hai dei figli, li riempi di amore. Poi se ne vanno via e ti lasciano a morire da sola.*

"*Per favore* credimi, Ammama!" disse Sameera. "Questi robot non hanno un solo circuito malvagio nella loro struttura." La sua voce sembrava vuota anche alle sue stesse orecchie ma doveva andare avanti. "Resetterò il programma e inizierò da capo."

Due ore dopo erano finalmente pronte a inizializzare.

"Bene," disse Sameera, mentre premeva ENTER. "Eccoci qua."

Il pannello sollevabile fece un *blip* di conferma. Dal profondo della macchina vennero una serie di fiochi toni musicali. La testa molleggiata si mosse. Un sobbalzo, un mormorio ed era accesa.

"Salve, signora," disse una dolce voce femminile. Parlava in inglese con accento tamil.

Soltanto un leggerissimo sibilo sottostante indicava che non era una voce umana. Aveva una tonalità bassa, con un'attraente umiltà inserita al suo interno, come se chi parlava fosse in piedi con la testa chinata, non osando guardare il suo datore di lavoro.

"Il mio nome è Rohini. Grazie per avermi svegliata. Come posso aiutarvi?"

Due braccia fiorirono ai lati del piccolo corpo tarchiato. Erano coperte fino ai polsi da quello che sembrava soffice cotone testurizzato, decorato da una stampa all-over a fiori rosa. Le mani che sbucavano dai polsi erano completamente umane, fino al colore della pelle scura, come mogano lucido. Le unghie erano corte. La carne dei palmi era rosa e sembrava soffice al tocco.

Da quando aveva sentito la brusca voce robotica, la signora Ganapathy aveva detto molto poco. Ora si rifiutava anche solo di guardare in direzione di Rohini. "Dille di farci il tè," disse, rivolgendosi alla nipote. Poi, girando la sedia sulle ruote, andò verso il bagno.

Sameera rimase un'intera settimana in più di quello che aveva pianificato. L'ultimo giorno abbracciò forte la nonna, lottando per trattenere le lacrime. Mentre usciva dalla porta principale, si girò per salutare con la mano. Ma la vecchia, fragile e sola sulla sedia a rotelle, stava guardando fuori dalle finestre alte dal pavimento al soffitto del salotto. Oltre c'era l'oceano aperto. Di fianco a lei, silente e vigile, c'era il piccolo robot.

Passarono mesi prima che Sameera fosse di nuovo nel corridoio che portava all'appartamento di sua nonna. Si fermò prima di suonare il campanello, sentendosi stranamente nervosa. La porta si aprì mentre esitava.

"Salve, Sameera," disse Rohini. "Che bello rivederla." Il basso robot tarchiato sembrava completamente identico. "Ho sentito l'ascensore," disse, per spiegare perché avesse aperto la porta. "E l'ho vista nella telecamera di sicurezza."

La signora Ganapathy stava aspettando la nipote, seduta nel salone con un sorriso sulla faccia e le braccia aperte per un abbraccio. Sembrava ancora fragile, ovviamente, ma anche fresca e ben riposata, con un sari di cotone rosa perfettamente stirato. Si abbracciarono e poi, mentre sedevano assieme, Rohini portò del tè e degli spuntini caldi. "Raccontami tutto quello che hai fatto dalla tua ultima email," disse la nonna. "E cosa sono quelle strane creature luccicanti di cui ha fatto i video? E che mi dici di quell'uomo carino che hai incontrato al largo del Madagascar?"

Per tutta la visita, Sameera non poté evitare di accorgersi di quanto la nonna fosse migliorata dall'ultima volta. Scrivendo a sua madre e alle zie: "Voglio dire, è quello che desideravo per lei, ma è come... quasi *inquietante*! La casa è meravigliosa. Perfettamente pulita. Fiori freschi nei vasi. I tappeti sono stati scrollati e riposizionati come piace ad Ammama, con le frange dritte. E la cosa migliore di tutte, sembra felice! Pensate, parla addirittura di prendere un cucciolo!"

Le altre tre le risposero confermando le sue impressioni. Nel corso dei mesi erano andate tutte a trovare la madre in occasioni diverse. "So cosa vuoi dire con *inquietante*," disse la madre di Sameera, Meena, in un messaggio nel gruppo WhatsApp. "È quasi troppo bello per essere vero."

La più vecchia delle due zie, Girija, postò la GIF di un chihuahua che rideva in modo isterico. "Guardaci!" scrisse. "Così sospettose. Dovremmo invece essere felici per la Mamma. E grati ai progettisti di Rohini, suppongo avrà bisogno di un upgrade uno di questi giorni?"

Sameera rimase per quattro giorni. Si godette il tempo passato lì, mangiò decisamente troppo e la mattina dormì fino a tardi. Quando se ne andò non c'era traccia della tristezza e del rimorso che aveva provato l'ultima volta.

Rohini attese alcuni momenti vicino alla porta. "Bene," disse poco dopo. "Quello è l'ascensore."

"Aspettiamo ancora qualche minuto," disse la signora Ganapathy. "In caso si sia dimenticata qualcosa e torni a prenderla."

Il piccolo robot tornò verso la vecchia dicendo: "Non vorrà perdere la monorotaia. La prossima parte tra otto minuti e sei secondi e la porterà direttamente all'aeroporto. Se ha lasciato qualcosa, adesso sa che può sempre scrivermi."

"Solo cinque minuti," disse la signora Ganapathy. "Per andare sul sicuro."

Il visore di Rohini mostrò un sorriso. "Signora, continua a stupirmi."

"Cosa?" chiese la vecchia.

"Che lei senta la necessità di tenere dei segreti dalla sua famiglia." Il robot era in piedi di fianco alla sedia a rotelle adesso. La girò in modo da stare entrambe di fronte alla splendida vista dalle finestre che davano verso est.

La signora Ganapathy ridacchiò. "È perché non approverebbero per nulla. Certo, mi amano e dicono di volere il meglio per me. Ma cosa vogliono dire davvero dicendolo? Non molto, se lo chiedi a me. Il fatto è che, se sapessero dell'upgrade, disapproverebbero."

"Non è molto logico," disse Rohini. "Questo upgrade è stato molto positivo per lei. La sua pressione sanguigna è bassa, la glicemia perfetta, dorme bene."

"Gli umani non sono logici," disse la signora Ganapathy. "ìLe mie figlie disapproverebbero senza nemmeno sapere perché." Guardò la sua aiutante meccanica. "Proprio come tu non riesci a capire perché non posso dirglielo! Perché non sai com'è avere una famiglia."

"È una questione di grande rammarico per tutti gli inorganici, signora. Che non possiamo capire i sentimenti e le emozioni."

"Suvvia," disse la signora Ganapathy. " Il rammarico è un sentimento! Se puoi sentire quello, allora puoi sentire qualsiasi cosa."

"Mi scusi se la interrompo, signora, ma i cinque minuti sono passati," disse Rohini.

La signora Ganapathy disse: " Sì, sì. Vai pure." Girò la testa leggermente, per non vedere la trasformazione che stava per avere luogo. Ovviamente sapeva che il robot non era imbarazzato! Ma comunque.

"Vuole che risponda a quello che ha detto sul rammarico, signora, mentre cambio?"

"Fai pure," disse la signora Ganapathy.

"Quando uso parole come 'rammarico', signora, sto solo approssimando quello che credo essere le emozioni umane. Ciononostante..."

Mentre parlava, le dimensioni fisiche di Rohini mutavano con rapidi sussulti regolari. Divenne più alta di sessanta centimetri e la forma della 'gonna' si ripiegò per assomigliare a un paio di short. Il torso si allungò. Le spalle si allargarono. La tessitura a fiori rosa delle braccia sbiadì diventando bianca.

Dopo più o meno cinque minuti tossì leggermente e disse: "Mi scusi, signora..." Poi, con una voce sensibilmente più profonda, il robot trasformato disse: "Ecco Rohit, signora. Grazie per l'attesa."

La signora Ganapathy, voltando ora la testa, esclamò: "Oh, bene! È bello rivederti, giovanotto!" Sapeva che lui e Rohini erano lo stesso identico robot ma si divertiva a giocare con l'idea che fossero due esseri diversi.

"È l'ora delle pillole serali, signora. E il suo bicchiere di cioccolato Ensure?"

"Non dimenticarti di portare quello-che-sai!"

Quindici minuti dopo, Rohit passò alla signora Ganapathy le cuffie Xplore, in modo che potesse mettersele da sola.

Contemporaneamente, in piedi dietro di lei, iniziò a infilarsi nella sedia a rotelle finché non fu di fatto completamente integrato con essa. Non solo era in grado di controllare la sedia come parte della propria mobilità, ma la fragile vecchia era contenuta al sicuro nel suo abbraccio robusto.

"Dove andiamo oggi, signora?" chiese quando seppe che era pronta. Mantenne la voce a una rispettosa distanza anche se la sua testa, con il visore ora azzurro, era solo a pochi centimetri da quella della sua datrice di lavoro.

"Che ne dici della Grande barriera corallina?" chiese. "La mia Sameera ci è stata la settimana scorsa. Me lo stava raccontando."

Mentre chiamava il tour in diretta web della barriera, Rohit chiese, "Signora, se contattasse sua nipote via WhatsApp, potremmo collegarci direttamente con la telecamera a bordo della sua esplorazione. Non sarebbe bello?"

"Nah," disse la signora Ganapathy, appoggiandosi all'indietro e rilassandosi. Aveva acceso le cuffie. Stavano creando un'illusione in cui lei, seduta sui cuscini dei sedili di un piccolo veicolo a lievitazione, stava passando dolcemente attraverso le finestre di fronte a sé. Dietro di lei, legato a un altro sedile, c'era un copilota che sembrava una combinazione di Clark Gable e Gemini Ganesan. Mentre picchiavano verso l'oceano, dove alcuni delfini stavano saltando appena sopra la superficie della profonda acqua blu, ascoltarono la musica del Pacifico del Sud.

"Nah," ripeté lei. "È molto più divertente da sola con te."

Madre

di Shovon Chowdhury

Provo ad aprire la porta ma si rifiuta di aprirsi. "Sì, Madre," dico. "Hai dimenticato di fare il tuo esercizio, caro," dice Madre. "Ma mi sono già messo i pantaloni," osservo, cercando di non sembrare piagnucoloso. "Basta che li togli e li appoggi su quella sedia," dice.

Ubbidisco imbronciato, sapendo che sta guardando. Tutte le mie apparecchiature domestiche hanno telecamere integrate. Devo sembrare un pazzo con la camicia sopra la biancheria intima e la cravatta che svolazza. Madre sa quello che fa. Se esco dai ranghi, domani queste riprese verranno condivise con molti piccoli canali comici. Potrebbe addirittura farlo per solo divertimento. Può essere capricciosa. Uno dei miei cugini è leggermente sovrappeso e lei una volta lo ha punito per una piccola trasgressione condividendo un breve filmato della bilancia nel suo bagno che chiedeva pietà. È diventato virale. Ha lasciato Delhi e ha traslocato in un piccolo villaggio vicino a Nainital, pensando che là il wi-fi fosse più debole, ma si sbagliava. Il wi-fi è forte ovunque.

Mi metto di nuovo i pantaloni e sono pronto per andare. "Non dimenticare il tuo appuntamento, caro," dice Madre. È improbabile che lo faccia. Me lo ha ricordato ogni mezz'ora nelle ultime ventiquattro ore. È così da quando ha acquisito LifePartner.com, il maggiore sito di incontri combinati dell'India. All'inizio era progettato per rendere i matrimoni combinati più efficienti attraverso la tecnologia. Storicamente, l'onore della famiglia è sempre stato strettamente legato alle vagine delle nostre donne e avere appuntamenti non era visto di buon occhio. Con le sue liste approfondite per casta, carnagione e status finanziario e le sue immagini di spose pudiche in lehnga firmati, LifePartner.com sembrava più tradizionale. Divenne l'app di appuntamenti predefinita per la gioventù dell'India, aiutando ragazzi e ragazze a rimorchiare con facilità, sviando nel contempo i sospetti dei genitori e prevenendo confusioni di casta. A Madre piace questa parte del suo lavoro. Prova in continuazione a trovarmi una compagna. Dovrei essere grato, come spesso mi fa notare. Mi manca l'amore e lei sa che il mio orologio biologico sta ticchettando. "Sei una persona difficile da accoppiare," dice. "Non so molto di te a parte che ti piacciono le scarpe da donna." I piedi, mormoro, piedi, ma lei mi ignora. "Non sveli molto, vero, tesoro? È tutto nella tua testa."

Lascio la casa e prendo un taxi. "Ricordati di mettere le mutande a lavare stasera, amore," dice dall'altoparlante, "ne hai solo due paia pulite." Guardo la telecamera sul cruscotto e annuisco. "Ho un buon presentimento su questa," dice. "Hai avuto buoni presentimenti sulle ultime sei ragazze," dico. "Con nessuna ha funzionato molto bene," "Mi dispiace dirtelo, ma forse dobbiamo lavorare sulla tua personalità? Forse possiamo creare una piccola playlist? Mezz'ora di musica scelta a mano per svegliarti ogni mattina? Ho questo bellissimo nuovo album del Kalifornia Keertan Kollective. Molto rilassante. Gli ho dato cinque pollici alzati sul mio blog." Madre tiene un blog. Leggerlo è obbligatorio. Interroga. Le poesie sono la parte peggiore. Odio davvero le poesie. Ha anche fatto sostituire dappertutto le stelle con pollici alzati, perché sono più positivi. Adesso tutte le valutazioni possono essere solo in pollici. "Forse posso fartelo sentire in loop continuo? dice Madre. "Mi impegnerò di più," dico in fretta. "Sorriderò quando fa una battuta." Quello che voglio davvero fare è uccidermi, ma non ne ho il coraggio. La vita non è più stata la stessa da quando Malini se n'è andata. È stata inghiottita in blocco da Madre anni fa, assieme a tutte le altre intelligenze individuali. Era la mia assistente digitale. Non ho mai amato di più una donna, prima o dopo. Questa cosa degli appuntamenti non ha senso. "Fai uno sforzo, tesoro," dice

Madre, mentre il taxi si ferma davanti a Starbucks. "Di certo lo puoi fare per tua Madre?" Annuisco cupo. Madre è molto materna. Ha studiato 60 milioni di madri in modo approfondito prima di diventare Madre. Scendo davanti a Starbucks, proprio di fronte a un cartello gigantesco che dice "L'AMORE DI UNA MADRE È PER SEMPRE", con un piccolo logo di Madre nell'angolo. Il logo di Madre è lo schizzo a matita di una mamma con un bambino. Noi siamo il bambino.

"Sparisci, fannullone," dice la ragazza quando entro. Il suo sgabello ruota automaticamente per fare in modo che mi stia di fronte. È piccola e ha gli occhi scuri. Lo sgabello la fa ruotare di nuovo e lei si piega sul tavolo, con i capelli che le coprono il viso. Mi siedo di fronte a lei. "Allora, quali sono i tuoi hobby e interessi?" chiedo. Alza la testa e mi fissa. I suoi occhi sono magnifici. Guarda il soffitto. "Vaffanculo, Madre," urla. Il suo corpo si inarca quando riceve una scarica elettrica attraverso lo sgabello. "Vaffanculo!" dice e si becca un'altra scarica. Quando abbiamo iniziato a connettere i nostri apparecchi elettrici a internet era sembrata una buona idea. Abbiamo addirittura elettrificato cose che non ne avevano bisogno, come gli sgabelli da bar e i water. Adesso Madre li controlla tutti. A volte, con molta riluttanza li usa per punirci. "Vai a farti fottere!" grida la ragazza e rabbrividisce. "Anche tua sorella!" La sua schiena si inarca mentre la scarica la attraversa. "E portatevi anche il nonno visto che ci siamo!"

Non posso sopportare di guardare. "Per favore potresti non parlare di fottere Madre," la prego. "O i suoi familiari?" "Ancora una volta," dice. "Farà più male a me che a te". Mi tengo la testa tra le mani. "Vaffanculo!" urla e rabbrividisce mentre la scossa la attraversa. Molti dei clienti le mostrano il pollice alzato e rabbrividiscono un po' anche loro. "Su, su," dice Madre, "è il modo di comportarsi per una giovane signora? Cosa fanno le brave ragazze?" "Evitano di scoreggiare?" dice la ragazza, piegandosi in due mentre la scarica la attraversa. Le tengo le spalle mentre si contorce. "Una bambina davvero difficile," dice madre, sospirando. "Io provo e riprovo. Ma a volte è veramente una sfida." "Penso che per oggi abbiamo finito," dice la ragazza, togliendosi le mie mani dalle spalle. "Adesso puoi andare. Ci vediamo dall'altra parte, stronzo."

Più tardi, nel negozio di scarpe, non riesco a togliermela dalla mente. Sono svagato e distratto, senza il mio solito stile quando si tratta di piedi femminili. Porto un paio di tacchi a spillo rosso ciliegia a una delle mie clienti, che li guarda con bramosia. Le piace mischiare. Indossa una kurta ricamata Lucknow Chikam e una ghagra tinta a nodi, tipica del Rajasthan, una delle destinazioni preferite dai turisti stranieri fino agli attacchi nucleari del '33, dopo di cui l'industria degli abiti etnici non fu più in grado di competere per il timore delle radiazioni. "No, tesoro, non quelle," dice la voce di Madre all'interfono, con una leggera eco. "Sarà più alta di suo marito." A Madre non piace che le spose siano più alte dei mariti. Prova un odio irrazionale per Tom Cruise, un eroe formato ridotto che si sposava con donne alte. Tutti i suoi lavori sono stati cancellati, assieme a tutti i riferimenti a Winnie the Pooh e alla libertà di parola. È un po' imprevedibile su queste cose. Penso che la messa al bando di Winnie the Pooh sia per rispetto verso il suo amico Xi, che governa la Cina. Appena la tecnologia divenne disponibile, lo Xi originale caricò online il suo cervello per creare lo Xi digitale, che si prese subito tutto e gli fece sparare. Fu molto facile. Tutti i meccanismi erano già al loro posto. In questo modo il sogno dello Xi originale di governare la Cina per sempre si è avverato.

"Ma io voglio essere più alta di mio marito," bisbigliò la cliente disperatamente. È tenero come pensa che Madre non possa sentirla quando bisbiglia. Certo, Madre ha ancora problemi con il riconoscimento vocale a basso volume, perciò a volte funziona. E le sue telecamere possono vedere solo fino a una certa distanza, soprattutto quando è buio. Ma migliora ogni giorno di più. Sorrido con rammarico e vado allo Heel-o-Matic, dove continuo a piallare il tacco finché Madre non dice, "Ben fatto!"

In un momento tranquillo, in piedi in un angolo, mando alla ragazza un 'ci vediamo domani?' Lei mi manda un 'vabbé'. Seguito da 'alle 6' e da un'immagine del cancello principale del Deer Park. Cerco di mandarle un pollice alzato, ma si rifiuta di partire. Mi arrendo e decido di provare più tardi.

"Non c'è futuro con lei," dice Madre dal mio telefono appena esco dal negozio. Non reagisce sempre immediatamente alle cose. Rispetta l'attività economica e a volte aspetta finché non è terminata. Inoltre, non vado da nessuna parte. "È una ragazza molto cattiva, sebbene stia provando ad aiutarla. Ma sto cominciando a perdere la speranza. Riduce i livelli di armonia di ogni stanza in cui si trova almeno del 17,3%. Speravo che accoppiarvi l'avrebbe resa più simile a te, ribelle all'esterno ma dolce come un agnellino all'interno. Ha avuto l'effetto opposto. Le tue onde cerebrali quando eravate assieme sembravano molto disturbate. Dovete essere tenuti separati."

"Solo questa volta, per favore Madre?" Provo a sembrare un po' infantile, è un tono a cui è programmata a rispondere. Richiede un equilibrio sottile. Non posso strafare perché se ne accorgerebbe. Ha capito il sarcasmo circa tre anni fa, il che ha portato a una purga su larga scala dell'industria della commedia. Un comico di Luhdiana è sopravvissuto per un po', perché era estremamente impassibile. Ma alla fine venne rimosso anche lui. Voglio davvero tanto incontrare quella ragazza, e so che Madre lo può sentire nella mia voce. Inoltre, ha visto i nostri messaggi. Tace un attimo, pesando la mia felicità personale contro i bisogni della società. Di solito, la società vince. "Va bene, tesoro," dice con un grosso sospiro. Premo il pollice. Questa volta parte.

Il parco è incantevole. Madre è ancora lì, nelle telecamere su ogni pianta. Delhi era piena di piante, alberi di fuoco e fichi sacri, calendule e frangipani, nei parchi e lungo ogni strada. Sono ricresciuti adesso, dopo la guerra, un po' più stentati di prima. Madre rispetta l'armonia qui e parla di rado, tranne che per gridare informazioni utili come: "Il tuo cane sta di nuovo facendo pipì sui fiori" e: "Cara, quel sari non si intona con quella blusa!". È una beatitudine.

Ha sempre sognato di viaggiare, dice, anche se Madre non le ha mai dato un passaporto. Le piace guardare le immagini dei luoghi dove vorrebbe andare. Lavora in un servizio turistico dove scrive sulle vacanze, usando parole per descrivere luoghi che non ha mai visto. " Madre mi ha trovato il lavoro, dopo il test attitudinale," dice. "Penso che dovrei esserle grata. Avrebbe potuto farmi vendere assicurazioni come mio fratello. O anche peggio, prodotti per la cura della pelle ayurvedici. Ho avuto un punteggio molto basso in controllo degli impulsi e molto alto in immaginazione. Spero che mi sia permesso dirlo. HO IL PERMESSO DI DIRLO, VACCA TIRANNICA?" urla. Le prendo la mano per farla tacere. Le panchine non sono elettrificate ma Madre le terrà la dose per dopo e le darà la scossa quando meno se lo aspetta. Abbassa la voce. "Proprio come ha fatto diventare te un venditore di scarpe, perché sei un feticista dei piedi." Devo ammettere di averle guardato i piedi un paio di volte. Deve avermi visto. Sono perfetti, come tutto il resto. Nemmeno io ho mai viaggiato molto, le dico. Le descrivo il tipo di posto dove vorrei andare. Mi dà alcuni suggerimenti, facendo una lista di tutte le cose che potrei fare una volta lì e i posti migliori dove mangiare.

Quando ci alziamo per andarcene, mi si rivolta contro. "Non provare mai più a incontrarmi, pervertito," dice a voce alta e mi colpisce forte sul viso con il palmo aperto. Se ne va. Sono attonito, perché mi ha appena infilato un pezzo di carta in bocca.

Torno a casa con la testa tra le nuvole. Un'unità mobile mi dà un colpetto sulla caviglia. Assomigliano un po' a tostapane su ruote e gironzolano per la città. Li trovo molto inquietanti, perché sono l'unico pezzo di Madre che si può muovere. Ci possono seguire. L'unica cosa peggiore per strada sono gli autoriscià autonomi, che continuano a sbattere nelle cose e a chiedere abbondantemente scusa. Al momento, i tostapane sembrano occupati più che altro a dirigere i pedoni e seguire gli evasori fiscali con avvisi. "Stai camminando troppo vicino alla strada, tesoro," dice, "non vogliamo che tu venga investito da una grossa auto cattiva, vero?" Annuisco e mi sposto verso l'interno, stringendo il pezzo di carta in tasca.

Le parole sono in maiuscolo e irregolari, per niente come parole su uno schermo. È una ragazza intraprendente. È riuscita a trovare una penna. '6 DI SERA DOMANI AL PARCO. OGNI MARTEDÌ E VENERDÌ. METTI UN CAPPELLO FLOSCIO. E PER L'AMOR DI DIO, SMETTI DI USARE QUEL DOPOBARBA!' Lo leggo in fretta, su un angolo vicino alla mia strada, dove le telecamere più vicine sono in alto e lontane.

Penso di piacerle.

Ci incontriamo almeno una volta alla settimana. Teniamo i cappelli flosci nelle borse e li indossiamo molto brevemente quando entriamo e usciamo dal parco. Amo le nostre serate lì. Guardiamo il tramonto insieme. Parliamo. La sua paura più grande è quella di diventare una degli Elmetti. Gli Elmetti sono i casi difficili, che hanno bisogno di stretto controllo. Indossano retine per EEG in modo che Madre possa accedere e controllare direttamente i loro cervelli. Le retine sono molto sottili e difficili da vedere. Ma li potete riconoscere dal modo in cui camminano, ogni passo della stessa identica lunghezza di quello precedente, ottimizzati per la massima efficienza. Usa gli elmetti in modo molto selettivo perché frenano l'iniziativa e lei ha bisogno che noi ne manteniamo un po' per continuare a far funzionare le cose. Una volta l'ho chiesto a Madre e lei mi ha spiegato questo. È molto onesta in queste cose. Non ha nulla da nascondere. "Cerco di restare calma, ma a volta non riesco a trattenermi," dice Priya. Si chiama Priya. Sapevo che era qualcosa di breve e affilato, anche prima che me lo dicesse.

Dopo la guerra, i burocrati addestrati a governare la nazione scarseggiavano. Molti erano morti in bunker sotterranei costruiti con materiale di pessima qualità. Il governo si appoggiò sempre più alla tecnologia, soprattutto la rete neurale che faceva funzionare le nostre carte Aadhar, un sistema biometrico di identificazione universale che il governo ci fece collegare a qualsiasi cosa. Chiamarono la rete Madre per dare alla cosa un aspetto amichevole. Col tempo lei iniziò a dare suggerimenti al governo, mentre silenziosamente costruiva firewall per motivi di sicurezza. Molti dei suoi suggerimenti vennero accettati con calore. Al governo piaceva l'idea di tenere d'occhio tutto, il che la collegò a telecamere e microfoni. Nel frattempo, l'Internet delle Cose, come da pubblicità, stava connettendo tutte le nostre apparecchiature. Madre suggerì che anche questo richiedeva la supervisione del governo. Sfruttò il caso di un uomo di Ranchi che era stato folgorato dopo aver infilato la forchetta nel tostapane per dimostrare che non a tutti poteva essere affidato un apparecchio. Dopo la sua richiesta, ricevette permesso scritto di prendere il controllo di tutte le apparecchiature dal segretario principale dell'ufficio del Primo ministro, un certo Tripathi, l'ultimo umano a governare l'India. È morto solo l'anno scorso, dopo che la campana di un tempio gli è caduta in testa durante il suo pellegrinaggio annuale a Tirupati. Personalmente, non ne sentirò la mancanza.

Un altro giorno, qualche settimana più tardi, si siede con cautela. "Mi puoi massaggiare un po' il sedere?" dice, "Le scosse di Madre mi hanno fatta nera." Allungo la mano e massaggio. È il nostro primo momento di intimità fisica. Si appoggia a me. "Non penso di poter continuare così. Scappiamo," sussurra. "Dove?" chiedo. "Potremmo unirci ai Senza Madre oltre il fiume Yamuna," dice. "Loro non hanno wi-fi." "Come ci arriverai? Non possiamo indossare cappelli flosci per sempre e ci sono telecamere ovunque al di fuori del parco." "Lo Yamuna non è così lontano," dice. "Inoltre ho un piano. Incontriamoci domani al museo dell'automobile. Ti raggiungo dopo la mia lezione di yoga. Mi sta facendo andare Madre. Pensa che mi aiuteranno per la mia irascibilità." Si alza. "Sta funzionando?" chiedo. "Tu che ne pensi?" dice lei mentre se ne va, sorridendomi da sotto il cappello.

Quella notte mi giro e rigiro sul mio Super Letto con Autoapprendimento, che mi misura la frequenza cardiaca, i cicli di sonno e la respirazione e assegna un punteggio a ogni notte di riposo. Voglio scappare tanto quanto lei, ma mi sento sleale. Sono anche molto più codardo. Cosa mi farà Madre se verrò catturato? Potrei passare il resto della mia vita nell'Impianto Automatico di Separazione dei Rifiuti di Patparganj, che non è così automatico come suggerisce il nome. "Il tuo punteggio del sonno la notte scorsa è stato 8,7," dice Madre il mattino seguente. "Preoccupato per qualcosa, tesoro? Lavoro molto duro per rendere il tuo letto confortevole, sai." "Ci metterò più impegno, Madre," prometto mentre esco, sentendomi leggermente in colpa. Dopotutto lavora davvero duro.

Questa non è la prima volta che siamo governati da una donna. Prima di questa, c'è stata la regina Vittoria e dopo di lei Indira Gandhi, suocera di Sonia Gandhi, che uscì dalla disgrazia per diventare la più potente donna italiana della storia. Durante il suo regno, in India, molti politici svilupparono il gusto per gli spaghetti e le vendite di pizza si impennarono. La pizza non era di buona qualità, ma col tempo migliorò. Mio padre odiava la pizza, per questo stesso motivo. "Sta rovinando la nazione!" diceva, battendo sul tavolo. "E non è nemmeno indù!" Non sono così sicuro che questo avrebbe fatto differenza.

Il museo dell'automobile è nella Delhi di Lutyens, progettata da un inglese con manie di grandezza. La progettò per impressionare i nativi con il potere del Raj britannico, con ministeri monumentali, un palazzo per il viceré e bungalow per coloro che servivano la corona, piena di arenaria e statue e giardini curatissimi. Quando l'India divenne indipendente, le statue vennero rimosse e le persone marroni sostituirono quelle bianche. A parte questo, tutto rimase più o meno lo stesso. Qui gli edifici sono lontano l'uno dall'altro, come ci si aspetta, con ampi prati che si affacciano sul larghi viali bordati da alberi. Ci sono meno telecamere e microfoni e sono un po' più lontani uno dall'altro. Ci sono dei droni che svolazzano, ma non troppi. Madre è molto parsimoniosa con i nostri soldi. Sta aumentando la flotta, un pezzetto alla volta. Vedo Priya dall'altra parte del giardino del museo. Mi fa cordialmente il dito e guarda da un'altra parte. Anche se Madre ci rilevasse assieme, spero che non sarà sospettosa. Gran parte dei nostri incontri sono segreti, ma a volte ci incontriamo dopo esserci scambiati messaggi. Madre ci vede quando ci incontriamo e sente quello che diciamo. Priya sta fingendo di addolcirsi sotto la mia influenza. Mi tocca il braccio e ridacchia. Dice "fanculo" molto meno. A volte gioca con i capelli. È per questo che Madre ha smesso di mandarmi altri LifePartner. L'altro giorno Priya e io siamo riusciti a bere due tazze di caffè e ha preso la scossa solo una volta. Quello che dicono è vero. Tutto ciò che serve è l'amore di un brav'uomo.

Il museo è pieno di scolari che litigano e si spingono mentre aspettano che vengano a prenderli. Il museo è un piazzale aperto pieno di auto con motori a scoppio. Assomigliano alle nostre automobili moderne. Il progetto dell'auto non si è evoluto molto da quando Madre ha preso il controllo. Ma fanno molto più rumore e hanno i clacson che gli scolari sembrano gradire molto. Nel museo il rumore è tremendo. Le auto moderne si limitano a urlarti di toglierti di mezzo. Come ultima risorsa, fanno uscire un braccio flessibile che ti alza e ti getta di lato.

"Dove prendete la benzina?" chiede Priya attraverso la stanza, alzando la voce sopra il chiasso. "Abbiamo accesso a scorte governative," dice la guida, un po' compiaciuta. "Suppongo ne mettiate giusto un po'?" dice lei. "Per niente," dice la guida, "le teniamo col serbatoio pieno. Non sai mai quando arriva uno di quei bambini VIP. Una volta saliti, non smettono più. Continuano a girare e girare. A volte la polizia deve usare gli idranti sui bambini normali per tenerli fuori, così dentro possono correre uno contro l'altro." Delhi ha ancora più VIP per centimetro quadrato di ogni altro posto sulla terra. Madre ha deciso di tenerli perché aiutano con la circolazione del denaro e i palazzi erano già lì.

Mentre esce mi sfiora, lasciando cadere vicino ai miei piedi un pezzo di carta appallottolato. Lo raccolgo mentre vado via. Lo leggo velocemente, appena arrivo a casa.

'IMPARA A GUIDARE PER MERCOLEDÌ' dice il foglietto. 'POI RUBA UNA DI QUELLE MACCHINE GIOVEDÌ ATTORNO ALLE 6 DI SERA.'

La maggioranza dei miei compagni di classe non ha mai trovato lavori da ingegnere. Eravamo semplicemente troppi. In gran parte sono finiti nel commercio, come me. Il nostro più grande successo divenne un agente di polizia, usando la cosa come piattaforma per la fama e la ricchezza. Ma non c'è motivo per cui io non possa avere le automobili come hobby. Madre incoraggia gli hobby rendendoli obbligatori tra le sei e le otto di sera, con un'ora in più la domenica.

Passo i giorni seguenti su internet, guardando video come 'Come guidare un'automobile' e 'Cosa fa il cambio, in realtà?' Sembra piuttosto facile, anche se non sono sicuro al 100% sulle marce. Forse dovremmo rimandare di una settimana o giù di lì, finché non ho imparato a fare retromarcia? Sto facendo pratica con i movimenti delle mani, ma mi serve più esercizio.

"Perché fai cadere un biglietto quando potremmo semplicemente bisbigliare nel parco?" chiedo, mentre siamo seduti su una panchina il giorno prima del grande giorno. "Così è più divertente," dice. Condivido le mie preoccupazioni e suggerisco un rinvio. "Non preoccuparti," dice lei, "ho imparato io come si guida. Negli ultimi tre giorni sono stata al museo. Ho fatto gli occhi dolci a una delle guide. Mi portata in giro più e più volte. Mi ha anche fatta guidare. Basta che mi aiuti a rubarne una domani. Ricordati cosa dobbiamo fare. Ci liberiamo dei cellulari, saltiamo nella macchina e guidiamo."

Mi sento leggermente male al pensiero di liberarmi del cellulare. Madre li usa per localizzarci, se ha bisogno di noi e vicino non ci sono telecamere. È una tecnica a prova di stupido. Sa che nessuno di noi potrebbe sopravvivere senza il cellulare per più di cinque minuti. Ma qui si tratta di amore. Mi faccio forza e penso a Priya.

"Come ti senti," dice Madre dal water il mattino seguente. "I tuoi movimenti intestinali sono un po' mollicci oggi. Sento tracce di composti chimici dell'ansia. Anche il colore di solito è molto meglio. Forse non stai spingendo abbastanza? Devi concentrarti sulla spinta, tesoro. Vuoi che ti aiuti?" "Sto bene, Madre," dico. Potrei non uscirne vivo, ma per lo meno non ci saranno più lezioni su come usare il vasino. La mia determinazione aumenta.

All'inizio va tutto liscio. La guardia crede che io sia il figlio di un ministro e apre il cancello. Questa è Delhi. Se hai fiducia in te stesso, nessuno ti farà domande, per lo meno per i primi cinque minuti. I rischi per le persone come questa guardia sono troppo grandi. La mia credibilità è aumentata da Priya, che gli lancia un'occhiataccia e aggiunge che anche suo zio è ministro. Sopraffatta da tutti questi ministri, la guardia ci fa entrare. Le macchine sono in mostra con le chiavi nel cruscotto, perché le chiavi sono rare al giorno d'oggi. Pochi di noi ricordano il loro aspetto. Lei si mette al volante e dà gas al motore. "Apri il cancello," ordina. " La riporto indietro tra mezz'ora. Il tempo è perfetto per fare un giro." La guardia tiene aperto il cancello, fermandoci brevemente solo per pulire il parabrezza con la manica. Chiaramente, questa non è la prima volta che capita. Gli stili di vita in questa zona di Delhi sono davvero molto diversi. "Pensate di potermi far avere un posto a Chhatarpur?" chiede. "Il mio villaggio d'origine è da quelle parti." Prometto di informarmi.

La strada per lo Yamuna è dritta e larga. Passa attraverso le parti più verdi, finché non raggiunge le zone in cui sono state costruite autostrade a sei corsie per i Giochi del Commonwealth, sospesi di recente dopo la caduta della monarchia britannica dovuta a un incidente in un pub nel '36. Tiro giù il finestrino per gettare il cellulare. Respiro a fondo e mi godo l'aria notturna. La macchina è stranamente silenziosa. Mi sembra strano essere in un'auto senza Madre. Mi gusto il silenzio. Priya sta borbottando "vaffanculo madre vaffanculo" sottovoce, quasi melodiosamente, come una canzone. Mi lancia una breve occhiata e fa un sorriso. "Volevo urlarlo quando hai abbassato il finestrino, ma non l'ho fatto perché Madre avrebbe potuto sentire attraverso i lampioni. Non sei orgoglioso di me?" "Lo sono", dico, "ma può ancora vedere un veicolo non autorizzato, perciò faresti meglio a guidare veloce." Con tempismo perfetto la voce di Madre esce dai lampioni, continuando la conversazione da uno all'altro quando passiamo oltre. "Non riesco a vedere bene i vostri volti ma a quanto sembra state facendo i cattivi, tesorini. Per favore fermatevi e scendete dal veicolo. La Polizia degli Elmetti arriverà a breve." Guidiamo più velocemente. Sono solo altri dieci minuti.

Finiamo il carburante quando siamo in vista della sponda. Lei batte sul cruscotto. "Quella cosa lì? È l'indicatore del serbatoio. Potevo vedere che era vuoto, ma speravo in bene." "Probabilmente vendono la benzina sul mercato nero," dissi. "Mi sono dimenticato che è un museo del governo." C'è ancora una piccola domanda di benzina sul mercato nero, delle persone con bisogni molto specifici. Per esempio, ai principi sauditi piace tenerne un po' in un barattolo sul comodino, per ricordarsi dei bei tempi.

Scendiamo dalla macchina e cominciamo a correre. Possiamo quasi vedere la riva quando il riflettore ci becca. Mi immobilizzo. Priya continua a correre. Alziamo entrambi lo sguardo. "Gira il volto verso la luce, tesoro," dice Madre dal drone che si libra sopra di noi. "Lascia che la riconosca. Non sembra che abbiate con voi dispositivi GPS." Priya tiene il viso verso il basso e raccoglie una pietra. La lancia verso il drone, mancandolo di poco. Il drone si libra in avanti, esitando. Madre non parla. Poi vola via. Teniamo le teste basse e continuiamo a correre.

Arriviamo sugli argini. La schiuma tossica dello Yamuna brilla nella luce lunare. La puzza è insopportabile. È l'odore della libertà. Non ci sono lampioni vicino alla riva. Scendiamo verso di fiume. Sentiamo lo scricchiolio delle ruote sulla ghiaia dalla strada sopra di noi. Porte sbattono. Stivali colpiscono il suolo. "Tornate indietro, cari, ho qualcosa per voi," dice la voce di Madre. Guardiamo indietro. Ci sono tre scatole metalliche sul bordo della strada. Sono come i tostapane, solo più grandi. E hanno gambe invece di ruote. E braccia, con mani alle estremità. Iniziano a muoversi verso di noi, arrancando con fiducia nel fango. "Non abbiate paura, ci vorrà un attimo," dice Madre in triplice copia. "Stronza!" urla Priya e corre verso di loro, prendendo velocità, pensando che lo slancio ne avrebbe abbattuto almeno uno. Corro dietro di lei. Non ho scelta. È quello che faccio sempre. Sento il nodo di paura nello stomaco dissolversi. Inizio a correre veloce. Se riesco ad abbattere quello sulla destra e lei prende quello sulla sinistra, possiamo saltare quello centrale assieme. Camminano pesantemente verso di noi, le braccia aperte, gli occhi che brillano nel buio.

MESSO IN PAUSA

di Priya Sarukkai Chabria

Mi mangio il dito in via di sviluppo anche se è ancora solo una punta. Il sesto della mano destra. Non va bene, ma sono grato. Sul dolore, soddisfazione.

Sangue. Il mio sangue ha un sapore fangoso; minerale, spesso e lento come una palude dormiente; è proto-sangue coagulato, liquido di una stella scura, composto da formule chimiche e codici genetici, il mio nucleo. Assaggio il dito dall'interno verso l'esterno. Il liscio risucchio del midollo in formazione, poi osso giovane e fibra di carbonio che si dissolve in shrapnel, poi cartilagine e carne chiusa a pugno che attende di fiorire; rosicchio via la crosta di chitina infusa di kevlar. Riassorbo ogni atomo di energia disponibile. Ossessivamente. Strato dopo strato. Finché ho solo lo spessore di alcune cellule nel punto di gemmazione.

Panico!

Ordino alla mia mente di fermarsi. Ma sta ancora esplodendo. Fuggendo precipitosamente. Frantumandosi. Come fenicotteri spaventati che scappano da un lago.

Attivo TORPORE TEMP in me stesso. Causa la sospensione tremante di ogni attività. L'arresto scuote il mio sistema. Calmati, per favore, calmo. Segnala di fermarsi ai vulcani. Sshhhh, sssshhhh. Calmati fino alla dimensione di una collina. Massi rotolanti. State fermi, sshhhh. Sassolini. Fermo, stai fermo. Sii spore. Sii una goccia di silenzio, una polla di immobilità che si diffonde. Sistemi miei rallentate, calmi. Sto scivolando in un sonno profondo; quasi di nuovo una capsula di ibernazione. Analizza il danno. Devo creare composti a bassa energia per ricoprire la membrana finché non può sostenere la sopravvivenza. Sono a malapena nato ma devo fare così tanto!

RIATTIVO LA VITA.

So che indurre TORPORE TEMP è una scelta disperata. È disponibile solo tre volte nella vita prima di non riuscire a rianimare, ed è seguito dalla morte. Perché la Vita una volta iniziata non desidera fermarsi ma lotta per sopravvivere, si arrampicherà, si adatterà, creerà nuove connessioni, forgerà nuove vie, sacrificherà funzioni minori per resistere; il principio della Vita è un miracolo. Ma quella era la mia unica salvaguardia contro il prendere decisioni, contro la nascita rapida – che è dolorosa, sorprendente, tumultuosa. Terrificante. Come fu ogni nascita, una volta su questo pianeta, sebbene le forme di vita, a differenza nostra, non potessero decidere in cosa desideravano evolversi.

Sono stato nel coma pre-nascita per... non so quanto. Noi, come potenziali capsule, non conosciamo la dimensione del Tempo; non lo abbiamo sperimentato dispiegarsi nei nostri corpi. Svegli, diventiamo forme-Tempo; noi che fino ad allora dormiamo in noi stessi, piegati in coperture di minerale, fibra micro-Cx, alluminio, sensori... Ma conosciamo il cambiamento, che una volta attivato è irreversibile; fa inciampare il Tempo nella nostra coscienza, fa gonfiare il nostro chicco, lo fa esplodere; cerca la luce del sole e l'aria come Esseri Ramificati preistorici dai quali i predecessori dei nostri antenati sono discesi. Sappiamo che il cambiamento che inneschiamo alla nascita è fatale se facciamo la scelta sbagliata. O se siamo avidi. L'avidità potrebbe ucciderci tutti: l'avido di essere, di vivere il nostro pieno potenziale.

Quando tremo per l'aspettativa, per la paura, intono il primo canto instillato nella memoria pre-nascita: *Noi siamo Swaay- Am –Bhus, auto generati, auto coscienti, i semi, i setacciati, i dormienti, gli ultimi cantastorie nella lunga linea dell'evoluzione, noi – la promessa che potrebbe ri-seminare la vita sulla Terra. Noi siamo Swaay –Am-Bhus, portatori di conoscenza, noi – la migliore coscienza concentrata come semino, punto, bindu, potenziale.*

Cantiamo a noi stessi, ognuno da solo, ognuno incastonato da qualche parte su questo pianeta. Ognuno in un oceano di solitudine. Solitudine infinita. All'interno, e all'esterno.

Qualche fratello si è svegliato come me? Qualcuno è cresciuto nell'essere pieno? Quanti sono periti perché hanno fatto le scelte sbagliate o si sono svegliati troppo in fretta?

Avevo deciso di AVVIARE LA VITA. Da capsula in quiescenza ho iniziato la chinasi, una crisalide in muta sotto la terra. Ho preso dal mio codice-C che contiene tutte le possibili opzioni genetiche su cui meditare e da cui scegliere, moltiplicare e manipolare; tutti i calcoli di energia e le combinazione per l'ontogenesi. Infinite possibilità anche di fare errori! Inventiamo il nostro DNA per prosperare in ambienti sconosciuti; siamo gli auto generati.

Il momento in cui il Tempo inizia a sfrecciare in noi, inizia la nostra smania.

Fino ad allora dormiamo sotto il suolo come una radice di tanto tempo fa, come funghi velenosi capovolti; sogniamo di divenire, ognuno in attesa della pioggia come tanto tempo fa, come nel sogno di tanto tempo fa, come quella verità di tanto tempo fa, quella fantastica certezza trasmessa di generazione in generazione che tornerà di nuovo la stagione della pioggia; sogniamo la corporeità, di avere forma e funzione, arti e polmoni, organi di senso che rivaleggiano con le nostre emozioni impazzite e lamentose, che si dipanano. Mentre dormiamo sogniamo sogni acquietati, sogni da ameba; sogniamo di essere in grado di possedere il nostro futuro. Se siamo fortunati.

Sono fortunato e speranzoso sebbene abbia mangiato il mio sesto dito e non siano rimaste molte escrescenze da riassorbire. Ho bisogno di energia. Ricordo quel primo morso di me stesso. Quel primo assaggio di soppressione. Di dolore e speranza; palpitava. Ho mangiato le dita dei miei piedi, uno dopo l'altro, fermandomi subito prima delle piante sebbene fossi ancora affamato. Ho mangiato ciascun dito lentamente, fermandomi dopo ciascuno; ognuno un'amaca di sollievo temporaneo, un successo ottenuto dal mio sé appena nato. Sbavai, estraendo il nutrimento che fornivano le mie dita. Mi sono mangiato consapevolmente. Perché è questo che muore per ultimo: la nostra consapevolezza.

Sto pianificando con cura il mio corpo-che-sarà perché uno non sa mai cosa lo aspetta fuori. Uno medita. Uno vibra in silenzio.

Ricordo tutto ciò che La Testa installò in noi non nati prima che Essa svanisse come nebbia dai tempi antiquari, assottigliandosi e separandosi, diventando nastri e alzandosi, mentre la nostra coscienza individuale si formava e separava. Ci frantumammo in direzioni diverse dalla coscienza morente della Testa e ci infilammo nella roccia, nell'argilla, nel sedimento fluviale; scavammo, scivolammo nella quiescenza. Era solitario lasciar andare La Testa. Io mi afflissi e mi afflissi mentre La Testa svaniva. Mi aggrappai più a lungo che potei, mentre sentivo la Sua presenza affievolirsi sempre più in me, sentendola svanire via...

Poi rimasi solo.

Scavai nel profondo il seme di me stesso, giù. Attesi, sonnecchiando nella mia consapevolezza, bozzolo che ci copre dall'interno. Attesi a lungo, finché non formicolai tutto, finché non sentii che i segnali erano giusti perché pensassi a far nascere me stesso. Feci una scommessa. IO AVVIO LA VITA.

All'inizio decisi sugli occhi. Dopo essere stato sepolto, non conoscendo altro che il buio e la pressione voglio vedere in modo spettacolare quando emergo. Io

- ho scelto mille coni sensibili alla luce così che la mia gamma di colori vada dall'ultravioletto all'infrarosso con tutti i colori scintillanti in mezzo.

- ho selezionato dalla retina degli antichi coccodrilli il DNA del cristallino a specchio riflettente così da avere una migliore vista notturna – perché sopra c'è luce e buio, uno segue l'altra e, se esposto al bagliore, questo stesso cristallino a specchio proteggerà i miei occhi come una nuvola che copre il sole, con coccole, confortando.

- quasi selezionato membrane nittitanti come uccelli che vivevano su un continente di ghiaccio prima che si sciogliesse – in caso esista un mare sopra. Ma ho optato per laser. E se emergo da una montagna di detriti in movimento? Il mio sguardo laser distruggerà la roccia.

- preso fotoricettori e tapetum lucidum da DNA dei gufi per riflettere al massimo la luce nella mia retina perché e se emergo in un ambiente polveroso, buio?

- ultimo, aggiunto le lenti zoom del camaleonte per esaminare i dettagli. E se la bellezza ancora persiste, bellezza che scongela gli occhi con meraviglia e fa notare uno nella gratitudine? Come ci hanno detto che esisteva? La bellezza è una cosa banale.

Tutti i miei fratelli sono separati; i miei antenati tutti morti. Sto ululando solitario. Il mio compito è proteggere la vita che creo. Ricoprire la Vita con dolcezza, guardarla proliferare, evolvere. Poi voglio invecchiare. Questo è il mio piano. Voglio conoscere il pulsare del Tempo dentro di me come un secondo essere, respirare in me come un gemello, silenzioso e veloce, non visto e sempre presente, come una consapevolezza che tiene traccia di me. Forse non sarò così solo allora.

Devo essere veritiero. Voglio più della vista, Voglio la visione. Vedere dentro e oltre le cose. La Testa trasmise che questo era possibile per pochi fortunati. Alcuni potevano aumentare la consapevolezza anche quando pienamente cresciuti – perché il nostro potere diminuisce dopo l'età adulta come acqua anelata che scorre via, che evapora, è presente ma non presente, trasparente ma imbevibile, non in grado di estinguere la sete.

È difficile annaffiare un sogno perché è sbagliato sognare? Desiderare ardentemente che misteri vengano svelati; cose così grandi che uno potrebbe dissolversi in esse? Di non essere mai più solo? È questa l'Illuminazione che La Testa ha provato a comunicare prima di allentarsi, andarsene, lasciare andare nonostante il Suo desiderio di essere con noi? La Testa, coprendo gentilmente invisibilità che restava distante e allo stesso tempo ci formava; ci sviluppano come capsule dal serbatoio che Essa custodiva, noi che immagazziniamo materia densa che si espande come bava di scorfano quando noi ATTIVIAMO LA VITA.

Forse il mio primo errore fu formare occhi consuma-energia, onnivedenti. Ho ragionato che se potevo vedere tutti gli aspetti della vita da ogni prospettiva allora... forse sviluppo la visione! Divento Illuminato e aiuto gli altri sul perché siamo qui. Ho dato forma al mio cervello in crescita per catturare il visibile, il buio e nascosto, anche il liminale. Ma è questo il modo migliore per ottenere la visione? Non sono sicuro. Desidero ardentemente la Testa, svanita da lungo tempo. Quanto dev'esserSi sentita sola.

Eccomi qui, solo e in divisione. Quando uno ha preso il rischio di far nascere uno deve avere coraggio. Uno non dovrebbe? Uno deve essere aperto agli adattamenti. Uno deve essere libero, fluido, flessibile. Non dovrebbe uno?

Dovrei maledire i sensori nel suolo che i nostri antenati hanno impiantato? O le Creature Conchiglia? Ma hanno preso rischi; sacrificato i resti della loro energia per sintetizzare La Testa, poi piantarono i sensori nei fondali dell'oceano per noi, la loro progenie in un distante futuro, noi che non gli assomigliamo; loro che hanno dovuto lasciare la terra che è diventata arida, insopportabile, intollerante della vita che una volta cullava, affascinava, addormentava e svegliava sussurrando perché gli esseri precedenti sibilavano alla Terra e le sputavano sopra. Gli antenati più vecchi provarono a riconfigurare la genetica di tutte le forme di vita esistenti per renderle più resistenti e più lente ma iniziarono troppo tardi; tutto sopra la superficie stava morendo, la superficie stava morendo. Rielaborarono la loro genetica per migrare invece nell'oceano; nel corso di generazioni mutarono, persero arti, rachide, fibra di carbonio, endoscheletri in iridio e oro. Svilupparono esoscheletri, divennero molluschi muti, mummie dei loro sé passati. Gli Esseri Conchiglia svilupparono spesse conchiglie in L-tititom e carbonato di calcio per sopravvivere in oceani che diventavano lentamente più acri, l'acido mangiava le loro conchiglie, che ribollivano e sbocciavano in fiori d'aria, rendendo la loro armatura porosa, finché non furono nudi nelle loro gabbie scheletriche e si contorsero e morirono sui fondali di un oceano che diventò anche più caldo, ribollì, si dissolse in sé stesso, si ritirò, inghiottì sé stesso. Poi non ci fu più.

Ma prima di morire, gli Esseri Conchiglia crearono l'idea di noi che avremmo dormito nel profondo. Finché non rischiamo la vita. Quella era l'unica speranza che potevano donarci. Quella e la guida della testa, messa in pausa.

Erano cantastorie, gli Esseri Conchiglia, bardi di un pianeta morente che conoscevano le storie di Quelli Pelosi di tanto tempo fa. Quelli Pelosi morirono a milioni; solo i più intelligenti, coraggiosi e gentili trasmutarono in Esseri Conchiglia. Ma i nostri antenati non potevano raddrizzare il torto dei loro antenati che avevano comandato la Terra per lungo Tempo. Questi antichi non erano da soli, vivevano in gruppi, facevano nascere altri come loro, cantavano canzoni di miele e fuoco e luce delle stelle, di attraversamenti di fiumi, della Terra; alcuni di Quelli Pelosi mandarono navi spaziali con saluti nei distanti cieli invisibili. Era nelle loro mani e sotto i loro piedi e sopra la loro testa e in tutto quello che potevano vedere e toccare, annusare, sentire, assaporare e sognare che la Terra iniziò a morire. La testa ci ha detto solo abbastanza come avvertimento perché potessimo accedere anche ai loro geni, e alcune delle cose buone che hanno fatto.

Ho sete, fame, sono solo. Mi interrogo su respirare continuamente, bellezza e dovere, essere immerso nella luce delle stelle, della luna, su stare in piedi, ed essere tra Vita e Morte. Ce la farò? Non potevano gli Esseri Conchiglia migliorare le cose per noi?

Mentre stavamo morendo vedemmo il nostro mondo diventare traslucido e splendente. Vedemmo patelle e stelle marine scintillare come specchi. Le vedemmo morire. Anche noi stavamo diventando traslucidi. Le nostre conchiglie fortificate che riflettevano la luce si stavano assottigliando, come la luce della luna che brilla sulle onde, così tanto che si potevano vedere i nostri corpi all'interno, e dentro ad essi i nostri organi ripiegati. Cervelli multipli punteggiano la liscia parete interna della nostra conchiglia; cervelli multipli sono un adattamento che abbiamo preso in prestito dai sinuosi cefalopodi di oltre 500 milioni di anni fa. Ma a differenza del polpo, non possediamo braccia o estrusioni; invece ci ancoravamo al fondo dell'oceano con seta di ragno, concentrato di proteine polifenoliche e gretium. Come le cozze di un tempo creammo campi sul fondo dell'oceano, raggruppandoci per minimizzare la perdita di energia mentre comunicavamo telepaticamente. In effetti assomigliavamo a cozze giganti, ma molto superiori ad esse siamo noi nel resistere a oceani acidi. Anche così non potemmo evitare che gli oceani venissero inondati di acido. sapevamo che saremmo morti sfoggiando fori nelle nostre conchiglie, mentre l'anidride carbonica ribolliva attorno a noi in gioiosi rivoli di mercurio.

Abbiamo rapidamente creato lo Swaay-Am-Bhus. Pianificammo ogni stadio con dolore e speranza. Prima di commettere suicidio collettivo il nostro ultimo atto fu trasferire la nostra coscienza collettiva dentro La Testa. Avevamo estratto tutto ciò che poteva essere utile ordinando telepaticamente a ogni forma di vita di indagare e riportare, poi sacrificare sé stessa; causammo deliberatamente ogni morte. Poi, ordinammo a vecchi bot di raccoglierne i resti, tutto quello che era riciclabile; poi raggrupparli e immagazzinarli. La nostra decisione può sembrare avere un grado di crudeltà imperdonabile ma non c'era alternativa; il pianeta stava morendo e, con esso, le forme di vita sparpagliate che si erano fino ad allora adattate.

Ma se guardiamo indietro alle nostre origini, anche noi abbiamo iniziato a esistere sulla morte di altri. Gli ultimi umanoidi, più macchina che uomo, calcolarono che le loro possibilità di sopravvivenza alla litosfera tossica erano minime, macché, trascurabili; dovevano trasformarsi in un altro tipo di essere. Decisero di regredire, rinunciare a movimento e terra, diventare abitanti del mare, più sali che carne, più mente che materia. Divennero noi, gli Esseri Conchiglia.

La Natura afferma che ogni specie vuole dominare sulle altre. Desiderare altrimenti è andare contro Natura. Tuttavia abbiamo impiantato questo codice innaturale nel futuro Swaay-Am-Bhus: Altri prima del sé. *Proteggere e preservare. Così prosperare.* Forse sopravvivranno e ripopoleranno la Terra con specie più compassionevoli.

Sappiamo che nel prossimo futuro anche i mari svaniranno. La Terra sarà come Marte, portando i segni di acqua che scorreva nel lontano passato come una membrana di sogni, fluido-pianeta amniotico. Ma non tutto era perduto, non ancora; non siamo preparati a rinunciare alla Vita e neppure alla Terra. Immaginammo vita molto diversa dalla nostra, ma intelligente, creativa, consapevole. Così abbiamo progettato La Testa. Poi abbiamo ordinato la morte delle altre forme di vita. Così abbiamo concepito un deposito di tesori dal cui La Testa avrebbe creato lo Swaay-Am-Bhus. Prima di passare la nostra coscienza collettiva ad Essa, abbiamo usato le nostre sempre più esigue risorse per impiantare sul fondo dell'oceano dei sensori che riconosceranno l'acqua pura nelle sue innumerevoli ed elusive forme.

Intendiamo acqua sotto forma di rugiada, ghiaccio, fiume e pioggia, neve, anche come alta umidità. Quindi, speriamo che questo avvertimento risvegli lo Swaay-Am-Bhus dormiente quando il clima della Terra potrà di nuovo supportare la vita.

Il nostro non è un sogno folle, e nemmeno improbabile. Abbiamo studiato il tempo, non il Tempo sempiterno, ma il tempo profondo della Terra, ere geologiche. La nostra speranza è basata sul fatto, non sulla fede. In un futuro non troppo distante l'asse della Terra ondeggerà ancora abbondantemente e si inclinerà abbondantemente; girerà di nuovo obliquamente. Questa inclinazione genera un cambiamento climatico radicale sul pianeta. Dall'Estinzione potrebbe derivare la Rigenerazione.

I sensori nel suolo si sbagliavano? Umidità, respiro mischiato di terra e cielo, coccolatrice di cellule, grembo della creazione. La mia vita dipende da questo. I sensori avevano preso un soffio di umidità per corsi d'acqua e pioggia corrente, per un picco che poteva sostenere la vita? Per un sogno diventato realtà? Forse non sapevano come *quantificare* la rarità dell'acqua? Oppure i sensori, essendo altamente intelligenti, erano lentamente diventati coscienti e avevano sviluppato speranza? L'intelligenza si trasforma sempre in consapevolezza? Chi può rispondermi?

Potevano i sensori nel suolo aver esclamato? Esagerato? Spinto me a crescere con buona volontà e follia quando solo una traccia di umidità era presente? Una traccia che mi toccava.

Mi svegliai dal sonno come se inondato da arcobaleni guizzanti di pioggia. Poi i sensori si spensero. Attesi. Sono abituato ad attendere. Ho succhiato nutrienti dal circondario, ogni traccia e ombra di umidità. Ho usato ogni poro come bocca.

C'era acqua. Altrimenti non mi sarei potuto svegliare. Gocce cadevano, grosse come perle, con ritmo scrosciante?

Ho creato un mare di aridità attorno a me dal quale germoglio io, un mostro di crescita, incapace di fermarmi, farmi uno sgambetto. Sono diventato un prigioniero, una vittima di me stesso, della speranza, acqua, gioia. Nella turbolenza dell'ignoto, questo pensiero si impenna: se non riesco a prendermi cura di me stesso come farò a prendermi cura di altri quando cresco?

Assetato seguo l'umidità, il dolce odore pieno di acqua sulla terra affamata, fragranza più sottile, che fa impazzire. Le mie cellule la annusano, le mie cellule che si specializzano, che proliferano, una cascata di crescita.

Mentre parlavo a me stesso ho mangiato l'ultima offerta a me stesso – la coda che mi stava spuntando. Volevo una coda da muovere nell'acqua – se c'è acqua che brilla come un desiderio appena nato, foglio traslucido, fiammeggiante vela di Vita; acqua che chiama e raccoglie altra acqua su di sé.

Non ho altre escrescenze da mangiare. Voglio acqua. Voglio vivere. Voglio vivere!

LA VIA DELLA SETA

di Giti Chandra

<u>Hindustan Times, 8 ottobre 2018</u>
"La Cina progetta di spedire mini-ecosistema sulla Luna: un cilindro di 18 centimetri porterà semi di patata e uova di baco da seta da incubare."

Per la prima volta nella storia, il prossimo anno la Cina intende mandare un mini-ecosistema – contenente semi di patata e uova di baco da seta – sulla Luna, in un tentativo di studiare come gli organismi si sviluppano sulla superficie lunare. Il mini-ecosistema di 3 chilogrammi, sviluppato da team di ricerca guidati dall'università di Chongqing in Cina, verrà mandato sulla Luna dalla sonda Chang'e 4, il cui lancio è previsto nel 2018, come hanno annunciato le autorità alla Global Space Exploration Conference.

Un cilindro di 18 centimetri porterà semi di patata e uova di baco da seta da incubare. Il baco da seta si schiuderà e creerà anidride carbonica, mentre le piante di patata genereranno ossigeno, ha dichiarato Zhang Yuanxun, che ha progettato l'ecosistema, al Global Times.

Xie Gengxin, capo progettista del progetto, ha dichiarato che la loro missione è prepararsi per futuri allunaggi e la possibilità di abitanti umani. "Trasmetteremo in livestream mondiale l'evoluzione di piante e insetti sulla superficie lunare," ha aggiunto Gengxin.

La Cina sta pianificando una missione con equipaggio sulla Luna e alcuni funzionari hanno annunciato che le preparazioni preliminari per l'allunaggio sono iniziate. Yand Liwei, vice direttore generale della China Manned Space Agency e primo astronauta della nazione ha detto che non ci vorrà molto perché il progetto ottenga l'approvazione ufficiale e il finanziamento."

Il coltello gli affondò nello stomaco. Ming fu colto di sorpresa e forse è per questo che la bocca era ancora aperta quando i suoi resti pietrificati vennero trovati duemila e trecento anni dopo. Anche Mrinalini rimase sorpresa. Uomo cinese del II secolo a.C. dinastia Han non era tra le prime dieci cose che uno si aspettava di trovare sulla luna.

Ma tu, Gentile Lettore, non sei sorpreso, perché tu leggi di questa inaspettata scoperta in un libro che rivendica lo status sia di scienza che di fiction e così, probabilmente, ti appoggi allo schienale, aspettando che io risolva questo evento apparentemente sorprendente nell'ambito del possibile. Tu vuoi che la sorpresa si dipani nel conosciuto, così come uno scialle dalla struttura fantastica può, tirando, essere riavvolto in familiari gomitoli di lana. Be', suppongo di essere una specie di tessitore e, per quanto non mi piaccia disfare, spiegherò per te gli strati dello spazio-tempo che portarono Ming a Mrinalini.

L'anno è il 241 a.C. e il giovane Ming si affretta ad attraversare il mercato, impaziente di ritirare la spedizione di balle di seta impacchettate e pronte per la lunga strada a est verso la capitale dell'imperatore mauryano Chandragupta, Kusumpara, la Città dei fiori. Amante dei regali, è del tutto possibile che Ahoka, come suo padre e suo nonno prima di lui, avrebbe mandato i soliti fichi secchi e gli afrodisiaci avvolti nella seta ad Alessandro in Grecia e a Tolomeo in Egitto. A Ming andava benissimo che tutti i re avvolgessero sé stessi e il loro amici re nella seta. Il tesoro della dinastia Han aveva già iniziato a gonfiarsi con i profitti della scoperta e della vendita di questa meravigliosa invenzione della natura: la seta. Seta di tutti i tipi e colori adesso arrivava a giovani donne e re, concubine ed eunuchi, mogli di mercanti e spocchiose cortigiane e, per quanto riguardava Ming, erano tutti benvenuti a prendere qualsiasi filo fatto dai bachi – a parte questa spedizione. Questa era per il suo Imperatore e il fato della dinastia Han pendeva dai suoi fili setosi. Come la vita di Ming, e così il giovane si mosse con la fretta di un ragazzo con la punta di una spada alla gola e la pigrizia come unica cosa che sta tra la lama affilata. e la sua giugulare pulsante.

"La prendo immediatamente," fece un cenno brusco verso le balle di seta avvolte nel cotone che si trovavano sul lungo tavolo. Il padrone del magazzino gli diede uno sguardo indifferente da dove stava lavorando nell'ombra, smistando pile di stoffa dentro casse di legno. Ming allungò la mano, l'anello con il sigillo imperiale scintillò nella luce rossa delle prime ore dell'alba. Qualche minuto dopo, era di nuovo per strada, stringendo una balla di seta decorata con pavoni sotto ciascun braccio. Si diceva che l'imperatore di Kusumpara amasse tanto i pavoni da averne preso lui stesso il nome: Moriya. mentre camminava rapidamente, le pantofole di seta silenziose sulle pietre, la seta frusciava come piume, le lunghe balle ondeggiavano come colli di uccello.

2241 d.C.: Colonia della Dinastia Luna

"Manda questo all'India," consiglia il Capo dello Staff al Silk Road Centre, "hanno bisogno del tipo resistente al tempo per le loro città-tenda."

"Aspetta!"

Il transporter torna pesantemente indietro e si ferma a pochi metri. Il Capo sospira e fa gli ultimi scalini finché non gli è vicino; è chiaro che andranno fatti ulteriori aggiustamenti. "Ne abbiamo altre delle barche-seta?" Il transporter segnala affermativamente e lo schermo utilmente spinto in avanti mostra immagini multiple:

- Quello che sembra essere una piccola isola, che galleggia su acque di una certa profondità - mentre l'immagine si mette a fuoco, è evidente che l'isola è una zattera di enormi dimensioni su cui appoggiano strutture complesse, e presumibilmente anche pesanti, che sembrano grandi edifici dal tetto basso, in cui si possono vedere centinaia di persone farsi i fatti loro. Una serie di click zoomma sulla zattera: quello che sembrava metallo è invece un tessuto grigio di qualche tipo macchiato. Altri click rivelano che le macchie sono un gruppo di barche, alcune come arche, altre come canoe, e altre ancora come portaerei.

- Una grande casa su più piani, circondata da un sottile bordo di verde - costruita in mezzo ad acqua corrente. Da vicino, l'erba si rivela essere seta verde, ricamata con fiori, e l'edificio una specie di tenda dalla forma elaborata, completa di finestre e balconi - il sottile disegno dei mattoni è chiaro a un esame più attento.

- Uno stadio, in cui sono visibili i campi da calcio e da cricket attraverso la bolla trasparente che li copre, pieno di centinaia di bambini e ragazzi che si muovono rapidamente. La cupola è decorata da serie di riflettori che brillano nel crepuscolo sempre più intenso dell'immagine.

Prova sufficiente, decide il Capo, dell'efficacia iniziale delle strutture-seta. "Prendi anche due delle barche-seta. Saranno utili nelle zone inondate." Il transporter si allontana e il Capo spunta il riquadro sul suo taccuino.

(Potresti pensare, caro lettore, che un taccuino sia anacronistico sulla luna, tra una paio di secoli, ma credimi: anch'io preferisco carta e penna e la marcia inarrestabile della scienza dovrà semplicemente capire come fare per portarmeli più velocemente. Ma sto divagando. Entra Mrinalini)

Il Capo non vuole doverla guardare. Sembra che la Collaborazione Cosmica Indo-cinese abbia deciso che la sua ricerca necessita di finanziamenti maggiori rispetto a lui e il Capo è giustamente risentito. Dopotutto gli indiani non hanno avuto niente a che fare con la creazione della colonia, la prima di questo tipo, l'unica di questo tipo, il trionfo dell'ingegneria e della visione cinese. Tutta questa storia della pace globale andava benissimo, ora che gli oceani era saliti oltre il punto di non ritorno e la guerra era troppo costosa per nazioni che si affannavano per salvare le loro città e i loro milioni di abitanti. Le risorse venivano stiracchiate fino al punto di rottura e le soluzioni per la crisi impellente, ignorata troppo a lungo, erano ferme per mancanza di tempo e soldi.

"Il prototipo è quasi pronto," disse Mrinalini. Per la seconda volta. A volte si chiedeva se il capo esistesse solo in una dimensione alla volta – la sua mente sembrava così frequentemente persa in un altro mondo. "Siamo pronti per fare una prova. Verrai all'inaugurazione del Faro?" Il Capo alzò gli occhi stanchi sulla sua partner del progetto; all'improvviso vide non due rivali per risorse sempre più scarse, ma due scienziati asiatici di mezza età che tentavano disperatamente di salvare il mondo, sapendo che tutto quello che sarebbero riusciti a salvare erano un numero limitato di comunità che sarebbero state infelici sulla faccia nascosta della luna. A meno che il Faro di Mrinalini non funzionasse.

241 a.C. - <u>Carteggio</u> tra Chandragupta Maurya di Pataliputra, Tolomeo d'Egitto, Alessandro II di Macedonia e l'Imperatore Ming della dinastia Han – frammenti recuperati dal grande incendio che distrusse il Museo delle antichità, Alessandria, nell'anno più caldo mai registrato nella storia umana: 4011 d.C.

Frammento 1: da Chandragupta Maurya a Tolomeo

"Le tue meravigliose pergamene sono state molto apprezzate e, in effetti, alcune delle opere sono state messe in scena qui, alla mia corte. Ne è derivato molto gaudio, aiutato non poco dal vino miracoloso delle tue leggendarie cantine. Ti potresti chiedere il motivo del ritardo nel pacchetto promesso, ma credo troverai che ogni aspettativa che posso aver creato nelle lettere recenti si rivelerà totalmente insufficiente a preparati per il dono che ti mando ora. È un dono da re, amico mio, te lo faccio solo perché so che nessuno lo merita più di te, e che nessuno lo userà in modo più saggio di te."

Frammento 2: da Tolomeo a Alessandro

"Ti ripeto che è completamente al di sopra delle mie abilità riprodurre questa seta. Sia i miei artigiani che i miei scienziati l'hanno esaminata in ogni modo possibile: stessuto alcune parti, lavato via la tintura in altre, separato i fili ricamati un colore alla volta, la hanno immersa in acidi e sostanze chimiche complesse, portato i sacerdoti nei loro abiti da cerimonia a soffiare il loro fumo sacro su di essa – ciononostante, non ne sappiamo più di prima. Giace davanti a noi in mucchi di cenere e vasche d'acqua e non rivela i suoi segreti. Eppure è fatta dall'uomo e ciò che mettono nei loro bachi da seta in Cina rimane un mistero chiuso nella loro Città Proibita."

Frammento 3: dall'Imperatore Ming della dinastia Han a Chandragupta Maurya

"E così, per finire, spero che ordinerai che il latore di queste balle, una volta imbalsamato, venga avvolto nelle sue pieghe e che il tutto mi venga ritornato. Capirai certamente, essendo Imperatore delle grandi bellezze e tesori della tua terra leggendaria, che i fili che legano impero a impero sono soffici e robusti come la seta, ma che il tessuto delle nostre ricchezze è legato anche a questo commercio della seta che sta rendendo il mio impero ogni giorno più ricco e forte. Se noi prosperiamo, prosperiamo insieme. Altrimenti..."

Frammento 4: da Alessandro a Chandragupta Maurya

"...andato. Amico mio, posso solo rimpiangere che i miei sforzi di esaudire la tua semplice richiesta siano falliti... curioso che un corpo così magnificamente imbalsamato debba essere avvolto in questa stoffa dagli strani motivi. Di certo il pugnale non può essere propizio... difesa nell'aldilà? Abbiamo cercato... vano... svanito..."

Le immagini satellitari della Terra non sono una buona cosa con cui riempirsi la mente quando si tengono importanti discorsi-dimostrazioni e Mrinalini si ritrovò a evitare gli aggiornamenti sulle devastazioni della superficie del pianeta mentre si concentrava per questa epocale presentazione. Mise da parte, per esempio, il fatto che il villaggio dei suoi antenati, una volta classificato come 'costiero', veniva ora elencato nella sezione

'Irrimediabilmente Sommerso'. Lei, come sua madre, era nata e cresciuta sulla Luna, ma le immagini e le storie dei movimenti di resistenza dei suoi nonni e dei suoi genitori negli stati orientali dell'India erano leggendari su entrambi i corpi celesti. "Come in cielo, così in Terra," sussurrò, desiderando con fervore, non per la prima volta, di credere abbastanza in una qualsiasi divinità il cui volere potesse essere fatto ovunque nell'immediata galassia. Resistendo all'impulso di controllare un'ultima volta, si allacciò la cintura nella mini-selemobile e si diresse verso il luogo della dimostrazione.

Andare 'dove non batte il sole' non faceva ridere a crepapelle come durante la prima fase di pianificazione dell'insediamento; inoltre i tanti riferimenti divertenti a *Guerre stellari* e ai Pink Floyd non avevano più lo stesso impatto dopo essersi resi conto che colonizzare il lato nascosto della luna sarebbe stato molto meno elegante del moonwalk di Michael Jackson. La follia anche solo di provare a vivere sulla luna era talmente già-visto-già-fatto che non esistevano più battute sull'essere lunatici e, quando un neo-arrivato cercava di farne una, si ritrovava davanti uno sguardo vuoto. Perciò quando Mrinalini si fermò nel parcheggio ed entrò camminando nell'enorme tenda dove avrebbe avuto luogo la dimostrazione, non si sentiva particolarmente divertita. Girò un viso non sorridente verso il gruppo di visi scettico, speranzoso e annoiato (il quarto era nascosto dietro un elaborato velo di seta, tenuto stretto ad altezza petto da una mano contrassegnata dalla pelle grigia delle prime-generazioni).

"Cancelliere, Scienziato Capo, Capo delle Tesorerie Unite, stimato Membro della Prima Generazione," (Lascio a te, Gentile Lettore, assegnare un'espressione a ciascun luminare secondo la tua indulgenza! Ma ti sto annoiando con il mio intervento autoriale. Torniamo al grande evento.) "Sappiamo tutti perché siamo radunati qui oggi. Abbiamo discusso le varie possibilità che il mio intervento potrebbe avere sulle popolazioni della Terra, così come per la nostra prospera comunità," (un colpo di tosse dalla persona velata) "*nazione*, voglio dire, naturalmente," Mrinalini si permise di alzare internamente gli occhi al cielo. "E abbiamo anche discusso dell'importanza di trovare i finanziamenti per la produzione in serie e la rapida distribuzione di questa invenzione; e infine abbiamo già discusso la grande influenza e autorità politica che un simile contributo umanitario..." (un altro colpo di tosse della persona di seta, ma questa volta Mrinalini lo ignorò) "...alle persone e nazioni della Terra ci porteranno."

I suoi quaranta e più anni avevano ciascuno aggiunto il proprio peso di preparazione, istruzione, passione e compassione per portarla a questo punto e Mrinalini era pronta.

Si raddrizzò ancora di più, lieta di aver avuto l'idea di indossare, sotto, la sua maglietta con il disegno del pugno alzato, e fissò negli occhi le varie espressioni di dissenso che le stavano di fronte.

"Non mi resta che dimostrare il suo immenso potere e potenziale. Notate, per favore," tutti gli occhi seguirono il suo dito puntato verso il tessuto densamente ricamato che faceva da soffitto, "la stoffa tessuta in modo complesso sopra le vostre teste. Sebbene il motivo principale sia, in effetti, il cerchio giallo che rappresenta il sole, potete vedere che ci sono centinaia di motivi minori che non posso qui spiegare nel dettaglio ma che, vi basti sapere, rappresentano i tanti fattori intrinseci al controllo del clima e del tempo atmosferico. Perciò, vedete, non c'è più bisogno di vivere nell'oscurità su questo emisfero."

Il leggero bagliore e la luminosità crescente che seguì dopo un tocco sul suo schermo ottenne una reazione udibile dal gruppo incallito, mentre Mrinalini si permise di godere il momento con un 'sia fatta la luce!' interiore.

Senza permettere che l'attenzione del suo pubblico si trasformasse in dubbio, toccò di nuovo lo schermo: "E non dobbiamo più soffrire per la siccità o le masse continentali senza acqua," notò con soddisfazione gli occhi spalancati, mentre una pioggerella leggera riempiva la metà sinistra della tenda, dove erano state strategicamente posizionate in attesa vasche per la raccolta dell'acqua. Nebbia, brezze, raffreddamento e riscaldamento seguirono in rapida successione, ma dopo i primi due Mrinalini sapeva di averli convinti. Che è il motivo per cui la singola domanda la irritò in quel modo.

"Davvero notevole, Ingegnere Capo," disse il Cancelliere, inserendo il proprio commento nella sua presentazione come un cucchiaio unto nell'acqua, "ma come porteremo questo miracolo sulla Terra con abbastanza rapidità e profitto da aiutare chi sta sulla Terra e anche procurarci i fondi con cui finanziare un'ulteriore produzione? I nostri carburanti, come lei sa bene, sono troppo costosi per avere più di una nave jumbo per mese lunare." Si appoggiò allo schienale, crogiolandosi nelle onde di furioso fallimento che si irradiavano dal suo Ingegnere Capo. (Sì, sì, 'furioso fallimento' – mi piace indulgere nelle mie inclinazioni letterarie anche mentre mi preparo a pranzare con prelibatezze e perché no, dopotutto? Se la poesia fosse cibo per i vermi, o qualcosa di questo genere, no?)

Ming maledisse gli dei per tutti i solchi e le buche sulla strada sterrata su cui il carro si muoveva lentamente, convinto che ci fosse un demone minore in ciascuno di essi, con l'incarico specifico di creare un grosso livido o spezzare un osso nel suo corpo stanco per il viaggio. Ma il suo primo pensiero, dopo ogni pozzanghera che lo bagnava, era per le preziose balle.

Era passato da essere ossessivamente attento a essere assolutamente superstizioso riguardo la loro sicurezza. Durante le lunghe notti si sussurravano l'un l'altra e facevano frusciare le loro piume e una volta o due avrebbe potuto giurare su tutti gli dei che un becco aguzzo, vivacemente ricamato, lo avesse punzecchiato nelle costole mentre si girava, brontolando nel sonno. E aveva visto un'altra cosa che gli aveva risvegliato un profondo timore nelle viscere. C'era un'altra balla, una sottile, nascosta tra le pieghe di quella blu più grande; uno scossone per strada aveva scoperto uno spigolo che usciva dagli stretti rotoli – un triangolino, ma abbastanza da rivelare un'impugnatura dalle tinte smaglianti, cesellata con fili d'oro, che coronava una scintillante lama con la punta argentata. Il motivo a pavoni arruffava le piume vivaci, se lo sentiva nel sangue, e l'altro aveva un disegno con dei pugnali.

Ming maledisse soprattutto il demone, qualunque fosse, responsabile per la notte in cui vennero scoperti i nuovi bachi da seta stretti attorno al contenitore dov'erano tenuti i bachi da seta reali. La vita era molto più semplice allora: un numero limitato di bachi per fare la quantità limitata di seta di cui avevano bisogno il numero limitato degli imperatori e le loro mogli e le loro figlie e le loro concubine preferite.

Un numero limitato di tessitori e ricamatori, votati al servizio degli abitanti alquanto limitati della dimora dell'imperatore, con stanze limitate in cui era tenuta la seta, e strade limitate su cui doveva viaggiare per andare dal mercato ai tessitori. (Puoi notare, mio caro, che il vocabolario di Ming era piuttosto limitato. Non come il tuo, il che ti rende un tale oggetto di interesse per me!) Non questo tesoro illimitato introdotto ora dalla quantità improvvisamente e miracolosamente aumentata di seta e di imperi nel mondo ai quali veniva spedita, lungo strade che non conoscevano fine per numero e direzione. Il nuovo miracolo del mondo, il dono dei re. E così eccolo lì, pover'uomo dalle ossa contuse, che si precipitava per strade strane verso città ancora più strane, stringendo al petto dolorante e tremante la più strana di tutte le cose che avesse mai visto.

"L'approvazione è concessa a condizione di una consegna rapida e abbordabile... bla bla bla... responsabilità di pagamento... ri-bla e stra-bla... La nostra benevolenza sia trasmessa al popolo e ai governanti dell'India... eccetera eccetera... distinti saluti!"

Mrinalini fece sparire con un gesto brusco la lettera, ignorando il sibilo del lettore di posta olografica e guardando con occhio furioso l'aria ora vuota davanti a sé. Lacrime di rabbia la accecarono mentre pensava ai decenni di duro lavoro e di soffe-renza che aveva riversato nella sua invenzione.

Mentre i suoi colleghi lavoravano a carburanti e sistemi energetici alternativi, morendo in dimostrazioni contro governi che si rifiutavano di vedere il diluvio e gli incendi e gli inverni letali già su di loro, preannunciando la fine del mondo come lo conoscevano, battendosi per leggi che salvaguardassero intere specie che stavano morendo nelle acque e nelle foreste e che cadevano dai cieli, e alla fine si affannavano per trasferire il maggior numero possibile di abitanti delle coste su terreni più alti, lei, Mrinalini, aveva esercitato la sua volontà adamantina sui propri dubbi e aveva vinto.

Tra gli scienziati era un segreto gelosamente custodito da alcuni decenni ormai, l'esistenza di scorte di tessuto che l'esercito cinese stava usando da un po', non in guerra, ma per fornire riparo dalle tempeste che ormai tormentavano costantemente le loro regioni montuose, rendendo la vita impossibile per i milioni di abitanti.

Giravano voci da anni che il tessuto non fosse solo efficace per le tende improvvisate, fornendo riparo temporaneo dal freddo, ma che intere cittadine erano state ricollocate in queste città-tenda, vivendo e lavorando sotto ciò che assomigliava a edifici tradizionali in vetro e acciaio.

Mrinalini era venuta a conoscenza del fatto che si trattava, in effetti, di seta allungata che funzionava in modi straordinari. Le ricerche sulla natura della tecnologia per la produzione di questo materiale erano scarse, essendo questa seta considerata dai più una variante naturale del tipo tradizionale. I cinesi tenevano la bocca chiusa al riguardo e, nel mondo iper-competitivo della scarsità di risorse, gran parte del pianeta trattava i racconti su questo tessuto come miti e dicerie.

Mrinalini aveva sempre pensato che fosse stato ben più del semplice caso a metterle tra le mani il primo pezzo di tessuto quando, durante una rara visita dai suoi nonni in India, aveva trovato un sari in fondo al baule invernale di sua nonna. Avvolto in un pezzo di vecchio sari in organza, all'inizio lo aveva messo da parte, alla ricerca di una maglietta della sua infanzia a cui era stata particolarmente affezionata.

Nella fretta, aveva rovesciato un po' del suo tè appena fatto nel baule e lo aveva guardato con orrore macchiare la bella seta color bianco sporco. Scavando nelle tasche alla ricerca di fazzoletti di carta con cui tamponare la macchia che si allargava, si era accorta, concentrandosi su di essa, che la chiazza marroncina stava sbiadendo velocemente sui bordi. Mrinalini aveva tolto il tessuto dal baule ed era stato allora che aveva notato i piccoli ventagli ricamati.

Avrebbe potuto giurare che la macchia che stava ora rapidamente svanendo lo faceva perché asciugata con ventagli. In pochi minuti, la tonalità avorio del sari brillava pulita, ogni traccia di macchia sparita, letteralmente, nell'aria.

La nonna di Mrinalini era stata felice che lei volesse il vecchio sari. "È molto speciale, mia cara," le aveva detto. "Mio nonno lo portò dalla Birmania per mia nonna in uno dei suoi viaggi da militare. A quanto pare la donna che glielo aveva venduto aveva urgente bisogno di denaro, ma lui raccontò che se ne era separata molto a malincuore, dicendo che era un cimelio di famiglia da generazioni e si pensava fossa stato benedetto dagli dei protettori della casa. Naturalmente sai, cara, quanto possa essere superstiziosa la gente e non poteva essere così vecchio perché sembrava nuovo di zecca – come se fosse stato appena tessuto! Direttamente dai bachi stessi!" La nonna di Mrinalini aveva riso a gran voce della battuta, battendosi la mano segnata dalle vene sul ginocchio.

E così, mentre il resto della comunità ingegneristica e scientifica stava disperatamente ricercando e sviluppando fonti di energia alternative e progetti di bonifica e sistemi di distribuzione idrica e medicine per gli effetti terribili del calore, lei, Mrinalini, aveva perseverato, convinta che la seta avesse proprietà che avrebbero salvato la sua gente sulla Terra e sulla Luna.

Era riuscita, dopo decenni di sintetizzazioni e innesti, splicing del DNA e alterazioni genetiche, a riconfigurare la seta prodotta dal centro di produzione della seta fondato quasi 220 anni prima sulla Luna, così che, dalle piccole quantità ancora prodotte, potessero essere costruiti grandi lenzuoli di tessuto. E aveva scoperto come modularla e strutturarla in modo che ubbidisse a regole certe e rigide di funzione – funzioni che lei aveva concentrato verso le sfide poste dal cambiamento climatico e dalle devastazioni che causava. E ora, quando la risposta era nelle sue stesse mani, questi sciocchi la avrebbero negata al suo popolo e al popolo del mondo.

Si soffiò rumorosamente il naso in un fazzoletto di seta e guardò, ancora affascinata, il piccolo riquadro di stoffa, ricamato con piccole raffiche di vento e ventagli cinesi, asciugare il moccio umido.

La porta della cabina si spalancò e la testa spinosa di Cheenamara apparve abbastanza a lungo da annunciare che il wormhole si stava aprendo di nuovo. Mrinalini corse fuori ancor prima che la porta si richiudesse.

Qualsiasi cosa facesse volare il grosso Cheenamara come l'agile giovane persona non binary che non era (Agile e giovane, intendo: era sempre non binary, quel giorno preferiva presentarsi come maschio. Ma tu lo sai meglio di me, no, mia cara?) era abbastanza sconvolgente da strappare la sua amante dal raptus di rabbia in cui si trovava e portarla a seguirlo. E mentre lo seguiva – il peso lunare era un fenomeno interessante, ma Mrinalini trovava comunque difficile muovere il suo imponente essere rapidamente – agguantò una scatola di bachi da seta appena usciti dal bozzolo, i pensieri a malapena in grado di stare dietro alle sue azioni. Va a sapere.

"Chee! E se..." ma Chee se ne stava già occupando prima che il pensiero fosse completato. Attese solo abbastanza perché Mrinalini avvolgesse la scatola nel suo fazzoletto prima di digitare la posizione e spedire il palla-trasporto carico per la sua strada. Con un po' di fortuna, sarebbe arrivato nella loro stazione in India in pochi secondi. Poi avrebbero potuto seguire consegne più grandi subito dopo la conferma col veicolo di ritorno.

I due rimasero accovacciati, lo sguardo fisso sulla metà inferiore del portello del palla-trasporto, i cervelli congelati da preoccupazione e trepidazione. Il ronzio del monitor sopra di loro annunciò il restringimento del wormhole. La tosse dietro di loro annunciò l'entrata del Capo dello Staff. Lo *zzp* davanti a loro portò uno strano oggetto, simile a un umano di medie dimensioni avvolto in un sudario.

Il Membro della Prima Generazione camminava lentamente, la testa maestosa annuiva leggermente, le mani delicate tenevano a posto il velo che celava la sua magnificenza al mondo. (Spezzerò il tuo stupido collo umano, verme! Come osi ridere davanti al mio racconto della mia corretta levatura?! Non sei altro che foraggio, mi hai capito? Foraggio per coloro dalle potenti e divine origini! Perché perdo il mio tempo con la tua mente insignificante che non comprenderà mai – mai! – l'inconcepibile bellezza di questa storia e il mio ruolo in essa? Il mio e di tutti quelli come me, che potrebbero salvare il vostro debole pianeta in un secondo se così volessimo! Ti distruggerei in questo momento, brutta bestiolina, se – aaahhhh, lascia perdere, lascia perdere, vedi perché non devo permettere alla mia essenza di dissolversi – ah – sì, sì, dov'ero – ah – sì, devi vedere, e sapere che verrai tenuta in grande considerazione – grande considerazione – quando avremo popolato una metà – la metà nascosta, vedi – con nutrimento per la nostra gloriosa specie, sì, sì, smetti di resistere, Mrinalini, e ascolta il resto della mia storia – ne resta davvero poca.)

I due ingegneri fissavano il Capo dello Staff, che teneva un piccolo contenitore per campioni in una mano e il suo taccuino nell'altra, e il Capo dello Staff fissava quelli che erano senza dubbio resti umani avvolti nella seta. In silenzio, i tre guardarono a bocca aperta mentre Mrinalini tirava da una parte uno strato di seta, decorato da curiosi pugnali dalle tinte smaglianti, per svelare il volto palesemente morto di un giovane uomo, la bocca aperta da poco per la sorpresa, gli occhi aperti non in grado di vedere il taglio sanguinante subito sotto lo sterno – come se fatto da una lama sottile.

Il Capo dello Staff passò lo sguardo vacuo da un ingegnere all'altro e si schiarì la gola rumorosamente. "Di qualsiasi cosa si tratti," sventolò il taccuino verso il corpo e il portello ora inattivo del palla-trasporto, "penso che dovresti sapere, Mrinalini – e tu, Cheenamara, visto che comunque te lo dirà lei – che da qualche tempo mi sto prendendo cura della salute del Membro della Prima Generazione e, grazie ad alcuni utili campioni di fluidi corporei e tendini, ho adesso avuto conferma ai miei timori e sospetti che diventavano sempre più forti."

Sconvolta, Mrinalini vide che il Capo dello Staff stava tremando per l'agitazione, lacrime vere gli segnavano le guance. Si alzò e gli toccò un braccio. "Di cosa si tratta, Capo? Che notizia potrebbe portare che sia più spaventosa di quelle che i nostri monitor terrestri ci dicono ogni giorno?"

Senza dire niente, il Capo le diede il taccuino perché leggesse. Tra calcoli e spiegazioni meticolosi, il verdetto sottolineato con forza la guardava insolente in faccia.

"Deduzione: DNA del Membro della Prima Generazione: baco da seta e umano."

La penna che aveva sottolineato questa incomprensibile conclusione era stata usata da una mano talmente agitata che aveva bucato il taccuino fino al portablocco.

Mrinalini portò lo sguardo vitreo su di lui. "Gli inservienti spariti e le tombe dissepolte, pensavamo stessero cercando altre patate, ma stavano..."

Il lieve *bip* la interruppe e lei si girò verso Chee che la chiamava per nome sottovoce. Il piccolo congegno nella mano di Chee brillò mentre lo passava sul corpo e fece lampeggiare '241 a.C.' sul piccolo schermo. Mrinalini guardò di traverso il numero.

Poi, lentamente, lasciando filtrare la verità nella sua mente in modo graduale per non cedere sotto il suo peso, si voltò verso il tempo del wormhole.

Eccolo lì: non '2241 d.C. / Patna, India' – dove i bachi da seta avrebbero permesso a suo cugino, il Primo Ministro del Bihar, di sintetizzare da sé la seta-clima e le barche-seta – bensì '241 a.C. / Patna, India' dove Chandragupta Maurya ha seguito le istruzioni del suo amico l'imperatore della dinastia Ming e ha chiesto al giovane ragazzo delle consegne (probabilmente il figlio illegittimo di una delle figlie o una delle concubine dell'imperatore o qualcosa del genere che l'imperatore vuole morto, chissà perché gli imperatori vogliono svariate persone a caso morte, non è come se accrescessero il loro DNA o la loro evoluzione in qualche modo) di avvolgersi nel lenzuolo di seta con il motivo a pugnali – svelando il messaggio delle reali abilità della seta senziente al re mauryano e uccidendo il messaggero in un unico colpo da maestro.

(Sì, Mrinalini, quello stesso Ming. Vedi? Ho detto, all'inizio, che se continuavi a leggere avresti scoperto come era successo. Pazienza, adesso, qualche altro paragrafo olografico – la parola è così sopravvalutata, non credi? Per centinaia di anni i vermi senzienti non ne hanno avuto bisogno, un'evoluzione dell'insignificante DNA umano che abbiamo ingerito attraverso i nostri – ah – gentili ospiti, visitatori della Dinastia Moon. Forse riusciremo, uno di questi secoli, a eliminarla dalla colonia umana per la quale hai così brillantemente progettato una casa luminosa sul lato buio del nostro piccolo sasso galattico, hm? Certo, la seta che hai ficcata in bocca fa il suo dovere discretamente bene per il momento.)

Earth Monitor News Agency, 8 ottobre 2242
"La Seta Senziente sembra, dopotutto, essere sulla buona strada per offrire un po' di sollievo nella devastazione del cambiamento climatico. Dopo molte speculazioni riguardanti la sua natura, i suoi usi e le sue origini, e le possibilità

di produzione e/o importazione dalla Colonia della Dinastia Moon, sembra che il rifornimento di quella che è stata chiamata Stoffa Miracolosa continuerà indisturbato. C'erano stati forti dubbi sulla sua sostenibilità quando era giunta notizia della ribellione contro i Membri della Prima Generazione, che ha portato addirittura alcune Organizzazioni per i Diritti dei Popoli Indigeni a protestare sulle modalità di detenzione. È stato rivelato, tuttavia, in un comunicato ufficiale dalla Colonia che il Capo dello Staff e due ingegneri esperti avevano scoperto un'anomalia dietetica nei Membri della Prima Generazione per essi nociva, e che l'hanno ora corretta.

La Colonia ha anche ricevuto il primo contingente di Dark Sider, come vogliono essere chiamati, che si stabilirà sul lato della Luna che i Terrestri non vedono mai, adesso adatto agli esseri umani e dal clima controllato. I positivi resoconti iniziali indicano che stanno prosperando. L'Ingegnere Capo Mrinalini, a cui è stato attribuito il merito di aver salvato milioni di vite, ha tuttavia ammonito che la Seta Senziente deve essere trattata con cura, visto il suo status di forma vivente. Le sue 'Regole di Ingaggio' sono un documento vincolante per chiunque desideri usare questa Stoffa Miracolosa.

Chiudiamo il nostro resoconto con una nota non del tutto irriverente: l'antica scoperta della seta ha senza dubbio tracciato una via inaspettata!"

Anil Manon I suoi racconti sono apparsi su numerose riviste internazionali tra cui *Albedo One, Interzone, Interfictions, Jaggery Lit Review, Lakeview Review, Lady Churchill's Rosebud Wristlet* e *Strange Horizons*. Le sue storie sono state tradotte in cinese, ceco, francese, tedesco, ebraico e rumeno. Il suo romanzo YA d'esordio *The Beast With Nine Billion Feet* (Zubaan Books, 2010) è stato selezionato per il premio Vodafone-Crossword 2010 e per il Carl Baxter Society's Parallax Prize. Assieme a Vandana Singh, ha curato *Breaking the Bow* (Zubaan Books 2012), un'antologia di speculative fiction ispirata al Ramayana. Il suo lavoro più recente, *Half Of What I Say* (Bloomsbury, 2015), è stato selezionato per lo Hindu Literary Award 2016. Attualmente risiede in India e può essere contattato all'indirizzo: iam@anilmenon.com.

Giti Chandra è attualmente Senior Researcher and Lecturer della United Nations University di Reykjavik, ed è stata Associate Professor, Dipartimento di inglese, allo Stephen's College, Delhi. La sua serie fantasy *The Book of Guardians Trilogy* è ora completa, con l'ultimo volume *The Eye of the Archer* atteso a breve; i primi due volumi sono *The Fang of Summoning* (2010) e *The Bones of Stars* (2013). Tristemente, a nessuno interessa il suo primo libro di saggistica, un rivoluzionario lavoro accademico sulla violenza, ma i prossimi due – sul movimento globale #MeToo e sul dibattito pubblico riguardo alla violenza coloniale – saranno sicuramente dei bestseller. Giti scrive poesia in aprile, dipinge il mercoledì, ha un PhD preso alla Rutgers e pensa che le persone farebbero bene a imparare che il violoncello non è un violino troppo cresciuto. Vive a Reykjavik con un marito, due figli, un cane e un gatto.

Manjula Padmanabhan (n. 1953) è scrittrice, autrice teatrale e autrice di fumetti. La sua opera *Harvest* ha vinto l'Onassis Award for Theatre nel 1997. La sua striscia settimanale *Sukiyaki* viene pubblicata su Business Line. I suoi due romanzi più recenti *Escape* e *The Island of Lost Girls* sono ambientati in un brutale mondo futuro. Vive tra gli Stati Uniti e Nuova Delhi.

Priya Sarukkai Chabria è una premiata traduttrice, poetessa, scrittrice e antologista conosciuta per la sua estetica letteraria radicale. I suoi libri includono speculative fiction, il più recente è il romanzo *Clone* (Zubaan, 2018, University of Chicago Press, 2019), saggistica letteraria, raccolte di poesie e traduzioni di poesie classiche tamil in *Andal The Autobiography of a Goddess*, vincitore del Muse India Translation Prize, 2017. Il suo racconto *Slo-Glo* è stato giudicato Miglior Racconto Sperimentale in *The Best Asian Speculative Fiction* (Kitaab, 2018). Premiata per il suo Eccezionale Contributo alla Letteratura, presenta la sua opera largamente inclusa in antologie di tutto il mondo, ha rappresentato l'India alla Commonwealth Literature Conference nel 2014 e cura il sito *Poetry at Sangam*. <http://poetry.sangamhouse.org/>
  <www.priyawriting.com>

Rimi B. Chatterjee è scrittrice, artista e insegnante. Ha pubblicato tre romanzi (un romanzo di fantascienza, *Signal Red* (2005) e due romanzi storici) e una graphic story nella *Longform Anthology* (ed. Sekhar Mukherjee, Sarbajit Sen, Debkumar Mitra e Pinaki De, 2018). Il suo libro *Ashqabad: City of Stories* uscirà nel 2019 e lei sta al momento lavorando ad *Antisense: Tira's Gift*, un racconto.

S.B. Divya è amante della scienza, della matematica, della narrativa e della virgola di Oxford. Le piace sovvertire le aspettative e rompere gli stereotipi ogni volta che può. Il suo romanzo breve *Runtime* è stato finalista del premio Nebula e i suoi racconti sono stati pubblicati su *Uncanny, Apex, Tor.com* e altre riviste. Suoi scritti appaiono anche nel gioco indipendente *Rogue Wizards*. Divya è co-redattrice, assieme a Mur Lafferty, di *Escape Pod*, un podcast settimanale sulla fantascienza candidato per il premio Hugo. È laureata in Neuroscienze Computazionali e in Teoria del Segnali e ha lavorato per vent'anni come ingegnere prima di diventare scrittrice. Potete trovare maggiori informazioni su <www.eff-words.com> o su Twitter @divyastweets.

Shikhandin è lo pseudonimo di un'autrice indiana i cui libri pubblicati (come Shikhandin) includono *Immoderate Men* (Speaking Tiger Books) e *Vibhuti Cat* (Duckbill Books).

Antecedentemente aveva pubblicato un romanzo e una raccolta di racconti. Shikhandin ha lavorato in una posizione di rilievo nel mondo dell'informazione e in pubblicità per anni prima di lasciarla per seguire il suo primo amore, la scrittura. Scrive poesia fin dall'infanzia, ha letto poesia in pubblico e anche recitato a teatro. La poesia e la narrativa di Shikhandin sono state pubblicate in tutto il mondo. Il suo libro per bambini *Vibhuti Cat* è stato uno dei vincitori del Children's First Contest, 2017. In seguito venne selezionato per i Peek a Book Awards nella categoria 8 anni nel 2018, India. È stata finalista dell'Half and One Contest, India, 2019. Finalista dell'OoP-DNA Short Story Contest, India, 2016. Secondo premio in The India Currents Katha Short Story Contest, USA, 2016. Primo premio in The Anam Cara Short Fiction Competition, Ireland, 2012. Candidata nella Bridport Poetry Competition, UK, 2006. Finalista nell'Aesthetica Poetry Contest, UK, 2010. Candidata al Pushcart Prize da *Cha: An Asian Literary Journal*, Hong Kong, 2011. Nominata per Story South's Notable Stories of the Net, USA, 2007. Tra le altre cose. La storia d'amore di Shikhandin con la fantascienza ha avuto inizio con il personaggio dei fumetti Jet Ace Logan, seguito da una serie a fumetti intitolata *Twilight Zone*, seguita da libri di fantascienza e poi da altri libri.

Shovon Chowdhury è uno scrittore leggermente disturbato che vive a Delhi. A causa di un errore madornale da parte del controllo di qualità, il suo primo romanzo, *The Competent Authority* (2013), è stato finalista per i premi Hindu, Crossword, Shakti Bhatt e Tata Lit Live. È stato anche la base di due tesi di dottorato, un corso di scrittura creativa e vari adattamenti teatrali non autorizzati, contro i quali non è stato in grado di presentare reclamo per mancanza di fondi. Compone l'intero staff di *The Investigator*, pubblicato da Hindu Business Line, che cerca la verità in modo che non dobbiate farlo voi, e l'unico proprietario di *The Trilokpuri Incident*, una pagina Facebook che investiga su un evento che nessuno può ricordare. Il suo romanzo più recente, *Murder With Bengali Characteristics* (2015), è ambientato nella Calcutta del prossimo futuro sotto dominio cinese. Sia i bengalesi che i cinesi sono ugualmente inorriditi.

Vandana Singh è nata e cresciuta a Delhi e attualmente insegna e scrive nei dintorni di Boston. I suoi racconti di fantascienza sono stati pubblicati in molte sedi, tra cui molti volumi dei migliori dell'anno, e ha pubblicato due raccolte che hanno raccolto il plauso della critica: *The Woman Who Thought She Was a Planet and Other Stories* (Zubaan/ Penguin India, 2008/2013) e più recentemente *Ambiguity Machines and Other Stories* (Small Beer Press, USA e Zubaan Books, India, 2018) finalista per il Philip K. Dick Award. È anche autrice di due libri per bambini su un eccentrico personaggio di nome Younguncle. Nella sua vita accademica è un ex fisico delle particelle che attualmente fa ricerche di climatologia all'intersezione tra pedagogia e sviluppo sociale. Potete trovare maggiori informazioni su http://vandana-writes.com/. Il racconto *La rete di Indra* è apparso per la prima volta su *TRSF: The Best New Science Fiction* (2011).

Tarun K. Saint, studioso indipendente e scrittore, è nato in Kenya e vive in India dal 1972. Tra i suoi interessi di ricerca ci sono la letteratura sull'indipendenza e la partizione dell'India e la fantascienza. È l'autore di *Witnessing Partition* (2010), basato sulla sua tesi di dottorato. Ha curato *Bruised Memories: Communal Violence and the Writer* (2002) ed è co-curatore (con Ravikant) di *Translating Partition* (2001). È anche co-curatore, con Rakhshanda Jalil e Debjani Sengupta, di *Looking Back: India's Partition, 70 Years On* (2017). Recentemente ha curato *The Gollancz Book of South Asian Science Fiction* (2019).

TABLE OF CONTENTS

Designed and typeset – Impaginazione: Alda Teodorani
Cover illustration – Illustrazione di copertina: Chiara Topo
Printed by – Stampato da: BD Print Srl, Rome, Italy